Chasing the Son

THE GREEN BERET SERIES

For Comrade-in-Arms: David Boltz, USA Special Forces, Team Sergeant ODA 055, B Company, 2d Battalion, 10th Special Forces Group (Airborne). May Valhalla Welcome You.

Prologue

Early 1970's

It was three in the morning when Lilly Chase pulled her battered Chevy into the trailer park. She was upset with herself because once again she'd allowed the manager of the Foxhole to foist off some of his closing duties onto her, therefore making her an hour late. Jenny, the sweet girl who lived two trailers down, had a not so equally sweet mother, who didn't appreciate her daughter being left to such late hours attending to Lilly's not quite two month son.

Lilly's head was full of what lie would suffice to explain, instead of admitting the truth. That she could lose track of Jenny and little Horace long enough to make things that shouldn't be important, but simply because someone asked, matter more.

It was Horace's father's only real complaint about her. The fact that 'no' was such an unfamiliar word to Lilly, that she'd put the very people she loved the most in the sad reality of her absence rather than say one little word, that was actually her right as a human being.

Closing up wasn't even in her job description. She was exhausted after a long evening of dancing for money in the Foxhole. She wasn't a stripper, the Officer's Club did have some limits, but the gaze of desperate second lieutenants going through Infantry Officer Basic at Fort Benning stripped her as effectively as if she took everything off. The Foxhole was a small bar off from the main bar, which was where higher rank ruled. The Foxhole was where the fresh meat came to blow off steam. Lieutenants to be sent to Vietnam.

Lilly was so busy pondering shameful truths about herself that she nearly hit the car filling her allocated parking space. For the briefest of moments she felt the flash of righteous anger that came over her every time she came home late and had to drive around and find somewhere else to park. But it lasted only for a moment, not just because righteous anger wasn't a weapon in her repertoire of emotion, but because she was registering the fact that no one living in this trailer park had a car so new. Or with government issue plates.

She put her car in park and turned off the engine. It sputtered for a few more seconds, the way any car that's never seen a service has to in order to wheeze itself through the rattling gasp between on and off.

While the car died, she sat there, willing herself to believe the possibility that her husband hadn't just died at the same moment. He could be wounded or missing. He could be in jail, awaiting a court martial, because, really, she'd already seen the soul of her impatient husband in their equally impatient son, Horace Junior.

What a ridiculous name for a baby. She had tried to fight it, but most women newly pregnant will make some promises, especially to a husband shipping out to war. She thought of the fact that his father had never seen him and now never would. She wondered what it was going to be like to be as a widow at nineteen. She thought all this in the few seconds it took to jump out of the car and run to the concrete block steps. And the door was already opening as she reached for it. A uniformed officer, a captain, was cradling her baby in his other hand. She could see Horace's tiny fingers reaching up, searching for the breast that wasn't there, instead fumbling over rows of ribbons and a Combat Infantry Badge. He had a green beret on his head, cocked at that same angle all those men her husband served with wore that little piece of cloth that mattered so much to them.

For the rest of her life she'd always remember that hand searching for what wasn't there and she'd feel the rush of grief all over again.

Another officer, a first lieutenant, aged beyond his years by the ribbons on his chest, helped her in and to the couch, where Jenny should be sleeping. But he was explaining in odd words that made no sense that they'd sent Jenny home.

They hadn't delivered the punch line yet, but she knew it absolutely, as sure as she'd ever known anything, so the words were hardly worth listening to.

Lilly began to cry, because no one sends the babysitter home, except to spare even the babysitter the bad thing these two men needed to tell her. The captain didn't even hand Horace Junior to her, so she knew that this was her time to dissolve, to disintegrate emotionally for the time they could allow her, because soon they would be gone and she'd be alone with the feeling which she'd imagined so often.

This new explosion in her chest, doubling in size every second could continue to grow and eat her alive, except for the fact that her dead husband had left her the one part of himself that would keep her from sliding down the hole of her own grief—their son.

For a few minutes she didn't hear their words, but allowed the feeling free rein to pulsate. And when it was a tiny fraction from ripping through her ribs and devouring her, she reached out for her baby. Through sheer force of will she stopped that feeling right there and then. She didn't care about the officers who were being so kind. She pulled up her shirt and the bra beneath it and Horace's fingers clasped on her and his tiny mouth nuzzled against her until he found the realness of all the mattered to him right now.

These men, these Green Berets, did not look at her like the naïve lieutenants in the Foxhole. If she'd bothered, she'd have seen tears in the captain's eyes and the fear in the lieutenant's who probably had his own wife at home with their own baby.

All she knew in the moment was that she was *not* feeding her baby her pain and never would. All the doubts she'd had about herself as a mother, which she'd written to her husband about for so many months, were as easily vanquished from her soul, as she allowed in all the words he had written back to try to reassure her about herself. That he believed in her. In fact, she realized now, they were not even close to the truest part of herself. Sometimes life shows you the truth in ways that aren't so easy.

The men asked if there was anyone to stay with her and she wanted to laugh. Of course there was. She was holding him in her arms.

After they went out, not really reassured but relieved by her new resolve, she heard them start her car. Move it. Pull their car out. Pull her old car into its righteous slot.

She moved Horace to her other breast and thought that for just this moment everything was in its rightful place. For now, everything was as it should be.

A little while later, when he was sleeping in the bassinet next to her bed, the bed where he'd been conceived, Lilly went to the built-in drawers made of the same cheap wood that filled the entirety of the trailer. She found the letter that Horace Sr. had enclosed inside his most recent letter. Maybe some part of him knew that he needed to write some words that weren't meant just for her. Impart something directly. She had gripped the thin envelope with such force, that even now, weeks later, it still bore the marks of her fingers.

She carried it to the kitchen, not a long walk, and used her sharpest knife to carefully slit open this most precious thing, marked on the outside simply: *To My Son.*

He'd told her so much in the few weeks they were together, and written even more words after deployment, enough for a lifetime. They would have to be. So she didn't even glance at the page as she carried it back to her room. She moved the few stuffed animals off her bed that were still there, because until now she'd been a girl who needed the matted bunny and worn teddy bear of her own childhood. She carefully set them on top of the dresser for when they would become her son's, because in the space of an hour she'd fully become the woman whom Horace Sr. had loved from the second he met her.

If being in love makes you stronger and better and more than you could ever hope for on your own, then her brief time with Horace Sr. had fulfilled all of love's obligations. It would have to be. A lifetime's worth.

She sat on the edge of the bed. Careful not to let one single tear stain the paper. And she never would in the years that followed as she read it to her son every night. She began to read to her son his father's words, actually her father quoting another poet, something she completely understood, which would forever belong only to their son.

"*If you can keep your head . . .*'"

Twelve Years Ago

She exited the Combat Talon at 30,000 feet altitude and offset from the border eighteen miles. Arms and legs akimbo, she became stable in the night air as her mind counted down as she'd been drilled.

She pulled the ripcord and the parachute deployed at an altitude greater than that of Mount Everest. She was on oxygen, and had been on it for forty-five minutes prior to exiting the aircraft. The ground, and objective, were over five miles below vertically and over three times that horizontally, leaving no time at the moment for her to enjoy the view.

She had a long way to fly.

She checked her board, noting the glow of the GPS and then double-checking against the compass. She began tracking to the north and east. Then she looked about. She was high enough to see the curvature of the Earth. To the west, there was a dim glow from the sun, racing away from her, leaving her a long night of fell deeds ahead. Far below there were clusters of lights: towns, not many, spread about the countryside. She remembered the nighttime satellite imagery and aligned the light clusters into a pattern to confirm both the GPS and the compass. While she was reasonably certain the aircraft had dropped her in the correct place, mistakes had been known to happen and it was on her, not the crew racing back to the safety of the airfield. She also had to factor in the wind, which would shift directions as she descended through various altitudes.

Her hands were on the toggles attached to the risers of the wing parachute, specially designed for this type of operation. Despite the thick gloves, the minus-forty temperature at altitude was biting into her fingers.

It would get warmer as she got lower.

Hopefully, not too warm.

She'd trained for two weeks to be able to do just this jump. The normal time to fully train a Military Free Fall candidate was four weeks: one in the vertical wind tunnel at Fort Bragg, then three out at Yuma Training Ground, in the clear Arizona weather. Like all her training, hers was quicker, harder and compressed. She'd been assigned individual instructors, hard-core Special Ops veterans who knew better than to ask what the female 'civilian' was doing in their school. She didn't even have a name, just a number.

They followed orders, just as she was following orders.

She shook her head. Too much time to think as she descended. The time was necessary as she was crossing from a neutral airspace into not-so-friendly airspace. She'd already passed the border, the 'point of no return'.

It did not occur to her it was only the point of no return as long as she didn't turn the chute around and fly in the opposite direction. If it had occurred to her, she wouldn't be here in the first place, as such people were not recruited into her unit.

Which also had no name. It didn't even have a number. It just was what it was. Those in it, knew they were in it. Those outside of it, didn't know it existed. A simple concept but profound in its implementation and implications.

Her chute did have a slight radar signature, but not a significant enough one to bring an alert, definitely less than that of a plane or a helicopter; more along the lines of a large bird. And she was silent as she flew through the air, a factor that would come into play as she got close to the ground.

She checked her altimeter, checked the GPS, checked the compass for heading, confirmed location by lining up the towns against the imagery she'd memorized.

Halfway there; both vertically and horizontally.

She was making good distance, almost too good. But better to overshoot and track back than fall short. She dumped a little air, to descend faster.

Of course she had to be on time. She had the small window every covert meeting had: two minutes before, two minutes after. Outside that window her contact had strict orders not to meet. To evade. And the mission would be a scrub. A failure.

It would be a long walk back.

As she passed below five thousand feet, she flipped down her night vision goggles from their position on her helmet. The world below lit up in various shades of green. She could see the outline of the lake she was using as a final reference point, the flat surface reflecting the quarter moon, confirming her location. She focused on the drop zone, a small, square field, barely big enough to allow her to land her chute in it.

A infrared strobe light was flickering in the middle of the field. Invisible to the naked eye, it was a clear beacon through the goggles. It went out for a few seconds, then back on, repeating a pattern.

The pattern that meant it was safe for her to land. At this altitude, if the no-go signal, non-stop flickering, had been present (or no signal at all), she still had time to peel off and land at least a couple of miles away and go into her escape and evasion (E&E) plan.

She dumped more air, quickening her descent, aiming for the light, estimating that she would land about a minute early. At two hundred feet she dropped the rucksack full of gear on its lowering line so that it dangled below her.

As she reached the treetop level, she flared, slowing her descent. The ruck hit terra firma, and then she touched down lightly, right next to the light, the chute billowing down to the ground behind her. She quickly unbuckled her harness, looking about through the goggles. A person appeared, moving out of the tree line toward her.

She was pulling her submachine gun free of the waist strap when the person raised a hand, not in greeting, but with something in it. Her gloved fingers fumbled to bring the sub up.

The taser hit her on the arm, sending a massive jolt through her system and immobilizing her. She collapsed, unable to control her body. As she curled up on the ground, she could see others coming out of the tree line, armed men, weapons at the ready.

Her muscles wouldn't respond. Not even her tongue.

Someone knelt next to her and reached toward her face. Fingers dug into her mouth and probed. The 'suicide' was ripped out of its hide spot in the upper right side of her gum.

How had they known about that?

Compromised. She'd been comprised right from the start.

The person who'd removed her suicide option spoke. "We've been expecting you. We have quite the welcome waiting for you."

Her muscles wouldn't work as her gear was ripped off her body. And then her clothes, until she was lying naked in the small field. Her hands were chained behind her back, the cuffs cinched down, but not too hard, a small fact she processed but found odd.

Her legs were also shackled, but the restraints were padded on the inside.

Like a sack of meat she was lifted by four men and carried. It was cold, the air biting into her naked flesh, but she barely noticed it, her muscles still trying to recover from the massive electrical shock; along with her brain from the betrayal. There was a van underneath the trees and she was tossed in, onto a carpeted floor. Someone grabbed a chain off one wall and locked it to the shackle chain between her legs.

The chains were thick.

She lay on the floor, staring up the van's roof as the engine started and they began driving. There were two men in the back with her, seated on either side. Despite her nakedness, they seemed barely interested in her; they had their weapons at the ready across their knees. Their demeanor told her they were professionals, men who knew how to use their weapons. They had small, bulletproof windows next to their seats and gun ports, and they alternated between glancing at her and watching the world outside.

They drove for a long time, hours. Movement returned to her muscles and she covertly tested the restraints, she had to, one never knew, but these were professionals. She was cold but knew better than to ask for a blanket or her clothing. If they wanted her covered, she'd be covered. Everything they were doing was according to a script, one she knew most likely ended badly.

For her.

Summer a Year and Half Ago

It is difficult to determine where the sea begins and the land ends in the Low Country. The line between the two is not a fixed one, fluctuating with the tide, which moves in concert with the moon and its phases. Such uncertainty in nature is at odds with the certainty with which the Military Institute of South Carolina seeks to instill discipline in its cadets, especially the first year ones, the 'rats' at the bottom of the pecking order. Particularly during their first few weeks at the Institute, in late August, when the fierceness of the Corps is blasted onto the boys trying to become men; or more accurately, trying to become cadets, as manhood sometimes requires different skills from those of the Institute.

But you could not tell an Institute graduate that. As was done to them, they bequeath onto those who follow.

The Institute is located on the northern edge of the City of Charleston, South Carolina, along the banks of the Ashley River, a few miles before it meets the Cooper River. At the confluence of those two bodies of water, the southern tip of Charleston, is the Battery from which the first cannon shots of the Civil War were fired. At least *most* say the first shots of the Civil War were fired that day on 12 April 1861, but true historians can point to many prior shots that portended that war; perhaps Harpers Ferry two years previously? Perhaps Bloody Kansas? Perhaps Nat Turner and his slave rebellion in Virginia in 1831 or, closer to home, the Stono slave rebellion in South Carolina in 1739? Perhaps during the Revolutionary War when the nagging problem of slavery was knowingly left for a future generation to deal with in blood? Regardless, it was the firing on Sumter that ignited the flame that had been smoldering since the founding of the country and the ratification of its flawed Constitution. It was only extinguished after more than seven hundred thousand soldiers, North and South, gave their lives. No one knows exactly how many civilians and slaves perished.

The Military Institute of South Carolina, M.I.S.C. (or Miss C, as it is known more intimately among cadets and graduates), saw glory in battle during the Civil War, although it also saw defeat in war for the state and the cause it served. Such a mindset could be the basis of a character disorder if evidenced by an individual. But when instilled in the fabric of a place like the Institute, it became myth and lore and spirit. The very fiber of the place. While Civil War re-enactors gather every so often to pitch their tents and pretend to be in the days of yore, the stone ramparts of the Institute were rooted in the past and *were* the days of yore.

State, City and Institute are intricately linked. While West Point, founded by Thomas Jefferson, boasted the United States Army, the Great Chain across the Hudson, the Revolution, Sylvanus Thayer, (Benedict Arnold) and other long ago historical footnotes at its birth, the Institute was part of Charleston, part of its heritage, part of its embroilment in politics and commerce and indeed, secession. And while the Military Academy ticks off as graduates: Presidents (2), five star Generals (3), astronauts (18), Medal of Honor winners (74) and others who served the country, the Institute was more subtle, its graduates spread into the very fabric of Charleston and its economic, political and cultural life.

And if you asked, and even if you didn't, an Institute man would tell you Charleston is more important than the country; and that they would be willing to lay down their lives for Family, Institute, City and then State, with Country coming fifth. Which might partly explain why those first cannon were fired from the Battery at the hulking presence of Fort Sumter, a man-made island, not even native to the place, built with New England stone piled onto a sand bar out in the harbor, which meant even its foundations were an anathema to the South. And, as any Institute man will tell you, again whether you want him to or not, there were Institute cadets and graduates manning those cannon in 1861.

That's not to say the Institute didn't send graduates to bleed and die for their country, whether it be the Stars and Bars, and afterward, the Stars and Stripes. Many a monument on the campus gave testament to that, along with the Wall of Honor, listing the graduates who gave the ultimate from the Civil War to the ongoing War on Terror.

There are a lot of names on that wall, each representing a man, an Institute man, in his prime, snuffed out.

Strangely, not the only strange, the Institute is a state college, partly funded by the great state of South Carolina. And while it called itself a military school, it was actually more a facade of a military school since only those cadets who signed ROTC contracts were obligated to serve in the military upon graduation, unlike West Point or Annapolis or the Air Force Academy whose cadets forked over five years of their lives upon graduation. Then again, they didn't fork over any tuition, while the Institute could cost a pretty penny to attend, despite the State funding.

The Institute, founded in 1845, served a very different purpose than churning out second lieutenants. The need for a military school in South Carolina had grown out of the same institution which later caused those cadets and graduates to fire that cannon in 1861: slavery. Pre-Civil War, South Carolina's white inhabitants were outnumbered by slaves almost two to one. And South Carolina, despite its relative small size, had more slaves than any other state except Georgia and Virginia. The Stono Rebellion in 1739 cost 21 whites and 44 blacks their lives. It resulted in legislation such as a requirement for white males to carry their guns to church on Sunday as it was the most opportune time for a slave revolt to occur. Closer to home, in Charleston, a freed black named Denmark Vessey plotted a revolt in 1822 that was pre-empted and Vessey and 34 other black men were hung.

Those kinds of numbers and events kept city fathers up late at night in Charleston. The threat of insurrection was ever-present.

There were some who helped found the Institute in 1845 who even remembered what had happened in Haiti beginning in 1791 and culminating on 1 January 1804: the only successful slave rebellion resulting in the formation of a state in a modern era. More importantly, they remembered that after Haiti was formed, the white minority was massacred.

Thus the leadership saw a pressing need for a well-armed militia, as laid out in the Second Amendment, which needed well-trained leaders. And thus the Institute.

And so the Institute is an integral part of South Carolina history and especially that of Charleston's. There is no city that can compare to that which lies between the Ashley and Cooper Rivers. Forrest Gump would have been told to move along, politely, but fiercely, if he'd tried sitting on a bench in Charleston telling his tale of chocolates in a box. His kind did not belong to Charleston, but rather to the lesser city to the south, Savannah, which was founded by boatloads of criminals, a fact of which any Charlestonian would be glad to remind you.

From the mansions south of Broad, to the Market, all built on a peninsula surrounded on three sides by water, Charleston is a wonder to walk by day and full of brooding shadows by night. It's a city that fairly screams 'here there be secrets' and it is to Institute Men that such secrets are given along with the keys to those closets in which they lurked. And Institute Men often went far beyond the bounds of the city and state, serving in Washington as representatives of their fine State, where secession was born.

Thus, to be an Institute graduate is to be given a cracking of the door into a special world. But even that wouldn't be enough for every cadet. Because there were Institute men and then there were the Institute Men of blood, of family, which even the fierceness of four years in the crucible of the Quadrangle at the heart of the Institute, could not grant. At best, one could be on the edge of the true power and benefit from it, but there is no substitute for being born to the right parents and having the proper blood coursing in one's veins. Old Charleston families held onto their lineage with a fierceness and pride that would make those descended from the Mayflower weep with envy, if they ever wept given their New England stoicism; those Northerners are as hard as the stones from their part of the country that blighted Charleston Harbor and formed the foundation of Fort Sumter.

Of course, the issue of race is also something that has not been untangled from the legacy of the Institute. While putting down a slave insurrection is no longer in the un-written mission statement for the Institute, the mindset cannot be weeded out of both the institution and the city.

And those issues were something Harry Brannigan and a classmate were going to be shown this particular evening. That no matter what they were willing to endure, they were outsiders and always would be.

It wasn't just the name: Brannigan, which reeked of Ireland and pubs and potatoes. Even his first name did him no favors: Harry. He'd already endured more Potter jokes than anyone should. It was mainly that he was from far away, from Oklahoma, taking a spot that should have gone to a native son if not of Charleston, then of South Carolina. While this wasn't directly his fault, it was his price to pay. What he could not know, what most would not know until it was too late, was that no matter how much sweat and blood he paid to the Corps, admittance would never be granted to the South of Broad club.

That club of high birth, privilege and money, was where the real business of the Low Country took place and where the true power resided. One challenged it at his peril.

At the moment, Harry was focused on simple survival. It is an axiom of military training to 'break down' a boy and make him into a man. It never seems to occur to those inflicting this training that perhaps they might break some blossoming good men in the process, turning them into something entirely else.

Only three weeks into his time at the Institute, Harry had already gone on a Magical Mystery Tour. To the sound of the Beatle's album, a rat was sent from upperclass room to upperclass room inside their company. Each upperclass room kept the rat for the official ten minutes of hazing, and then, in order to comply with regulations, dismissed the rat with specific instructions on where to go next: another upperclass room. For another ten. And another. And so on. It was efficient in that each upperclass room only had to spend ten minutes hazing, while the rat spent every minute until Taps under the crucible.

It hadn't been *that* bad and Harry had sensed he was being tested. Could he take it? Would he lash out?

Harry had taken it, kept his mouth shut except for a direct response and learned the cardinal rule of surviving as a rat: be a ghost. Don't make waves, don't stand out, don't draw attention.

That seemed contrary to the concept of 'man-building' in Harry's opinion, but he knew his opinion meant squat compared to that of the Institute and the upperclass.

But Harry now had a problem. Just after an evening meeting of the football team, upon which he was trying to gain a spot on the roster as a safety, he'd pinged back to his room, pinging being a nice way of saying marching at 120 steps per minute, eyes forward, neck braced back, squaring every corner, walking at the far wall of every corridor, taking only the single, furthest stairwell reserved for rats, up to his fifth floor room.

He'd made it inside just as Taps began to play, taking a moment to inhale deeply in the relative (no locks on door, subject to upperclass intrusion at any time) safety of his room, when he noticed his roommate was missing.

This was troublesome for two reasons. His roommate was technically on bed rest as mandated by the infirmary. So Cadet (rat) Wing should have been in bed. And even if not on bed rest, Wing was required by regulation to be in the room at Taps.

And, more to the point of the moment, Wing was Chinese-African American.

It might be the second decade of the 21st century to the rest of the world, but at the Institute, it might as well be Jim Crow combined with the fervor of 'America for the Americans', yada yada. In a way, things would have been easier for Wing if he'd been 100% black. The cadets would have known where he fit (on the bottom) and treated him accordingly, but the Asian was a wrinkle which they couldn't iron out by turning to tradition. So they used the hazing hammer to slam at it, trying to see what the result would be.

Wing was on bed rest after being run ragged the past week (including Magical Mystery tours for three consecutive nights). Not the most impressive physical specimen to start with, he'd finally collapsed in the dining hall at breakfast. The norm was to suck it up. Get up, get to class, make it through the day. Instead, Wing had opted to go to the infirmary. If he'd been able, Harry would have talked him out of it, but he never had a chance, only finding out in between his second and third classes when it was too late. Going to the infirmary was a big step in the wrong direction among the Corps of Cadets; a sign of weakness. Worse, cadets were wondering if Wing had 'ratted out'; told the officials what the cause of his physical condition was and named names. Not that anything would come of it, hazing being as much a part of rat life as breathing, but it showed a lack of fortitude and willingness to be part of the system. If he ratted out as a rat (redundant yes, but reality) then how could one trust him later in life?

Harry checked his roommate's closet, trying to see what uniform was gone to get an idea where he might have gone. He didn't miss it at first, but then he realized what was absent: Wing's grey raincoat. And his M-14 rifle and parade bayonet.

It wasn't raining outside; indeed it was a muggy, 95 degree Low Country August night. And there wasn't a parade scheduled after Taps.

Harry faced that decision point every man faces in his life: do nothing, cover your ass, go to bed.

Or he could go searching for his roommate.

The correct Institute answer was obvious—hit the rack and ignore the issue.

At West Point plebes quickly adopted an unofficial motto: cooperate and graduate. At the Institute, it wasn't the same. Sort of an *every man for himself,* rats on a sinking ship philosophy. Those who climbed to the top made it; those who were on the lower decks went under. It is a fact that when drowned sailors or fishermen are recovered from their wrecks, boot marks are often found on the shoulders and tops of heads of the dead bodies caught below decks.

Harry didn't owe Wing any particular loyalty. He barely knew the guy. Harry was a rat in a sea of snakes called upperclassmen who relished nothing better to do than feast on a rat out of his quarters after Taps. There was an adult somewhere on campus, a tactical officer, but the unwritten rule was the Tac stayed out of the barracks, never passing through the sally ports into the inner sanctum, especially at night, allowing hundreds of young men free rein inside a class system that not only allowed, but fostered abuse.

Harry stripped off his 'As For Class Grey' and put on his athletic shorts and shirt, the name Brannigan emblazoned on the left chest, right above the Institute crest with its motto: *Duty, Loyalty, State*. Harry tied his running shoes. Took a deep breath. Then slipped out of his room.

He heard a clicking noise echoing down the empty corridor, the steel taps on the heels of the shoes worn by the Charge of Quarters, CQ, making his rounds, turning off the hall lights. Harry cut into the rat staircase and descended. Down six stories, below ground level, to the Sinks, as the basement level of the barracks was called. There were indeed sinks there, along with communal showers, lockers, weight rooms, and storage areas for the upperclassmen to put their civilian clothes for their weekend jaunts into Charleston and beyond.

Why he went down, Harry couldn't explain, but it was instinctual. Even with only three weeks under his belt at the Institute, Harry was getting a feel for the place. While the Institute proudly displayed cadets on parade on the large field in front of the barracks every Saturday morning, it had a dark, morbid side to it, hidden deep inside the battlements, so Harry went deep.

Reaching the level of the Sinks, Harry paused. There was a smell to this level, one no cadet would ever forget: musty locker room with a tinge of fear and desperation. Harry cocked his head and listened.

There was the muted echo of several voices raised, threatening, humiliating, taunting. A familiar sound to every rat. But there was an edge to this cacophony, a threat. A darkness that caused Harry to reconsider his plan. There was something else and it took Harry a few moments to recognize it: drunkenness.

He was at a second decision point, where the stakes were higher. Harry sensed if he went down the corridor into the Sinks, he was never coming back the same. Not to the life he'd had planned out in conjunction with his benefactor, Doc Cleary. It didn't occur to him that the stakes might be even higher than that.

But then he thought of what Doc would say, what Doc would do, and to hell with the plan, he pushed open the stairwell door and headed down the corridor toward the hazing.

And for the first time he heard his roommate scream.

Chapter One
The Present—Wednesday Evening

"You broke my heart, Horace," Erin Brannigan said. "You broke it when I was seventeen, and then you broke it again when you came back. You put your life on the line, searching for a boy that didn't exist. I couldn't believe it. But I saw it. It was like you were going out of your way to slap me in the face with your every action."

A cool breeze swept over the pool near them, blown in off the Caribbean Sea onto this isolated side of the island. Chase's friends waited offshore for him to finish what they all believed was one last mission to close this clusterfuck out.

Chase did what would have been unthinkable just five minutes earlier, turning to Sarah Briggs for amplification. "All this over a teenage fling?"

Sarah sighed, and Chase could clearly see it in her eyes now, something he'd seen in a handful of men in combat. She was one of those who had no real fear outside of them. A psychopath, through and through. One to whom everyone was like the large chess pieces outside Erin's office back on Hilton Head. Pieces to be moved and played. She was topless, reclined in her chaise, sporting only a bikini bottom, but there was no allure to her nudity and she wasn't pretending any more. She'd fooled Chase, fooled him bad, drawn him into a battle with the Russian Mafia and she'd gotten away clean, with all the money. She'd faked her death somehow and disappeared.

Until now.

But Erin Brannigan was a wild card; Chase had been stunned when she walked out of the mansion and joined them.

"Horace," Sarah said, with a hint of exasperation, "Erin is upset because you walked away when she got pregnant."

Chase blinked in stunned disbelief and Sarah leaned forward, her first surprise of the unexpected meeting. "You never knew?"

Chase could only shake his head.

Sarah glanced over at Erin, who was perfectly still. She wore a simple sundress and was the last person Chase had expected to run into when he'd infiltrated this island to deliver the economic coup de grace to Sarah for her deceptions and lies.

"Don't act like you didn't know," Erin said, her voice cold.

"Of course he didn't," Sarah said, nodding in understanding. "He nearly got killed trying to find my kid, who didn't even exist. You don't think he'd have given a shit about his own?"

"I called you," Erin said to Chase. "I wrote you."

Chase's mind was racing, thoughts tumbling over one another in a confusing cascade: what had happened to the child? Did she have an abortion? Adopt it out? Raise it? "I didn't know. I was in Beast Barracks at West Point. We couldn't get calls. Or even letters, for those two months. Nothing."

"He's telling the truth," Sarah said to Erin. Backing from a psycho wasn't exactly what Chase was looking for at the moment, but he was too rattled to care.

"Shut up!" Erin finally cracked, screaming at Sarah. "How the hell can you know?"

"Because if he'd have known, he'd have crawled over broken glass to help you," Sarah said. Her head was swiveling back and forth between the two of them, as if sorting out a Gordian Knot from so many years ago, and looking for her own angle to play. "You gave up," Sarah suddenly realized, staring at Erin. "You made a feeble attempt to contact him, just to cover yourself, and then you just gave up. Because you *did* know he'd come back. He'd give up West Point, everything. He'd have come back for you and for the child. You did understand him. Even if you don't know you did. You didn't want him to do that, and, ultimately, you didn't want him."

Chase felt stupid, listening to them talk about him as if he weren't even part of this, when he most definitely was, but Sarah's words sent a chill through him on another level.

"No," Erin said. She seemed confused. "My father. He wouldn't have it. When we didn't hear back from Horace right away, he said I had to leave. I had to go to my mother's in Oklahoma. That she'd take care of me. My father got rid of me. Just like you did, Horace," she hissed at the end, drawing her hatred back to the present.

Chase took a step toward Erin. "I'm so sorry. I *would* have come. I'm sorry you had to go through it alone. I'd have held your hand."

Sarah laughed, sending Chase's thoughts tumbling into freefall.

"Horace! Erin knew you so much more than you ever knew her. She didn't want you there holding her hand while she got an abortion. Because she didn't get one. She didn't want you there holding her hand while she gave birth to your son."

Chase's knees buckled, and he almost fell. "My son?"

Sarah got to her feet, finally putting the pieces together. She was focused on Erin. "That's what this has all been about to you, isn't it, you bitch?" There was real anger in her voice. The betrayer, betrayed. "This has been a game to get Chase here, right now, because you knew he'd show up. You want to hurt him. All you've ever wanted to do is hurt him. It was never about the money. Why? Why, Erin? Why was that so important to the point you'd get us both killed to do it?"

"Because he left me," Erin said.

"I didn't leave you," Chase protested weakly. "I had to report to West Point."

"You left me," Erin said. "Everyone left me."

"You never asked me to stay," Chase said. "We have a son?"

"You left me," Erin said, and then her right hand snaked behind her back and she brought the gun out.

Chase didn't even attempt to lift the MP-5 as she brought it to bear at his head.

She was the mother of his son, two intertwined facts so staggering he was incapable of even protecting himself.

The shot startled him.

Erin looked down at the small black hole in her upper chest, just over the top of her sundress. From hard experience Chase knew the exit wound wasn't as pretty. Erin gave the slightest of smiles. "His name is Horace, too."

And then she crumpled, in the inelegant way the dead do, to the tiled deck, blood pooling underneath her body.

At least Gator hadn't used the Barrett, was the bizarre thought that went through Chase's brain as he looked down at Erin's body. The massive .50 caliber round would have blown Erin in half.

Chase turned to Sarah.

Her face was white. "I didn't know she was crazy like *that*, Horace. You have to believe me."

Chase stared at her, the weight on his heart gone. "The money—whatever's left—will switch accounts in"—he looked at his watch—"twelve minutes."

Sarah stiffened. "What?"

"Sarah." Chase shook his head. Clearing it. Feeling a warm glow growing deep inside. "I might have my faults, but stupid isn't one of them." He reached into his waterproof bag, tied to his waist, and pulled out the USB key. "My acquaintance in black ops programmed this. He did what I should have done. As soon as I called him on my way down to see Karralkov, he checked on you. He learned *you* didn't have a son. Or a husband. He knew who you were, and what you were. But he let it play out for his own reasons. And it worked for him. You might be good, Sarah, but he's in a world you can't even imagine.

"Before I left the *Fina*, I sent a retrieval code so that it automatically moves your money to several pre-programmed destinations. There's nothing you can do to stop it." He checked his watch. "Eleven minutes." He turned and headed back toward the cliff and ocean.

"Horace?" Her voice had lost all its allure.

Chase turned. "You know, if I can find you, so can someone else. And they're looking. Hard. Karralkov had friends. And the bettors, those whose millions you took, they aren't happy, either."

He opened the gate and took the stairs down to the beach. He threw the USB key into the water, took off the running shoes, and retrieved his fins. He couldn't see the *Fina* at this level, but knew it was just a couple of hundred yards offshore. He whistled, and heard Chelsea's short bark. Chase whistled back, turned in that direction, and dove into the water heading toward his dog and his friends.

It was over, but it wasn't over.

It was just beginning.

He had a son, and his son's mother was dead.

It was all just beginning.

But once more, Horace Chase was heading into the murky future without much information.

He was going to have to correct that.

He began finning, heading toward the *Fina* and his teammates and his dog.

And his new future.

Chapter Two

Wednesday Evening

The balcony commanded a superb view of Charleston Harbor and the only complaint Mrs. Jenrette had about the view was that Fort Sumter was still out there with the flag of the Federalists flying high over it. The National Park Service lit it with a spotlight every single night, as if taunting the city that had taken it down by force so many years ago and replaced it with the Stars and Bars.

"Mrs. Jenrette?"

The grand dame lifted her right hand off the arm of her exquisite cane chair ever so slightly, a signal for the supplicant to proceed. He was a man in his late sixties, awkward in this subservient role, cloaking himself in it only on this balcony. To the rest of Charleston he was a ruthless lawyer with only one client: the most powerful family in the city.

Like many things in that rarified world full of secrets, that wasn't quite true.

Charles Rigney walked up next to the wooden railing, smartly blocking Fort Sumter from view, a silent acknowledgement between the two of them. He was six and a half feet tall, had played forward on the Institute basketball team many years ago, and was bald as a billiard ball and lean as a cue stick.

"Yes, Charles?" Mrs. Jenrette said, a voice dripping in magnolia, Charleston, and age, swirled with the essence of power that came naturally from birth and exercised without restraint for decades. She had once been as physically commanding as the view, an inch shy of six feet, willowy and graceful, with long auburn hair. She'd broken many a beau's heart when she was a debutante; as a young married woman, she'd brought attention to herself and her husband, as he escorted her about on his arm. Men envied him, women hated her, and the truly insightful knew she was more than beauty: she was the brains behind the throne. Even in her later married years, as her hair turned silver and she disdained coloring it and cropped it back, she was still a marvel. But now, in her early nineties, the realities of arthritis and age had worn her down, literally shrinking her a few inches and making any excursion out of chair or bed a painful endeavor. Only the voice and the surroundings reminded one of who she was.

"The invitation list for the Ball has been finalized," Rigney said.

He didn't have to specify *what* ball, as there was only one that mattered in Charleston: the St. Cecilia Society Gala, held once a year. Which evening it was held was a closely guarded secret and at the whim of Mrs. Jenrette, who'd reigned as president of the Society for eighteen years. It was never reported on in the local newspaper and spoken only of in whispers. No one got in unless invited and no one was invited unless they were a member of Society of St. Cecilia, a dwindling, but still very powerful social circle, the most powerful one in Charleston. Mrs. Jenrette had 'come out' at that ball three quarters of a century ago.

Mrs. Jenrette sighed. This used to be one of her favorite tasks, an annual display of power. Even she admitted, only to herself, that she dipped into the well of petty once in a while, scratching a line through this name or that, for some slight, real or imagined. There was no point being powerful without some of the perks. But now, implicit in it, was a deep pain. And the realization the odds were rather good it would be her last one.

"There are no other men in my line," Mrs. Jenrette said. "It dies with me."

"It need not," Rigney said, daring an argument that she always shot down. But it was late, and the large glass carafe on the table next to his patron was two-thirds empty, indicating she'd imbibed more than usual. Perhaps, for once, reason might prevail in this matter. "No woman was President before you. Perhaps the rules can be changed. You have a daughter. And she has a daughter."

"But no living son or grandson; no male heir to carry on the name." Mrs. Jenrette scoffed: "The men did not elect me. It passed to me when my husband and son moved on from this mortal coil in the crash, since no one was willing to step up during a difficult time. When I move on, no woman will set foot in the inner council. And they will never allow me to change the rule: only direct male descendants of founding members of the Order of St. Cecilia may become members."

"It is a dwindling pool, ma'am," Rigney pointed out. "Half of the houses south of Broad are now owned by strangers."

"Turncoats," Mrs. Jenrette stirred angrily. "Youngsters selling out their family homes for money."

"They *need* the money," Rigney gently pointed out. "Their parents did not provide as well for them as they should have. As you have so generously provided for your own family."

"Tread carefully," Mrs. Jenrette said. "Those parents were, and those still alive *are* my friends."

"Yes, ma'am," Rigney said.

Both were silent, the only sound the waves breaking on the rocks lining the Battery. It was late and the park south of the house was empty of tourists. There were those wondered if that was why Mrs. Jenrette always chose the night to be out there. She would never be caught out on the porch during daylight any more, not when some yahoo tourist from Ohio with a camera could capture her image. Whether it was from a sense of privacy or vanity was up for debate. That and the fact that three years ago one of the tour guides who drove the carriages that clopped through the streets was regaling his captive audience with a tale of the Battery so inelegantly false in historical accuracy, belittling the bravery of the men who'd fired the cannon, that Mrs. Jenrette had gone inside and brought one of her deceased husband's guns out and fired a load of bird shot at the poor young man. No one was hurt, but Mrs. Jenrette had begun a retreat into the cloak of darkness.

"What is the status of Sea Drift?" Mrs. Jenrette asked, touching on her final project, her legacy to the Low Country.

"It will be in three days, on Saturday. All is as I briefed you yesterday."

"And the Bloody Point Course?" she asked, referring to one of the three defunct golf courses on Daufuskie Island.

"Ownership is still buried under several shell companies, but I'm getting closer to finding out the true owner so we can proceed."

"It has to be completed by Saturday. You don't have much time."

"I know. But even if it isn't completed, we can go to our alternate plan. Block off easement to the course, which will make it worthless. The owner will then have to show themselves and sell."

"One would think so," Mrs. Jenrette said. "But the true owner has not showed themselves yet, and we've put good money on the table. Perhaps this mystery owner knows more than they should?"

Rigney had no answer to that speculation.

Another silence played out.

"Mrs. Jenrette . . ." Rigney began, a bit uncertain, which he knew was a mistake as she snatched on that like a cobra.

"What is it man? Speak."

"There's been a development." Rigney had thought this over on the short walk from his house (not waterfront) to her's (owning the waterfront). "Someone has been making inquiries concerning the whereabouts of Horace Brannigan, whom we know as Harry Brannigan."

"I assume you mean someone other than us," Mrs. Jenrette said.

"Yes."

"So what is the development?"

"It's on Hilton Head. As you know, his mother, who had nothing to do with him since birth, disappeared a few months back. We checked into it and couldn't track her, which is suspicious in and of itself. But now a man named Farrelli is making inquiries about both the mother and the younger Brannigan."

He continued, not giving her a chance to ask questions, and knowing her dislike of having to ask.

"Farrelli has connections with New Jersey. Organized crime connections. He launders money for New Jersey through several restaurants on the island and has been trying to expand his operations as much as possible. Protection. Gambling. Escort services."

"A gangster." Mrs. Jenrette's voice dripped derision for the criminal element; conveniently ignoring her own family history and the truism in America that behind every great fortune lay criminal activity somewhere in the past.

"Yes, ma'am."

"Why would he be interested in Brannigan?" Mrs. Jenrette asked.

"We suspect he's asking on behalf of someone else."

"Who?"

"We don't know."

Mrs. Jenrette tapped her finger on the arm of her chair, a sign of extreme agitation those who were close to her would recognize, except there were few of those. Rigney was one.

"We knew Brannigan was of poor blood," she finally said. "Why the Institute would allow such a person in to the Corps, is beyond me. And, as usual, your news is not news. I also have heard rumors that someone is asking of Brannigan. I believe we must pursue that angle further."

"Of course," Rigney said, not surprised that she'd already heard. Whispers came to the old woman, even though she rarely left the house, creeping to it, like the vines which crept up the brick walls on the back of the house.

"I'm bringing in someone new. He's an Institute man, class of '08."

"Young," was Rigney's immediate assessment.

"I thought that would be beneficial," Mrs. Jenrette said. "Closer in age to my grandson's classmates and those who were involved." When Rigney didn't say anything, she continued. "He's young, but he's sharp. Commissioned in the Army upon graduation. Branched Infantry. Airborne and honor graduate of Ranger school. Served with the 101st Airborne in Afghanistan for one tour; awarded a Bronze Star for bravery. Then into the Ranger Battalion at Hunter Army Airfield, outside of Savannah. Multiple short deployments to combat zones; awarded a Silver Star. He resigned his commission four months ago and moved back here."

"'Back here'?" Rigney repeated. "What is his family name?"

"Dillon."

"From Charleston, you say?" Rigney was running through the families of Charleston in his brain and coming up short.

"North Charleston," Mrs. Jenrette amended. "He attended the Institute on a football scholarship. A good man. Tough. Single family home, raised by his mother who works as a paralegal, but he's taken his opportunity and made the most of it."

"How much are you paying him?" Rigney asked.

"I'm not," Mrs. Jenrette said. "You are. If he succeeds, you will put him through law school and give him a place with your firm. Like me, you have no successor. If this young man works out, that might well be his position."

"Mrs. Jenrette, that's—"

She cut him off. "If he succeeds in this task he will be a valuable asset. He will be bound by spilled blood. Sometimes I fear that is a stronger bond than blood in the veins. He is waiting in the library. I have not met him in person yet."

"If you've not met him," Rigney said, "how do you know he is up to the task?"

"I did some research," Mrs. Jenrette said, vaguely. "He's waiting downstairs. Please bring him to me, Charles."

Rigney disappeared through the French doors behind her. Mrs. Jenrette signaled and a silent figure who'd been practically invisible all this time appeared out of the shadows at the rear of the porch. The butler, an old black man, dressed in a white starched shirt with a bow tie, and black trousers, poured her another drink from the pitcher. Task accomplished, he faded back into the darkness.

Rigney appeared, accompanied by a younger man, three inches shorter, but broad and well built. He wore a suit much like Rigney's, except purchased from a store much farther down the pecking order in men's clothing. He had light-colored hair, cut short in the military way. There was a scar on the right side of his face, and a pockmark below and to the outside of the eye.

"Mister Dillon," Mrs. Jenrette said.

"Ma'am." Dillon stood near the railing, at attention, just short of the way a rat would be braced at the Institute. But his eyes were moving, shifting about, taking in his surroundings.

"Did you ever think you'd stand here?" Mrs. Jenrette asked. She didn't wait for an answer. "I am sure you have walked the Battery. Looked at these houses. What did you think when you did so?"

"I thought they were quite magnificent," Dillon said.

"An impersonal observation," Mrs. Jenrette noted. "What did you *feel*?"

Dillon didn't hesitate. "Ambition."

Mrs. Jenrette laughed, a surprising sound. "Honesty. I so enjoy an honest man. Most use words to obscure the matter, but you cut right to it with a single utterance. Do you understand the situation I've explained to you over the phone?"

"You want me to find Harry Brannigan," Dillon said.

"Then you *do not* understand."

"Excuse me, Mrs. Jenrette," Dillon quickly interjected. "I was not certain if you wanted me to speak plainly in front of others."

Mrs. Jenrette cocked her head, confused. "But Mister Rigney already knows."

"There is another present," Dillon said, nodding toward the shadows.

"There is *not*," Mrs. Jenrette said with the certainty born of centuries of slavery and servitude. For Mrs. Jenrette and her generation the 'help' was like the furniture. Something useful and functional but certainly not a concern in any other matter.

At least that's the way it was in almost every big house in Charleston and appeared to be in Mrs. Jenrette's mansion.

"Yes, ma'am," Dillon said. "You want me to find Harry Brannigan and kill him."

"Partially correct," Mrs. Jenrette said. "I want you to kill him and bring me his heart, since he has torn mine out of my chest. It is the proper punishment to return in kind what he wrought on my family. It is the tradition of honor."

"It is, ma'am," Dillon said.

"Are you saying that to placate me or because you believe it?" Mrs. Jenrette challenged.

Dillon bowed his head ever so slightly. "*Lex talionis.*"

"Mister Rigney?" Mrs. Jenrette asked.

Rigney spoke up, impressed. "Mister Dillon is referring to the Latin, where a retaliation is authorized by law. A form of an eye for an eye."

"Whose law are you using in your reference, Mister Dillon?" Mrs. Jenrette said. "Certainly not the law of the State or the Federals."

"The Code of the Corps of Cadets of the Institute," Dillon replied. "And, more importantly, as you noted, of the tradition of the city of Charleston."

"Indeed," Mrs. Jenrette said. "Indeed. Retribution must be made." She slumped back in her chair, simply an old woman mourning her grandson for a moment. "I miss him every day. Worse than any pain I imagined a human could experience; in many ways worse than the day I lost husband and son. My heart was ripped out that day and will never return. All that is left is the hole and the darkness that consumes it. The only solace that can come is when you bring me that murderer's heart."

"I will do that," Dillon promised.

"Good, good," Mrs. Jenrette murmured. "What happened to your face?" she suddenly asked.

"I was shot in combat," Dillon said.

"And you have made a full recovery?"

"Yes, ma'am. It was a while ago. The bullet was removed during surgery."

"But it entered your brain?"

"It did, but only tangentially," Dillon allowed. "The doctors say there is no permanent damage."

"And what do you say?"

Dillon hesitated ever so slightly. "I am fine."

She abruptly shifted the discussion as she was wont to do. "Why do you believe you will succeed where more experienced men have failed?"

"I believe they've been going about finding Brannigan the wrong way," Dillon said. "They've been trying to discover where he went. I believe we have to uncover where he came from. That will give us an idea where he would go. In Afghanistan, when searching for a high value target, we learned that going to the village of their birth yielded excellent results. It was strange how often these hardened guerilla fighters would return to that place when they felt they were being cornered. When they feared the Predator circling overhead, getting closer and closer."

"You mean going to Oklahoma for Brannigan?" Mrs. Jenrette said. "We've been over that. If you're—"

Dillon dared interrupt. "Oklahoma is indeed a dead end, Mrs. Jenrette. Since I spoke with you over the phone, I've looked at the reports. That trail is cold. The only tie Brannigan had there, his maternal grandmother, is dead. But two events make me believe we must look much closer. To Hilton Head. His mother lived there, although he didn't know it. And she has recently disappeared. And the inquiries by this Farrelli fellow are curious. Someone is using him. We must discover who. It might be his mother. If we can find the mother, we should be able to find the son."

"I have been thinking," Mrs. Jenrette said. "I have little else to occupy my time." Which was a lie, of course since Mrs. Jenrette was the wealthiest woman in Charleston and still ran the business hands on. "What about the father?"

"There's nothing in the reports about who that might be," Dillon said.

"I know. But a father must exist, unless this was an immaculate conception."

"Yes, ma'am. Another reason to go to Hilton Head. Harry Brannigan was conceived there. We know that. Erin Brannigan was not sent to Oklahoma until she was four months pregnant. However, it's likely the father was the teenage son of one of the hordes of tourists who visit the island. A summer fling, since the father had no role in the child's life and there is no father of record in any document. It's possible the father doesn't even know he has a son."

"Likely, but not certain," she said. "The only solace I take is that my husband and son were not alive when Greer was taken from us. It would have destroyed them."

She fell silent and neither man dared intrude on her thoughts.

"Is that all?" Mrs. Jenrette finally asked.

"No, ma'am. I've read the report from the Institute about the—" he fumbled for words for the first time—"incident. And—" His fumbling had fumbled as Mrs. Jenrette cut in.

"My grandson's murder, you mean."

"His murder," Dillon corrected. "Something's missing in it."

"What?" Mrs. Jenrette demanded.

"If I knew it wouldn't be missing," Dillon said. "I don't know what it is. But I sense there is something lacking. I want to interview the personnel involved."

"They've been interviewed," Mrs. Jenrette said. "They are the sons of people I do business with and mingle with socially. Very important people. One of them is the senior Senator from our state."

"Thus their interview was incomplete," Dillon pointed out. Another silence played out.

"So," Mrs. Jenrette finally said. "You want to know how far you can push these young men?"

"Yes, ma'am. I believe they are holding something back."

"I'll deal with their parents as needed," Mrs. Jenrette said. "Go as far as you feel you need to. But remember; they are of fine families."

"Yes, ma'am."

"And Senator Gregory is not a man to be trifled with, so deal carefully with his son."

"Yes, ma'am."

Rigney stirred. "We must conclude business with two of these parents on Saturday. Are you certain," he said to Mrs. Jenrette, "that now is the time to investigate? Can't it wait until after this deal is completed?"

Mrs. Jenrette's eyes flashed with anger. Her voice was like a whip. "There is *nothing* more important."

Rigney's dedication to his profession caused him to press the issue. "This deal is worth two hundred million dollars, Mrs. Jenrette. It's taken over a year to pull together and—"

Mrs. Jenrette lashed out. "And you still don't know who owns Bloody Point! So it is *not* completely pulled together."

"We have enough to make it work," Rigney said. "I must look after your family interests, ma'am."

"What family?" Mrs. Jenrette snapped.

"Your daughter and—'

"My daughter is provided for by her new husband and she bears *his* name," Mrs. Jenrette said. "My family ended when Greer was killed. *Nothing* is more important than avenging his death."

Rigney conducted a conversational withdrawal. "Yes, ma'am."

Mrs. Jenrette shifted back to Dillon. "And I need not remind you that the Institute makes it own rules, beholden to no one outside those walls. My reach extends only so far despite the millions my husband and I have bequeathed to the place. The ranks of the Institute Men close rapidly if threatened."

"Yes, ma'am."

"But perhaps, since you wear the ring, you will be able to penetrate those ranks."

"Perhaps."

"What else?" Mrs. Jenrette asked.

"I believe those three areas of focus will yield results," Dillon said.

Mrs. Jenrette held up a finger. "Bearing with Mister Rigney's concerns about discretion, I will have someone check into Mister Farrelli and the mother on Hilton Head. You talk to the Institute people."

Dillon glanced at Rigney, obviously not happy about being sidelined in one part of the inquiry, but he responded: "Yes, ma'am."

"Don't worry, Mister Dillon," Mrs. Jenrette said, not missing a movement in the dark. "You will travel to Hilton Head when needed, armed with more knowledge than you have now."

"Yes, ma'am. But may I ask, who will you use for the initial inquiries there?"

"An old family friend and another Institute man," she said. "Merchant Fabrou."

"The Quad," Dillon said.

Rigney stirred and was about to say something but he didn't get a chance.

"You have heard of them?" Mrs. Jenrette asked.

"They are whispered about at the Institute, ma'am" Dillon said. "While you are spoken about."

"A well turned comment," Mrs. Jenrette said, obviously pleased in the way those in power are when hearing what they believe is a truth. "The Quad wields some degree of power in our younger sister city down in Savannah. They are useful at times. This is one of those times.

Additionally, as you know since you've read the reports, Mister Fabrou's son, Jerrod, was involved in the incident, so he has a personal stake." She shifted her attention. "You will talk to Merchant and ask him to investigate further, Mister Rigney?"

"I will." He paused. "But do you think it is wise involving Fabrou in this so close to the closing on Sea Drift? We will be seeing him on Saturday."

"Hush," she chided him. She reached out and opened a drawer on the small table to her left. She fumbled inside and drew out an object. She held it out, hand shaking from age and the weight of it. "Take it."

Dillon did as she commanded.

"Recognize it?"

"It's a ceremonial bayonet for the M-14 rifle," Dillon said. He pulled back on the hilt, exposing the metal. "The blade has been chromed. It's what we use at the Institute for ceremonies and parades. Every cadet, except Toppers who have swords, is issued one along with his rifle."

"It's the weapon used to kill my grandson," Mrs. Jenrette said. "Brannigan's fingerprints were all over it. I want you to use it to kill Brannigan and cut out his heart. Understand?"

"Yes, ma'am."

"Mister Rigney will provide you with everything you need. Go now. God speed."

Dillon pivoted, a maneuver he'd learned on the Quadrangle at the Institute as a frightened seventeen year old. He marched off the porch, bayonet in hand.

Rigney remained. "I don't think involving Merchant Fabrou or the Quad is wise. Nor do I think having Mister Dillon interview those young men this week is prudent. Why not let it go until next week, when the deal is done?"

"I know you don't," Mrs. Jenrette said. "But Fabrou will think I'll be indebted to him. He will believe he has gained an advantage over me. All great philosophy regarding power is essentially the same; whether it be Sun Tzu or the Godfather. To survive and flourish it is always best to keep friends close, but enemies closer. And Fabrou knows Farrelli. They have done business before. Mister Dillon will eventually go down to Hilton Head and in doing so he will discover what Mister Fabrou is up to. Fabrou will show his true colors in how he handles this. I do not trust the man, even though he has agreed to Sea Drift." She stared at Rigney. "And that is why this is being done now, *before* we meet on Daufuskie on Saturday. I sense another entire level to this entire affair. What it might be, I have no idea. But there are secrets, Charles. And they might be very dangerous secrets."

"Yes, ma'am."

"And, as I told Dillon. Fabrou's son, Jerrod was there."

"You fear Sea Drift is at stake in this?" Rigney asked, finally understanding why she wasn't willing to wait.

"Of course it's involved," Mrs. Jenrette said. "There are no coincidences. There are no accidents. I need to find out how and why."

"And Senator Gregory?"

Mrs. Jenrette closed her eyes briefly. "He is the most powerful man in the state and one of the most powerful on Capitol Hill in Washington. He has great plans for his son, Preston. Who, I believe, has even greater plans for himself. I had hoped that my dear Greer could work with Preston, the two of them forming a powerful union; his family's political might with my family's money. In fact, Senator Gregory and I had discussed it several times. But that is not to be."

Silence reined for over a minute. Rigney thought Mrs. Jenrette had fallen asleep, but her voice was sharp when she suddenly spoke. "I do not have much more time, Charles. I *will* have my satisfaction before I pass. This has gone on too long."

"Yes, ma'am."

"I will also have my legacy in Sea Drift."

"Yes, ma'am."

"You may go." Rigney departed.

Mrs. Jenrette looked out at Fort Sumter, the flag a distant, bright speck, illuminated by the spotlight. One could almost imagine the Stars and Bars there as it was impossible to make out details at this distance. It was a fantasy she indulged in sometimes. What a world that would be! Full of honor and elegance.

She was not unaware that there had been a very dark side to that world and that it had been unsustainable from the start. The ability to be practical had always served her well.

"Your thoughts?" she finally said.

The butler broke his silence. "Doctor King said the law of an eye for an eye leaves everyone blind."

"For all his peccadillos," Mrs. Jenrette said, "he was a wise man."

"But you're going to ignore his wisdom, aren't you ma'am?"

"Yes, Thomas. I *am* old and not much longer for the world. And I know it is blasphemy to you and many others, but I do not believe there is anything beyond the stillness of death." She chuckled with no mirth. "And if there is, I am surely damned for my long litany of offenses."

"That is true," Thomas said.

A wry smile twisted the old woman's lips. "I can always count on your for honesty. Would you join me for a drink?"

"I would," Thomas said. He came out of the darkness and poured them each a full glass, handing one to her. He grabbed a nearby chair without asking and sat down in it with a grateful sigh. He was an old man, with a fringe of white hair around his wrinkled black skull. He wore glasses with thick black frames. His dark suit was crisp, the white shirt starched, the bow tie perfectly knotted. He took a sip. His hands betrayed a harsher life, the fingers gnarled and twisted with arthritis.

"They came after my grandson, Thomas. My grandson; the last of our family name. I did not expect that."

"You can't be certain it wasn't an accident, as they said it was."

"I can't afford the luxury of chance," Mrs. Jenrette said. "Maybe it was just bad luck and cruel fate. But I don't have the time to believe that. I must act as if there was, and is, a plan afoot and poor Greer's death was part of it. You understand, don't you?"

"I do."

"And the timing of these inquiries via Farrelli. Just days before Sea Drift is to close. That cannot be coincidence after a year of nothing."

"It is odd timing," Thomas said. "But the connection is not apparent."

"That is what we must uncover in the next few days," Mrs. Jenrette said.

"Yes, ma'am."

"Something is on your mind?"

"I do not believe Mister Rigney is trustworthy."

"My husband trusted him. He graduated the Institute with Mister Rigney's father, who handled my husband's affairs and then his son, Charles, handled my son's affairs. They developed the Sea Drift plan together. My son worked together with him for four decades."

"I know," Thomas said. "But you are not your husband or your son. I sense Mister Rigney resents having to answer to you. And he resents you are not a man. Or an Institute graduate as he and your son and husband and his father and every man of importance in this city."

"Of course he resents me," Mrs. Jenrette said. "But he is the horse I must ride to the end of this race. It's too late in the course to switch."

"Yes, ma'am."

Mrs. Jenrette gave a low laugh. "That's your disapproving 'yes, ma'am, Thomas."

"Sea Drift is very important. I suppose my anxiety is showing through."

"I understand." She switched topics. "Your network of information, as usual, seems to be proficient. This Dillon character seems capable. I appreciate the recommendation."

"You're welcome."

"Now that you've seen him, what do *you* think of him?"

"I believe he might surprise you," Thomas said.

Mrs. Jenrette's head snapped to look at him. "How so?"

"A feeling. There is a depth to him. And he has seen some terrible things."

"How do you know that?"

"I've seen terrible things," Thomas simply said.

"Hmm," was all she had to say on that. "As Mister Rigney said, we are at a delicate time for Sea Drift. I feel adrift, Thomas."

"It has been a hard road these past few years," Thomas said.

"We need to make it through Saturday," Mrs. Jenrette said. "And we need to find young Mister Brannigan. When those are complete, then I can rest."

Chapter Three

Wednesday Evening

"You killed the mother of my son," Horace Chase said, without the anger, recrimination or what might pass for normal emotion attached to such an inflammatory statement.

But the situation was anything but normal. Chase had just climbed up the ladder on board the *Fina*, a converted river patrol boat to join his comrades: Dave Riley, Kono, and Gator and Chase's dog Chelsea. It was Gator who'd fired the fatal shot at Erin Brannigan, the impetus for Chase's statement, back on the island in the Caribbean off their port bow, a dark silhouette in the night.

"What?" Gator was startled. "Erin?"

"Erin?" Dave Riley echoed, holding the rope attached to the zodiac Gator had just driven up in. "Our Erin?"

Chase had a submachinegun slung over his shoulder, water dripping off his combat fatigues. He dumped the fins on the deck. Chase was a tad under six feet tall. His hair was turning gray and cut tight to his skull. As he peeled off the wet shirt, he revealed a dozen various sized pockmark scars on the right side of his body, the result of a Taliban grenade. There was also a bullet mark on his stomach, left of center.

The fourth member of the team, Kono, was up above them, in the cockpit of the patrol boat, silent, as he usually was. But he moved forward, leaning over the bulletproof glass lining the cockpit, listening.

"I had to shoot her," Gator explained to Riley. "She drew a gun on Chase."

"I'm still at Erin being there," Riley said. "How was she connected to Sarah Briggs? And you *didn't* shoot Briggs?" he said, indicating Gator.

The huge ex-Ranger shrugged. "She didn't have a gun. Actually, she didn't have much. No top. Not my type." He added with a hard look at Chase who'd made her his type for a disastrous couple of days.

"Explain," Riley said to Chase. Dave Riley had retired from Special Forces years ago. After working security for several gigs, he'd tossed it in and moved to Daufuskie Island, taking over his Uncle Xavier's small-time bookie operation. Raised by his Puerto Rican mother after his Irish father skipped out, Riley was a long way from the Bronx where he'd grown up. He was a slight man with dark skin, sporting an inevitable slight beer belly, and his once-thick hair was thinning and greying.

"I have a son," Chase began. Then he quickly relayed what had transpired between himself, Erin and Sarah. When he finished, Kono made his first contribution.

"Should have suspected Erin," the Gullah said. "She said Briggs was dead after checking her right here on the deck of this boat. Then we find out Briggs not dead. She lied."

"Yeah, obvious now," Riley acknowledged. "We should have made some sort of connection there. But we missed a lot of things." He shook that off. "Erin say anything more about your son other than he was named Horace?"

Chase sat down, running his hand through Chelsea's mane as he tried to collect this thoughts. A Shepherd-Chow mix, dark-colored, Chelsea was a gift from his landlord when he'd lived in Boulder, Colorado and worked as a F.L.I.: Federal Liaison Investigator. That job seemed long ago and far away.

"No," Chase said. "Just that Erin had to leave Hilton Head when she was pregnant and go to her mother's in Oklahoma. He'd be—" Chase did the math—"around nineteen now. Give or take a few months."

"If you're the daddy," Gator pointed out.

"I'm the father," Chase said.

"If there's a child," Gator persisted.

Chase started to get up, toward Gator, which would prove futile given Gator's bulk and quick temper.

"Hold on," Riley said. "Gator's right. How do you know she wasn't just fucking with you? This whole thing has been a mindfuck from the start."

"Then why would Erin have gone in on the scam with Briggs?" Chase asked.

"Money," Kono said.

"No." Chase pointed at Gator. "You knew her."

"Not that well," Gator said. "We chatted a few times. I thought she was cute. But she didn't, you know, respond."

"She said she had a partner," Chase said. "A woman?"

Gator shook his head. "Not that I knew of." He seemed happier. "Maybe that's why she didn't respond to me."

"Another lie," Riley said.

"What?" Gator was off a beat on the conversation.

"Why didn't you ask Briggs?" Riley asked Chase ignoring Gator's wounded manhood. "She knew, right?"

Chase nodded. "Yeah. She brought it up."

"Then she knows something," Riley said. "Why didn't you question her?"

"Time," Chase said. "We had the op timed."

"We had it timed because we thought she'd have security," Riley said. "Think clearly. Did Briggs know about the child *before* Erin said anything?"

Chase had to focus, realizing he'd lost his professional anchor and was making bad decisions. "Yes."

"So the two of them discussed it," Riley said. "Then it's likely Sarah Briggs knows more about your son."

"Shit," Chase said. He'd been caught between revenge and surprise and the shock of Erin's death right after finding out they'd had a child together. Well, not exactly together other than the conception.

"There was no security?" Riley directed the question to Gator.

"I didn't see any," Gator said, "and there was no reaction to my shot."

"All right then," Riley said. "That changes things. Then let's go back and ask her again."

"What?" Chase said.

"We go back," Riley explained. "Talk to Sarah Briggs. Find out what she knows about Erin and your son. She was counting on secrecy to protect her, not guards. It didn't work." He wasn't waiting. Riley pointed to Kono. "Hold the boat here." To Gator. "You come with us and bring the big gun. We'll take the zodiac. We'll do commo checks every thirty minutes. We miss two, Kono, you can head home."

"Not," was Kono's response to that and the others knew better than to argue with the Gullah. A descendant of the former slaves and freedmen who populated the coastal barrier islands off of Florida, Georgia and South Carolina, Kono was part of a unique culture that had its own traditions and language. He was much a part of the Low Country as any person could be. A solidly built black man, Kono sported a shaved head with unblemished chocolate skin. He was barefoot, his feet more sure of the deck than any man-made shoes. He wore jeans that had seen better days and an untucked Hawaiian shirt. On his left hip was a machete.

Riley went over the side, into the zodiac Gator had used to transport himself into his sniping position on the island. Chase clambered over the side behind him. Gator climbed back into the rubber boat, the big .50 caliber Barrett sniper rifle cradled in his arms.

Without another word, Riley cast off and they roared toward the beach.

As they neared the shoreline, Riley leaned close to Chase, speaking loud enough to be heard over the outboard engine, but low enough that Gator couldn't hear. "Get you head out of your fourth point of contact, Horace. This woman wrapped you around her finger and tossed you. Then Erin dumped her thing on you. You don't do well with women."

No shit, Chase thought. A divorce, losing Sylvie back in Boulder, then Sarah conning him, and on top of her Erin lying dead ahead of him and lurking long ago in his past. He was coming full circle, and it wasn't a pretty one, more like a whirlpool.

Riley was watching the surf. At just the right distance, he cut the engine and pulled it up. Their momentum carried them onto the beach. Riley jumped overboard with a stake on a rope. He slammed it into the beach as Gator hopped off and headed to the left to assume his overwatch position.

"We take the stairs," Riley said.

Chase followed him and they took the creaking wooden boards two at a time. Riley had an MP-5 at the ready and Chase was backing him with the same.

They made it up the cliff to the plateau holding the mansion.

Erin's body lay where it had fallen, blood congealing. Her body had not been covered. Sarah Briggs was nowhere to be seen.

They double-timed past the body and into the house. They moved fast, but tactically, the odds were likely that Sarah had already getten out of there as quickly as possible.

They were wrong.

They came upon her standing a balcony overlooking the cliff and the ocean, a cell phone in her hands, talking forcefully.

She saw them and switched off the phone, then tossed it in an arc. It landed in the pool.

"Calling the cavalry?" Riley asked.

"If I have, perhaps you should go back to where you came from."

"Perhaps not," Chase said.

"Forget something, Horace?" she asked as they joined her. Her tone was casual but her body was tense. At least she'd put a robe on.

"Tell us everything about Erin and her son with Chase," Riley said.

Sarah laughed, a low sultry sound, regaining her balance. "You left in a rush, Horace. All pumped up about being a daddy. And threatening me, thinking you destroyed my life. Must have felt good to get those last digs in. Did you toss that USB drive?"

"I tossed it," Chase said.

"And I tossed my phone, so we're even."

"Who were you talking to?" Riley asked.

"Like you said. Arranging transportation out of here before bad people come to do me in. Am I too late? Are you bad people?"

"Why'd you toss it?" Riley demanded.

"I don't want you two showing up at my next place," Sarah said. "Hell, I didn't expect you to show back up here. That money from SAS is gone?"

"It's gone as far as you're concerned," Chase said.

Riley cut in. "Was Erin lying?"

Sarah deigned to look at Riley. "How are the nerves, Dave? You a little shaky?" She picked up a flute of champagne. "Need something to steady things out?"

"I'm fine," Riley said.

"Sure, sure. Pills help? All you vets get happy pills, right? VA passes them out for free so you're willing to stand in line while dying, right?"

"Was she lying?" Riley repeated.

"Why would Erin lie?" Sarah said. "I admit she is, was, very good at it. Better than me, and I've been told I'm among the best. But lying about having a son? None of what happened would have played out the way it did if that little tidbit wasn't true. I didn't figure it out until too late. After we were here. And she started talking just a little bit. She finally let me in on the big secret about a week or so ago. I didn't think much of it, although it did explain some of her actions since she never seemed into the money. But I never thought you'd find us, Horace. I did start getting worried Erin would leak our location somehow to get you here since she'd obviously never let it go and people who can't let things go always want to dig that knife in deeper and then end up falling on it themselves, as she did. Honestly, since you want honesty, I was planning on getting away from her shortly. She was a liability and unraveling. I appreciate your help in that matter, although it was more extreme than what I had in mind."

Chase stepped up next to Riley. "You're done."

"Oh, Horace, Horace." She shook her head. "You are *still* so naïve. Yes, you got *a lot* of the money. By the way, do you mind if I ask where it went? To your account perhaps?"

"No," Chase said, but nothing more.

"Of course not. Honest Horace wouldn't do that. One then assumes your secret friend in the dark world who tracked me down for you. Spooks. They play people. Today your friend gives me up. Tomorrow he'll give you up if it suits his needs. We're just pieces on the board, moved about and sacrificed without a second thought."

"We've been around," Riley said. "We know how the game is played."

"Oh yes," Sarah said, "you have. And look where *you* ended up, Dave Riley, former Green Beret. Running small-time book on Daufuskie Island. Taking over your Uncle Xavier's nickel and dime operation. I made more off one regular season football game than you could make in a lifetime running that gig. Drawing your pension from the government for decades of service and giving up your physical and mental health. How much do you get a month for all that traveling around the world getting shot at?"

Surprisingly, Riley laughed. "You're buying time. You've got people coming."

"Perhaps."

"And how do you know about spooks?" Riley asked. "You ran an off-shore gambling site. Not espionage."

"Any time there's considerable money involved," Sarah said, "you can be sure the spooks come around like moths to the light. Whether it be tracing the money or wanting it."

Riley took two steps and put the muzzle of his pistol in her face. "Tell us what you know about Chase's son."

"You won't shoot me," Sarah said with absolute confidence. "You're not capable of doing that in cold blood."

"Good point," Riley said, lowering the muzzle of his weapon and putting it back in the holster. "You *might* have me pegged." He stepped back. "But if I give the signal, Gator will put a fifty caliber round right through you. Probably a head shot. Blow it right off your shoulders. Isn't pretty. You remember Gator, don't you? You think he'll hesitate to shoot you?"

Sarah stirred, enough of a realist to understand that was indeed a possibility given it was Gator who had his finger on the trigger. "Nothing more than what she told you. She got pregnant from Horace's summer romp before he went off to West Point." She shifted attention to Chase. "She made a feeble attempt to contact you. If it had been me, and it wouldn't have been since I wouldn't have been in that situation in the first place, but if it was, I'd have shown up at West Point and put on quite the performance, maybe in the middle of that big parade field there, what do they call it?"

"The Plain," Chase said.

"Smack dab in the middle of the Plain," Sarah said. "Made you accountable. But Erin wigged out. She didn't tell her father who was the planter of the seed producing the little bugger germinating inside her. Why, I have no idea. Did her father not like you, Horace? Did she know she couldn't count on you? So her father banished her to Oklahoma to live with her mother. She gave birth. And then she was done with the kid, dumping him with her mother. She went to college somewhere in the Northeast. Got her vet degree. Worked a bunch of places, but when her father died a year ago, she ended back up on Hilton Head, living in his old house. She never knew what happened to the kid."

"Bull," Chase said.

"Gator shooting me won't blow secret little parts of my brain onto the wall spelling out anything," Sarah said. "She told me several times she'd wanted nothing to do with the kid and I believed her. She wanted nothing to do with her mother and her mother wanted nothing to do with her after she gave birth. Erin didn't even try to see Horace Junior again. She told me her mother died two years ago. She didn't go out there for the funeral and had no idea what happened to the boy. Probably ended up with her mother's family out there in Oklahoma as far as she thought. Which wasn't far. She certainly never checked on it."

The earpieces both Riley and Chase wore crackled with a report from Gator. "Two SUVs inbound. About six or seven minutes out."

"You've got company arriving," Riley said to Sarah.

She nodded. "I know. I called them. I was remiss not having security on site, but I enjoy my privacy and hired muscle standing around ogling isn't my thing. I have my kinks but that's not one." She shifted to Chase. "Horace, you and your friend did cost me a lot. Far, far more than all of you are worth combined. But only a fool would have all their assets in one place. I've got enough squirreled away here and there to live the rest of my life in reasonable comfort. And enough to pay the gentlemen coming down the road to kill you and your friends. And police up the body you so inconveniently left behind."

"Not if we kill you first," Chase said.

"You would have done that the first time you visited me here," Sarah said.

"The people you stole from will catch up to you," Riley said.

"But I won't be here," Sarah replied. "I got caught once. I won't get caught again. And I doubt they're coming tonight. I'll have time to pack. Seriously, you should just email or text next time you want to talk or threaten. Tick, tock, gentlemen."

Their earpieces came alive. "Three minutes out," Gator reported. "Two SUVs, I count at least six inside."

"Tick tock," Sarah repeated.

Riley drew his pistol once more. "I'm tired of being dicked with. You think you know me, but you don't. Chase won't kill you. Not his nature. But me, I truly don't give a rat's ass about you. You caused a lot of men's deaths. One more death doesn't make a bit of difference at this point. I've killed over less; and by less I mean killing someone simply because he's wearing a different uniform than I am or is in the wrong place at the wrong time. Seems a personal killing is more legitimate." He pressed the tip of the pistol against Sarah's forehead. Her eyes swiveled up to meet Riley's.

"Well, okay. Maybe I misjudged you there, Dave. Seriously, fellows, I'm telling you all I know. Erin wasn't the talkative type. We only hooked up halfway through our little excursion and she spent most of her time here cooped up, moping about. Not fun company at all."

"And?" Chase said.

Sarah smiled. She tilted her head back, turning slightly, sliding the muzzle down her cheek to her mouth, which she opened. Before Riley could react, she put her lips lightly around the end of the barrel.

Riley did the totally unnecessary movie move of pulling back the hammer on a double-action pistol.

But it sounded good. And he assumed Sarah had seen enough movies to know what it meant. He was just a finger twitch away from ending her, especially after this latest last stunt.

Sarah pulled her mouth back and blew Riley a kiss. "Okay, darling, okay. So that doesn't do it for you. Every man is a little different, but in the end, they're all the same. The only thing she said about Chase was that after you called and said you were coming, she checked out your mother's place on Brams Point. She was surprised to learn your mother had died. And that the man she was living with, Doc Something-or-Other, had disappeared. Maybe she was looking for you?"

"Two minutes," Gator warned. "Want me to delay them? Blow a tire or two out?"

"Hold on," Riley said into the throat mike. "You're still lying," he directed at Sarah.

"His name is Horace Brannigan," Sarah said. "That's it. That's all I know. I swear on—" she faltered, trying to come up with something she could swear her life upon.

She couldn't which told one all they needed to know about Sarah Briggs.

"Gator, shoot some tires," Riley ordered.

The roar of the Barrett firing echoed through the night air. A second shot followed the first.

"Not only is their ride down," Riley said, "but your friends are going to be hesitant to advance with a big gun out there having the advantage on them. So we have time. How much cash do you have here on site?"

Sarah was startled by the sudden change. She started to shake her head, but the pressure of the barrel on her forehead prevented that. "Not much."

"I'm really growing tired of your lies," Riley said. "You were boasting about it a minute ago. How much?"

"Two and hundred and fifty thousand," Sarah said.

"So half a million," Riley said. "Degenerates always half down in lies and double down in bets. And you're degenerate, Sarah. Let's get it." He pulled the gun back slightly.

Sarah opened her mouth to protest, but there was something in Riley's eyes that stopped her. She got up then walked into the master suite behind the balcony. She went to a painting, took it off the wall, revealing a safe with a keypad.

She quickly tapped on the pad. As it swung open she reached, but Riley was faster, shoving her back away from it.

He glanced in, then reached in and retrieved a pistol lying on top. "Nice try. I'd have killed you. You can thank me later."

Chase had silently followed them, still trying to catch up to reality. Riley stuck an arm into the safe and swept the contents out onto the wood floor. Bundles of cash, jewelry, two more guns, several passports.

"Cover her," Riley said to Chase.

Riley knelt and quickly looked at each passport, checking the names. Then he divided the money, expediently eyeballing two piles without counting. He reached in his combat vest and pulled out a lighter. He broke it in half, then poured the fluid onto one pile of money. He put the passports on top of that.

"That's your take," Riley said. "We're taking the other." He emphasized the point by quickly stuffing that pile into a bag he pulled out of one of the closets. It was a Gucci, but recognizing such wasn't in Riley or Chase's repertoire. "Now. Last chance. Everything about Horace Brannigan. or I burn your money and your passports. You won't be going anywhere before some very bad people get here."

The deep roar of the Barrett echoed.

"Keeping their heads down," Gator reported over the radio.

Riley retrieved another lighter out of his combat vest.

"Little anal on the lighter thing, aren't you?" Sarah said.

"They're useful. It's an old survival habit from my winter warfare Army days." Riley flicked it. "What haven't you told us? The other half, just like the money?"

Sarah eyed the passports. "That's pretty much it. Seriously. Okay. I put out some queries, to see if I could find little Brannigan."

Chase finally found his voice. "Why?"

"Leverage, Horace," Sarah said. "One can never have enough leverage."

"Against me?" Chase asked. "Or Erin?"

"Both." Sarah sighed. "I didn't think I'd ever see you again Horace. But Erin was here. I still needed to control her." She shrugged. "And I was curious. You have to admit, there is a certain, hmm, shall we say, pathos to the tale."

"Did you get anything back?" Riley asked.

"He's definitely not with Erin's family in Oklahoma," Sarah said. "I had a very discreet agency out of Oklahoma City do the checking. They lost the trail about a month after Erin's mother died. He disappeared from Oklahoma and never came back. And that, gentlemen, is it. I didn't pursue it further."

Riley stared at her. "I think you might be telling the truth. At least part of it." Then he shook his head. "But you're still lying, Sarah. There's more to all this than you're telling us."

"I've told you everything," Sarah said.

"Doubtful," Riley replied. He nodded at Chase. "Grab the bag. Let's go."

As he turned, Riley tossed the lighter onto the pile. The money and passports roared into flame.

The last they saw was Sarah Briggs, arms folded, passively watching the small pyre that contained her cash and fake passports burn.

* * *

Sarah Briggs, at least that was the name she was currently using, watched the pile burn to ash, then walked to the balcony. There was no sign of Chase or Riley. Ghosts disappearing back into the darkness.

A phone rang and she went over to her nightstand and opened it. There were a half dozen 'burners' in there and she pulled out the one that was buzzing.

"Fix your damn tires," she ordered the man calling her. "I have to be at the airport, ASAP."

She hung it up, then reached under the bed and pulled out a black leather shoulder bag. She dumped it on the bed. Handcuffs, whips, dildos and various other devices tumbled out. Along with a leather binder. She picked up a particularly large dildo and unscrewed the base. She shook and a thick wad of hundred dollars bills fell out. Then she put her finger in and pulled out the passport that had been jammed in there, curved around the interior. She began flexing it, straightening it out.

She'd learned long ago that men, whether they be customs, police, or even criminals, would never search the device. They'd laugh, make comments, but never touch it.

Thus the perfect hiding space. She repacked the bag, then went to the closet.

There was work to be done.

Chapter Four

"Three can keep a secret if two are dead," one of the three said.

The other two responded: "Except for the Ring."

They put their fists together, Institute rings shining on their left hands. It was a complicated move, but they managed to bump rings with each other. They were seated in a booth in the back of the High Cotton Bar on East Bay Street in Charleston. It was an upscale place, full of tourists and a scattering of locals. It was early afternoon but several empty glasses littered their table, a sign of nerves not as steady as their oath. For two of them, at least. The third had a half-full glass of water in front of him.

"I heard this Dillon guy was a bad ass on the football team," one of the men said. He was the youngest of the three, having just graduated and not yet taking his 'position' at his daddy's firm in Savannah.

"Jerrod, *I* was a bad ass on the football team," the biggest man at the table said; he was seated on the same side as Jerrod. He was a former lineman for the Institute team, whose gut had not seen the inside of a gym since graduation. The mound of flesh pressed up against the table. His name was Chad Mongin Jr., a first name he hated, but his father had been a Chad, his father's father had been a Chad and so on down the line until some fellow who'd stepped off a boat in Charleston harbor carrying the name Chad from whatever country he'd departed from. Thus he came from a long line of Chad's. And the last name, Mongin, represented a family that had come to the Low Country in 1685.

Despite his size, it was obvious to any observer, and there was one, that Chad was not the dominant figure at the table. That honor fell to a young man sitting alone on the other side, dressed casually in expensive jeans, and a button-down shirt, layered under a sweater. He was a page in Esquire come to life with his brown hair, sculpted cheekbones, and overall model looks. Those pages where they showed other men how they were supposed to dress and look, although most could only do the dress since looks had something to do with genetics.

Preston Holland Gregory was the son of the senior Senator from South Carolina and chairman of the Select Committee on Intelligence. While Chad might fit in at a toga party chugging beer, and Jerrod in a library perusing literature, Preston would fit perfectly in the halls of power, which is what all twenty-two years of his life had been directed toward and his future portended.

"Gentlemen," Preston said, not calling his friends by their names, since he actually didn't consider them his friends, although they didn't know that. "My father's aide informed me that this Dillon fellow comes from Mrs. Jenrette and—"

"Shit," Chad muttered. "When is that old witch going to let it go?"

"I do not believe," Preston said, "she will let it go as long as she breathes. Hopefully, that won't be very much longer. Nevertheless, we are to cooperate with this Dillon chap." He said that with the slightest of English accents, an affectation he'd started at the Institute and was growing stronger each month, since no one pointed it out to him. It might have been too much *Downton Abbey*; or the fact he was heading off to Oxford for graduate school in a few months and his subconscious was preparing him. Or he might simply be one of those dicks who need affectations like a fake English accent.

"I don't like it," Jerrod said, looking nervously around the bar. "We told the investigators everything they needed."

"There are deeper forces at play," Preston said. "People are coming after our parents. Our parents, who are finalizing a deal with Mrs. Jenrette concerning Sea Drift on Saturday." He nodded at Jerrod. "I know your father has a lot of capital tied up in the Sea Drift proposal."

"My father doesn't exactly fill me in," Jerrod said.

Chad snorted in derision. "My family gave up too much on the island, but they still have a slice. An important one."

"Yes," Preston said. "And your family will be well paid for that slice." He looked at one, then the other. "We are the future. We can do much better than our parents have."

"Your father is a United States Senator," Jerrod noted. "What more do you want?"

Preston simply smiled back at him, without saying anything.

Chad downed his drink in one quick swallow. "You two might. My family squandered almost everything."

Preston graced both of them with a smile. "Don't worry old chaps. I've got both *your* interests in mind despite what our parents do. We're the next generation of the Ring. But we're going to be bigger than our fathers. We're going to own everything of importance from here to Savannah. And then we move on to Atlanta and Washington."

"You sound like Sherman," Jerrod muttered.

"Fucking Brannigan," Chad cursed. "Why did he have to show up in the Sinks?"

"It really—" Preston paused as a figure loomed up to their table. Dillon was wearing a long black overcoat, jeans and a black T-shirt.

"How y'all doing?" Dillon asked, a bit heavy on his own southern accent. He didn't wait to be invited, but slid in next to Preston, who could not hide his irritation at the close proximity of another human being and scooted away, until he was trapped against the wall.

Dillon pointed. "Jarrod Fabrou, right? Chad Mongin? And you must be Preston Holland Gregory. Your pappy is the Senator, is he not?"

"Did you check our yearbook photos?" Preston said, trying to reclaim some ground. "Or Google us?"

Dillon ignored the question. "I've been watching y'all for a little bit. Habit of mine. In Afghanistan, I'd have my platoon set up recon at least twenty-four hours before we were supposed to hit a target. I was never a fan of those midnight swoop-ins with no advance eyeballs on the target. Those can go to shit in a heartbeat. At first my company commander wasn't thrilled with, having to detail a chopper to send the recon element in. But it worked so well, eventually every platoon in the company was doing it."

"You were in combat?" Jerrod asked.

"No," Dillon said. "I'm making it up because I'm a liar."

An awkward silence followed, one that Dillon allowed to last.

Preston finally stepped into the breach. "We're here as requested. Is this in reference to the unfortunate incident with Greer Jenrette?"

"No," Dillon said. "I want to conduct a survey on how much you enjoyed your time at the Institute. Whether you would recommend the experience to other high school seniors seeking to better their lives."

"Listen," Chad began, leaning forward, his gut pushing the table toward the other side, but Dillon's palm on the wooden top halted it. "We agreed—"

"To come here and answer questions," Dillon said. "Not ask them."

"So ask," Preston said.

"The Quick and the Dead," Dillon said.

The three exchanged glances.

"That's what you were doing that night, wasn't it?" Dillon asked, not quite a complete question, almost a statement. "With Wing? And Greer Jenrette?" He didn't wait for an answer. "I used to think bayonet training was over-rated and out of date. But then I was with a squad that got trapped inside a hut. In the middle of Bum-fuck Nowhere Afghanistan. It's actually a pretty country if you don't have to fight in it. Fantastic snow-covered mountains. Sweeping vistas. And hard-ass fighters who will gut you in a heartbeat. Speaking of gutting, that brings us back to bayonet fighting. The Quick and the Dead. That's what the cadre screamed at us rats when we did bayonet training. Remember?"

He looked at Chad. "You must have been on the bayonet committee, right? All the football players were. I was. Easy duty. Scream at rats. Make them practice all that parry, thrust, recover crap. Then the fun part. Put helmets and pads on them and make them beat the shit out each other with pugil sticks. Of course, sometimes we forgot the helmet and the padding.

"Funny thing is, the last recorded bayonet charge by the U.S. Army was in Korea in 1951. But the Brits, they actually did one in Iraq in 2004. Low on ammo, a unit of Brits charged some ragheads and scared the living piss out of them. Still, there are a lot of other martial skills the time could be better spent on than using the bayonet, which is why the U.S. Army has actually done away with the training. But we keep it at the Institute, like we keep a lot of things at the Institute that have outlived their actual usefulness. Like close-order drill. No use for that in combat. Not like we're redcoats facing Napoleon at Waterloo.

"But that's not the point of bayonet drill. It's actually designed to reverse what we were taught growing up—you know the Christian thing: love each other, blah, blah, blah. Most people are actually kind of reluctant to kill another person. Any of you fellows ever kill anyone?" Dillon stared at each one in turn. Jerrod didn't meet his gaze; Chad did, but said nothing and Preston simply stared back.

"Anyway, the goal of bayonet drill is to get soldiers to drop that reverence for life, other people's lives that is, and get them wrapped up in the chaos and emotion and adrenaline-pumping insanity that is combat. And I assure you, it's pretty much that. Kipling's unforgiving minute. Got to keep your head, yada, yada. So that's why there's all the screaming and yelling and getting in your face during bayonet drill; besides the fact we liked screaming and yelling and getting in rats' faces as upperclassmen, didn't we? Not like you can do that in the regular army with real troops or in a law office or a board meeting. Real soldiers and real people don't put up with that kind of bullshit."

"Do you have a question in all of that?" Preston asked.

"Patience Grasshopper," Dillon said, drawing blank looks from the others. "No Kung Fu for you, eh? Probably never watched Monty Python either. I like the oldies. Anyway. Back to the Quick and the Dead. I vaguely remember hearing rumors while I was a cadet that there was this group called the Ring." He held up his hand, showing his Institute ring. "You know, ring-knockers. I got one." He rapped the top of the table. "But a special group of cadets were invited into this secret group called the Ring; me I wasn't invited 'cause I don't have the lineage. Got to be born into it apparently. Is that correct?"

None of them said anything.

"Anyway," Dillon said, "I'm digressing. I heard rumors that some members of this Ring group would take rats and make them fight each other, just like with pugil sticks, but with their

M-14s and their chrome-covered bayonets and using body armor to protect the vitals." He reached into a pocket on his long coat then pulled out the weapon Mrs. Jenrette had given him. He slapped it down on the table with a solid thud. "Like this one. So tell me. Is that true?"

Chad's mouth was open, his brain trying to process the long string of words in which Dillon had wrapped them. Jerrod was staring at the bayonet as if it were dripping blood. Which left Preston.

Preston clapped once, then twice, then several more times, mockingly and slowly, until he stopped. "Bravo. Bravo. A command performance. But which part of 'is that true' do you want the answer to? You implied quite a few things. Most of them incorrect."

"Was Greer Jenrette killed interrupting a forced Quick and the Dead?" Dillon asked.

"You know he wasn't," Preston said. "You've read the investigation."

"I don't know anything for certain." Dillon leaned back in the booth and looked at all three, a sweeping gaze. "I didn't finish my story about the hut. Me and six other Rangers were trapped there. We had one man badly wounded, but medevac couldn't get to us. Dust storm down in the lowlands where the choppers were based. And things were getting mighty grim. Ammo was running low. And the enemy was gathering, building up for one last rush. By the way, if you ever get into combat, you'll learn quickly you can never carry enough ammunition." Dillon smiled without humor. "But I don't foresee that in any of you-all's futures. Not a one of you signed an ROTC contract. Anyway. We ended up fixing bayonets. I mean, I gave the order. Just like they do before a parade. Except these bayonets weren't chrome plated—" he pulled the blade out of the scabbard—" but cold steel. Razor sharp. Had a fellow in the platoon that loved sharpening 'em for everyone and he was good at it so we all let him. Some backwoods good old boy, or should that be good young boy, from Arkansas. Good man.

"So there we were, bayonets at the ready, some of us down to a couple of rounds, some of us out. And the rest of my platoon, they came running. Three miles, gentlemen. Full gear. The gunners carrying the pigs, the M-60 machineguns, which weigh twenty-two pounds and each also had a basic load of ammo. Some of them were carrying over a hundred and fifty pounds of gear. And those sons-a-bitches ran three miles and rescued us."

He fell silent. As Preston opened his mouth to speak, Dillon cut him off.

"And that, gentlemen is true loyalty. That is the bond that can never be broken. So I don't know what little bullshit ceremony you all just did fist-bumping rings together, but I guarantee you, it can be broken, and I *will* break it if I have to."

"It appears you will not leave until we repeat what we've already said." Preston folded his arms across his chest. "We had Wing and Jenrette in the Sinks. A sweat party. You remember those?" He didn't wait for an answer. "Raincoats in the showers in the summer. Water turned full hot. Making them spout off rat poop. You remember, don't you?"

Dillon didn't respond.

"Everything would have been all right, except Brannigan showed up," Preston said.

"With a bayonet," Dillon said.

"No." Preston shook his head. "We had the bayonets. It was Wing's. We had him bring it. Along with his M-14. Jenrette had his too. We had them do close-order drill before turning on the showers. A warm-up, so to speak."

"Speaking of speaking." Dillon gestured at the two men on the other side of the booth. "Either of you do any?"

"Let me finish," Preston said. He didn't wait for permission. "Wing had gone to the infirmary earlier that day. But he didn't rat out. Just got bed rest. Still, going to the infirmary is what a loser would do. We were giving him a chance to man up."

"And Jenrette?" Dillon asked. "Why was he there?"

Preston looked across at Jerrod, who finally spoke: "You saw us 'bumping rings' as you call it. We belong to a special, uh, club, that—"

"The Ring," Dillon said.

"The Ring," Preston confirmed.

Jerrod continued. "Jenrette is old Charleston. His mother runs St. Cecilia. A very powerful woman."

Dillon gave a cold smile. "I've met her."

"Exactly," Jerrod said, growing a little more animated and confident. "So Greer Jenrette would eventually become part of the Ring. His birthright. But we do have to make it a bit of an ordeal."

"You went through this ordeal?" Dillon said, staring at Jerrod.

"I did."

"Right," Dillon said. "Musta been tough."

"Hey," Chad said. "We got to talk to you, but we don't have to take crap off of you."

"Please continue your tale," Dillon said.

Preston picked up the thread. "We had Wing and Jenrette down in the Sinks. Have you talked to Wing yet?"

Dillon shook his head. "But I plan on it."

"You'll see what I mean when you do," Preston said. "We figured we'd make it easy on Jenrette. Wing isn't exactly a devastating physical specimen. We planned to have them sweat for a while. Then maybe let them go at it against each other a smidge. Gentlemanly stuff. Do some boxing."

He fell silent.

"And then?" Dillon prompted.

"Then that dickhead Brannigan showed up," Chad said. "All fired up. Telling us to fuck off. To leave his classmates alone. He grabbed Wing's bayonet and—"

"It wasn't on his rifle?" Dillon asked.

"Negative," Preston said. "It was on a bench in the showers. Sheathed. Along with Wing's rifle. And Jenrette's rifle and bayonet."

"So you big bad three ring-knockers were scared of a single rat waving a chrome bayonet around?" Dillon asked.

"It was steaming down there," Preston said.

"Because you'd turned the showers on full hot," Dillon said.

"It was steaming down there," Preston continued. "We were all hot and sweaty. We'd been bracing those rats for over an hour. Brannigan just busted in and everything got a little crazy. Next thing we know, Jenrette's got the blade in his chest. And Brannigan's gone. Ran away like the shitty coward he is."

"Were you drunk?" Dillon asked.

Chad and Jerrod exchange glances, but Preston answered.

"Unfortunately, we'd had some drinks. Honestly, that's why we feel so bad about it. If we'd been completely sober, perhaps we'd have reacted quicker and handled it better."

"But you're not drinking now, Preston," Dillon noted.

Preston didn't say anything to that.

"So that's it?" Dillon asked.

"That's it," Preston said. "And it's all in the official inquiry, so you wasted our time bringing us here."

"No Quick and the Dead?" Dillon asked.

Preston rubbed his forehead while Jerrod was looking toward the front of the bar, eager to be gone.

"Listen—" Chad began, but then the waitress came by.

"Get you boys another round?"

"No," Dillon snapped, in such a tone that she immediately went away.

Preston turned awkwardly on the bench to face Dillon. "Brannigan stabbed Jenrette. All three of us saw it. Wing saw it. All four of us testified to that. Brannigan's fingerprints were on the bayonet. It was in Jenrette's chest. Brannigan fled. We reported the incident to the duty office right away. Why are you wasting our time?"

Dillon looked at each of them, one at a time. "You-all would never let me in this Ring of yours, would you?"

"It's not our call," Jerrod said. "There's a list and—" He came to an abrupt halt as Preston kicked him under the table.

"Wing and Brannigan would never be let in either, right?" Dillon asked.

The three graduates stared at Dillon without a word.

"You sure y'all have told me everything?" Dillon asked. "On your word of honor as Institute men?"

"Yes," Preston said.

Dillon stared at Chad.

"Yes," Chad said.

Dillon shifted his hard gaze to Jerrod who failed to meet the gaze and simply mumbled: "Yes."

"Alrighty then. Guess I have to take your words for it." Dillon stood and slid out of the booth. The three also exited the booth as Preston threw a hundred-dollar bill down on the table.

The three headed for the door, but then Preston turned and came back, leaving the other two staring after him out of earshot.

"Waiting for change?" Dillon asked.

"What if you *could* join the Ring?" Preston asked.

Chapter Five

Thursday Afternoon

Hilton Head Island is shaped roughly like a shoe, with the flat of the sole facing the Atlantic Ocean on a long strand of hard-packed beach. The back of the heel points toward Port Royal Sound and the top of the shoe abuts the Intracoastal Waterway. Roughly halfway up where the island faces the Intracoastal, Broad Creek cuts in a wide path, almost dividing the island in two. As the seagull flies, it's twenty miles north of Savannah and ninety miles south of Charleston. The island is twelve miles long and only four wide at its broadest.

People who lived there liked to say it was the second largest barrier island, topped only by Long Island, but technically that wasn't true as Hilton Head is actually two islands, only one of which is a barrier island, but that's splitting hairs and the island. The first Europeans set foot on it in 1521, some wandering Spanish. It was the English, of course, who gave it a name, when Captain William Hilton stopped by in 1663 and decided to name the north end Hilton Head, after, imaginatively and egotistically, himself.

Of more immediate interest, the island is in a rather unique position as far as the law. It boasts no police force of its own, instead relying on the Beaufort County Sheriff's Department. Given that Beaufort is only about ten miles straight distance away, that doesn't seem like a big deal, but the actual drive requires one to come off Hilton Head and drive west a good distance, then drive north, skirting the tidal marshes, then back east. It is an indication of how much emphasis the sheriff's department places on policing the Island that there is no permanent substation.

It was more than just geography. Between distance and the desire not to interfere with tourism, the hand of the law rested lightly on the island. Underneath that, Hilton Head was a cesspool of vices from the numerous escort services that catered to all those golfer's foursomes, to the gambling and the drug smuggling. Money flowed and some of it flowed to the sheriff's department, pulling that light touch back even further.

Dave Riley had known this ever since arriving in the Low Country and talking with his Uncle Xavier before the old man passed away. Horace Chase was a relative newcomer, but he was learning fast.

The two of them were seated at a table at the end of Chase's deepwater dock, extending 240 feet out into the Intracoastal. A metal gangway led from the deck where they sat to a floating dock below them, although the dock was in pretty bad shape, several of the floats having lost their buoyancy and water threatening to cover the entire thing. When they first got back, Chase had gone ashore to feed Chelsea and grab a small cooler full of beers before rejoining Riley out here.

"You need to pull some maintenance," Riley observed as he tipped back a cold one. It was the day after their Caribbean excursion. After dropping them off on Thursday afternoon, Kono and Gator had gone off to do whatever the two of them did, the less known about the better; they were extraneous beneficiaries of the light hand of the law in the Low Country. Unlike Chase, Kono had mentioned something about pulling maintenance after the fast, hard ride back to the coast.

"I haven't exactly had time," Chase said.

"Haven't made the time," Riley said. "So. What now?"

The house Chase had inherited from his mother was in Spanish Wells, a community on a spit of land between the Intracoastal Waterway and Broad Creek. Only one way in by road and the same way out. Almost every house had a deep-water dock in the back, either on the Intracoastal or on Broad Creek, and many sported large, expensive boats on lifts.

There was no boat at the end of Chase's dock.

"You know," Chase said, "I've yet to see any of those boats get used. It's like they're trophies."

"Boats are more expensive to operate than most people realize," Riley said. "Plus, as you noted, the people owning them are working too hard to find the time to enjoy them."

Chase turned his attention back to Riley. "The first question is: Should we believe what Sarah Briggs told us? And, by the way, why did you burn the money and passports?"

"Same answer to both question," Riley said. "She's a liar. That's why I burned her passports. Make it harder for her to run. Gives her enemies some time to catch up and finish her off which I think would make the world a better place. And when I say she's a liar, I'm not saying we shouldn't believe what she told us, but we need to understand she only told us half the truth. I view that as a form of lying."

"'Never lie to a Ranger'," Chase quoted on of Rogers' Ranger Rules. "She paid the price."

"We should have killed her," Riley said.

"That's not who we are."

"What bothers me," Riley said, "is that she knows that and counts on it. Maybe we need to adapt."

"Become murderers?" Chase asked.

"I don't know about you, but I aint too certain exactly *who* I am. We've both killed. Let's not fool ourselves."

"So should we believe her about Oklahoma being a dead end?" Chase asked, implicitly agreeing not to go down a philosophical rabbit hole about killing.

"Yes," Riley said. "The key to a successful lie is to tell enough of the truth. She led with that, so I believe it. But let's take a look at it from her point of view. She wants to find your son. For whatever reasons, although I think she was pretty up front about that—possible leverage if she needed it down the line. Most likely on Erin, but also on you if the need arose. Briggs plays angles. It's why she's still alive and there's a decent chance she'll probably stay alive a while longer despite our efforts.

"So," Riley continued, "it seems to me that she'd check further into Erin. After all, she wouldn't believe everything Erin was telling her. And it also seems like trying to find his mother might be first on young Harry's agenda." Riley had a sudden awareness. "That's why Sarah checked into it. She knew Erin had this connection with you. And if you found out somehow, you'd come looking."

Chase shook his head, but he wasn't disagreeing. "It's weird for me to imagine that there's this person, this young man, out there, who I brought into this world."

"You didn't do much," Riley said. "Contributed a little sperm, is all."

Chase gave him a hard look; Riley simply met the look and raised an eyebrow. Chase's anger dissolved. "Yeah. It's just strange. But you mean to tell me if you found out you had a kid, it wouldn't turn your world upside down?"

Riley granted him that. "All right. But for all you know, Horace Junior is studying coeds at some college or traveling Europe or working at a Starbucks. You should be glad Erin had nothing to do with raising him. Unfortunately, she was raised by her mother, so I'm not thinking that was the best thing either, but who knows? Maybe crazy skips a generation?"

Chase shook his head. "Erin was raised by her father. She never said much about her mother. Her parents split when she was young." His forehead furrowed.

"I sense a great thought," Riley said.

"Cardena said something strange," Chase said. He was referring to the spook who'd given them Sarah Briggs' location and several months earlier had a Predator fire a Hellfire missile to take out Karralkov's yacht. "I didn't make much of it at the time, but he's not the kind of guy to say throwaway lines."

"Don't seem like it," Riley agreed.

"He asked me why I was so keen to go after Briggs' son—"

"Her non-existent son," Riley had to throw in as he reached into the cooler then pulled out another pair of beers, handing one to Chase.

"Why I was so keen to go after her son. He said something along the lines of—'it's not like he's your son'. That's a little odd, isn't it?"

"Maybe you should call him?" Riley suggested. "And it was odd that Sarah mentioned spooks, like she had some experience in the area. Seems she—" he paused as his cell phone vibrated on the wooden table. He snatched it up: "Riley."

A voice with a distinct New Jersey accent was on the other end. "Mister Riley, how are the trade winds blowing today?"

"The words and the music don't match," Riley said. "The words indicate someone used to the ocean, the music says Jersey, Mister Farrelli. The only connection I make between New Jersey and the ocean is sleeping with the fishes."

Farrelli laughed. "I try. Can't fault me for that. But you know, we got the Jersey Shore. Lots of oceanfront although Sandy did a number on a fair stretch. Heard you had a little expedition recently."

Farrelli Riley mouthed to Chase. "Where did you hear that?"

"A little birdie whispered it in my ear."

"And?"

"And some things are going on," Farrelli said. "People asking questions. I don't like it."

"One of those people Sarah Briggs?"

Farrelli answered with his own question. "You had that animal doctor, Brannigan, with you guys when you did that thing, didn't you?"

"What thing?" Riley said.

"Don't fuck with me," Farrelli said. "You wanna talk or not?"

"I wanna talk," Riley said.

"Then come here and talk." The phone went dead.

Riley quickly relayed the conversation.

"So Sarah did make inquiries about Horace here," Chase said.

"At least about Erin," Riley said. "We don't know if she asked about the son. Your son," he amended. "Told you—Sarah Briggs only tells half a truth. Even if it served her better to tell the whole truth, someone like her will still lie. It's in their DNA. And I'm not sure I buy her reasons for the inquiry. She didn't expect to see you again. And I don't see why she needed leverage on Erin. As she said, she was growing tired of her and saw her as a liability. My take is that she *is* the type of person who will kill if someone's cramping their style."

"Why would Farrelli call you about her?"

"Good question," Riley said. "And one I have to talk to him to find out the answer."

Chase was looking at his house, just above the low steel seawall that separated beach from grass. Unlike the McMansions on either side, his was one of the few remaining original single-story houses left in Spanish Wells.

Riley got up to leave. "What?" he asked, seeing the look in Chase's eyes.

"I haven't paid a utility bill since I moved in," Chase said.

"So?"

"So who's paying for the electric and water here? Didn't even realize it. And where did Doc Cleary go?"

"You lost me," Riley said.

Chase nodded. "You're right. I've had my head up my ass. There's a lot more going on here than is apparent."

"Well, good," Riley said, not having a clue what Chase was talking about. "Get your head out of your ass. I'm going to talk to the mob. If I don't come back, keep the cannoli." With that he headed down the long wooden dock, hopping over some of the rotting boards that looked ready to give way.

Chase followed him, walking slowly, thinking hard. He had the sense that he was at the surface of a deep pool and there were dark secrets down in there; Erin's admission of a son just being the first. Significant, but part of something more.

He stepped off the wood walkway onto the struggling grass lawn that sloped up about six feet to the back of the house. Almost all of Hilton Head Island is a flood zone; a strong enough hurricane hitting at the right time with a tidal surge would pretty much wipe the island off the map. Which brought something else to mind: who was paying the insurance on the house? Backing up from that: was there insurance on the house? Being military, either living in on-base quarters or being deployed, Chase had never owned a home before. While the deed was in his name, he realized not much else was.

While old, the house had charm, if one considered a tree smashed down through the living room roof charm. Chase did, which gives one insight into his character. The tree was still alive, its roots still in the earth outside and he'd patched around it, incorporating it into the house. There were three bedrooms: a master with its own bath on the north end and two guest rooms on the south sharing a bathroom. The tree living room was in the center with a large wood-burning fireplace built into the wall fronted by a brick hearth. Chase figured if the storm-damaged tree began to die, it would provide a ready source of wood for the fireplace.

He had vague childhood memories of a Christmas spent here with his mother and Doc Cleary. Old Doc. He'd been Old Doc when Chase was a kid; a distinguished white-haired man, tall and thin, with rimless glasses that always slid down his nose. Chase had spent that one Christmas and several summers here, including that last fateful summer before he went off to West Point and Beast Barracks. The summer he met Erin Brannigan.

He passed by the concrete pool, another thing he hadn't gotten around to, the surface covered with algae and about four feet below being full; at least there wasn't a gator nesting in it. Chelsea ran up to his side, accompanying him as he went in the back sliding glass doors.

Chase went to the battered footlocker in the living room that held a lot of his gear. He dialed in the combination then opened it. A letter lay on top and he took it out and carefully unfolded it. It was stained with blood, Chase's, since he'd received the letter in Afghanistan just prior to being wounded and medevacked to a hospital in Germany.

My Dearest Horace.

We are both at war, but I fear I am losing mine. The cancer has spread too quickly.

Fate has dealt you a final card from the father you never knew and the man I hardly knew. Don't be like your father. Don't be too brave. Come back from the war.

I know we haven't spoken in a long time. I know you don't want to hear this. I blame myself for that. But maybe someday you'll think better about me. I hope you will.

Sometimes there are broken people. Like me. Like you. I was trying to do the right thing for you. Now I know I did wrong by giving you your father's legacy. The Medal of Honor and the Academy appointment that came with it, and all afterward. But maybe it isn't too late.

Even broken people should get another chance.

Be a good man.

With my dying love,
Your Mother.

PS: In my will, there's a house. An old house. But it's a good house in a good place. It will be yours. It's the house we spent the summers in on Hilton Head in the Low Country. It's from an old friend. He's a good man. You won't understand now, and will think the wrong thing because you tend to think the wrong thing first. It's all I can give you now.

He looked at it a little differently now. What had she meant by 'all afterward'? And that 'it isn't too late'? What had she known? He had to agree she was on target with him thinking the wrong thing; he had plenty of evidence of that.

Chase folded the letter, put it back in the footlocker. He saw the other letter. The one he rarely read. The one from his father to him. IF.

IF. Chase knew he'd failed the test. And he wasn't certain he could ever make it up.

And below the letter was the Medal of Honor. Still in its case. Sealed. His mother, Lilly had never opened it.

Of course his father had chosen Kipling.

The strange thing was, Chase intimately understood one thing in that poem: the Unforgiving Minute. That was the essence of combat. His father had known and now he did too.

There was no forgiveness from that minute.

He put the letter in the locker and closed it. He sat down on top of it with a heavy heart. Chelsea pressed her head against his thigh. He took out his cell phone and dialed a number he knew by heart now. He was surprised when it was answered on the second ring.

"Horace, Horace, Horace. Heard you were down in the Caribbean recently and not for a vacation."

"You told me where to go," Chase pointed out.

"True," Cardena said. "But you left her alive."

"You got the money."

"I could have taken the money," Cardena said, "without you going down there."

"Why did you give her up to me?" Chase asked.

"Duh. Are you listening? To kill her."

"You knew I wouldn't."

"I was counting on Riley," Cardena said.

"You don't know him that well."

"Apparently you're a bad influence. The old Dave Riley was stone cold. He's gone soft."

"He's older and wiser."

"Horace, you're always one conversation behind," Cardena said. Chase had first met him at Denver International Airport while on the trail of a drug smuggling ring. He'd been told that Cardena was DEA. That wasn't true. In the end, Chase had learned he'd been played by Cardena to accomplish a mission with multiple goals, one of which was to cause the death of a CIA agent. Who Cardena worked for, Chase had no clue. And he'd never met the man face-to-face since that one time at DIA.

"Why do you care about Sarah Briggs?" Chase asked. "I thought your concern was Karralkov, and he's no longer among the living, thanks to you."

"The world is very large," Cardena said, "yet it's also a lot smaller than most people realize. But you didn't call me to discuss philosophy."

"I was thinking about one of our conversations," Chase said. "You asked me why I was going after a boy who—"

"Didn't exist," Cardena said.

"Who wasn't my own," Chase finished. "Turns out, it appears I do have a son. Just found that out from my trip to the Caribbean."

Chase waited, hoping Cardena would fill the silence with something, anything.

Finally the other man spoke. "Horace, why are you such a shit magnet? I mean, seriously. I thought getting you out of Boulder would induce you into quiet retirement. But you went from the frying pan into the fucking bonfire."

"You'd miss talking to me," Chase said.

"Not really. And now it looks like you've stepped into another pile of shit."

"What do you mean?" Chase asked.

"You think killing Karralkov solves everything in that neck of the woods?" Cardena asked. "It just gets the Russians out of things; for the time being."

"What's going on?"

"Sarah Briggs isn't who you thought she was," Cardena said.

"I know that."

"No, Horace, you don't. You think she's some hustler who ripped off a bunch of money using an offshore on-line betting web site. What, do you think she just started there? Came out of nowhere? We all have histories."

"What are you talking about?"

"You'll figure it out, Horace. Or maybe you won't."

Chase decided to stop tap dancing around. "I'm trying to find my son. I think you know something."

"I know a lot of things," Cardena said. "But keeping track of your spawn isn't one of them. You really should have killed Briggs. She's a loose end that's going to come back to haunt you some day. Sooner than you expect. Just like this son is a loose end that's been out there for almost two decades. Really Chase, your house is not in order."

Chase glanced at the tree crashed down through his living room and wondered if Cardena knew about that and was speaking both literally and figuratively.

"What do you know about your son?" Cardena asked.

"Nothing."

"Might I suggest you keep it that way?"

"Why?"

"You wouldn't follow my advice anyway." Once more his question went in a different direction. "Is Dave Riley still assisting you?"

"He is."

"Interesting," Cardena said.

"Why?"

"Nothing."

Another throwaway that meant something, Chase knew.

"Unfortunately for you," Cardena continued, "I do not have a dog in this hunt. I believe that's a popular saying in your current part of the world. But I'd watch your back. This is bigger than just your boy."

The phone went dead. Chase stared at it, wondering at the vague threats Cardena had floated out there. He saw no reason why Sarah Briggs would come after him. Yes, she might want revenge, but she was the type of person who valued money over revenge.

Which made him wonder if money was still involved somehow. Briggs hadn't checked on Erin and his son out of boredom. She had a stake in things. But what was that stake?

Chase made a couple more quick calls, confirming that the house's utilities were still in Doc Cleary's name and payments were automatically processed out of an account from a local bank. The bank wouldn't tell him how much was in the account, but the woman Chase talked to confirmed that it was an active account, with deposits being made, as well as the bills being paid. But she would tell him nothing further, citing privacy laws.

Finally he called Kono.

The Gullah answered on the fifth ring. "Speak."

Chase could hear the *Fina's* engines in the background. "I need to speak to Tear."

"What for?"

"I need to find out about Doc Cleary." *And my mother*.

There was a silence, then Kono replied. "We be there in forty-five minutes. Take you to him."

* * *

Dillon hesitated in the sally port before entering the Quadrangle, the heart of the Institute. Surrounded on four sides by battlements topping the square barracks, the Quadrangle was the formation area for the Corps. A concrete square, a hundred and fifty yards to a side. Barracks loomed up on all sides, six stories high. All the walls were covered in grey stone. Hanging on inner walls were battle flags, all those in which Institute Grads had participated, from the Civil War forward.

There were a lot of them, practically the entire history of America's wars.

Painted onto the concrete area were squares, black and white, a checkerboard, which the Corps ostensibly used for lining up the sixteen companies and also for conducting close-order drill. Unofficially, the Quadrangle's squares were useful in hazing with upperclass cadets treating the checkerboard as such, moving rats around on it at their whim.

Dillon lifted his hand in front of his eyes and stared at it. There was no tremor, no sign of weakness. but still he was hesitant to proceed. Crossing through any of the sally ports, stone arched tunnels from the outside world into the Quadrangle through the walls made up of barracks, was reserved for cadets. No civilians were allowed in. Even as a graduate, Dillon felt an invisible barrier blocking his way.

It was mid-class, which meant cadets were either in assigned classes in the various academic buildings, in the library, or in their rooms if they had a free period. Dillon had Wing's schedule and he knew Wing wasn't in class. He'd checked the library and the rat wasn't there either. That left one place.

Dillon stepped through and marched at an angle across the Quadrangle.

"Hold!" a voice rang out.

A Topper, a senior cadet by the insignia on his sleeve, came walking toward Dillon as if he owned the Quadrangle, the concrete, 'and the earth underneath all the way down to hell', a common saying among the cadets.

"No civilians in the area!" the Topper yelled as he got close.

Dillon held up his hand, showing his ring. That stopped the Topper in his tracks. "Sorry, sir. But, well . . ."

"No problem," Dillon said. "I've got to see someone and I have permission from the Superintendent."

The Topper reverted to rat behavior, snapping to attention, jaw tucked in tight. "Yes, sir."

Dillon moved on but he realized his hands were tightened into fists; he almost laughed. Multiple combat deployments and he still reacted to a screaming Topper like a rat. And that made sense he thought as he entered a stairwell. He'd been a rat in this maze, broken, trained, conditioned. Time had softened the conditioning as long as he was away from the lab. But back in the heart of the maze, it was all coming back.

He didn't notice that behind him, the Topper had taken off running.

Dillon bounded up the stairs two at a time.

He shoved open a fire door, vaguely remembering hanging from the top of it during one hazing routine, his fingers raw and bleeding. He strode down the corridor, almost wishing to get confronted now, his blood up.

Dillon kicked open the door and Second Year Cadet Wing leapt to his feet, the shoes he'd been shining falling to the floor.

There was no roommate replacing Brannigan, even after all this time. Wing was an undesirable and the other cadets kept him isolated. Dillon looked around. The room was in inspection condition, everything in its place. There were still textbooks on Brannigan's bookshelf.

"Sir?" Wing was confused by the man in civilian clothes standing in his doorway.

Dillon suspected he could go up and choke Wing and he'd still keep his brace.

"Tell me about Jenrette and Brannigan," Dillon ordered.

Wing blinked. He was rail-thin and Dillon could see a tremor in one of his cheeks. The kid was close to a breakdown even though he was no longer a rat.

"Sir, may I ask a question?"

One of the four responses allowed a cadet to a superior. *Yes, sir; No, sir; No excuse, sir; Sir, may I ask a question?*

"Yes."

"Who are you, sir?"

"I'm the man who's asking you about what happened that night in the Sinks when Cadet Jenrette died."

"Sir, I made an official report as required by regulations," Wing said.

His voice irritated Dillon and Dillon realized this was exactly the kind of person he'd helped terrorize when he was an upperclassman. But for some reason, Dillon also saw in Wing one of the privates in his Ranger platoon, a skinny little Korean, not even a citizen, who'd enlisted for the right to gain his citizenship. And the son-of-a-bitch had turned into hell on wheels once the bullets started flying.

He'd been killed in action, still not a citizen.

Dillon sighed. "Sit down, Wing. My name is Dillon. Class of '08. I'm doing a follow-up at the request of the Superintendent. Just dotting the I's, crossing the T's, sort of thing."

Wing blinked, confused. "Sir?"

"Just tell me in your own words what happened that night. Sit."

Wing dropped in his chair as if shot. Dillon grabbed the chair from the empty desk on Brannigan's side of the room. He noticed that there was a picture frame propped up; the one allowed a cadet on the desktop by regulations. A white-haired woman with a kind smile gazed at the camera.

And then Wing told his version, which was almost word-for-word the version in the official report. It was obviously well rehearsed. Dillon waited it out, watching Wing's face, trying to determine if he were telling a story or a fact.

Twenty minutes later, when Wing was done, Dillon didn't know. The account matched what the three ring-knockers had said in the High Cotton. Despite the time that had passed, the kid was still shell-shocked by his rat experience. Dillon was sure he could tell Wing to open the window here on the fifth floor and step out and the kid would do it.

"You're absolutely sure of that account?" Dillon asked. "Brannigan just went nuts and attacked Jenrette?"

"He was trying to help me, sir," Wing said. "It was an unfortunate accident."

"Then why did he run? Why didn't he wait and tell his version?"

"He was scared, sir."

"Of?"

Wing spread his hands, the first human sign since Dillon had entered. "Everyone and everything! And Jenrette. His family. They practically own Charleston. We all knew it. I was shocked when I saw him down there in the Sinks. They hazed him, hard sometimes, but we figured he was bullet proof."

Dillon knew Wing was wrong. Sometimes the Corps went after the biggest names in the rat class. In a bizarre way, many upperclass knew it was the only window of opportunity in their lifetime to belittle and embarrass those powerful people. He also now knew that they were testing Jenrette for the Ring, a group Dillon had heard rumors of, but nothing more, while he was a cadet.

"Why are you doing this, Wing?" Dillon asked. He could see the question had confused the rat. "Why are you attending the Institute?"

"My father wishes it so," Wing said. "He believes we must become part of our country."

"The country is bigger than the Institute."

Wing met Dillon's eyes. "My father believes one must go through the fiercest fire in order to be accepted."

Dillon noticed that Wing kept glancing toward the door. "What's the matter?"

"Sir, I've got to get to—"

And then the door flew open and a half-dozen cadets dressed in grey, their heads covered with black hoods came rushing in. They had broom handles in their hands.

For a moment, an important moment, Dillon thought they were after Wing.

As the first stick came whistling toward his head, Dillon reacted as he'd been trained in the pits at Ranger School and brought his forearm up in a block. The stick broke on the bone. And then they were on him.

Another stick struck right behind his ear, a stinging blow, but Dillon lashed out with a side-kick, catching one of the cadets in the stomach, doubling him over. As more sticks bounced off his body, blow after blow, Dillon, arms up protecting his head, snap-kicked another cadet in the crotch. The cadet screamed and fell to the ground.

Dillon bull rushed, arms still over his head, knocking over the remaining four like pins, making for the door, when two men dressed in civvies and with the same hoods appeared in the doorway, one of them wielding an axe handle. Dillon caught a glimpse of it, the ring on the hand holding it, but at that moment the end of a broomstick jabbed him hard in the kidney and he saw stars as exquisite pain exploded from the spot.

And then he saw nothing as the axe handle struck him on the side of his head.

* * *

Charles Rigney, Attorney at Law, Institute graduate, scion of Charleston society, was not a pleasant sight to see in the raw. His arms and legs were scrawny, and his chest was almost sunken, the imprint of his ribs apparent. His skin, except for his golfers tan, was pale white. His chest hair was grey and uneven, the result of a treatment for baldness that had set his body's natural hair-generating system out of whack.

He screamed as the whip lashed across his derriere.

"You can't leave a mark!" he complained, which earned him a second strike.

The blows actually wouldn't leave a mark, not even enough to earn the scream, but the intent was key here. The image.

Sarah Briggs knew about image and intent.

"Charles, Charles, Charles," she said as she walked around to face him. He was tied, hands and feet apart with spreader bars, the top bar looped over a hook dangling from the ceiling; his feet on the cold, tile floor.

While Rigney was naked, Sarah was dressed in an incongruous outfit for the scenario. A gray business suit, white blouse and moderate high heels. Not the leather and thigh-highs one would expect given the whip, but Sarah liked to mix things up. Men were simple creatures and it paid to keep them off-balance.

Plus she hadn't had a chance to change since flying in to Charleston this morning.

And she had other business that needed to attending to later in the day.

They were in the basement of Rigney's home, in his wine cellar which doubled as his dungeon. His wife knew about the room and was quite happy to stay out of it and let him do whatever perverted little things he liked to do in there with whomever was willing to do it. It made her job being married to him that much more bearable. Not an unusual arrangement in Charleston's high society.

"Mrs. Jenrette is focused on the boy?" Sarah asked.

"Yes."

"Yes who?" Smack.

"Yes, Mistress."

"And what are you going to tell Mister Fabrou?"

"That the deal is set, Mistress."

The whip snapped and Rigney squealed.

"About the boys!" Sarah demanded.

"That all is as has been, Mistress," Rigney said. "Harry Brannigan is still missing. That his mother is missing."

"And if he gets wind of the boy's father asking around?" Sarah asked.

"To let you know right away, Mistress."

"Anything else?"

The silence lasted a moment too long. Sarah expertly snapped the whip, the leather tip hitting the end of his erect cock.

This time the scream was real, echoing off the racks of wine bottles that lined the room; Rigney's wife wasn't going to totally give up the room to her husband's kinks. She mixed practicality with functionality.

"Tell me!"

"Mrs. Jenrette has brought in a new investigator."

The news was so surprising that Sarah missed that he forgot the 'mistress'.

"Who?"

Rigney quickly told her about Dillon.

"Damn it!" Sarah said when he finished. She punctuated the comment with a lash across Rigney's back, which brought forth a real scream.

And left a mark.

"I'm sorry, Mistress," Rigney said with a whimper, but Sarah's brain was already racing.

Sarah went over to her leather bag and reached in. She put down the whip then pulled out a rubber glove and some lubrication. She squirted a generous portion of lube onto the glove then went to the strung-up lawyer.

"Very good, Charles," she said as she took his cock, already hard from the whipping, in her hand and began to stroke him. She was off to his side, where he couldn't really see her.

As she worked him, she had a phone in her other hand and was checking her text messages.

"You're a good boy, Charles," she said, almost as an afterthought as he moaned and squirmed and finally came. She finished checking her messages and arranging two more meetings.

Sarah tucked the phone away and ripped off the glove, dropping it to the tile floor. She hit the winch that lowered the spreader bar and unlocked his wrists and ankles.

"What are you going to do?" Rigney asked as he toweled off.

"Nothing has changed, Charles," she said, as she looped the strap of the bag over her shoulder. "You just make sure everything goes as planned on Saturday."

Then she opened the vault door and left the naked Mister Rigney behind.

She took the servant's entrance out of the house, which really pissed her off.

* * *

Riley drove his 125cc dirt bike across the Cross Island Bridge to Sea Pines Circle. Then straight through the roundabout onto Pope Avenue. He cut left off Pope into a shopping center. He parked and then walked up to the blacked-out glass door to the left of New York Pizza, which was doing a modicum of business.

Riley opened the dark door and stepped inside. The guard who usually stood just beyond wasn't there. Riley stood still, letting his eyes adjust to the relative darkness. The interior was decorated with mid-80s fashion; lots of leather, velvet and dark wood. It was missing the glittering disco ball, but Riley was pretty sure it was in storage somewhere in the back. It was technically a restaurant but unlike most restaurants went out of its way to discourage traffic. It was one of those places a person had to know existed, then know someone who knew someone who would let you in.

Riley looked toward the bar on the left. Farrelli was seated there alone, a bottle of water in front of him next to his cell phone. He waved Riley over.

"What happened to the muscle?" Riley asked as he took a stool one away from the mobster.

"I'm not expecting trouble," Farrelli said. He had long legs and deep-set, almost hooded eyes, and a large Roman nose. His hair seemed sparser than last time Riley had visited. His scalp was covered by liver spots.

"What if trouble finds you?" Riley asked.

Tony 'Can of Tomatoes' Farrelli nodded. "That happens on occasion. But your taking out Karralkov made my position here on Hilton Head much more comfortable."

"Nobody's replaced him yet?"

Farrelli smiled. "I have."

"Well congratulations to you," Riley said.

"I'm sure some other Russian or Ukrainian or Latvian or 'ian' from Eastern Europe will try getting a piece of the action," Farrelli said. "They're criminal entrepreneurs who've survived Czars, Stalin, Hitler and communism. America looks like a squalling baby to them, ripe for the taking. I'll deal with it when it happens."

Riley reached into his pocket and drew out a thick envelope counted out from Sarah's stash and put it in front of Farrelli.

"And what is this?"

"Paying off Detective Parsons' note. With the vig."

Farrelli slipped the envelope into the pocket on his sports coat without looking inside. "He give it to you?"

"What does it matter where it comes from?" Riley asked. "It's paid." Riley had met Parsons during his investigation into Sarah Briggs phantom child. He'd learned that Parsons was into the mob for twenty large-- $20,000. Some of it was a gambling problem, but some was also trying to get the best medical care for his son, an Army Ranger who was missing both his legs thanks to an IED. The VA only went so far and more importantly, so fast.

"Forgive my manners," Farrelli said. "Would you like something from behind the bar? Feel free to help yourself."

"I'm fine," Riley said.

Farrelli indicated the bottle of water. "My doctor says I'm not sufficiently hydrated most of the time. I told him to choose his words more carefully."

"You called me," Riley reminded him.

"Ah yes. You done me a solid with Karralkov so I figure I owe you. That Briggs woman contacted me around a week ago. Asking me about that veterinarian, Erin Brannigan. And asked me to check into her having a son, named Horace or Harry. Whatever. Say, isn't Horace the same first name as your buddy Chase?"

Riley didn't answer because he knew Farrelli was playing.

"Didn't really get anything on her," Farrelli said. "And you and her and your other miscreants was buddy-buddy anyway, so you know more than I do."

"And the son?"

"Nada."

"So why am I here?" Riley asked.

"To pay me the money?" Farrelli laughed. "Something else, but I think it's connected. Someone from the Quad came to visit me. Merchant Fabrou."

"From Savannah?"

"From the Quad. They run Savannah."

"Educate me further," Riley said.

"Military Institute of South Carolina graduates who control a large portion of business in Savannah and outward from there."

"Okay. And?"

"He wanted to know what I knew about someone named Harry Brannigan. Which is pretty damn close to Horace Brannigan, don't ya' think?"

"It is."

"He heard I was asking around so he was asking around."

"Lots of that going 'round, it seems."

Farrelli laughed. "I assume your friend Chase wants to know about this guy with roughly the same name?"

"Well, the second Horace would be a Junior," Riley said. "Whom the first, the Senior, did not know existed until our recent expedition to the Caribbean."

"Ah!" Farrelli soaked that in. "Must have been a bit of a surprise for Horace Senior, eh?"

Riley was playing connect-the-dots. "What does Fabrou want with young Horace a.k.a. Harry?"

"Your guess is as good as mine," Farrelli said, "but he did intimate that any information would return a profit to the provider of said information. A profit to the tune of fifty large. I suppose that would be significant to some."

"What the kid do, kill someone?" Riley meant it as a joke, but the second it left his mouth he had a bad taste.

Farrelli's eyes peered out from their recesses in his skull. "I got the feeling that might well be the case. Fabrou is a careful man and a powerful one. For him to trek up here from Savannah, well he took his yacht, which is actually quicker than driving, but for him to come here, to talk to me, means someone more powerful than him is pulling his strings. Someone with an urgent need to find Horace Junior. And I don't think it's to tell him he won the lottery."

"But you know nothing?"

"I didn't say that," Farrelli said. "I told Fabrou that."

Riley waited.

"And I wasn't lying," Farrelli said. "I just didn't know that Harry Brannigan was connected to Horace Chase. Now that I have those two pieces, things make more sense. Fabrou told me that, let's call him Harry so we can skip the Junior and Senior stuff, Harry disappeared about eighteen months ago. Know who else disappeared around the same time?"

"Doc Cleary."

"Right. Everyone thought it was 'cause Lilly Chase died. The woman who lived with him the last several years."

"And Horace's mother."

"Right," Farrelli said. "But now we know she was also Harry's grandmother. 'Curiouser and curiouser'. That's Shakespeare, right?"

"Wouldn't know."

Farrelli closed his eyes for a moment. "Nah. Alice in Wonderland I think."

"Possibly," Riley said.

Farrelli shrugged. "Maybe not. I get stuff confused sometimes."

"So Lilly Chase dies and Harry—wait a second. What do you mean, he disappeared? That means he was somewhere. Where was he?"

"Fabrou told me," Farrelli said. "At the Military Institute in Charleston. A freshman."

"Huh." Riley processed that but wasn't sure what to make of it. "Is that why Fabrou wants to know about him? Some connection there?"

"Perhaps."

"Okay," Riley said. "So Lilly Chase dies. Harry quits school and disappears. And Doc Cleary disappears."

"Sails off into the sunset, or sunrise," Farrelli said. He jerked a thumb toward the beach which was at the end of Pope Avenue.

"Likely they disappeared together," Riley said.

"A distinct possibility."

"But you didn't tell Fabrou this."

"I didn't have the key piece you just provided."

"Will you tell him?"

Farrelli picked up the water bottle and peered at it as if the answer were inside. "I don't need the money."

"That's not an answer."

Farrelli had an edge to his voice. "And I don't have to answer your questions. You're here at my discretion."

Riley saw movement out of the corner of his eye and two men wearing dark suits were now flanking the door.

"You think I'm trouble?" Riley asked.

"I *know* you're trouble," Farrelli said. "Fabrou is trouble of a different sort. Without Karralkov and the Russians around, there's a power vacuum. I've been sticking my beak in, but so has the Quad. I don't want to go up against them. They don't use guns. They use bank accounts. And theirs is bigger than mine. I would prefer to have my interests run parallel to the Quads rather than perpendicular or head-on."

"So you're gonna tell him."

"But not today. Today is your day."

Riley got off the stool. "Thank you for today."

"Hold on," Farrelli said. "This is bigger than Harry or Horace or Doc. There's a big deal being bandied about. A land-grab for Daufuskie, which I'm sure interests you." Daufuskie was reachable only by boat and was where Riley made his home and ran his anemic bookie business. It was also the island about which Pat Conroy had written in one of his first books about: *The Water Is Wide*. And Jimmy Buffet had sung about it in his song *The Prince of Tides*. It had gone through hard economic times during the down turn and the three golf course had gone under, taking the large resort hotel with them. It was close to reverting back to pre-resort wilderness.

"I heard something is in the works," Riley said.

"I know Fabrou wants it," Farrelli said. "The resort and the golf courses. And somebody in Charleston wants it. There's a project called Sea Drift, which would cover almost the entire island except for the few private houses left. All three golf courses, the resort, the beach. Except one of the golf courses, Bloody Point is owned by someone else."

"Who?"

"No one really knows."

"So?"

"Here's the kicker," Farrelli said. "There's an appropriation in Washington that's hiding in a desk, waiting until the resort and golf courses are bought out. It allocates Federal funds to build a causeway to Daufuskie from the mainland. You know what that would do to the value of the land?"

"Increase it?"

Farrelli laughed. "You're a funny guy, Riley. Hell, you couldn't afford to live there if people could drive on. Same thing happened on Hilton Head years ago before there was a bridge.

Developer came in and bought up most of the land. *Then* the bridge was built. That's why they were able to build all those gated communities: one person owned the entire thing."

"Okay," Riley said. "What's that got to do with Harry?"

Farrelli spread his hands wide. "I have no idea. Perhaps they ain't connected except for the players involved. But we're talking potential profit in the hundreds of millions here. When the stakes get that high, people tend to act aggressively and often irrationally. I'd be careful if I was you."

"What's you stake in Daufuskie?" Riley asked.

"Me?" Farrelli laughed. "I'm keeping my money closer to home. I don't have enough to play in that arena."

"All right," Riley said.

"But here's the thing," Farrelli said. "There's going to be a meeting on Daufuskie on Saturday. Word is the deal is going to be closed. One company owning Sea Drift and who has what percentage of it. Fabrou, Charleston folk, whoever."

"Why are you telling me this?"

"I think it's connected to what you're checking out."

"Chase's son?"

"I told you last time we talked that I don't like getting families involved in business."

"How can there be a connection?" Riley asked.

"That's the key question."

"Why are you doing Sarah Briggs' bidding?" Riley asked. "You told me money isn't that important to you."

"Money is very important to me," Farrelli said.

"So how much did she pay you to find out about Erin to make it worth your while? More than fifty large, obviously."

"That's none of your business," Farrelli said. "But let me tell you. Briggs is bad news. You shoulda whacked her when you had the chance. In fact, if I was you, I'd shoot first next time you see her."

"You think there's going to be a next time?" Riley asked.

"Who knows?" Farrelli shrugged. "Ah, fuggedhdaboutit. Who the fuck knows what's going on?"

Riley nodded. "I appreciate the information, Mister Farrelli. And your giving me today."

Riley went to the door, passing between the two goons and out into the sunlight.

Behind him, Farrelli sighed. He got up and walked behind the bar. He grabbed a bottle of wine and opened it. He poured himself a large glass, satisfied he had reached the water hydration quotient for the day.

He walked back to his chair and sat down.

A few minutes later the door opened, throwing in a beam of sunlight and a woman silhouetted in it.

"Ah, welcome!" Farrelli said.

Sarah Briggs walked past the two bodyguards. She sat down on a stool, right next to Farrelli.

"May I offer you something?" Farrelli asked.

"What did you tell Riley?" Sarah asked, ignoring his hospitality. "I saw him leave."

"Lucky you," Farrelli muttered.

"What did you tell him?"

"Nothing," Farrelli said.

"Bullshit," Sarah said. "You play every side, then you are allied with no one."

"I just run my business here," Farrelli said. "I take no one's side. And, I do not appreciate being spoken to like this. Especially in my own place of business."

She reached into her leather bag to retrieve the binder. "I've already had the transfer notarized." She pulled out a sheaf of papers and turned to the last page. "You only have to sign."

"Isn't that backwards?" Farrelli asked. "Doesn't the notary have to witness the signing?"

"Not *my* notary."

Farrelli sat up straighter on his stool and folded his arms. "And what if I decide not to sign?"

"We have a deal."

"We had a deal."

Sarah closed her eyes briefly, then graced him with a tight smile. "Sign Bloody Point over to me. I gave you the money to buy it. You keep your percentage. That was the deal."

"Too many people are asking questions," Farrelli said. "And I don't believe you've told me the truth about what will happen. Fabrou intimated that this deal is much bigger than I thought."

"We have a deal," Sarah repeated.

"Fabrou will make me a better deal," Farrelli said.

"That's not how it works."

"It works the way I say it works," Farrelli said.

Sarah got off the stool and walked around the bar. She found a bottle of chilled champagne in a fridge under the bar. She slowly opened it, then took down a flute and filled it. She returned to her stool.

"You have no idea how long this has been in the works," she said. "Not quite a long con, but a long plan. You ever hear that joke about the woman wearing the fur coat?" She didn't wait for an answer. "An activist is screaming at her: *'You know how many animals died for that coat?'* And she replies: *'You know how many animals I had to fuck for this coat?'*."

"Yeah," Farrelli said. "Cute. But not my problem."

"Au contraire, Mister Farrelli," Sarah said. "You're making it your problem."

Farrelli thumped the bar with a thick forefinger. "You're in my joint, on my island. Be careful."

"I am very, very careful," Sarah said. "And that's what should concern you. Yes, I've fucked for this deal, but I've also killed and kidnapped. As they say, I'm in this from the feet up, full throttle, all the way; whatever cute one-liner you choose to use."

Farrelli stared at her, a frown on his forehead.

Perhaps re-assessing.

Sarah pointed at the papers still on the bar. "Please sign as we agreed, Mister Farrelli. I will not ask again."

"No, you won't," Farrelli said. "And you keep it up, you won't be speaking any more either." He nodded at the two burly men. "You want to leave here in one piece, I suggest you pack your crap up and get outta here."

Sarah lifted up the flute of champagne and downed it in one long drink. She put it on the bar. "I told you this was a long time in the planning and making." She stared Farrelli in the eyes. "Think. Think hard. Tick, tock. Tick, tock. You think I didn't anticipate Fabrou making you an offer? This is a game. With very high stakes. I'm so many moves ahead of you, you're not even on the board, Farrelli. Sign."

Farrelli looked down at the paper, then up at Briggs. "Who the fuck are you?"

"You should have asked that question a long time ago," Briggs said. "Not that I'd have given you a straight answer. Sometimes I don't even remember who I am. You might find that strange, but if you've been through what I've been through, you'd understand. But I doubt you would have survived what I've been through." She smiled, but there was no warmth in it. "An old friend, a woman who taught me a lot of what I know had a saying: *'I've been everywhere but the electric chair. Seen everything but the wind.'* And here I am now." For a moment Sarah Briggs looked human; a tired woman fighting the hard fight.

The moment didn't last long.

"Please sign."

Farrelli raised a hand and gestured for the two men.

Instead they turned and went out the door.

And Farrelli looked down at the very sharp dagger Sarah had poking him in the groin. "I will start by removing your balls. Which leaves you still able to sign. But if that's not enough, then I will cut your cock off and shove it in your mouth. Which leaves you still able to sign and has the advantage of shutting you up." She spoke like she had some experience in the matter. "Then I will jab you with this." With her other hand, she held up a needle. "You will be infected immediately. Which leaves you still able to sign. But you will already be a dead man. And the infection will be a most horrifying death. Irreversible. I've seen it."

Farrelli's face was flushed red, anger competing with embarrassment and acceptance of reality. "How did—"

"Don't ask how, Farrelli. I'm in a bad mood. I've had a terrible week with a bad day piled on top of it and the day isn't over yet and there're still miles to go before I rest. I'm sick of dealing with the people in this asshole of the world. So. Ten seconds. Sign or I will neuter you, then kill you."

To emphasize her point, she pushed the point of the blade farther into his testicles.

Farrelli picked up the pen and signed.

But Sarah didn't pull back the blade. With her free hand, she put the papers into her binder, which then went into her bag. "Now you suppose I would back out, happy to have achieved my goal. Correct?"

Farrelli nodded.

"But again, I am not stupid and I have thought all of this through." She laughed. "Funny thing is, there's a woman in Charleston who would have paid considerably more for this land than Fabrou. The fact you didn't find out who that is tells me that you're not very clued-in; not like you think you are."

"Jenrette," Farrelli said. "I know about her."

"Very good," Briggs said. "Why didn't you go to her?"

"I tried. I called her several days ago. She wouldn't deal with me."

Briggs nodded. "The old broad has standards. So you were playing everyone. As usual. That's a dangerous way to make a living, Mister Farrelli."

"I got connections in Jersey. They will not take kindly to my being injured."

"Who said anything about injuring you?" Briggs said. "But I do have to factor in that Italian temper. That Cosa Nostra desire for revenge. I will be forever looking over my shoulder, won't I?"

Farrelli said nothing. He stared at her, face expressionless.

Faster than he could react, she pulled the dagger back and had it at his neck. "Stay still."

A muscle twitched in Farrelli's cheek, but he obeyed her.

Sarah smiled. "All right then." She slipped the bag over her shoulder. "I'll take my leave then." And then she jabbed the needle into his thigh.

"Fuck!" Farrelli yelled as Sarah back up.

"Be glad I lied, by the way," Sarah said. She slowly backpedaled as Farrelli jumped off his seat, his hand fumbling underneath his jacket for his gun. "It works fast. Not painful, well not for long. And looks like a heart attack to a coroner."

Farrelli opened his mouth to say something, but no words came. His eyes bulged. He dropped the gun before he could bring it to bear, both hands going to his chest. He dropped to his knees, still trying to say something. Then fell face forward with a solid thud into the floor.

Chapter Six
Thursday Afternoon

Dillon regained consciousness slowly and painfully. He was lying on the floor in Brannigan's and Wing's room, cold tile pressed up against his cheek. He didn't open his eyes right away. Someone could be waiting and his head hurt enough as it was.

He listened.

It was quiet. He didn't sense anyone in the room, but he didn't trust that. He waited until he felt in sufficient control of his faculties and his body. Then he rolled, coming to his knees, hands up in a defensive posture.

The room was empty.

"Fucking Wing," Dillon muttered, then he had to smile. "Fucking Wing," he repeated.

He knew it wasn't the cadet's fault. Had to be the Topper from the Quadrangle. Or worse: someone from the Supe's office had alerted the cadets. The Corps was infamous for protecting their own and Jenrette's death was a dark spot that everyone wanted forgotten. He'd gone into their den and paid the price.

Apparently Mrs. Jenrette's influence did extend only so far as she had warned. Dillon understood the fundamentals from the Institute and the Corps point of view: Greer Jenrette was dead, Brannigan was gone, let it alone. The Corps had closed ranks and he was on the outside, ring or no ring.

Dillon got to his feet. He looked in the mirror. There was a bruise on his right cheek. Running his hand over his head, he found a lump was forming where the axe handle had struck. He had a bad headache, but time would cure that.

The ass-whupping was something he'd have to cure some other way.

He headed for the door and then remembered something. He went back to what had been Brannigan's desk. He was sliding the back off the picture frame to remove the photo, when something fell out.

Another photo. This one was of a woman, not quite as old as in the one that had been covering it, and a white-haired man with spectacles. They were standing on the rear of a sailboat. The name of the boat was visible on the stern: *Epodes*

A piece of where Brannigan came from.

Dillon opened the drawers. Nothing.

He looked around the room, then remembered something from his own time at the Institute. He went to the air vent and used his Leatherman to unscrew the cover. He reached in, then up and to the right. As it had been in his own room, there was a small shelf there, a convenient place for hiding things, such as booze, porn or whatever the powers that be at the Institute deemed contraband. While it was a familiar spot for cadets, investigators would not know of it. Wing didn't strike Dillon as the type who would even try to hide contraband.

Dillon's hand closed on something, a leather pouch. He pulled it out. It was closed with a leather lace, which he untied. He emptied it into his hand. A silver bracelet, tarnished with time. Dillon frowned; he doubted it was something Harry would wear; it was woman's jewelry. He looked inside and there was something inscribed: *With You I Should Love To Live; With You I Should Love To Die.*

Dillon considered the photo and the bracelet. Someone had left in a hurry. Which is what the official report said: after the incident in the Sinks, no one at the Institute had seen Harry Brannigan again. He'd run fast.

Dillon put the bracelet back in the pouch and then put it in his pocket. He left the room. He took the stairs two at a time and hustled across the Quadrangle, feeling many eyes looking out at him until he made it into the sally port and out of the cadet area.

* * *

"She's supposed to be dead," Hannah said.

"She isn't."

"That's the name she's going by now?" Hannah asked. "Sarah Briggs?"

"Yes." Cardena was seated across from her in her office three hundred feet underneath the 'crystal palace' that was the headquarters of the National Security Agency at Fort Meade, Maryland.

Hannah was head of the Cellar and while her office was underneath the NSA, she was not part of that organization, nor did she answer to it. She answered only to a Presidential Executive Order authorizing from the dark days of early World War II giving her free rein as judge, jury and executioner of all the inhabitants (and there are many) of the covert world that the United States ran.

"And she was involved in the Karralkov incident?"

"Correct," Cardena said.

Hannah fixed her subordinate with eyes the color of dark chocolate. "And you did not make the connection as to who Sarah Briggs truly was?"

"No."

Hannah was in her late forties, in good shape, the result of a daily workout regime that was intense and brief, as she begrudged the time she spent on it. She had blond hair with gray roots, cut to her shoulders. She was known only by Hannah; no last name, no title.

"That's unfortunate," Hannah said. "But you did authorize a Predator strike that took out Karralkov's boat. And saved Sarah Briggs."

"Yes. I was focused on Karralkov. I misjudged."

"Partly," Hannah said, which was a strong rebuke coming from her.

"I've alerted an asset, one who knows one of those involved in events in South Carolina."

"Knows how?"

"They worked together long ago when the asset was CIA and the person involved was in Special Forces. The asset also has a stake in the Sarah Brigg's case."

Hannah rubbed her forehead, a surprising sign of weariness, one Cardena had never seen before in his boss. Cardena was short, wiry and dark-skinned. His hair was completely gray. His eyes mirrored what Hannah was exhibiting: exhausted and haunted.

"Westland." Hannah did not frame it as a question. "What happened with, let's call her Sarah Briggs in order not to get confused, was before my time. Under Nero's reign. Westland was her handler in that unit. I suggested the unit be disbanded and it was."

"Before my time also," Cardena said, as much of an excuse as he was going to attempt with Hannah.

Hannah allowed him that. "Nero thought Briggs was dead. He wouldn't have closed the file if he had had any suspicions she was still alive. I suppose we have no idea how she escaped, if she did escape. She might have been turned."

"Nothing," Cardena said. "I've been able to track her back only to Hilton Head, fronting this off-shore gambling site. Before that, nothing until we go all the way back to her jump into Russia."

"Odd place for her to show up."

"The gambling site was hacked several times by the Russian mob. Paid off millions of dollars."

"So the hack might not have been a hack," Hannah said. "Perhaps money laundering and she was in on it. Which would explain how she got out. We know the Russian government and its organized crime elements are almost the same thing. Putin is no fool. He wields power and makes deals as needed. One might say he's the biggest crook of them all in Russia."

"That's a possibility if she'd been turned," Cardena said. "But she was well trained against torture and interrogation."

Hannah could not tell Cardena that it would not have been difficult to turn Sarah Briggs given the circumstances around her capture.

"She also had a suicide option," Hannah said. "Obviously that wasn't used."

Hannah leaned back in her seat, deep in thought and Cardena waited on her. She was thinking of the 'greater good'. How the ability to truly make the hard decisions for those two words was an extremely rare trait. One few humans possessed. Most were ruled by fear; those who weren't ruled by that most prevalent of emotions tended toward extreme self-interest. Neither were for the greater good.

She was located in such close proximity to the NSA because it was the greatest collector of information in the history of mankind. It sorted a considerable amount of that information into intelligence. Hannah needed intelligence in order to make those hard decisions for the greater good.

Another person might have some empathy for the woman called Sarah Briggs. Might want to understand who she was, why she did what she was doing. Empathy was not in Hannah's arsenal.

"This is a Sanction in the hands of the field agent," she said.

Cardena cleared his throat.

"Yes?" Hannah asked.

"The way Briggs has resurfaced after escaping Karralkov has caused me to investigate why. She's involved in some sort of land deal south of Charleston. There are other parties involved. One of them is Senator Gregory."

"How so?"

"The land involved is on an island. Gregory quietly pushed through an appropriation for a causeway to be built to the island, which would then be developed as a resort, vastly increasing the worth of the land. But the existence of this appropriation has been kept under wraps. Additionally, Briggs has involved elements of the New Jersey mafia in acquiring a piece of land on the island. It's complicated, but there appear to be irregularities involved in Senator Gregory's involvement."

"Is Briggs connected to the Senator?"

"Not that I've been able to find," Cardena said.

Hannah considered the information. "Send backup for Westland. She's to gather information. It's up to her to determine when the backup will conduct the Sanction. Inform me about the depth of the Senator's involvement. He's a powerful man and it's always good to have leverage on such people."

Cardena stood. He waited a second to see if she had any further orders.

When there was nothing he left.

The heavy door swung shut behind him, leaving Hannah alone, as she usually was. There were no windows in the office, not that there could be. No personal touches. It was austere, much like her mind. If Cardena had known her background, he would have been surprised: she'd been a suburban housewife in St. Louis before being hand-picked, recruited without her knowledge, tested under fire and then blessed by her predecessor, Nero, to take his place. Because she had that most critical of talents: she could remove herself from the process and analyze, judge and order a Sanction without compunction.

She was not swayed by emotion, by money, by ambition. To her the greater good was the scales on which she made decisions.

The same scales that had tipped against Sarah Briggs so many years ago.

* * *

Kono had his hand lightly on the wheel of the *Fina*, expertly guiding the former patrol boat through the shallow waters north of Port Royal Sound. Hilton Head was to the south. Several rivers flow in the Sound, primarily the Broad River, but there were also the Coosawhatchie, the Colleton, the Chechessee and the Pocotaligo. With that many coming in, the place was a maze of islands, swamps, marshes and waterways.

Parris Island was to the west, where the Marine Corps did its own version of turning boys into men; they were much more effective at it than the Institute, because their mission was to prepare soldiers for combat, although, again, in the end the definition of what it meant to be a 'man' was up for grabs. Kono had the *Fina* on a waterway cutting through St. Helena Island, a path few boaters would attempt and one that was entirely dependent on understanding the tide. Chase and Gator flanked him on the bridge as they finally came out in Trenchards Inlet.

"Pritchards Island," Kono said, nodding at the land ahead. "No man other than Tear live there."

"University of South Carolina has it set aside for research," Gator explained.

"No man allowed," Kono said, ignoring his sometimes partner-incrime, "or else face bad spirits. Blackbeard buried many a sailor in the beach there. Many of my people are buried there after escaping from working the rice."

Kono cut throttle and the patrol boat slowed. An old dock, looking like it hadn't been used in decades, was ahead. The pilings were rotting and several boards were broken. A rowboat was to the left of the dock, flipped over. It looked like it had been used recently, the wood in good shape.

"I remember this place," Chase said as he spotted a crumbling concrete structure beyond the surf line, nestled among the palmettos.

"Old Coast Guard station," Kono said. He pointed to the right. "Good view of shipping channel during big war."

"You took me here when we were kids," Chase said.

"Aye," Kono acknowledged. "To let Tear see you. But you never seen him."

Gator grabbed a line and jumped into the water. He tied the *Fina* off.

Kono pointed to the flag on the bow. "Recognize it?" It was a black flag with a white skeleton holding a chalice which it appeared to toasting from and in the other hand a spear that was thrust through a heart.

"No," Chase said.

"Blackbeard's flag," Kono said.

"Cheery," Chase said. "He's waiting," he added as an old man appeared in the open doorway of the old Coast Guard building.

The old Gullah was wearing denim coveralls and a black turtleneck. Like Kono, he was barefoot. His white beard flowed down to his belt buckle. His dark skin was wrinkled and worn.

"You let me talk," Kono said as he and Chase went ashore. "He speaks English but it's easier if he and I talk in Gullah. Okay with you?"

"It's okay with me," Chase said. "How he'd get the name Tear?"

"He cried for a long time once," Kono said simply.

Chase's cell phone buzzed, picking up the signal off a tower on Parris Island. "Hold on." He recognized the number and answered it. "Go."

"Chase, Riley. Briggs did have Farrelli checking after Erin. And your son. He does go by Harry Brannigan, not Horace Junior. And he disappeared at the same time as Doc Cleary."

"So they're together," Chase said. He wasn't too thrilled with Harry, but he'd never liked Horace much either. His mother had named him after the poet for some strange reason she'd never explained.

Of course, he'd never asked.

But his son being with Doc Cleary relieved a lot of his angst.

"Most likely," Riley said. "And get this: he was a student at the Military Institute of South Carolina before he disappeared."

Chase had attended West Point primarily because he'd been given an automatic appointment; tendered to the son of a Medal of Honor winner. Chase had never known his own father, killed in Vietnam, and it shook him to realize that his son was in the same predicament. But why would he go to M.I.S.C.? Then he remembered: Doc Cleary wore the ring.

"Any idea why they took off?" Chase asked.

"Nope."

"Any idea where they are?"

"Nope. But there's some guy, Fabrou asking around for him. He's involved in a land-grab for Daufuskie. Not sure how that's connected in any way, but it might explain why Doc got out of town so fast and took Harry with him."

"All right," Chase said, more confused than when he'd answered the phone, but now armed with one key piece of information: his son was with Doc Cleary. That was a comforting thought. He turned the phone off and joined Kono with the old man.

Gator remained on board the *Fina*.

The two were talking in their native tongue, bits of which Chase could understand.

When Chase came up, Tear held up a hand. "Let us speak so he can hear," he told Kono. He smiled at Chase, revealing a single missing tooth in the front center. "I was Marines long time ago. Vietnam."

Chase nodded. "I was Army."

"Not as good as Marines," Tear said.

"So says every Marine," Chase allowed.

Tear laughed. "You are blood friend to my great nephew here," he indicated Kono.

Chase nodded.

"You have a son. One you didn't know you had."

"Yes. I just found out he's with Doc Cleary," Chase said.

Tear nodded. "Doc took boy in when he come down from Charles Town. Then Doc and boy take sail." He waved a hand toward the water. "Doc can set a good sail." Tear sat down on the concrete step.

"Do you know why my son came down from Charleston?" Chase asked.

"Bad things happen up there in that place," Tear said.

"The Military Institute?" Chase asked.

Tear nodded. "Bad place. Bad spirit near the water. I crab there when younger. Never liked going by."

"Do you know exactly what happened?" Chase asked.

"Someone die," Tear said. "Word is your son to blame."

"What?" Chase was surprised at this twist. "Who died?"

"Son of big woman in Charles Town." He gave a slight smile. "Old Mrs. Jenrette. Been around longer than me."

"Did my son have something to do with this death?" Chase asked.

Tear looked at him. "He there. What truth is, I don't know. Doc say your son not at fault. I believe him." Tear straightened his back with effort. "Getting old is no fun. Doc used to give me medicine and take care of me. Now I have to use VA. Not as good as Doc. My advice? Don't get old."

"It's better than the alternatives," Chase said.

Tear laughed. "True, that be true." But the smile was gone from his face. "Doc protects your son. As he protected your mother until she passed. Lilly was fine woman. Doc knows he can't bring boy back until old Mrs. Jenrette dies. Which not be long word is I hear."

The pieces of the puzzle didn't fit in Chase's mind. "Someone from Savannah, a guy named Fabrou, has been asking about my son. Do you know of them?"

"Fabrou big man in his own mind," Tear said. "Easy thing to be. But dangerous man. He owns big piece of Daufuskie. That island name go back, all the way to Yammacraw Indians who lived there before white men, or even black men, come. These islands we came to as free men a long time ago. We live here free now."

"What does Daufuskie have to do with Doc and my son?"

Tear shrugged. "Everything in this land connected."

"Do you know where Doc and my son sailed to?"

"Ocean be wide," Tear said. "Once they gone out on ocean far from land, I can no longer hear them in the rhythm of the tides." He indicated the Low Country around them. "And last I speak with Doc, he not coming back unless it safe for your son. And not safe. Mrs. Jenrette from Charles Town whose son died; she wants your son dead. A heart for a heart is what she say."

Chapter Seven
Thursday Evening

"You do not look well," Mrs. Jenrette informed Dillon.

"I'm fine," he replied.

She was in her study, a large room off of her master bedroom. On one side were double doors leading out to the second floor balcony, which ran the entire front of her mansion on South Battery Street. The shadows were slanting from the trees in bloom outside as the sun headed down in the west.

"Proceed," Mrs. Jenrette said. She was seated behind an ancient, wooden desk, the top large enough to land a helicopter. The surface of the desk was covered in Plexiglas and underneath that, covering the expanse, was a map of the Low Country coastline from Frances Marion National Forest in South Carolina down to Savannah and Tybee Island in Georgia. Dillon stood in front of the desk, flanked by chairs, neither of which she had offered to him.

He quickly related events at the High Cotton and the Institute.

"You do not believe the accounts given by Monsieur's Gregory, Mongin and Fabrou?" Mrs. Jenrette said at his conclusion.

"I believe they are withholding some information," Dillon said.

"How do you propose to get more information out of them?"

"I'll go for the weakest link," Dillon said.

"Who do you believe that is?"

"Jerrod Fabrou."

"Hmm," Mrs. Jenrette said. "The Gregory boy, Preston, is very sharp. His great-grandfather came from low birth. A smuggler. His grandfather made a fortune during Prohibition, running booze all along the coast, bringing it in from the islands, using the secret ways his father had taught him. I remember him. He made sure his son, Preston's father, was legitimate." She laughed. "So Thaddeus Gregory went into politics, which I view as more wicked than smuggling. But his name is clean. And the family has high hopes for Preston. Given the father is a United States Senator, you can only imagine how truly high their hopes are."

"He's a dick," Dillon said.

"A succinct assessment," Mrs. Jenrette said, "but be careful of him."

"I will."

"And the Institute? Are they hiding something or simply protecting their image?"

"Aren't they the same thing?" Dillon asked. "The Corps will always close ranks. The Superintendent told me I could go to the barracks but that was the extent of his assistance. Whether he called over to someone in the Corps, or someone in his office did, or it was simply the Corps reacting, it doesn't really matter. Cadet Wing is backing up the official account." He reached into his pocket and pulled out the photo. "I found this on Brannigan's desk." He took a couple of steps forward and put it on the deck. He had to lean far forward to slide it in front of her.

Mrs. Jenrette picked up a pair of reading glasses and peered at it. "Doc Cleary. I do not recognize the woman."

"I'll find out who it is," Dillon said.

"Doc Cleary," Mrs. Jenrette repeated in a low voice. "I remember when he wasn't so old. He was quite the dashing cadet at the Institute. A most eligible bachelor in his own rights although his family wasn't on par. Came from dirt, and I don't mean that in a disparaging way, but the fact is, his folks were farmers up-country in the Piedmont. They did well, but not that well. Ran into some hard times and got foreclosed on. But Doc, he moved on from the Institute. Worked his way through the Medical University of South Carolina here in Charleston. Then moved down to Hilton Head."

She put the photo down and Dillon reached across to pick it up.

"Bear with me one second," Mrs. Jenrette said. "Thomas, can you tell Mister Rigney to come up."

"Yes, ma'am." Thomas moved out of his corner in the office and through the double doors to the hallway. He was gone for less than a minute and returned leading the lawyer.

Rigney nodded at Dillon as he came to a position in front of the desk.

"Take a seat, gentlemen," Mrs. Jenrette finally allowed, indicating the two high-back chairs facing her desk. She did not notice that Rigney took his chair somewhat gingerly.

"Mister Rigney, what did Mister Fabrou uncover?"

Rigney pulled a thin manila folder out of his leather briefcase. "It's a bit confusing. A woman named Sarah Briggs asked Mister Farrelli to make inquiries about one Erin Brannigan; mother of our subject."

"Who is Sarah Briggs?" Mrs. Jenrette asked.

"It's a false name," Rigney said. "Used by a woman who ran an offshore gambling site. She's disappeared, along with a lot of people's money. And somehow that was connected to Karralkov. Who is no longer with us."

"Go on."

"Farrelli was able to uncover little, but he called me earlier and said that someone else is asking, not just about Erin Brannigan, but more importantly, about the boy."

"And who is this?" Mrs. Jenrette asked.

"A man named David Riley," Rigney said. "Apparently, he's a friend of the boy's father, one Horace Chase."

"Ah!" Mrs. Rigney remembered. "The photo, Dillon."

He stood and brought the picture back to her.

"Yes," she remembered. "Lilly Chase." She tapped the woman on the photo. "She co-habitated with Doc Cleary. Not a scandal on Hilton Head, where they are mostly drunkards, sinners and fornicators, but rumor of it reached here." She smiled. "We have many drunkards, sinners and fornicators here in Charleston but we are much more discreet about it." She continued to stare at the photo.

"So," Mrs. Jenrette finally said. "Lilly is the grandmother. This Horace fellow is the father. Erin Brannigan is the mother. The family tree is falling in place. But where is Harry Brannigan now?" When Rigney didn't answer, she sighed. "Tell me what you do have."

"This Riley character is a small-time bookie on Daufuskie Island," Rigney said.

Mrs. Jenrette's head snapped up from the picture. "Daufuskie? How is he connected to the the Brannigans?"

"He's connected to Horace Chase," Rigney said. "They were both in the Army. Special Operations, although somewhat different eras. Riley retired about a decade ago and Chase just recently, after doing a stint as a Federal agent."

That got Dillon's interest. "Special Forces or Special Operations Forces?"

"What the difference?" Rigney said.

"Special Forces is a subset of Special Operations," Dillon said. "Gives me an idea of their training and their attitude if I know exactly."

"I'll check on it."

"This Chase fellow is no longer a Federal agent?" Mrs. Jenrette asked.

"No, ma'am. Farrelli wouldn't tell me exactly what happened, but Riley and Chase were apparently just involved in an incident involving the Russian mafia; indeed, it appears they are the reason Mister Karralkov is no longer a factor in the Low Country."

"Impressive," Mrs. Jenrette said. "I would owe them a debt of gratitude except for the family connection between Mister Chase and young Mister Brannigan. I fear I must bring sorrow to Mister Chase's life as his son has brought to mine."

"The other news," Rigney said, "is that these two men are also trying to find Harry Brannigan. Apparently Mister Chase did not realize he was a father until just recently."

Dillon stirred. "They might do the job for us. I would assume, given their backgrounds, they are rather capable."

"They might," Mrs. Jenrette allowed. "But then they would also come between us and what I desire. Go to Hilton Head tomorrow," she ordered Dillon. "But for tonight, follow up with the Institute as we discussed. I believe they have given you cause for action."

Dillon rubbed the mark on his face. "They have." He nodded. "I think pressuring the younger Fabrou will give me leverage with the elder one." He turned to Rigney. "Tell me more about these guys: Riley and Chase. Do they work alone?"

"I'm getting more information on them," Rigney said. "A couple of nefarious character named Gator and Kono work with them at times. Both are known smugglers. Usually alcohol to avoid taxes."

"Sounds like they're following the footsteps of Preston Gregory's family," Dillon noted.

"Not exactly," Mrs. Jenrette said. "There was a much larger profit margin during Prohibition." She waved a hand, dismissing that topic. "If Mister Chase finds his son first, it might make your task more difficult."

Dillon nodded. "I'm talking to Jerrod Fabrou tonight. Then I'll go to Hilton Head tomorrow. It sounds like Mister Fabrou is already involved. I'll give him some more motivation."

"Very good," Mrs. Jenrette said.

"There was also this," Dillon said, pulling the leather pouch out. He opened it and put the bracelet on her desk.

Mrs. Jenrette picked it up. She read the inscription out loud: "*'With You I Should Love To Live; With You I Should Love To Die'*." She nodded. "Horace."

"Chase?" Dillon said.

Mrs. Jenrette laughed. "They don't teach the classics at the Institute do they anymore? My husband had to take Greek and Latin there."

"I took Farsi," Dillon said.

"I suppose that's more useful in these days," Mrs. Jenrette said. She wiggled the bracelet. "The saying. It's from the Roman orator and poet, Horace. There are versions of it though, depending on how it's translated. It's more common to translate it as *'With you I should love to live, with you be ready to die'*."

"What about the boat's name?" Dillon asked.

"*Epodes* is a form of oration or poetry that Horace used," Mrs. Jenrette said. She closed her eyes and recited: *"'Then farewell, Horace, whom I hate so. Not for thy faults, but mine'.* There's more but that's Lord Byron's ode to Horace's words."* She tossed the bracelet back toward Dillon. "Find me the man I want. I don't need to know his personal stuff." She seemed bothered by the bracelet. "You may go."

Dillon took the bracelet and left Rigney with Mrs. Jenrette and her servant.

"How goes Sea Drift?" Mrs. Jenrette asked.

"We're still on schedule to close the deal on Saturday," Rigney said. "My concern is any action by Mister Dillon toward Mister Fabrou could compromise that."

"If it does, it does," Mrs. Jenrette said.

Rigney looked less than pleased.

"And Bloody Point?" she asked, tapping her desktop, indicating the third golf course on Daufuskie; the one not under her or Fabrou's control.

"I've peeled away another layer of a shell company," Rigney said. "It's pointing to the New Jersey mafia."

"Farrelli," Mrs. Jenrette said.

"Yes. And that's a problem."

"Why?"

"Mister Farrelli suffered a heart attack just a couple of hours ago. He's dead."

Mrs. Jenrette absorbed that information as she opened a drawer and took out a pack of cigarettes. She lit one and inhaled deeply. She immediately began coughing, but didn't put the cigarette out. "I quit like the doctor suggested over twenty years ago," she said. "Doesn't matter now."

Rigney didn't say anything.

"So whoever killed Farrelli now owns Bloody Point," Mrs. Jenrette said.

"My contact in the Beaufort Sheriff's office told me it looks like a heart attack. Farrelli's two guards said he just keeled over at the bar in his restaurant."

Mrs. Jenrette inhaled once more. This time she didn't cough. "If you believe it was a heart attack, Charles, darling, then my husband had a stupider man that I thought at his side all these years."

A muscle rippled on the side of the lawyer's face, but he didn't respond directly. "I don't understand why someone would hide the fact they own the course so deeply. It's been out of business for over two years now and not worth much."

"*Apparently* not worth much," Mrs. Jenrette amended. "If someone knows of the appropriation Senator Gregory is sitting on, they know the land is worth much, much more. Enough to kill Farrelli. Someone is playing their own hand in this business," Mrs. Jenrette said. "I want that course. I want to own it by the closing. Before Fabrou gets to it. It will give me more leverage with him."

"Yes, ma'am."

"Find out who took it from Farrelli. His guards are lying."

"Yes, ma'am."

"And the easement for the causeway?"

"The Mongin family is willing to sell, but they want to see what Fabrou offers. I've given them a deadline."

"It's stupid for us to be bidding against Fabrou," Mrs. Jenrette said.

"I've talked to the head of the Mongin family," Rigney said. "He understands your concern."

"Very well. You may go."

After he departed, Mrs. Jenrette turned and looked at Thomas. "The Institute has always been a pain. It believes it owes its allegiance to no higher power than itself. The Superintendent often forgets that the Institute requires funding. From the State and from people like me. If I find out he's been lying to me—" she left her threat unsaid. "Sea Drift is important, Thomas."

"I know, ma'am."

She finished the cigarette, then took another out. She offered the pack to Thomas. He accepted one. He lit his, then hers.

"There's another player on the table," Mrs. Jenrette said. "A serious player willing to kill." She shook her head. "It grows dark for me, Thomas."

"You're still-" he began, but she hushed him.

"You've never bullshitted me before, Thomas. Don't start at this late stage, please. You are the only person I can be around and be me." She closed her eyes for several moments. "I might be wrong, Thomas."

"About what?"

"It is the bane of old age to question one's life," Mrs. Jenrette said. "Especially when one's child dies before one and then a grandchild. That is a burden that can never be gotten rid of. That can never be answered. It is a wound that burns every moment. I know my last thought will be of Greer. Of how I failed him in some way."

"You were a wonderful mother and grandmother," Thomas said. He held up a hand as she started to respond. "As you said, I will not bullshit you. You were a wonderful grandmother to Greer. But—" he waved that hand, indicating the house and all that went with it. "But this life was not for him. He was too gentle a soul for it. Your husband, may he rest in peace, had a hard heart. He was able to live this life. And you have hardened your heart for your family. But now it's broken and the pain seeps in. You have done the best you can."

"But is it enough?" Mrs. Jenrette said. "Will it be enough?"

And to that, Thomas had no answer.

* * *

Sarah Briggs was on her hands and knees, her pants and panties pulled down to her ankles. Fortunately, she'd been able to grab two cushions off nearby chairs before being shoved into this position. One was under her knees, and now she lowered her head to the second one, turning her face to the side as Preston Gregory fucked her from behind.

"Oh yes, Preston, baby, oh yes," she murmured as she checked her watch. "Do Mommy. Do Mommy right. Make her your bitch."

Preston was in his own world (not a good one) eyes closed. He too was mostly clothed, his trousers and underwear (boxers not briefs) around his knees. His hands were on her hips and he was gripping her too hard (he was going to leave marks, she knew, but now was not the time to complain). They were in the Charleston field office for his father, the great Senator Thaddeus Gregory. It was deserted since the Senator wasn't in town and it was after five. She'd entered by the back door, which Preston had left cracked open.

That pissed her off.

Sarah Briggs (not her real name) was getting tired of coming and going from back doors.

That forced her to stifle a laugh as she realized the irony of that thought given her current position (literally).

Which reminded her. "Oh yes, baby. Do me. Do me. Do me."

She sometimes wondered if men really got off on that porno stuff, but had enough experience to know that, sadly, many did. As if she could be getting some enjoyment off of this guy's sick fantasy? At least he was in better shape than Charles Rigney. She wondered how Preston would feel if he knew she'd been with Rigney just hours ago. Would he care? That would be an interesting scenario, one which would tell her much about Preston. How much did he *really* want power?

Those men who really wanted it could not afford the luxury of jealousy.

"You bitch," Preston said, teeth tight together. "Bitch. Bitch. I'll show you. I'll show all of you."

His pace was picking up so she put some animation into her rear, gyrating slightly, but not enough that he'd pop out (that was always awkward) since he wasn't that endowed. From experience she knew there was a definite correlation between that lack and the desire for power, although her sample pool wasn't big enough to be statistically significant to publish a paper on it. Still. It was a pretty decent-sized pool.

She was getting real tired of this too.

So she reached back between her legs, between his legs, and fondled his balls. "Yes, yes, yes. You're the best. The best, Preston. Make Mommy proud. Make Mommy proud."

And, as always with him, that worked.

He slammed into her so hard, her head slipped off the pillow onto the wood floor. She bit back a curse. This guy had some serious Oedipal issues.

Which had been working quite well to her advantage.

Satisfied, Preston pulled out of her. Sarah stood, pulling up her panties and pants. She felt her forehead and worried the floor might have left a mark. Preston pulled off the condom (he wasn't stupid, nor she) and walked to the bathroom.

She heard the toilet flush.

The person who came back in was completely different.

"You have Bloody Point?" Preston asked as if meeting her just now.

"Yes."

"I'm surprised Farrelli signed it over," he said, as he sat behind one of the desks, putting it between them, a subconscious move that Sarah consciously noted.

"He took some convincing," Sarah said.

"How much convincing?"

"Terminal convincing."

Preston laughed. "Good riddance."

Sarah walked out of the office and down the short corridor for her turn in the bathroom. As soon as she was out of sigh, a side door opened and a man hustled in. Preston said nothing as the man grabbed her back, took her phone out, pulled the back off and pressed a small device into it. He put the phone together, into the bag and everything back in place and then was gone.

It took 14 seconds.

Sarah was back 30 seconds later. She paused, almost sniffing, sensing something was off, but not able to pinpoint it.

"Tell me more about this Dillon fellow," Sarah said.

"We took care of him," Preston said.

"Do you really believe that?"

He smiled. "No. It was worth a try, but he'll be back. Mrs. Jenrette is like an old dog with its teeth stuck in something. She just won't let go."

"It's personal for her," Sarah said.

"That old hag has run Charleston for far too long," Preston said. "A change is long overdue."

"You'll be sharing ownership of Sea Drift," Sarah said. "What change are you talking about?"

"Don't worry your pretty little head," Preston said.

"I need to know what's going on."

"Do you?" Preston asked. "You know enough." Preston looked at a clock on the wall. "I'm meeting Jerrod and Chad later this evening at the High Cotton."

"How are they bearing up?"

"Well enough," Preston said.

"Dillon will go after Jerrod," Sarah said.

"That would be a mistake," Preston said.

And that was why she had allied with him years ago. Sarah nodded. "He should go after Chad. But Jerrod's the obvious one."

"I'll take care of it," Preston said, as he got up.

"Get Chad to do his part," Sarah said.

"I will."

"And your father?" she asked.

He stared at her. "What about him?"

"Everything is on track there?"

"In terms of what?"

And Sarah Briggs knew she'd misstepped slightly. She waved a dismissive hand. "As long as you're in charge, we're good to go, right?"

"Right." Preston's voice was cold.

Sarah Briggs stared at him, realizing that perhaps Preston was a step past a sociopath and dabbling in psychopath; that was a significant step and one that she would have to monitor carefully. There were born psychopaths and then there were those who were made. She had a feeling Preston was the former. She knew she was the latter, which had always given her an advantage.

"Do you have what you promised?" he asked.

"Yes." She pulled a small vial out of her bag of many tricks. "Be very, very careful with it. Rubber gloves will protect you, but any of it on your skin could be fatal, even for someone like you, who is healthy. For someone who is in poor health it will definitely be deadly."

"It looks like a heart attack?" Preston said as he walked over then took the vial.

"Yes. Unless a pathologist knows exactly what to look for, it's undetectable. And my understanding is that the homicide investigator and the coroner down here are less than average. They once listed someone who drowned as dying of natural causes."

Preston laughed. "It will never get to that. I can squash any investigation in the Beaufort Sheriff's department. I assume this is what caused Farrelli's heart attack." He went back to his seat behind what would be his father's desk when he deigned to hold court in this part of his home state. He put the vial on the top of the desk.

He looked at her, as if seeing her for the first time, and not like someone he'd just had sex with. "How do you know all this stuff?" Preston asked.

"A woman has to have her secrets," Sarah said, and knew right away that was the wrong answer.

"You're not an ordinary woman," Preston said. He pointed at the vial. "I assume what's in there is not found in the drug store. How did you get it?"

"I made it."

"How did you know how to make it?"

"Someone taught me."

Preston laughed once again. "You like your secrets, don't you? And Briggs isn't your real name. No doubt about that. And Sarah? Is that your real first name?"

She didn't respond.

"Ah, yes, keep your secrets," he said.

"Can I ask *you* something?" Sarah said as she sat down at another desk, putting it between her and his desk and him. "Since we're discussing secrets."

"What?"

"What really happened with Greer Jenrette that night at the Institute?"

Preston's face was a blank slate. "We were hazing Greer and some half-chink, half-black named Wing and another rat, Brannigan, came in, waving a bayonet. Greer ended up with it in his chest. A tragic accident."

"But a convenient one for you," she said. Her hand was in her purse, her fingers curled around the handle of a 9mm pistol, another 'toy' she carried .

"Greer was my friend," Preston said, with about as much emotion as discussing the weather on a nice day.

"But he was also your rival," Sarah said.

Preston raised an eyebrow. "What do you mean?"

"You, and him, were the next generation. Of power brokers in this town. And you would have been partners in Sea Drift. Eventually."

Preston folded his hands together, fingers interlaced and leaned back in the chair. He regarded her with his head slightly cocked to the side. "Why do you care? Doesn't it make things better for you that Greer Jenrette is dead?"

"'Better'? It almost destroyed the deal. I'm surprised Mrs. Jenrette is still pursuing it, given her motivation was to give it to her grandson." Sarah waited a moment. "There's an aspect to this you are unaware of."

"And that is?"

"Harry Brannigan."

"What about him?"

"His father is looking for him."

Preston steepled his fingers. "That's curious. How do you know this?"

"Hard as it is for you to believe," Sarah said, "I have access to information you don't have."

"This have anything to do with you suddenly disappearing a few months back?" Preston asked.

Sarah ignored the question. "His father is a dangerous man."

"My father is a powerful man," Preston said. "Very powerful, which makes him very dangerous."

"There are different types of power," she said. "And his father, named Horace Chase, is being helped by some other men, all formidable in their own fashion. Dave Riley is retired

Special Forces, as is Chase. They also have a couple of local hoodlums named Gator and Kono helping them."

"So? Are they any closer to finding Harry than Mrs. Jenrette?"

"No," Sarah said.

"So why are you telling me this?"

"I'm keeping *you* informed," Sarah said. "It's what partners do."

"So what should we do about Mister Chase and Mister Riley?" Preston asked.

Sarah smiled. "I've had a few run-ins with them. And once I found out about Harry Brannigan, I put out some feelers."

That got his attention. "And?"

"I don't think he's as far away as people think."

"Do you know where he is?"

"Not yet, but I'm working on it."

"Brannigan would be excellent leverage with Mrs. Jenrette," Preston said.

"I imagine he would. But also for Chase."

"Let me know if anything develops there," Preston said. He stood up to leave.

"Are we on the same page?" she asked.

"'Page'?" Preston seemed amused. "It's my script."

Sarah Briggs blinked in surprise. "And what script is that?"

Preston smiled. "The one where you're a subplot."

One more day, Sarah thought. One more day until the funds were released for the causeway by this nut-job's father. One more day until she sold her slice of Daufuskie and got the money.

"Perhaps you should give me a copy of the whole script," Sarah said. "So I can make sure I'm up to speed."

The change in Preston was as abrupt as the one where he re-entered the room. "Who the fuck do you think you are, bitch?" He stood up, shoving his chair back against the wall. "We finish this tomorrow. You get paid. Then I never want to fucking see you again."

He walked out, leaving her alone in the Senator's field office.

* * *

Dave Riley noted the rental car parked in front of Chase's house as he drove his motorcycle down the long gravel driveway. He had the covert ops instinctual initial response that whoever had come in the car was bad news. Everything and everyone was bad news until proven otherwise. He stopped short of the car and dismounted. He checked his pistol in its holster, making sure the draw was clear. Then he circled around, disdaining the front door and walked to the back. Someone was seated out on the dock.

A woman.

Which could only mean trouble. Even from this distance Riley knew it wasn't Sarah Briggs, which was a slight source of comfort. He walked across the dying lawn onto the wooden walkway. As he closed the distance he could make out more detail.

She had silver hair that glinted in the waning sunlight, which pretty much silhouetted her and made it impossible for him to perceive more. She was faced away from the setting sun and toward him. As he approached within twenty meters she got to her feet. She was slightly taller than Riley's height. Her shoulders were broad on an otherwise slender body and something about that triggered a memory deep in the recesses of Riley's brain, but he couldn't access it clearly.

He knew he'd met her before.

He kept walking. Her skin was as dark as Riley's. She wore a sleeveless white blouse and tan pants. She had a purse in her hand, and the way she kept the other hand in it told Riley she was armed.

He drew his pistol, action being the smarter part of discretion.

Riley halted ten feet from her, squinting to see her with the setting sun in his eyes.

"Not very tactical, Dave," the woman said. "Walking up on someone who has the sun at their back. I thought the green beanies trained you better."

"Kate?" Riley said, not quite believing it. "Kate Westland?"

"Well, at least you remember my name," she said.

Riley's next action surprised even him. He shoved the pistol back into its holster and threw his arms wide, as he came up and wrapped them around her, lifting her off the deck and twirling her around.

"Whoa, cowboy," Westland said. "I know it's been a while." But the smile on her face betrayed her true emotions.

Riley put her down and took a step back. "You haven't changed a bit!"

"Oh bullshit, Dave. Look at you. Less hair, bit of a beer belly, moving slower."

"Silver hair, wrinkles on your face, and your chest seems flatter than I remember," Riley said. But now he could see there was a dark streak in her hair, running right down the center, pitch black, most unusual.

They both laughed.

"Geez," Riley said. "How long has it been?"

"Twenty-four years," Kate Westland said. "Not that I've been counting. I've been busy. And you have too, I hear."

That set off a little alarm bell in Riley's head. He pointed at the table. "Take a seat."

Westland took one of the chairs and Riley sat across from her.

Before he could speak again, she held up her hand. "What am I doing here? Especially *now*? Right?"

Riley nodded.

"I retired from the Agency six months ago," Westland said. "I'm not on official business. I got a call from a guy named Cardena—"

"Oh, crap," Riley said. He'd done a mission early in his Army career with Westland, when she was the liaison officer the CIA sent to work with his A-Team. She'd been a South America area specialist. They'd worked together, and ended up fighting together, as they took down a Colombian drug cartel; and faced betrayal from their own side. It was Riley's introduction into the dark world of double-and triple-crosses.

He didn't miss it.

Westland smiled. "Yeah, he's the fucking Prince of Darkness of the covert world. I've had a few dealings with him over the years. But he's been reliable and his intelligence is always accurate. Let's be glad he's on our side. He called me yesterday. Told me you were involved in some dangerous things here. That's it."

"'That's it'?" Riley shook his head. "Hell the bad thing was over a couple of days ago."

"Apparently not," Westland said.

"That's not good," Riley said. "He didn't tell you what the bad thing was, did he?"

"Nope."

"But you came."

"I did indeed."

"Why?"

"I was bored," Westland said. "We work all those years for retirement, then it comes, and it's like, what the hell?" She laughed and shook her head. "I came because he told me you needed help." She leaned forward and reached across the table to take his hand. "Really, I came to see you." She looked down at his hand. "By the way, you didn't get married on me or start playing for the other side or any of that in the last twenty-four years did you?"

"Not that I recall," Riley said.

"Well okay," the former CIA agent said. "Cardena did tell me some things. He said you took down Karralkov."

"We did. But Cardena brought in the Predator that fired the Hellfire which finished him off."

She nodded. "Karralkov had some ties in South America and his name came across my desk a number of times. The world is a better place without him."

"Okay," Riley said. "And?"

"And Cardena said there was a woman named Sarah Briggs who was trouble."

"She was," Riley said. "And is. I should have killed her when I had the chance."

"If we killed everyone when we had the chance," Westland said, "the world would be shorter a lot of bad people and our consciences would be a lot heavier."

"So Cardena wanted you to come here for a reason," Riley said. "I assume it has to do with Briggs? Because he told Chase—do you know Horace Chase?"

"Never made his acquaintance, but Cardena said he's the one that dragged you out of the comfort of *your* retirement and got you involved in all this."

"Wasn't much of a drag," Riley said. "Like you, I was pretty bored. Anyway, Cardena told Chase, and I quote somewhat: that he didn't have a dog in this hunt. Since he sent you here, then he's most definitely got a dog in this."

"Are you calling me a dog?" she asked, with a smile.

"Absolutely not," Riley said.

"Cardena is known to misrepresent himself when it's to his advantage," Westland said.

"What a surprise."

"Tell me what the hunt is?" Westland asked. "You show me yours, I'll show you mine," she added with a smile.

Riley quickly updated her on the quest for Chase's son, starting with searching for Sarah Briggs invented son and ending with the current situation. When he was done, Westland sat silent for a few moments, processing it all.

"You turn," Riley said. He could see a speck approaching from the south, coming up the Intracoastal and from the large bow wake, he had a feeling it was the *Fina*, with Kono running the engines wide-open. Darkness was settling over the low country and the sunset across the Intracoastal was breath-taking, a blaze of red, partly obscured by long clouds.

"Two things," Westland said, following his glance. "Cardena was stingy with information but he did give me something, which helps explain why he called me. First, Sarah Briggs isn't her real name."

"What is it?"

"I don't know," Westland said. "Cardena wasn't specific, but I get the feeling her fingers are in a lot of pies in the shadow world. While some of those she ripped off might be after her, she's got some powerful friends who might take her in or give her cover."

"All right," Riley said, regretting once again not taking the shot; or at least letting Gator do the job. He doubted very much that Gator's conscience, if he had one, would be weighed down too heavily by the act. He'd yet to show any remorse over shooting Erin Brannigan.

"Second," Westland continued, "there's some sort of land deal going on with Daufuskie Island. And for some reason, Cardena gives a shit about it."

"You don't know why?" Riley asked. It was definitely the *Fina*, Kono arcing the patrol boat in toward the dock. Chase and Gator were flanking Kono on the bridge.

"Not exactly," Westland said. "I do have something of interest, but maybe it better wait until I can brief everyone."

"Roger that," Riley said. "One quick question though. Who exactly is Cardena and who does he work for? Like Dylan sings, we all gotta serve somebody."

"He serves a woman named Hannah," Westland said. Seeing that the name meant nothing to Riley, she amplified. "Hannah runs the Cellar."

"Still not ringing a bell," Riley said.

"If Cardena is the Prince of Darkness, then he serves Hannah, the Queen of all of the covert world." The boat was getting closer to the dock. "No one knows much about the Cellar," Westland said. "But essentially it's the cops for the covert world. Polices our ranks without ever having to enter a courtroom. Judge, jury and executioner. No one wants to go up against the Cellar. You do and you just vanish from the face of the Earth. It's been around a long time."

"Great," Riley said as he got up and went down the metal ramp to the floating (sort of) dock. He grabbed the line Gator tossed him and secured the boat.

"My son's with Doc Cleary," Chase said, leading with the headline.

"That's good news," Riley said.

But Chase was shaking his head. "Not that good. Apparently he was involved in a death up in Charleston and we have no idea where Doc and Harry are." Chase looked past him, toward the deck at the top of the ramp. "Who's the guest?"

"Kate Westland," Riley said. "I worked on an op in South America with her a long time ago. CIA, retired."

"What's she doing here?" Chase asked.

"Cardena sent her to help."

"What?"

"Let's go inside and get everyone up to speed," Riley suggested.

* * *

Years ago, Horace Chase had been told that an effective sniper was a man who could shoot another human being on nothing but an order and stop; also on order. The stopping is important.

He'd been told he was one of those people.

But he wasn't the only person who'd been told that.

And the instructor had failed to include half the population, since it also applied to women.

Across the Intracoastal Waterway, just short of half a mile, the sniper lay on a pile of small shells. The hummock had been built up by generations of birds dropping empty shells, the tide pushing them together in a linear mound. It was an uncomfortable perch, but the sniper had been in worse.

The sniper moved her scope from Westland, down to Riley and Chase and then Kono and Gator. She knew she couldn't get them all before they reacted. But the first one would be dead before the sound of the shot crossed the waterway. The second hit at just that instant. Then it would be a race against their reactions.

The only problem was the sniper's order was to hold.

To wait.

So with darkness settling over the Low Country, she switched from her optics to night vision.

And waited.

Chapter Eight
Thursday Evening

Doctor Golden had two file folders in her hand as she sat down across the desk from Hannah. The air hummed quietly from the powerful pumps keeping Hannah's sanctum in a slight over-pressure (to prevent biological or chemical agents infiltrating in). It had a slight odor to it, the result of the multiple filters it passed through before being allowed in.

Much like the people who made it to her office had to pass through multiple checks.

Doctor Golden was one of the few who made it all the way in. Tall, with dark hair that she kept pulled tight, she'd begun working with Hannah's predecessor, Nero, at almost the same time Hannah had.

Golden came out of the military's Special Operations Command, SOCOM, where she'd been doing groundbreaking work in profiling. While most people associated profiling with popular fiction and catching serial killers (after the fact), Golden had looked at it another way. She wanted to profile people *before* they did bad things. And to find certain types of people who might be the right fit for the extremely demanding jobs that filled the field ranks in SOCOM.

Her basic premise was that some people were genetically pre-disposed to become certain types of people, but for the extremes, there also needed to be an environmental trigger. For the criminals, it was usually abuse as a child by someone who was supposed to love them. For SOCOM, they were trying to adapt the training to exploit critical skills.

It was all well and good, but ultimately Hannah relied on Golden for personnel assessments.

Thus the folders.

"I thought Nero closed out Sarah Briggs' file," Hannah said.

"He did," Golden said. "I found it in his personal archives. And-" she hesitated.

"Go on?"

"It was never really closed. Since there was no confirmation of Briggs' death, it's still open."

"I don't understand," Hannah said. "If it's open, then it shouldn't have been in Nero's archives. It should be in my records."

Golden had nothing to say to that.

"Summarize," Hannah finally said.

"Very intelligent. Very effective. A top-notch agent, trained specifically for assassinations."

"How many ops did she carry out before she vanished?"

"Seven. All with maximum efficiency."

"Odd," Hannah said. "Then why would her unit send her into a blown op?"

Golden tapped the folder. "That's not in here."

"Please leave it," Hannah said.

Golden put the top folder on Hannah's desk.

"And Senator Gregory?" Hannah asked.

Golden shook her head. "This isn't the Senator's case file. It's his son, Preston Gregory."

"Go on."

"He came on the radar a year and a half ago when he was involved in a death at the Military Institute of South Carolina. I get alerts from the various public and private military academies since their severe environments can be a trigger for certain types of activities." Golden then relayed the same version of events that Dillon had received in Charleston.

"Sounds like an accident," Hannah said when Golden was done. "Why did you start a file?"

"The Senator is a powerful man," Golden said. "His son's desire to be even more powerful. Couple that ambition with a death, and I always find it suspicious."

Hannah considered that. "The situation is very dark and deep here. Sarah Briggs's file in the wrong place. As if Nero was paying special attention to it. And we know his attention was never misplaced. And Preston Gregory being involved in events that are brewing in South Carolina. Keep monitoring."

Golden stood up, dismissed.

"Leave Gregory's file."

* * *

Dillon took down Jerrod Fabrou in Charleston Library garage the way his platoon would hit a Taliban-controlled village: fast, fierce and ruthless. Stepping out from behind a concrete column, he jabbed the stun gun into Jerrod's back, then moved back, letting him fall to the ground, saving him from splitting his skull open by sticking out his foot and letting the head bounce off his toes.

Tucking the stun gun away, Dillon reached down and threw Jerrod over his shoulder, walked five feet to his car and tossed him into the open back of the SUV. He roughly grabbed Jerrod's arms, pulled them behind his back, and zip-tied them together at the wrists. Then he jabbed a needle into Jerrod's neck and pushed the plunger. He threw a tarp over the body. Then he slammed the door shut.

It was done in under eight seconds.

Dillon looked around. No one to witness and he'd spray-painted over the single security camera that could possibly have gotten worthwhile images.

Dillon got into the driver's seat and started the car. He drove out of the garage underneath the library onto Calhoun Street and turned right. He followed Calhoun to a brief right onto Lockwood and then onto 17 South. To his right front, the sun was setting, another day in the Low Country coming to an end, leading to what promised to be an interesting and long night. He crossed the bridge over the Ashley River, leaving Charleston behind.

He cleared the outskirts of West Ashley and continued until he saw the exit for Edisto Island on the left. He crossed onto the island, then took back roads, certain of his destination, not needing to use the GPS, although he had it on to double-check.

Always double-check. His platoon sergeant in Afghanistan had insisted on it and it had saved their asses more than once. Dillon had heard about the platoon leader who'd replaced the batteries in his laser designator but forgotten to reboot the system, thus designating his own position for a five-hundred-pound bomb.

That was bringing in a world of fatal hurt.

The paved road gave way to gravel, which, after one last turn, gave way to dirt. There were no lights from houses, no sign of civilization, other than the road. Dillon finally braked when he saw the dirt give way to wood. He left the engine running and the lights on, put the SUV in park, and got out. Walking forward, he stepped onto the old bridge. It was in decent shape and crossed a deep tidal cut. Dillon guessed it would hold the weight of his vehicle, but he wasn't planning on crossing.

He went back to his vehicle and opened the back. Jerrod was still unconscious from the shot. Dillon checked his watch. He had at least another forty-minutes with which to work. He quickly got to it.

Twenty minutes later Jerrod Fabrou was lying on the wooden bridge, near the edge. His hands were still zip-tied behind his back, his feet were also zip-tied together, a black hood covered his head, and, most ominously, a rope was tied around his neck.

The noose was not done professionally, as a hangman would with the long, stiff knot that would break the neck. This was a simple slipknot, but that would be sufficient. Dillon very much doubted that Jerrod knew how to make a true hangman's knot.

He went back to the SUV, turned the lights off, then shut the engine down.

Then he waited. He'd learned the art of waiting early in his military career and taken it to higher levels by going out with his hunter-killer sniper teams at least once a month while in Afghanistan.

Snipers knew how to wait.

Jerrod began to stir. Dillon turned the headlights back on. The creatures of the night were also beginning to stir, insects buzzing about. The strong smell of tidal flats filled the air. Dillon got out and walked over to Jerrod and kicked him, none too gently.

Jerrod cried out and began to 'worm', the movements a trussed-up person made while on the ground and disoriented.

"Stop moving," Dillon said.

Jerrod, of course, in panic mode, ignored the warning. Dillon knelt, putting his knee in the middle of Jerrod's chest. "Stop moving," he repeated. This time, with the aid of the knee pinning him to the wooden planks, Jerrod stopped squirming.

Dillon reached down and whipped the black hood off his head. He stood and backed off slightly.

Jerrod blinked into the headlights, disoriented. "What? Who are you? Where am I?"

Dillon was just a black silhouette in the headlights, looming over Jerrod. He held his hand out, turning it to and fro so Jerrod could see what he held between his fingers.

"Your ring," Dillon said.

"What are you doing? What do you want?"

"Look around," Dillon said. "This is where you're going to die if you don't do what I say. This is the last place you're ever going to see."

Jerrod's eyes grew wide. "Who are you?"

Dillon leaned over. "We met yesterday."

That clicked for Jerrod. "Dillon? What do you want?"

"I want the truth. What happened that night with Greer Jenrette?"

"We told you."

"Then you die here." Dillon pulled on the rope around Jerrod's neck. "See?" He grabbed Jerrod's hair and twisted his head so he could see that the noose around his neck was tied to a wood plank in the bridge. "It's low tide so the drop is about eight feet. The rope will stop you at seven. Just a single foot below your feet. Close, but not close enough. It will be enough to let you swing. Choke to death. Bad way to go."

"We told you the truth!" Jerrod exclaimed. Tears ran down his face. His eyes were on the rope, but then he looked up at Dillon. "You're a brother! An Institute man. You can't do this to me! We wear the ring!"

"Bunch of Institute men beat the crap out of me yesterday," Dillon said. "They didn't seem to care that I wore the ring. Were you there, Jerrod? Who had the axe handle? I recognized Chad. Can't quite hide him even with a hood on his head. But I think the guy with the axe handle was Preston. Seems his style. Attack in a pack. With a hood on."

"I wasn't there. I swear."

"Yeah," Dillon said. "I bet you weren't. Too much action for you. But you were there that night in the Sinks. What happened to Greer Jenrette?"

"Brannigan stabbed him. He didn't mean to. It was an accident."

"Bullshit," Dillon said. He put a foot on Jerrod. "Just a little kick and you go over. You'll be dead before the tide comes in to make your feet wet. And then the crabs will come. You'll make a good meal. Someone might find you some day, but when I reconned this spot, didn't look like any tires had been down the road in a while. Maybe your skeleton will be found. Maybe nothing."

"You won't kill me," Jerrod said. "That's murder."

"Oh, no," Dillon said. "It's suicide. There will be no reason to think otherwise. Distraught man takes his own life by hanging after having been involved in an accidental death at the Institute. There will be questions, of course. Did you walk all the way out here? Why here? Why so long after the incident? But you'll be dead. Just like there're questions about Jenrette's death, but no one wants to answer them right? So I don't think anyone will be too interested in *your* death either. Maybe your dad. But there will be no answers. Because only two people will know. And you'll be dead and I'll never tell."

Dillon leaned over once more, putting his face inches away from Jerrod's. "You're going to die very soon if you don't give me some answers. Tell me the truth. What happened that night?"

"Fuck you!" Jerrod screamed. "Fuck you!"

Dillon straightened and stepped back several steps. He considered Jerrod, trussed and noosed, screaming defiantly. In the movies in this situation the good guy was always sure the bad guy was hiding a truth, but Dillon wasn't certain. Jerrod *could* be telling the truth. Sometimes it was what it was. At least he'd said it had been an accident; manslaughter, not murder.

"Why did you guys pick Wing?" he finally asked.

Jerrod stopped screaming long enough to consider the question.

"We wanted to make it easy for Jenrette. He would have been inducted into the Ring his third year. But we had to at least test him."

"Like you were tested."

"Yes."

"I'm sure they picked someone similarly tough for you."

Jerrod didn't say anything to that.

"What was the test?"

"They were supposed to fight. After we had them sweat in the showers. Let them fight it out. But fucking Brannigan interrupted."

"There's something you're not telling me," Dillon said.

"They'll kill me if I betray them," Jerrod said. "They will. And you know what?" He tried to jerk himself into a sitting position, but that tightened the noose around his neck and he panicked, flopping back onto the bridge's plank roadway. "They're coming for me."

"What?" Dillon said.

"I was supposed to meet them at the High Cotton. What time is it? I'm sure it's after seven. They'll come looking for me since I haven't shown."

Dillon spared a glance at his watch. It was 9:30. "Where will they look? We're in the middle of nowhere."

"My phone," Jerrod said. "We all allowed each other to track our phones. We decided that after we met you yesterday. Turns out it was a smart move. They know exactly where I am right now."

Dillon reached in a pocket and pulled out the offending device. He hadn't exactly stayed up on technology while deployed. The phone was on and pushing the button he could see that there had been a half-dozen calls from Preston. "Not any more." He tossed it out into the dark, toward the water. He was rewarded with a splash.

"Doesn't matter," Jerrod said, gaining confidence. "They located it and are on the way."

"You trust them to do that?"

"Yes. And you won't kill me. Not over this bullshit."

"I think you read me wrong," Dillon said.

"Fuck you!"

Dillon sighed. *He* had read it wrong. Jerrod wasn't the weak link; he was the obvious one. He should have picked Chad. He could just imagine that tub of lard writhing around, pissing his pants, begging. Dillon had a feeling old Chad would give up anyone and everyone in this situation. But Jerrod was showing some spine. And the phone thing threw a twist in his plan; started a clock ticking. And he had no idea when he would run out of time. How long would Preston and Chad wait before searching for Jerrod? He figured he had about thirty minutes, then it was time to bug out. He didn't see Preston as being overly concerned about racing to help anyone else. But he would come, just to find out what was going on as it affected him.

"I've killed people," Dillon said. "The first time is really hard. And my first time, I didn't even do the killing direct. That's the thing about being an officer. We give orders for other people to kill. I know lieutenants in my unit who never fired their weapon the entire deployment. But they ordered lots of people killed. In a way, it's an easy introduction to a hard thing.

"We're taught to respect life. Because that's the way we're brought up. It's what religion tells us. But we're trained at the Institute, then during basic, during officer training, during Ranger School, to go against that instinct. Bayonet training for example. We talked about that, didn't we Jerrod?"

Jerrod just glared back from his prone position, the headlights fixed on his pale face, tears or perhaps sweat dripping down his cheeks.

"But until you do it the first time, you question yourself. Every man does. Tell me, Jerrod, have you ever killed?"

Jerrod shook his head.

"I'm talking not just a human. Ever go hunting? Surely your old man took you out with his buddies. Big guns. Boar hunting maybe?"

Jerrod continued to shake his head.

"Really?" Dillon said. "That's unusual for a Low Country rich boy like you. Anyway, I got a call in from a hunter-killer sniper team my second night there. They'd spotted a couple of dudes digging next to a road. Like who the fuck would be digging next to a road in Afghanistan at two in the morning except some dipshits putting in an IED? Right?"

Dillon took in a deep breath through his nostrils, smelling the pungent night air of the Low Country, a fragrance unique to that part of the world. Part life, part decay. Part land, part water.

"They wanted to engage. My first thought was, *Shit, I need to ask someone about this. Get permission.* But I looked around the CP and I realized *I* was the guy. There was no one for me to pass the decision on to. And everyone was looking at me, new boot L.T. in-country. *What's he going to do?*

"In Ranger school they beat into you that you have to be decisive. Even a bad decision is better than not making one. You can't stand in the kill zone trying to make your mind up when ambushed. '*Do something Ranger!*' they scream at you all the time. So I said 'take the shot' like I was in some damn movie.

"So they took the shot. Correction. Shots. Drop two dipshits." He shrugged. "Once you do it the first time, it loses its mystique. Every decision after that was easier. And I ended up eventually using my weapon. Killing directly. I stopped counting too. How many people I ordered killed, how many I killed." Dillon stepped up next to Jerrod. "So don't tell me I won't kill you."

Jerrod glared up at him. "You're good at making speeches. But if you kill me here, it's not combat. It's murder. And Chad and Preston are on the way. They'll know it wasn't suicide. So fuck you."

Dillon kicked out, the tip of his boot thudding into Jerrod's side. There was the sound of a rib cracking, Jerrod grunting in pain, the crying out in alarm as his body rolled, tipped on the edge of the bridge, and then he fell.

He came to an abrupt halt at the exact height Dillon had predicted. He stopped so quickly, both his loafers were jerked off his feet, landing in the fluffer mud a foot below.

Jerrod was screaming, his voice undulating up and down the spectrum of abject fear.

"Shut up," Dillon said, leaning over the edge of the bridge. "In case you haven't noticed, you're not choking."

And Jerrod did finally notice. The noose around his neck wasn't tight. A nylon strap just two inches shorter than the rope, coming down from a truss underneath the bridge, looping under Jerrod's arms and up the back of his neck was holding him up. Dillon had put the strap on Jerrod while he was unconscious.

"Your fucker!" Jerrod yelled.

Dillon sniffed. "Did you shit yourself?"

"Fuck you!"

"You did a good job protecting your asshole friends," Dillon said. "But next time, I won't be as nice."

Dillon put the ring on the edge of the bridge, above Jerrod's head. He walked away, got in his car and drove off, leaving Jerrod Fabrou dangling underneath the bridge, screaming into the darkness.

* * *

The 'dissemination of information' took a while. Chase went first, updating them on what he'd learned from Tear and Doc Cleary.

That part didn't take long.

Riley went next, relaying his conversation with Farrelli.

"Who is Harry supposed to have killed?" Chase asked, when Riley finished. "Tear said the grandson of some important woman in Charleston. Who?"

Kate Westland spoke for the first time. "Greer Jenrette."

All the men turned to look at her: Chase, Riley, Kono and Gator.

"How do you know?" Chase asked.

"Cardena briefed me."

"Old Lady Jenrette is a powerful woman," Kono said. "She runs Charleston."

Chase spread his hands toward Westland. "Pray tell. What did Cardena tell you?"

"There are two things going on," Westland said. The men were seated around the living room, Chase on his locker, Kono and Gator on the brick step in front of the fireplace, Riley on a branch of the tree. Westland had been sitting next to him, but now she was standing, a person obviously well versed in giving operational briefings. They only had a couple of lights on, dimly lighting the room.

She held up a single finger. "One is the thing that concerns you most immediately. Harry Brannigan." She looked at Chase. "Your son with Erin Brannigan." She held up the other hand, a single finger. "Two. Daufuskie Island. It's the center of a complex bidding war and land-grab."

"How are they connected?" Riley asked.

She pulled the fingers down but left her hands up. "The players. Mrs. Jenrette is one. The other is Merchant Fabrou, out of Savannah. His son was involved in the incident where Greer Jenrette died."

"I still don't see the direct connection," Riley said.

"I don't exactly know if there is one," Westland said. "I don't think Cardena does either." She dropped her hands. "I believe that's why he's gotten me involved."

"He didn't order you here?" Chase asked.

"I'm retired," Westland said. She nodded toward Riley. "Cardena dangled my old friend in front of me and I bit."

"Who is this Greer Jenrette that Doc and Chase's son had to run away?" Gator asked, focusing on the violent aspect. "And how did he die?"

"As was noted," Westland said with a nod at Kono, "he's the grandson of the most powerful woman in Charleston. He died during a hazing incident at the Military Institute of South Carolina around eighteen months ago. You son," she looked at Chase, "is the one who killed him. Allegedly. An interesting aspect is that no legal authorities were involved. The death was labeled accidental."

"What kind of accident?" Gator asked.

"A ceremonial bayonet in the heart," Westland said.

"Helluva accident," Gator said.

"Exactly Mrs. Jenrette's feelings," Westland said. "I believe she wants your son dead in return and that's why Doc Cleary is keeping him far away from South Carolina."

"Fuck," Chase said. "Did he do it?"

Westland shrugged. "That's the unofficial official version. More importantly, it's what Mrs. Jenrette believes. Greer was her only grandson." She put her hands together briefly. "And she's the guiding force behind Sea Breeze. Almost all of Daufuskie Island under one ownership, developed into a major resort on the east coast."

"There *was* a resort on Daufuskie," Riley said. "It went under. As did the three golf courses. It's dead. The island's practically uninhabited now. I don't see the plan. The land isn't going to be worth much more."

"Not if there's a causeway to the island," Westland said. "And it gets deeper. The upperclassmen who were present when Greer Jenrette died, supposedly at the hands of Harry Brannigan were Preston Gregory, Chad Mongin and Jerrod Fabrou."

Westland ticked off the first name. "Preston Gregory is the son of Senator Gregory. Who has the authorization for Federal funding for the causeway in his desk, just waiting to file it and the funds will be released. The word is that's going to happen on Saturday. And he's also head of the Select Committee on Intelligence."

"Oh crap," Riley said. "Now we know why Cardena and the Cellar want to know what's going on."

Westland pressed on. "Chad Mongin's family first came to the Daufuskie area in the 17th Century. They've been selling up their land for the past century, but they still own a key piece. The access point on the mainland where the causeway will start.

"Jerrod Fabrou is the son of Merchant Fabrou, a prominent businessman in Savannah. He's an Institute graduate who is negotiating with Mrs. Jenrette regarding Daufuskie. It appears they will share ownership."

She folded her arms. "Now you know what I know." Then she said: "Ah. Except one thing. There's another significant piece of property on Daufuskie that needs to be bought to make the resort complete: the Bloody Point Golf Course. Its ownership is buried under a number of shell corporations. Which were being investigated by the Treasury Department. They managed to dig down and find that Karralkov owned it once upon a time."

"Well—" Riley began, but she pressed on.

"Note I use the past tense," Westland said, gracing her old friend with a smile. "Prior to his departing this world care of Cardena, he was bought out. By another shell company. Owned by the Jersey mob and then devolved to a man you're familiar with: Alfonso Farrelli."

"The shit just gets deeper and deeper," Gator said. "Why don't we just invite everyone to Daufuskie and have a shoot-out?"

"If only it were that easy," Westland said.

"We don't give a shit about Daufuskie or this Sea Breeze," Chase said. "Did my son kill this Greer Jenrette? You avoided the question earlier."

"I avoided it," Westland said, "because I can't answer it. The only people who know what happened that night were in that locker room. One is dead. Four of them swear to one version. We don't have your son's version."

Chase spoke up: "Doc Cleary's not bringing him back until this is cleared up. So we won't get the other side of the story until then."

"Great," Gator said.

"How does Sarah Briggs figure into all of this?" Chase asked.

"That's the real question I need to get an answer to," Westland said.

"That's Cardena's dog in this hunt," Riley said. "Briggs. And if he's part of this Cellar, that means it's likely that Briggs is a former operative gone rogue."

Westland nodded. "It's likely."

"Then he should have a file on her," Riley said. "Which means you should have a file on her."

Westland shook her head. "There's a level where there are no files any more. Cardena simply told me that Briggs is dangerous and to find her and report back to him. That's it."

Riley started at her hard but there was nothing more forthcoming. He stood up. "All right. We're not gonna figure this out in the next five minutes. I say we sit tight for a little bit. Then come up with a course of action."

"Maybe you should have a chat with Farrelli again," Gator suggested. "I'll come with you."

"We'll go in the morning," Riley said. "For now, we hunker down for the evening."

Chase divvied out sleeping assignments. Then he sought out Riley. The two went out back, next to the slime-filled pool.

"Can we trust her?" Chase asked.

"I trusted her with my life on that op," Riley said.

"That was a quarter of a century ago," Chase pointed out. "And if she's working for Cardena, who knows what her real plan is, or more accurately his plan. We're getting side-tracked by this Daufuskie thing."

"No," Riley said, "we're not. We know where your son is. With Doc Cleary. Who isn't coming back until this issue of the death of Greer Jenrette is cleared up. So he's safe. And Mrs. Jenrette is involved in this land deal. There's something binding all this together. I just don't know what it is."

"Sarah Briggs," Chase said. "Westland is holding back on that. I'm sure there is a part of the black world where there are no files, but no one comes out nothingness. She knows more about Briggs than she's telling us."

"I agree," Riley said. "But she'll tell us when she wants to. For now, we can use her help."

Chase didn't look happy with that. "Everyone keeps saying we should have killed Sarah Briggs."

Riley nodded. "So let's kill her next time we see her."

* * *

"What did Dillon want to know?" Preston asked.

"Get me up," Jerrod demanded.

Preston and Chad were kneeling on the bridge, looking down at Jerrod, twisting and turning on the harness below them. Chad had a flashlight aimed at Jerrod, effectively blinding him.

"Just get me out of here," Jerrod begged.

"Did you shit yourself?" Chad asked, taking a deep sniff. He turned to Preston. "He shit himself." He laughed. "What a pussy."

"What did he want to know?" Preston persisted. He had Jerrod's Institute ring in in a plastic bag and was looking at it as if it were something new to him, even though he wore a similar ring on his own hand.

"Same as in the High Cotton," Jerrod said. "What happened that night with Jenrette and Brannigan."

"What did you tell him?"

"I told him the same thing we told him there," Jerrod said.

"Bullshit," Preston said. "You ratted on us."

"I swear," Jerrod said. "Would I be hanging here if I had?"

"Maybe you'd be dead if you hadn't," Preston said.

"I swear," Jerrod pleaded. "I kept to our story."

"I don't know," Preston said. "I don't think you have the balls to stand up to Dillon alone. You didn't come to the barracks when we beat the shit out of him."

"That was stupid," Jerrod said. "The Pelican Brief syndrome, you dumb fucks."

"What?" Chad asked.

"By beating the shit out of him," Jerrod explained, as best one could dangling from an old wooden bridge, "you made him want to know more."

Chad laughed. "I don't think so. He'll think twice before coming after us."

"Look around," Jerrod said. "He's already come after us. Or else why am I hanging here."

"He's got a point," Preston allowed. "Dillon is turning out to be a major pain in the ass."

"Cut me down," Jerrod said. "I need to get out of here. And turn that damn flashlight off. I can't see anything."

"Tell me what you told him and then I'll cut you down," Preston said. Chad turned off the light.

Jerrod's voice shifted into a whine. "I've already told you!"

"Your daddy is trying to develop Sea Drift for you, isn't he?" Preston asked. "To establish your power base."

"What the hell are you talking about?" Jerrod peered up. Preston and Chad were just dark figures up on the bridge now, lit partially by the headlights of their SUV. Jerrod had dangled for what seemed like ages since Dillon left, but was really only thirty minutes. His arms were numb and he stunk.

Under the circumstances it had been a very long thirty minutes.

"Mrs. Jenrette told my father she foresaw me and Greer working together," Preston said. "With Greer being the money behind my political aspirations." He laughed. "But a study of history shows that the power of the purse is what this country was founded on. He who has the money controls. And I will be beholden to no one. And I will not tolerate rivals."

Jerrod looked up. "I didn't say anything to Dillon. What happened that night stays with us. Within the Ring of just the three of us."

"But three can keep a secret only if two are dead," Preston said.

"Four know," Jerrod said.

Preston nodded. "Good point."

"And we swore an oath," Jerrod reasoned. "The person we have to find is Brannigan. And that's what Dillon is after. Maybe we let him do his job?"

"If he gets to Brannigan," Preston said, "then he'll learn the truth. And then he'll be after us."

"Not if you use your father's power to take care of Dillon *and* Brannigan," Jerrod said. "My father has people who do that kind of work too."

"Interesting," Preston said. "I do have some men standing by."

"Come on, Preston," Jerrod begged. "Let me up."

Preston got on his knees. He pulled a folding knife out and opened it. Getting on his belly, he reached underneath the bridge toward the nylon strap wrapped around the bridge trestle.

"The rope first," Jerrod pointed out. "Then pull me up. Or just cut the rope, then the nylon and I'll crawl out of here."

"I know," Preston said, and then he cut through the nylon.

Jerrod dropped two inches, then a couple more as the rope cinched down around his neck. His mouth was open as he tried to cry out, but nothing came out of his lungs and nothing was coming in.

"What the fuck!" Chad exclaimed.

Jerrod's feet were kicking, desperately trying to gain a foothold, but the ground was several inches below him. Close, but not close enough.

Jerrod didn't hear Chad or see them. He was experiencing flashes of light and a loud ringing in his ears. He couldn't think, didn't understand what was happening to him.

And then he lost consciousness. But not life.

His body continued to convulse, struggling against death even though the brain wasn't conscious. His face was distorted, livid, the eyeballs protruding.

Preston got to his feet and folded his knife. "I've read that the heart might keep beating for up to ten minutes," he said to Chad. "If you want to rescue him, go ahead. But he'll probably be braindead."

Chad wasn't rushing to the rescue. "Why did you do that?"

"I didn't do it," Preston said. "Dillon did. I'm willing to bet his fingerprints are all over that strap. And this ring if we need to use it."

Chapter Nine
Friday Morning

Riley sat on the seawall and watched Chase work out. The sun was rising from the east, on the other side of the peninsula, over Broad Creek, sending rays slanting through the trees.

A battered heavy bag hung from a two-by-four on the bottom of the dock walkway, just above the sand. Chase was doing turn-kicks, whacking the bag solidly. He was also breathing hard. It wasn't just a workout; it was a distraction from the matter at hand.

Riley turned as Westland came out, dressed in khaki slacks and a blue shirt. She had a cup of coffee in each hand and she extended one to Riley. She sat down next to Riley and reached down to scratch Chelsea behind the ears, making it an audience of three.

"Enjoying yourself?" Chase asked, as he took a break, punching a button on his watch that he'd been using to time himself.

"I'm feeling stronger by the minute," Riley said. "You?" he asked Westland.

"Definitely. I prefer nine millimeter at twenty paces, though."

"Don't we all," Chase said, grabbing a towel to wipe his face. He looked past them. "We've got company."

Coming down from the side of the house was an older man wearing a white sports jacket, and a red shirt underneath, not exactly a fashion mogul; misguided Miami Vice attire. His flat-top was right out of Parris Island. He was lean and weathered. His eyes moved about, checking everything and everyone out.

"Cop," Westland said with certainty. "And former military. Probably Marine."

"Beaufort's Sheriff Department," Chase confirmed. "He's a friend." He greeted the visitor as he arrived. "Detective Parsons."

"Horace," Parsons said. He nodded at Riley. "Dave."

"Detective," Riley said. "This is my friend, Kate Westland."

Parsons gave a slight bow. "Ma'am. Pleased to meet you."

"To what do we owe this honor?" Chase asked.

"A mutual acquaintance has gone to the afterlife," Parsons said. "Alfonso Farrelli."

"Did natural causes take him or his line of work?" Riley asked.

"It appears to be a heart attack," Parsons said.

"'Appears'?" Riley repeated.

"Yep," Parsons said. "And that's most likely what the official report will read. And it's what his two bodyguards swear to. Those boys say he collapsed right in front of them. They did CPR and called nine-one-one to no avail."

"And the reality?" Riley asked.

"First," Parsons said, "I wouldn't believe a word those two thugs said. Plus, I doubt they know what CPR is. And if they had performed it, there would have been bruises on the old man's chest. Nothing.

"Second. I had medical examiner take a closer look. She found a needle mark on his thigh. A recent one."

Chase spoke up. "So someone escorted Mister Farrelli out of this world."

"Yep," Parsons said. "Not that my department is going to look into it. My boss doesn't see the point of looking into the death of a mobster. Especially on Hilton Head. Especially when two witnesses swear to a natural cause. Heart attack it is."

"And you're telling us this because?" Chase asked.

Parsons ignored Chase and looked at Riley. "He was found with an envelope in his pocket. With a sizable sum in it."

"I understand he made loans," Riley said.

"The amount in the envelope equaled exactly what I owed him, plus the vig," Parsons said. "And the two muscle heads said you'd been to see him just before his fatal attack."

"We had some things to talk about," Riley said.

"Thank you for your kindness, sir," was all Parsons would say. He reached into his pocket and removed an envelope and tossed it to Riley. "I appreciate the gesture, but Mister Farrelli's departure cancels the debt out."

"Won't they miss this in the evidence room?" Riley asked, but he was already sliding it into a pocket.

"It never made it to the evidence room," Parsons said. "I was first detective on-scene and the body hadn't been disturbed other than getting the pulse checked. It would cause awkward questions if I had reported it and turned it in. Better for everyone all around."

"Roger that," Riley said.

"There's something else," Parsons said. "I pulled video from a security camera on a bank across the way; pans out to the parking lot and catches Pope Avenue and even across the street. Someone came to visit Farrelli after you. And departed just a minute before the ambulance call went in. Someone the two muscle heads didn't say had stopped by." He reached into a pocket and pulled out a thin stack of photos. He turned the stack so they could see the top one.

"Sarah Briggs," Chase said.

"Of course," Riley said.

Parsons handed the photos to Riley. "I assume by your reaction you are familiar with the lady."

"She's bad news," Riley said. He passed a photo each to Chase and Westland. "Sarah Briggs is what we know her by, but I have a feeling checking on that name will turn up nothing."

Parsons frowned. "Is she the one involved in that mess with Karralkov?"

Riley nodded. "You met her. Hair was shorter and blonde then. Renting a house down the street."

"Ah yes." Parsons nodded. "I remember; the one with the kid that didn't exist. I'm assuming she killed Farrelli. And assuming *you* didn't. I'm further assuming there's no way I could prove it. Another reason not to pursue this."

"How are Farrelli's friends in Jersey reacting?" Chase asked.

"Too soon to tell. But most likely they'll think it was a heart attack," Parsons said, "unless someone tells them otherwise." He looked at the three. "I don't plan on doing that. And I can assure you the two muscle heads won't."

Westland spoke up. "If that's the story they're telling, then they were complicit in the murder."

"They weren't very communicative," Parsons said.

"We can fix that," Riley said.

"Gator," Chase said.

"Gator," Riley concurred.

"I didn't hear anything," Parsons said.

Riley had another question. "You hear anything about some big land deal for Daufuskie?"

"All I've heard is Daufuskie is off limits," Parsons said. "Not that we go out there, but even our water patrol is to steer clear, especially this weekend."

"Any idea why?" Chase asked.

Parsons shrugged. "No clue. As usual, the powers that be, which means the people with money, are dictating how the law goes, or doesn't go in this case, here in the wonderful Low Country."

"We appreciate the information," Riley said. "Farrelli's guys, or ex-guys, still at the restaurant?"

"Last I saw. I believe they're still thinking about what to do next and they don't appear to be the quickest thinkers. I've seen swamp moss move faster."

Riley shook Parsons' hand. So did Chase. The detective gave another slight bow toward Westland. "A pleasure to meet you, ma'am."

And then he took his leave.

"I'll take Gator and Kono and talk to Farrelli's guys," Riley said.

"I'll go to the harbor master at Harbour Town," Chase said. "Maybe he'll have an idea where Doc Cleary would sail to and hide out. At the very least he can put the word out among his network. From what I remember Doc saying, people who sail are a pretty tight community."

"I'll go with Dave," Westland said. She stood and stretched. "I'll join you inside in a second. I want to enjoy the view a bit longer. You *do* have a beautiful place, Horace."

Chase nodded. "Thank you."

The two men headed into the house.

Westland waited until they were out of sight, then took a small mirror out of her purse. She angled it toward the water and then jiggled it, signaling in Morse code. It took only a couple of seconds, then she slipped it back in and headed into the house.

* * *

An effective sniper is one who accepts not taking a shot can be as successful a mission as taking one. The sniper watched the 'dots' and 'dashes' from the mirror, translating the Morse (dot-dash/ dot dot/ dot dash dot) into the three letters A-I-R that were repeated three times into what the mission briefing had been, and knew it was time to pack up.

She slithered back on the shells until she was concealed from the land on the far side. Then, still in a crouch, she stepped down into the waist-high water of a narrow inlet that ran toward the pick-up zone about two hundred meters away. It was going to take a while to get there, but she'd been in worse places.

She was wet, she was chilly, and she was hungry. Pretty much standard fare for an op.

As she moved, she made a radio call for her ride to come.

* * *

Dillon had had to pay $5 to enter the first gated community ever in the U.S.: Sea Pines Resort, on the southern end of Hilton Head Island. He didn't see the point of having a 'gate' if one could get in that easily. But tourists were the lifeblood of the island and even those who lived there had to accept that fact. So the gate was for those too cheap to fork over half a sawbuck.

Dillon drove down streets that were like tunnels, with large oaks on either side and Spanish Moss dangling from overhanging branches framing the way. He had to admit the place had atmosphere. There were bike paths next to the road and families were tooling about, apparently enjoying their vacation. Dillon had spent a couple of weeks on Hilton Head one summer, working a temporary job and he'd watched the families spend their week in an arc, driving onto the island full of excitement on Saturday and departing the following weekend bedraggled and hoping to get home and away from each other.

Harbour (spelled like that) Town was on the Intracoastal side of the island, an inlet that had been dredged out to allow yachts to dock at a series of piers. The original developer of Sea Pines had built a lighthouse in 1970 that had been the butt of many a joke along the coastal area, since one wasn't needed and it was designed as little more than a tourist attraction. The jokes stopped when the attraction worked. A popular golf tournament had its 18th Hole near Harbour Town every year and a camera was always up in the top of the lighthouse. Tourists paid another five dollar a pop just to climb up the ninety-foot high tower. And climb they did.

To see lots of trees and water and water and trees.

Dillon wasn't going to Harbour Town to climb the lighthouse. He parked his car then walked to the semi-circular harbor packed with yachts of varying sizes from rich, to so-rich-you-can-see-it-in-my-linear-feet of boat. As arranged, two men were waiting next to a zodiac tied off to a pier and Dillon went up to them. They checked his drivers license, then escorted him into the rubber boat, indicating he should sit on the small bench in front of the console. One of them then sat at the console and the other behind Dillon.

They moved slowly out past the breakwaters delineating the edge of the harbor and then the driver opened up the engine and the boat planed out, heading toward a large yacht anchored just off the Intracoastal, west of Hilton Head and opposite Daufuskie Island. Dillon estimated the yacht was almost one hundred feet long, not too bad, but not quite big enough to land a helicopter on.

The ride took less than two minutes and then they were at the larger boat. Dillon noted the name inscribed on the fantail: *Quad* and the Institute flag flying from the yardarm. The two men had yet to say a word.

"My dinghy's bigger than your whole boat," Dillon quoted, earning blank stares from the two.

Not *Caddyshack* fans.

While the driver kept the boat against a gangway, the other gestured. Dillon climbed on board, wondering whether he was supposed to render honors to the United States flag on the fantail or the Institute flag overhead. The Zodiac took off, heading back toward Harbour Town.

Dillon was escorted along the side of the ship, up another set of steep stairs, and then into a wardroom.

He was surprised to see that Merchant Fabrou was in a wheelchair. The man was only in his fifties but appeared sick, with hair dyed dark, contrasted against a pallid face. However, his voice was deep and southern as he 'greeted' Dillon.

"I only agreed to see you because Mrs. Jenrette requested it," Fabrou led with. He didn't extend his hand in greeting, nor indicate a seat for Dillon.

"Thank you, sir," Dillon said. Fabrou was seated to the side of a desk. Several plush chairs were scattered about the stateroom. Another hatch/door was across the way from the one through which Dillon had entered.

Fabrou must have noticed him staring at the wheelchair. "Hip replacement," Fabrou said. "Irritating as all hell. Had some complications. A damn infection."

"Sir, I—"

"I told Rigney everything I know," Fabrou said. "What do you want?"

Fabrou's reaction to his phone request for a meeting had indicated that Fabrou's son had not called him to tell of last night's activities. Dillon had thought that unlikely for several reasons, embarrassment being the primary one, but also because he had a feeling Preston wanted to play things close to the vest.

Dillon decided to lead with a hand grenade since it appeared the field was already deeply mined. "Sir, I don't think your son was honest with me when I talked to him about the event with Cadets Wing and Brannigan that led to the death of Greer Jenrette."

"Who the fuck do you think you are," Fabrou said, "coming onto my boat and saying that?"

"I'm representing Mrs. Jenrette regarding her grandson's death," Dillon said.

"Then find Brannigan," Fabrou said.

"I understand you've been asking around concerning that," Dillon said.

"I heard Farrelli, that wop who thinks he's a gangster, was asking around about it," Fabrou said. "I did Mrs. Jenrette the courtesy of giving her that information. Then I get Rigney showing up and now you asking me about it. And you saying my son's a liar?"

Dillon decided on a slight tactical retreat. "Mister Rigney said you were doing some checking about Harry Brannigan's location?"

"He's with Doc Cleary," Fabrou said.

Dillon was surprised at the secret revealing itself so easily. "And where is Doc Cleary?"

"Your guess is as good as mine," Fabrou said. He gestured about. "Somewhere on the ocean. Doc is one hell of a sailor. He could take that boat of his and go around the Cape if he wanted. Could be in Tahiti. I tell you one thing, Doc isn't coming back with that boy until Mrs. Jenrette is no longer with the living. Doc's a smart man. Unlike you, coming here and throwing weight you don't have around. You expect to do business in the low country any time in the future, boy?" Fabrou didn't wait for an answer. "You just pissed me off which means you pissed off the Quad. Which means you best not set foot in Savannah. And I'll tell you something else, boy. We're expanding. We're moving north. Charleston aint as powerful as it used to be."

"Sir, I assure you—" Dillon halted as the door to the wardroom which he'd come through was thrown open and Preston Gregory stood there, disheveled and mud-covered. He pointed at Dillon as he threw a noose on the deck. "That's the son-of-a-bitch! He killed your son, Mister Fabrou!"

* * *

The harbormaster in Harbour Town (redundant in Chase's opinion, despite the different spellings) wasn't a guy; it was a woman. A lean, grizzled, middle-aged (or older?) woman who looked like she'd been baked twice-over under the sun. Chase foresaw many visits to a dermatologist in her future.

"Yeah, I know Doc Cleary," she said in response to his query.

She was sitting at an old wood desk on the second floor of a building overlooking the boats that filled the harbor. A battery of radios sat on the long bench behind her. Various nautical gear, the purposes of which Chase didn't know, hung on the wall. She had several charts on the desk, one pegged down with a coffee mug, a bottle of whiskey, an ashtray and a sextant. He thought the bottle might be for show, but it was half-empty, so maybe not.

"How do you know Doc?" she asked.

"I inherited his house," Chase said.

That got him one raised eyebrow as she lit another cigarette. "Really? Nice place. I'm Zelda, by the way."

"Chase."

"Just Chase?"

"It's what most people call me," he said. "My first name is Horace but—"

"We'll stick with Chase," Zelda said. "Doc set sail a while ago." She closed her eyes briefly. "Year and a half or so."

"Do you know where he went?" he asked.

"'Where he went'? Hell, he could have went anywhere. And kept going. I've talked in person and on the radio to folks who sighted him all over the place. Antigua. Panama. Hawaii. Doc could cut the water. Might be circumnavigating. Something he had on his bucket list."

"Did he have a young man with him?"

"You mean Harry?"

Chase put a hand on the edge of her desk. "Could you tell me about Harry?" For some reason this complete stranger meeting his son made it completely real.

"Seemed like a nice kid," Zelda said. "Only met him once, just before Doc took off. They seemed in a rush. Heard there was some trouble up in Charleston. But Doc never said much. Why do you want to find Doc?"

"He's still paying the utilities at the place," Chase said. "I want to make sure I reimburse him."

"Right," she said. "You wanna do the right thing. He gave you the place, and Doc wasn't senile last I saw. If he's paying the bills, he damn well knows it. Don't worry about it."

"The boy is my son." It was the first time Chase had said it to a strange and it felt strange and exciting and scary all at the same time. "I've never met him."

With the cigarette dangling from her lips, Zelda stared at him. "Well, hot damn. Were you in prison?"

"The army."

"Sorta the same."

"I didn't know he existed," Chase said, a red flush spreading across his face.

"Okay, there's a story there and I'm sure it's interesting, but I got to ask: is Doc keeping the boy away from you?"

"No. As you said, he's afraid some people up in Charleston mean him harm."

"Fucking Charleston." Zelda reached out and picked up the bottle of whiskey. She grabbed two, not so clean mugs, then poured a couple of stiff drinks. She slid one across to Chase, who automatically picked it up.

"To Harry, your son," Zelda said.

"To Harry, my son."

As he lifted the mug to his lips he saw that Zelda was tipping hers back, emptying it, so he did the same.

She slammed hers down on the chart and Chase followed her lead.

"Sad to say, my friend, I don't know where Doc is. And you aint the first person to be asking about him. Some woman was here about a week ago asking."

Chase pulled out the copy of the picture of Sarah Briggs, which Parsons had given him. "This her?"

"Yep."

"What did you tell her?"

"Same as I'm telling you. No idea." Zelda shook her head. "Cold bitch. Wouldn't have told her even if I did know. Hope she wasn't the mother of your son."

"She's not."

"That's good." But Zelda was looking past him as there were several dull echoes, which Chase recognized as gunfire. "What the hell?" She grabbed a pair of binoculars then trained them on a yacht anchored outside the harbor, between the south end of Hilton Head and Daufuskie Island.

* * *

"He hung him, Mister Fabrou," Preston said, "trying to make it look like suicide."

A pair of guards had accompanied Preston in, and both now had guns in their hands, trained on Dillon.

Merchant Fabrou's face was even paler. "Preston. I need the truth. Are you saying Jerrod is dead?"

"Yes, sir, Mister Fabrou. We were supposed to meet at the High Cotton. Where this son-of-a-bitch confronted us the night before. Asking questions about Greer Jenrette's death. He didn't like the answers and he went to the Institute, asking more questions. Then he must have grabbed Jerrod. Kidnapped him. When Jerrod didn't show last night, I called, but there was no answer. I knew something was wrong. So Chad and I tracked the last location of his phone. On Edisto Island. And we found him—" Preston paused and took a deep breath, putting a quiver in his voice—"and we found him, hanging from a bridge there."

"He's dead?" Merchant Fabrou repeated. "My son's dead?"

Dillon knew an ambush when he was in one, although this was different from his combat experience. This wasn't going to get better with time. He did as he'd been trained in Ranger School. Act even if it was the wrong thing.

He darted for the door opposite where Preston stood, flanked by the guards. Surprised at the sudden move, the guards aimed, but didn't fire.

That gave him enough time to get through it and slam it behind him. He heard Fabrou screaming something and knew time was running out. Dillon ran along the side of the boat. The door behind him was thrown open.

"Stop!" Someone yelled and there was the sound of a shot.

He assumed it was a warning shot since he wasn't hit; or the guards were bad shooters.

He didn't wait to find out.

Dillon dove overboard, arcing into the Intracoastal while taking a deep breath.

Behind him, both guards stopped at the railings and fired, bullets plinking into the water, the sounds of their guns echoing across the Intracoastal.

* * *

Chase had followed the direction of her binoculars and saw the man dive into the water, then what appeared to be two men shooting into the water. The sounds of their guns were muted at this distance, but recognizable to those who knew guns.

"Someone pissed someone off," Zelda said.

"Whose boat is that?" Chase asked.

"The *Quad*," Zelda said without a pause. "Merchant Fabrou, out of Savannah."

"Going to call the cops?" Chase asked as he picked up a telescope off the wall and trained it on the boat.

"You haven't been here long, have you?" Zelda asked.

Chase saw a dark spot appear, the swimmer's head. He was moving fast, heading toward Daufuskie. The guards were firing, but the distance was growing greater, and their accuracy didn't appear up to par.

"Sheriff's department's got two boats," Zelda said. "They use those to cite people in small boats for driving drunk so they can collect on the tickets. They don't screw with people in big boats. You could slaughter a goat in a pagan sacrifice out there and no one gives a shit. You should see the party in the harbor during the big golf tournament week. Strippers on the masts doing their thing. Drugs being passed around like candy. The cops don't mess with the golden goose."

"They don't care if someone shoots at someone?"

"Not if the shooter is rich." She lowered the binoculars. "And they didn't hit anything. No harm, no foul. He looks okay. Probably just some good ol' boys fooling around."

It was obvious she didn't believe that.

"Why's Fabrou out there?" Chase asked, still watching through the telescope.

The guards had given up on target practice and disappeared inside. The swimmer was still heading toward the shore.

"Land deal," Zelda said. "They're going to build up Daufuskie. I didn't care much for all the golfers out there, but now it's going to be just like this place. Overcrowded and built-up. Can't say I wasn't cheering when those golf courses went under. It's a great island and I hate to see it turned to crap. But Fabrou and his ilk, they'll do anything for a dollar."

"Any idea who just jumped ship?" Chase asked, not expecting an answer.

"Young fellow," Zelda said. "Was taken out there by Zodiac just a few minutes ago."

Chase watched the 'young fellow' reach the shore and walk out of the surf, onto Daufuskie Island. Things were growing more interesting by the minute. He put the telescope back on the wall.

"If you hear anything about Doc's or my son's whereabouts, could you call me?" He gave her a card with his cell phone number.

"Sure thing."

His phone rang and he saw it was Dave Riley.

"What do you have?" Chase asked.

* * *

"Can I shoot them?" Gator asked. "A wound, nothing fatal."

"Let's talk first," Riley suggested as Westland drove her rental car down Pope Avenue and turned into the parking lot for New York Pizza and the no-name restaurant.

Gator and Kono filled the back seat, blocking the rear-view mirror. They were both armed, and Kono had his machete jammed in between them. Gator wore his usual Ranger T-Shirt, the gold letters rippling over his chest muscles. His body always looked on the edge of exploding, the muscles lined with veins as if wired with det cord. Alcohol wasn't the only thing the two of them smuggled and Riley knew Gator dealt steroids to the other body-builders in the various gyms on the island.

Westland parked the car and glanced at Riley with a raised eyebrow. "We good?"

"We're good," Riley said.

The four of them exited the car. Riley tapped Westland on the arm, indicating that Gator and Kono should take the lead. Gator threw open the blacked-out door and the other three hustled in behind him.

To find an empty restaurant.

Riley pointed to a door leading to the kitchen.

Gator took lead once more. As he pushed open the swinging door on the right, the one on the left swung in the opposite direction, with a no-neck guy, approximately Gator's size, coming out.

Gator was faster, sucker-punching the goon in the nose.

Blood exploded from the broken appendage, spraying over Gator's fist and the man's face as the tumbled backward. Kono slipped by Gator, catching the bat that was swinging at Gator's head with his machete, the razor-sharp blade slicing halfway through the wood, before coming to a halt.

Kono twisted the machete, taking the bat with it, thus disarming goon number two.

Gator kicked the man he'd punched and they could all hear ribs break. The man dropped to the floor moaning in agony.

"Hello," Riley said to Number Two.

Westland had a pistol in her hand, the muzzle aimed at his head.

"We've got a few questions," Riley said. "About the recently departed Mister Farrelli."

"Fuck you," Number Two said.

"I think Gator is right," Westland said. "Let's shoot him in some non-fatal spot." She lowered the muzzle. "Like his balls."

"Hey!" Number Two exclaimed. "Who are you people? You know who we are? Who we work for?"

"Your worked for Farrelli," Riley said. "But he's dead. And you betrayed him. So don't pull that 'we work for the mob' bullshit with me. I make one call to Jersey and you guys are swimming with the fishes." He caught Westland's slight eye-roll, but the goon didn't. "We work for the government," Riley continued. "The government that puts people in prisons that don't exist. Where no one comes back from."

The goon's eyes widened. "Hey. We didn't do nothing."

"Sarah Briggs," Riley said.

"Who's that?"

Riley sighed. He reached into his pocket and pulled out the photo. "Recognize her?"

"Oh yeah, the dame."

Riley wondered how many mob movies this guy watched. "Yeah, the dame. She paid you, right?"

The guy nodded. "Yeah. Ten large each."

Riley wondered if Farrelli had known his life could be sold that cheaply, but then he realized his life had been on the line for a paycheck that was much less than that every month.

"She said he was gonna have a heart attack," the goon said. "And he did. Pretty fucking smart of her to knows it was coming. She a doctor or something?"

Riley realized the guy actually thought that Farrelli *had* had a heart attack.

"'Never underestimate the power of human stupidity'," Westland said.

"You make that up?" Riley said.

"I wish. Robert Heinlein."

"Did she pay everything up front?" Riley's hopes rested on payment on the back end, where they could meet Sarah Briggs for the last time.

"Yeah," the goon said, crushing that hope.

"When did she contact you the first time?" Riley asked.

A deep furrow appeared in the goon's forehead as he tried to remember. The guy Gator had punched tried to get up and Gator hit him on the side of his head with his fist. The sound was like a mallet hitting wood and the guy flattened, out cold. Kono pulled his machete out of the bat.

"Like a month ago?" the goon guessed.

"How did you talk to her?" Riley asked.

He reached toward his pocket.

"Whoa!" Westland warned.

"Huh?" The goon was confused. "Just getting a phone."

"Go ahead," Riley said.

The goon pulled out a cheap cell phone, a burner. "She's on speed dial. Number one. She told us not to use it for anything else."

Riley took the phone. He looked at Westland.

"You never know," she said. "Stranger things have happened."

Riley punched in number one on the speed dial. It rang, then rang, then just as the third ring began, a voice he recognized answered abruptly.

"What?"

"Sarah," Riley said. "How you doing?"

She laughed. "I know that brogue. A mixture born in the Bronx, muted by a career in the Army, and twisted with too long in the Low Country. Dave Riley. How are they hanging my friend? You just can't enough of me."

"I've had more than enough of you," Riley said. "Why'd you kill Farrelli?"

"He was disagreeable," Sarah said.

"Regarding?"

"Our business arrangements. A man should keep his word."

"What about a woman?" Riley asked.

"Where's your friend, Horace?" Sarah asked.

"He had some errands to run," Riley said.

"Like tracking down his son?"

"You lied."

"Really?" Sarah laughed. "Do you think I owe you the truth or something? Seriously. But I tell you what. I think you and Horace owe me. You owe me for the money you took. Then the money you burned. And the passports. Those aren't cheap, you know."

Riley said nothing. Westland was still holding the gun on the one conscious goon. Gator was looking like he wanted to hit someone else. And Kono was checking the edge of his machete.

"And I'm going to collect," Sarah finally said. "I want you to get your friend, Horace. And then call me back."

"Why?"

"He's looking for his son, isn't he?"

"He is."

"Well, I've got him."

The phone went dead.

Chapter Ten
Friday

Preston knelt down in front of Merchant Fabrou's wheelchair. "I have your son's ring, Mister Fabrou."

The two guards came back in, reporting that Dillon had escaped. But Fabrou was still processing the devastating news that Preston had conveyed.

"What?" Fabrou said, trying to focus on the man kneeling in front of him.

"I have your son's ring," Preston repeated.

"Where is my son?" Merchant Fabrou asked. Some semblance of the message got through. "Where is his body?"

"I've had it taken care of," Preston said. He reached into a pocket and pulled out a plastic bag. He extended it to Fabrou. "Your son's ring, sir."

Fabrou took the bag with shaking hands. He opened it and reached in, retrieving the ring, hands shaking. Tears formed, as if the presentation of this band of gold was final proof.

Preston stood up and took a couple of steps back. "If you wish, sir, I'll make arrangements for your son's body to be shipped to Savannah."

Fabrou was turning the ring to and fro. His own Institute Ring glittered on his finger. "But what happened? How did he die? How did this Dillon kill my son?"

Preston looked at the two guards, then back at the old man. "Sir, maybe it's best if—" then he paused as Fabrou gasped. The old man dropped the ring, hands going to his chest. His mouth opened, trying to say something, but nothing came out except desperate gasps for air.

Preston took another step back. He looked over at the two guards. They looked at each other, then at Preston.

And remained where they were.

"Anyone can be bought, Mister Fabrou," Preston said.

The old man stared at him, hands to his chest, fighting for air. Preston walked closer and leaned forward, his face scant inches from the old man's. He whispered so only Fabrou would hear him. "I killed your son, Merchant. And now I've killed you. Your line is over. And you were betrayed by more than just your guards."

Fabrou's face was bright red and his eyes were losing their focus. He reached forward, toward Preston, who easily stepped back, out of the grasp.

Then Fabrou fell forward and hit the deck. He twitched for several seconds, then was still. Preston knelt and carefully retrieved the ring with the plastic bag, ensuring it was sealed inside.

Then he stood up. "Call it in once I'm gone," he told the two guards. "And next time I tell you to shoot someone, make sure you hit him!"

* * *

Dillon stared at Fabrou's yacht from the concealment of palmettos on Daufuskie, well above the water line. He was surprised the Zodiac hadn't been sent after him. Then he saw why as it headed toward Harbour Town with Preston Gregory in it.

One step behind. That was Dillon's summary of events so far. He was one step behind. If not more.

There was one person left for him to push, the person he should have gone to instead of Jerrod. Fortunately, his destination wasn't that far away, but that made sense since Daufuskie was where everyone was coming, all the elements for a perfect storm.

With a long, determined stride, Dillon began walking toward the narrow waterfront golf cart path that ran down the center of Daufuskie Island. Cars had long been banned from the island, even when the resort was open, the primary means of transportation being golf carts. With the death of the resort and all three golf courses, only a handful of people still called the island home, and almost of those were seasonal visitors on the north side.

The island was beautiful, with nature ruling, other than the golf courses and a few buildings. Native Americans had lived here for centuries. During the Yemassee War in 1715, a group of them had been massacred on the southern tip of the island, and thus Bloody Point had gotten its name. Gullah, freed black slaves, and runaways had settled the island for a long time, until most were pressed out when the resort had been built.

Now, with the resort bankrupt and the golf courses shut down, the island was reverting back. Something Mrs. Jenrette and Mister Fabrou were planning on changing.

* * *

"What?" Chase had not expected this turn of events.

"Sarah Briggs," Riley said. He explained shaking down the goons, getting the phone, and calling Sarah. He related the entire conversation.

Westland, Gator and Kono stood around them, on a dock underneath the Cross Island Parkway Bridge where they'd agreed to meet after accomplishing their tasks. The fact it was Riley who'd learned where Harry and Doc were, and not Chase, was a twist that was hard to process; much worse was the fact that Sarah Briggs said she had them.

"She's bluffing," Chase said. "Fucking with us."

"I don't think so," Riley said. "She killed Farrelli. She's got something going on, something big enough to take out a wise guy from New Jersey. She's not stupid. She knows if we could get those two idiots to talk, so can some muscle from the Garden State."

"Why don't we call her?" Westland suggested. "Find out what she wants?"

Chase put his hand out and Riley put the burner in it. "Speed dial one," Riley said. "And put it on speaker."

The five of them gathered in tight around one of the pylons that supported the pier. Chase opened the phone, hit speed dial one and then speaker. He put the phone on top of the pylon.

Sarah answered before it rang twice. "Horace, how are you?"

"I need proof of life," Chase said.

"Oh, Horace, right to the business as always. No chit-chat for you. No 'How do you do'? No 'How are things since I fucked you over'?"

"Proof of life," Chase repeated. "Hell, proof you really have him."

"Oh, I have him. And Doc Cleary. Irascible old coot, isn't he? Put up quite the fuss for a man his age. Got to give him credit, Horace. A good man to have your son with. Especially since you were never there for him. A boy needs a male role model. Someone in his life he can turn to. Someone he can emulate. Someone he can count on. Someone who is *there*."

"Proof of life."

"Horace, if you're going to just be a recording," Sarah said, "I can hang up now and save myself a lot of trouble. After all, you contacted me, not the other way around."

Riley spoke up. "Bullshit. You left the burner with Farrelli's two guys who you paid off. Both are mistakes unless they were deliberate. You should have killed both of them. And if you didn't, you certainly shouldn't have left them a phone to contact you. So you knew we'd check, and you knew we'd call. You're willing to have them give you up to the Jersey mob to draw us in with this call. So let's cut the bullshit."

"Leave it to the old man to figure something out," Sarah said. "But seriously, you guys are so far behind, you two will still be figuring this out in the old soldier's home. If you're alive to make it to the old soldier's home."

"Proof you have them and proof of life," Riley said. "Or this conversation ends now."

"Oh you boys. No fun at all. And we had fun didn't we Horace? Rocking around in your little rubber boat?"

When there was no reply, they could hear her sigh. "Give me a different number to send a photo to."

Riley rattled off his cell phone number.

"Call me back after you get the picture," Sarah Briggs said and the line went dead.

Seconds later, Riley's phone buzzed with a text message. He accessed it and then turned the face so they could all see.

Doc Cleary and a young man, tied down in chairs inside some kind of room with wood walls. On Doc's lap was a newspaper. The look on his face was resolute.

And Chase saw his son for the first time. It was difficult to tell in the photo, but he looked big, larger than Doc. With dark hair that had grown out since his Institute days, covering his ears and close to his shoulders. His face was well tanned, not unexpected after eighteen months at sea. He had a couple of days of beard, giving a dark tint to his face.

"Looks like you," Westland said.

Chase didn't know how to respond.

"Today's Island Packet," Riley said, referring to the paper, and nudging Chase out of his shock.

"Fuck," Chase said. "How did she get them?"

"She was on this well before we were," Riley said.

Gator spoke up. "We kill her next time we see her."

"We get my son and Doc back first," Chase said.

"Any of you recognize the place?" Riley asked, looking at Gator and then Kono.

They both shook their head. Kono pointed at a window in the left rear. "Get that larger, we might see something out there." Right now it was just a green blur.

"Okay," Riley said. "She has Doc and Harry. She didn't do that on a lark. She wants something. The question we have to answer before we call her back is how far are we willing to go to get them back? Based on her history, Briggs' price is going to be high. And I don't think it's going to be money."

No one responded as they pondered that.

"I can't ask you all to do anything," Chase said. "This is on me. I'm the one that has to pay the price, whatever it is."

"Oh, bullshit," Riley said.

"Yah," Kono added. "Bullshit. I owe you my life. A life for a life."

Chase looked at Gator.

The big man shrugged. "Whatever. Sounds like there's going to be some good action. I'm in."

Chase turned to Kate Westland. "You've got no stake in this. So—"

Westland cut him off. "I have a stake."

That surprised Riley. "Kate, just because I'm—"

"Shut up," Westland said. "It's got nothing to do with you, Dave. So don't get a swelled head. I've got a stake in this. Trust me."

"Okay," Chase said. "Let's see what she wants."

He hit speed dial on the burner. This time it went through five rings, Sarah taunting them with each ring.

Finally she answered. "Well, gentlemen? By the way, who am I talking to? Chase, of course. Riley. Who should know better. Is that big musclehead Gator there? And his sidekick, the Gullah?"

"Kono," Chase said. "Yes."

"Hell of a team," Sarah said. "You guys were damn lucky that Hellfire took out Karralkov."

"So were you since you were with us," Chase noted. "What do you want?"

"'What do I want'?" She was silent for a few seconds. "I want you to do whatever I ask of you in the next twenty-four hours. You do that and you get your son and the old man back. So hold on to that phone. It rings, you answer. It goes six rings and there's no answer, then your son and the old man are fed to the gators."

The line went dead.

"They here," Kono said.

"What?" Chase asked.

"She say 'fed to the gators'," Kono explained. "She's here. And she has them near here too."

"He's right," Riley said. "She'd want to keep her ace in the hole close by, and that's what she considers Doc and Harry. She thinks she's got us on kidnap retainer."

"She does," Chase said.

"At the moment," Riley said. "But she wouldn't have said twenty-four hours if it was something she wanted us to do right now."

"The land deal," Westland said. "Tomorrow morning on Daufuskie. It's got to have something to do with that. Everything is pointing to that."

Riley took charge. "Gator. You know some place where this image can be increased?" He held up his cell phone.

"Yeah," Gator said.

Riley handed over his phone. "Do it." He turned to Kono. "We need your boat at Chase's place at Brams Point. It's close to Daufuskie and hopefully wherever Doc and Harry are being held."

"Can do," Kono said.

The two of them left to accomplish their tasks.

"I think—" Riley began, but then his phone rang. "Yo."

"Riley, it's Parsons. You got an epidemic of heart attacks down there it seems."

"Who now?"

"Merchant Fabrou collapsed on his boat. I picked it up off the wires since they're dispatching a sea ambulance to his yacht in your neck of the woods. Report is that it's a heart attack."

Riley sighed. "Anything else?"

"Nope. Just thought you might want to know. Seems like the shit is hitting the fan. Might want to duck."

"Not likely," Riley said. "Thanks."

He hung up then relayed the information to the other two.

"I saw something," Chase said, "when I was in the harbor master's office. Kind of looked like they were trying to kill someone on Merchant Fabrou's yacht, but he got away."

"And where are the cops?" Westland asked.

"Don't ask," Riley said. As she started to ask, he held up a hand. "Seriously, Kate. Think Deadwood. Think Wild West. Think whatever."

"Okey-dokey," Westland said, obviously not surprised. "Got it."

"The guy they were shooting at got away to Daufuskie," Riley said. "So I'm thinking that's a good place to check out. Not like the ferry is running any more. And it isn't likely he's going to run into someone to bring him to the mainland. Island's almost deserted now since the resort went under. My boat is tied up here. We can head over there now and track whoever it was down."

* * *

Preston looked at the image, recognizing Harry Brannigan, despite the longer hair and the semi-beard. "Do you know where this is?"

The man holding the iPad with the picture was former Secret Service and now worked for Preston's father. Who'd 'subletted' him to his son as personal protection. He was a short man, with a burly build. His nose had been broken long ago and set improperly, giving it a slight cant. He often felt it was his appearance that had kept him from a promotion to the Presidential detail, blithely ignoring the fact he'd been cashiered for spending a night with a hooker on an advance detail and showing up for duty still somewhat drunk.

That didn't mean Jimmy Pappano didn't know his job. He'd put a tap into Sarah Briggs' phone while she was using the bathroom during her 'meeting' with Preston at the Senator's Charleston office. What the two had done hadn't disgusted him, as he'd seen much weirder and kinkier stuff in his time in Washington D.C. both in the Secret Service and working privately for the Senator.

Pappano nodded. "I tracked it off the towers. It's south of here. Wassaw Wildlife Refuge, which is east and a little south of Savannah on the coast."

Preston was in a second-floor suite in the Sea Pines Resort, where Presidents and other bigwigs used to visit annually for Renaissance Weekend. The event had since moved on to other locales, but it was a still a nice joint.

He was seated behind a large desk, covered with papers and plans: the future of Daufuskie Island as envisioned by the Sea Drift plan, but modified by Preston Gregory for Preston Gregory.

"Harry Brannigan," Preston said, staring at the image. "I assume the old man is Doc Cleary."

"She threatened Chase," Pappano said. "Told him he had to do what she said to get his son back."

"She's going to betray me," Preston said with certainty. "The fucking bitch is going to betray me. She lied to my face yesterday about Harry. She's going to use Chase and Riley to take me out."

Pappano had nothing to say to that.

"You saw her come out of Rigney's place?"

Pappano nodded. "One of my men was tailing her. She was in there about forty-five minutes."

"She's playing everyone," Preston said. "And so is Rigney."

"What do you want me to do?" Pappano asked.

"Go to Wassaw Island," Preston ordered. "Get them. Leave three of your men with me."

Pappano nodded. "Where do you want me to bring them?"

"My boat," Preston said. "You're going to need it to get down there. Then come back up. Clear?"

Pappano nodded. "Might get a little messy dealing with whoever she has guarding them."

Preston shrugged. "So be it. Going to get messy in a lot of places." As Pappano went to the door, Preston called out: "Send him in. Tell the men you're leaving to wait five minutes, then come in."

"Roger that." Pappano exited and Charles Rigney entered.

"Is something going on?" Rigney asked.

"Something is always going on," Preston said. "But everything is under control."

Charles Rigney gingerly sat down without asking permission—he'd work with the young man, but he would not kowtow to the youngster. "You're sure Merchant is dead?"

"Heart attack," Preston said.

"Incredible timing," Rigney said. "And quite prescient of you to have me get him to amend his will two months ago, before his surgery."

Preston tapped the side of his head. "I see the future, Charles. Stick with me and I'll take you places you've never considered."

"I suspect that is a possibility," Rigney said. "But I'll be cashing out as we discussed. I'm getting too old for all of this." He paused. "The word is that Farrelli also had a heart attack."

"You'd think it was contagious," Preston said. "You're certain the clause will work?" he asked, tapping the papers he'd just been perusing.

Rigney nodded. "Upon the unlikely event of the passing of both father and son, with no male heir, the Fabrou stake in Daufuskie passes to the State of South Carolina, earmarked as a wildlife refuge. But, as I showed you, there was a case twenty-two years ago where a parcel of land was passed to the State that way and the lawyer for the ex-wife had quite a bit of leverage in Columbia. A law was passed, retroactive, and now the state can waive its claim and the land be purchased at a price determined by the comptroller."

"And you know the comptroller," Preston made it a statement, not a sentence.

"As planned, the paperwork is already drawn up for that sale to you." Rigney indicated his brief case. "You'll be getting it for pennies on the dollar."

"And how much does the comptroller get?"

"Six hundred thousand."

"How much does he actually get once it passes through you?"

"Four hundred thousand."

Preston laughed. "Got to love capitalism. Anything can be bought. Anyone can be bought."

Rigney shifted uncomfortably in the chair.

"Do you believe that?" Preston asked.

"What?"

"That anyone can be bought?"

"I've never really thought about it," Rigney replied.

"Don't lie," Preston said. "You're a lawyer. Of course you've thought about it. And you've done it. I bought you from Mrs. Jenrette, correct?"

"Old man Jenrette screwed me in his will," Rigney said. "Rewrote it himself and cut me out. It wasn't what we'd agreed on. And I know the old lady isn't going to do anything for me. After all the years I've served the family. So it's not so much a case of you buying me; they ran me off."

"And Sarah Briggs?"

Rigney froze in the chair. "Who?"

"Are you fucking her?" Preston asked. "What special ploy does she use on you?"

Rigney's mouth opened, but nothing came out.

"The paperwork in your briefcase," Preston said. "Is it made out to me? Or is it made out to her?"

Rigney found his voice. "To you, of course."

The door opened and three men walked in. They spread out around the room, effectively circling Rigney.

"What's going on?" Rigney demanded.

"I've asked you that three times and you haven't answered," Preston said. "If I look in your briefcase, will the paperwork be made out to me for the Fabrou's portion of Daufuskie via the state or to her? I assure you, if you're lying to me, you will not leave this room alive."

Rigney closed his eyes. He sighed and then opened them. "There are two sets of paperwork in there. One for you. One for her."

Preston laughed. "Exactly what a good lawyer would do. Prepare for all contingencies. And I assume you've done the same with Mrs. Jenrette's property?"

"Yes."

"What has Briggs offered you?" Preston asked.

"Five million."

"And how does she propose to develop the island?" Preston asked. "She doesn't have the contacts."

"I believe she plans on selling it once the appropriation goes through."

"And Bloody Point?" Preston asked.

"She owns it now."

"You really think she'd pay you five million?" Preston asked.

Rigney shook his head. "No. But she's a dangerous person. I needed a back-up in case she turned on you and she was the only one left standing."

"I admire the planning," Preston said. He looked past the lawyer at the man directly behind him and nodded.

Rigney started to turn, but he was too slow. The man slammed an icepick into the base of Rigney's skull and twisted it once it had penetrated to the hilt.

There wasn't much blood at all.

Preston walked around the desk then retrieved Rigney's briefcase.

"Take care of the body and then we have to go out to Daufuskie Island to make another deal."

* * *

Mrs. Jenrette didn't like to leave her house. In fact, it was hard for her to recall the last time she'd passed out of the doors. And she most definitely did not like leaving Charleston.

She had a yacht, of course. One could not be rich in Charleston and not have a yacht, given there was water on three sides. She did remember her last time on it. A cruise with her husband, son and grandson. And now all three were gone. So it was with heavy heart she was supervising Thomas packing a small bag for a two-day excursion. Not far, just down the coast to Daufuskie Island and back. And she wouldn't be doing it if the stakes weren't so high.

"It will be done soon," Thomas said, as he closed the overnight bag.

Mrs. Jenrette was thinking about that last trip. A cruise to Europe and the Mediterranean. Her pile of bags had filled the foyer; and the mansion had a very large foyer. Who had she been back then? All the stuff; she'd give it all up to have Greer back.

"I will be glad," Mrs. Jenrette said. "I believe—" she paused as the house phone rang, a most unusual occurrence. Oly a handful of people had the number; otherwise a service handled her calls, logging them, noting the message, and supplying a summary.

Thomas walked over to the closest extension. "It says 'unknown'," he reported as he looked at the display.

"Might as well answer it to see who is disturbing me."

Thomas picked up the phone. "Jenrette residence."

He listened for a moment. "Who might I say is calling?" A frown flickered over his face. "I cannot bring Mrs. Jenrette to the line unless I know to whom she would be speaking." He put a hand over the receiver and spoke to Jenrette. "A woman. Says she must speak with you. It's urgent regarding Daufuskie."

Mrs. Jenrette twitched a finger, indicating he should bring the phone to her. She took the device. "Yes?"

"Mrs. Jenrette, my name is Sarah Briggs."

"Proceed." She nodded at Thomas and he picked up an extension to listen in.

"I just love your voice, Mrs. Jenrette. So southern, so much charm, so much power. Truly a marvel."

"Is there a purpose to this call, Mrs. Briggs?"

"You assume I am married," Sarah said. "I am not. But you can call me Sarah."

"I have no reason to assume familiarity with someone I do not know," Mrs. Jenrette said.

Sarah laughed. "So true, so true. Then I will get down to business. Seems everyone is in a hurry to get down to business these days. I was wondering about worth. How much things are worth on a relative scale."

"Speak more plainly or I will hang up."

"Sea Drift will be worth roughly two hundred million, won't it?" Sarah did not wait for a reply. "And the split was to be fifty percent Jenrette, forty percent Fabrou, five percent Mongin, if they won't sell out right, and the rest is allocated to acquiring Bloody Point. Five percent. Am I correct?"

"How do you know this?"

"Let's not waste questions," Sarah said. "If I am correct, then I know you know I know. We are most knowledgeable are we not?"

"I am knowledgeable," Mrs. Jenrette said, "which is why you are wasting my time telling me things I already know."

"That math would net me ten million," Sarah said.

Mrs. Jenrette looked at Thomas as she spoke into the phone. "Our invisible owner of Bloody Point has dropped her cloak and appeared."

"Indeed."

"You do understand that those figures were internal discussions and privy to only a handful of people. We never intended to pay full price for Bloody Point."

"I know. You were offering four hundred thousand."

"And while you might feel you are in the catbird's seat," Mrs. Jenrette continued, "understand that the land you own is worthless since we control access to it."

"As Senator Gregory controls releasing the appropriation for the causeway that will be built to the island once he releases the funds. By the way. How much does he get?"

Mrs. Jenrette gripped the phone tighter. "What do you want Mrs. Briggs."

"Told you. I'm not married."

"What do you want?"

"It's more a question of what *you* want," Sarah said.

"I want Bloody Point, but I won't be extorted," Mrs. Jenrette said.

"Fair market value given the causeway being built is not extortion," Sarah said. "Current market value without knowledge of the causeway, well, now that would be cheating, wouldn't it? And that's what your agent was putting out there publicly." Sarah's voice got sharper. "So let's not dance around pretending we're belles at the ball, Mrs. Jenrette when we're business women at a knife fight."

"Fine," Mrs. Jenrette said. "Ten million is fair market value given the causeway. I can have—"

"I want more."

Mrs. Jenrette was about to say something, but Thomas shook his head and mouthed: *Wait.*

"And *you* want more," Sarah said. "Don't you?"

"Speak."

"Harry Brannigan."

Mrs. Jenrette stood, one hand on the chair. "Go on."

"I have him," Sarah said. "What's he worth to you? Wait. Don't answer. I think we've gone past money now, haven't we? This is personal."

"It is."

"And it's personal for me too," Sarah said. "Seems we've both had our pound of flesh carved from us in the past and want retribution. Perhaps there is a way for us to both be satisfied."

"And how is that?" Mrs. Jenrette walked across her master suite to the French doors that led out onto the balcony running across the front of the house. She stepped outside. It was late in the day, the sun slanting rays across the harbor.

Fort Sumter was out there, still taunting her.

"You'll find out tomorrow," Sarah said. "But I will give you Harry Brannigan if you give me what I want. Tomorrow morning, Mrs. Jenrette. When I ask, you give me what I want. And we will both have our satisfaction." There was a short pause. "And I do want my ten million also."

* * *

Sometimes honor was a bad thing, but a man had to have a code. Doc Cleary most definitely regretted listening to Erin Brannigan beg to see her son over the radio three weeks ago. He'd known it was her by the information she had and he vaguely remembered her voice from so many years ago when Horace brought her around.

The fact she'd been gone for almost all of Harry's life was something he'd been willing to put aside to agree to her request for a clandestine meeting; after all, there was still Mrs. Jenrette to deal with.

The journey back had taken eighteen days, out of the Mediterranean, and then across the Atlantic to this hidden spot at Wassaw Island. He and Harry had waited two days until a boat showed up just the other day; but Harry's mother wasn't on board, but rather a woman leading a trio of toughs from the islands.

Cleary had seen their like before, but he'd never met anyone quite like Sarah Briggs. She'd only spent a few hours with them, grilling Harry about what had happened at the Institute, and Doc about what he knew about Horace, and then she'd departed in a small Zodiac driven by one of the toughs, who'd returned an hour later.

Since then, nothing. Except for once when they were tied to chairs, a newspaper was propped in his lap, and one of the toughs took their photo.

Proof of life. Doc had seen enough movies to know what it meant.

"Do you think she's going to sell me to Mrs. Jenrette?" Harry asked.

They were locked in the bow stateroom on the boat. There was a hatch above, not large enough to crawl through, but it allowed light through and it was cracked open, allowing ventilation. They had a small latrine and food was shoved through the door every so often, on a random schedule, whenever the three guards felt like cooking something up; usually island fare that was surprisingly good.

Doc had been thinking along the same lines, but not expressing it. They'd discussed escape plans (coming up with nothing viable against three armed men) and speculated where Harry's mother might be. Doc had told Harry what little he knew of Erin Brannigan.

They'd discussed Harry's father at length during their many months at sea. Doc could see Horace in Harry, in the strong jaw, and the tough physique, but he also saw his grandmother Lilly in the graceful way Harry had handled the sails and scampered about the deck and his eyes. For a long time it had pained Doc every time he looked into those eyes, because they reminded him of her; but he knew that was selfish and he'd put it aside, shelving that it in a bittersweet part of his mind.

"It's possible," Doc said, never one to obscure reality with wishful thinking. "She's a bitter old woman." He was seated on one side, on the narrow bunk while Harry was on the bunk on the other side. "She didn't use to be that way. I knew her a long time ago. But the deaths of her husband and son gutted her and she put everything into Greer. And then—" he left it unsaid.

"Maybe it's not a good idea to love someone that much?" Harry said.

"Oh no," Doc said. "Never regret love. But never turn it into hate. Bitterness kills the heart."

"Maybe I should have stayed and explained—" Harry began not for the first time.

Doc cut him off. "Let's not get into that again. Going up against Mrs. Jenrette is bad enough, but throw in Gregory, Fabrou and Mongin and no one would have believed you. We tried to get the truth, but when I learned what the official account was, we knew we had to go."

"Still—" Harry paused and cocked his head. "Someone's coming."

The noise of a boat engine came in through the cracked hatch.

"I assume our friend is back," Doc said.

On the deck, the three men Sarah Briggs had hired to sail here didn't know what to make of the approaching boat. In fact, they didn't know what to make of much of what they'd been doing. Her instructions had been brief: keep the two men locked up below, answer the cell phone she left with them and do whatever she instructed.

She had not called to tell them she was coming, or anyone else for that matter, so they drew their pistols.

On board Preston Gregory's boat, which barely made classification as a yacht at forty-two feet, Pappano stood on the foredeck. A sniper, another former Secret Service agent, who'd been on the CAT—counter-assault-team—and cashiered after being found drunk in a hallway during a Presidential trip to Europe. Pappano had hired him on previous occasions. The sniper lay prone, covered with a piece of canvas. A fold in the canvas allowed him to see out and gave a clear line of fire for his rifle. The muzzle of the weapon did not poke out; that was the sign of an amateur.

Slightly behind their counterparts in Special Operations, CAT still used the SR-25, also known in the military as the MK-11, for sniping. Essentially it was an upgraded version of the AR-10 chambered for 7.62 ammunition. The gun the sniper used also had a sound suppressor.

It might be a tad outdated. but it could get the job done.

"I see three," Pappano said.

"I confirm three," the sniper said.

"Terminate."

The first round hit the man farthest away, on the bridge of the boat, exploding his head like a melon. The second round was on the way before the first victim hit the deck. The third man had less than a second to react.

He was beginning to move when he too was killed.

It was all over in less than two seconds. The sniper stayed in position though, scanning the boat through his optics.

Just in case.

They pulled up next to the boat and Pappano led two men aboard as the sniper threw aside his canvas cover and provided overwatch.

Below deck, all Doc Cleary and Harry heard were three thuds above them and the other boat getting closer, then idling.

They heard the lock being turned, then the door was opened and a short man with a pistol in his hand filled the opening.

"Are you—" Doc began, getting to his feet, but the man had the gun up, aimed at them, answering his question.

"Turn around," Pappano ordered. "Hands behind your back."

Another man squeezed in and zip-tied their hands together.

"Come on," Pappano said, leading them up to the deck-level cabin.

The bodies of the three who'd held them captive were lined up on the floor.

"So you understand we mean business," Pappano said, pointing at the three dead men with the muzzle of his pistol.

"Who are you?" Doc asked.

"You don't need to know," Pappano said.

Doc and Harry were transferred to Preston's yacht, while one of Pappano's men took the helm of Sarah Briggs' boat. They got underway, edging out of the low country and into the open ocean, heading due east.

Doc and Harry were moved below, once more locked in a stateroom, this one with just a single porthole. Their zipties were cut just before the door was locked on them. Harry stood by the porthole, staring out at the open ocean. "Who do you think *these* people work for?"

"Not Mrs. Jenrette," Doc Cleary said.

"How do you know?"

"She wants *you* dead, not others. This is out of her league."

"Then whose league is it in? Why are we heading out to sea?"

"Harry." Doc Cleary said it calmly, sensing the agitation in his young protégé. "Remember the days we were becalmed in the middle of the ocean?"

Harry nodded. "Put your mind back in that place."

"We fight if we get a chance," Harry said. "I'm not going the way that couple went off of San Diego."

Doc Cleary knew what he was referring to: a couple took some men out for a test drive of their boat and ended up being tie together to the anchor and thrown overboard. A frightening way to go.

"We fight," Doc agreed, "but I think the fellow in charge wants us alive. Since he's already got three bodies on the other boat, two more wouldn't make much difference."

That seemed to satisfy Harry slightly. But then the boat slowed down. They could hear muffled voices. Then a muted explosion. Harry was leaning, trying to see. "They're scuttling the other boat. The one we were on."

"Getting rid of the bodies," Doc said. "Since we're not on it, I'd say we're useful for a while longer."

"They were people," Harry said.

Doc was surprised. "What?"

"Those three men," Harry said. "They held us prisoner, but we know they were just doing it for the money. They never hurt us. They fed us. They were people. They didn't deserve to die."

Doc Cleary looked at Harry. "True, true. Many who die don't deserve it. But many who live have a pain worse than death."

Harry turned from the porthole. "What do you mean?"

"We don't know anyone's true story," Doc said. "No one but you and me can say what truly happened at the Institute. I've regretted every day that I got you that appointment."

"You thought it was best for my future."

"I was wrong."

"You were," Harry said.

And that brought a smile to Doc's face. "I am so glad to hear you say that."

The engines revved up and the boat made a long arc, heading west.

"We're going back," Doc Cleary said. "We'll find out soon enough what's going on."

* * *

By boat, Riley meant an F-470 Zodiac. A dinghy; not a boat per se in the class of Sarah Briggs, and only fit to be used to transfer people back and forth to a yacht in the class of Preston Gregory's. But he was content with it, although almost every boat, especially around Hilton Head, was bigger than it.

He'd seen *Caddyshack* and enjoyed it.

He expertly drew the Zodiac up to the pier on the northern end of Daufuskie, cutting the motor as he looped a rope a stanchion. One other boat tied up to the pier, but otherwise the place looked deserted.

"Where are we going to look?" Westland asked, as he helped her off the boat.

Chase hopped up next to them.

Riley pointed at the other boat. "Whoever that is won't be far." He pointed. "Marshside Mama's, most likely. It's been closed but—" Riley nodded as he saw three men sitting at one of the outside tables.

"That's the guy," Chase said, pointing at one of them, "who dove off Fabrou's boat."

"The others are Chad Mongin Senior and Junior," Riley said. "Owned most of this island long ago, but sold most of it off. Now they have a place on the mainland, across the water. The elder is a degenerate."

"'Degenerate'?" Westland asked as Riley led the way along the dock toward the restaurant.

"Gambler," Riley said. "I cut him off long ago."

"How do you want to approach this?" Chase asked.

"I want to approach this from the perspective of finding out what the fuck is going on," Riley said.

They came up to the table. The three men stopped talking and turned to stare at them. Dillon was partially dry from his swim. The Mongin's were dressed in what was pretty much the uniform of the Low Country: khaki slacks and golf shirts.

"Hey, Mongin," Riley said, eyes on the elder.

"Riley," Mongin said.

"Who is your friend?" Riley asked.

"My name's Dillon. You must be Dave Riley." Dillon shifted his gaze. "And you're Horace Chase." He looked at Westland. "You have the advantage, ma'am."

"What a polite young man," Westland said. "I am growing more enchanted with the Low Country with each new encounter."

Chase addressed Dillon. "Saw you jump ship not long ago." He jerked a thumb at the water. "Merchant Fabrou not happy with you?"

The three at the table exchanged glances.

"We just found out that he had a heart attack," Riley continued. "Same as Alfonso Farrelli yesterday. Someone is wiping out the competition for this land-grab."

"He was fine when I left," Dillon protested.

"Then why did you jump ship?" Chase asked. "While getting shot at?"

"Preston Gregory," Dillon said. "He—" then he paused. "Shit. Preston is doing it. He killed Fabrou's son. Then he killed Merchant."

"Back up," Westland said. "What about Fabrou's son?"

"I grabbed him last night in Charleston," Dillon said. "I was trying to find out about what happened that night with Harry Brannigan—" he paused and looked at Chase—"what happened with your son that night at the Institute. I don't think they're telling the truth. I mock hanged him, but left him alive. But Preston showed up on the boat saying he was dead. Had his Institute ring, which I left there at the bridge. He killed him. Then he killed Merchant. Wiped out the Fabrou's. They were the other half of this deal."

As everyone absorbed that, Dillon turned to the two Mongin's. "You're next. You and whoever owns Bloody Point. And Mrs. Jenrette. Preston wants it all."

"Oh shit," Chad said, pointing. A fiberglass speed boat was roaring up to the dock, four men on board.

"Heart attack time is over," Chase said, checking his pistol.

"Preston is with them," Chad said. "We can talk to him."

"I doubt that," Riley muttered.

Un-noticed by the rest of them, Westland reached into her bag and hit a button on her phone.

* * *

The sniper was relaxing in the back of the idling MH-6 'Little Bird' helicopter, the roar of the engine a comforting sound. She wore a 'monkey harness', with a strap bolted into the floor. The measurement on the strap was exact, the result of many hours of experimentation.

When her headset crackled with the incoming alert, she checked that she had a round in the chamber (she knew she did, her finger was her safety, but one *always* checked), as the pilots lifted the bird up out of the small clearing where they'd been waiting.

On their display, a blip indicated where the alert had come from.

"Six minutes ETA," the pilot announced.

"Make it five," the sniper advised.

* * *

Riley, Chase and Westland formed a front guard as the two Mongin's stepped behind them. Dillon moved to flank Chase.

"You armed?" Chase asked him.

"Negative."

"Then get behind us," Chase suggested and Dillon ignored.

The incoming boat bumped against the dock and the four men jumped off, Preston and three hard-cases in long coats.

"We don't want any trouble!" Riley called out.

"Hello!" Preston Gregory called out. He had a metal briefcase in hand. "You must be Dave Riley. And Horace Chase. I know Chad. And Chad senior. And Dillon. We meet again. You left so quickly from Mister Fabrou's yacht we didn't have a chance to say goodbye. The lady is an enigma. Your name?"

Chase took half a step forward. "You killed Merchant Fabrou and his son. Are you working with Sarah Briggs?"

Preston cocked his head as if puzzled. His three men spread out, obviously trained. They all had bulges in their coats indicating they had automatic weapons on slings underneath them.

"We're outgunned," Riley whispered.

"No shit," Westland said in the same low voice. "Delay them for a couple of minutes."

"And then what?" Riley asked.

"Something you want to share?" Preston said, noting them whispering.

The two groups were about fifteen meters apart. Outside amateur range, decent range for an expert with a pistol, and deadly for experts with automatic weapons.

When no one replied, Preston looked past the front line to the Mongin's. "Gentlemen, can we come to an agreement on the access point? I believe you've been offered good money at a reasonable price."

Chad answered. "Damn, Preston. What are you doing? Why'd you kill Jerrod? And Mister Fabrou?"

"I believe the evidence points to Dillon as Jerrod Fabrou's killer," Preston said. "And his father suffered an unfortunate heart attack upon hearing of his son's death at Dillon's hands. So both deaths can be laid at your feet," he added, nodding toward Dillon.

"I don't think Chad is on your side any more," Dillon said.

Preston held up the metal case. "I think Chad is on the side of the money. Do we have a deal?" he asked the elder Mongin.

"Sarah Briggs is playing you," Chase said.

"What Sarah does isn't any of my concern," Preston said. "Whatever is between you and her is your business."

"Where does she have my son?" Chase asked. "Where?"

Preston shrugged. "Again, that's between you and her." He shifted his attention back to the Mongins. "I want the easement. Give me the signed documents you were provided with and my men and I, will be on our way. And you'll get what we agreed upon." He held up the briefcase. "You'll be richer, the Mongins I mean," he amended. "Not the rest of you. Unless they're paying you to stand in front of them."

"What happened at the Institute with my son?" Chase asked.

"Old history," Preston said. "Terrible accident. So on and so forth, old fellow. I believe Mrs. Jenrette still holds a grudge. You'll have to take that up with her." He waved that aside. "Do we have a deal, Mister Mongin?"

When there was no reply, Preston gestured. "Shoot Chad," he ordered. One of his men brought a rifle to bear, peering through the laser sight.

Riley, Chase and Westland pulled their pistols. The other two men whipped up their own automatic weapons.

"Easy, everyone," Riley called out. "This is a negotiation. Let's not make it the O.K. Corral."

"That would make you the Clanton's right?" Preston was grinning. "And I'm Wyatt Earp."

"Your hand is empty," Westland said.

"You must be Calamity Jane," Preston said.

"You're mixing your Westerns," Westland said. "Right now, a sniper has you targeted." She brought her other hand up, phone in it. "I give the word, you're dead."

"Oh, bullshit," Preston said.

"Warning shot," Westland said.

* * *

The sniper was on the skid, a kilometer and a half away. The MH-6 was stealth-enabled, with special rotors, engine, and other gear that kept its noise to around a kilometer radius, which meant it was silent at her kill range.

Which was the entire point.

The monkey harness held the sniper from falling as she leaned into it, rifle to her shoulder.

She hated warning shots. Waste of a bullet, but she also followed orders.

She shifted her aiming point from Preston's forehead to the metal case. She picked her aiming point, exhaled, found the sweet spot of not breathing and between heartbeats and caressed the hair trigger.

* * *

"Fuck!" Preston yelled as a bullet punched the case out of his hand, sending it tumbling to the ground.

The three guards went to their knees, searching through their sights for the shooter, with no idea from which direction the shot had come.

Preston was frozen, for once facing something he hadn't planned.

"Next bullet, you're dead," Westland said.

"We'll make the deal!" the elder Mongin cried out. "No one else needs to get hurt." He held up a leather satchel. "The paperwork is all set. Like we agreed."

"Get it," Preston ordered one of his men. "Give them the case." The guy looked like he was going to protest, then picked up the punctured case and scuttled forward, past Chase, Riley and Westland and exchanged for the satchel.

Preston began backing up. "Until we meet again."

"Kate, kill the son-of-a-bitch," Riley suggested, in a voice loud enough for Preston to hear.

"Then old Horace won't see his son," Preston yelled. "Kill me and he's dead."

"You said you didn't know where my son is?"

"I lied," Preston said.

"Hold," Westland said out loud.

* * *

The sniper had heard the conversation through the phone. She wasn't pleased to stand down because in her experience appeasing a bad guy just put off the inevitable. Which was usually a 7.62 mm round through the skull.

But orders were orders.

And Preston wasn't the target of this Sanction anyway.

* * *

"Where is he?" Chase demanded.

"No idea at the moment," Preston said. "But I'll know by morning. I'd love to stay and chat, but I've been shot at."

As Preston and his three compatriots got in the boat and pulled away from Daufuskie, Riley turned to face Kate Westland as Chase looked to the south, the direction from which they knew the round had to have come, having extensive experience working with snipers.

"Little bird, shooter on the skid," Chase said, spotting the small dot hovering just above the treeline.

"Cardena," Riley said. "He sent you."

"I told you that," Westland said.

"No," Riley said. "You said he told you about this and you decided to come. You didn't tell us he ordered you *and* the cavalry to come here. Why?"

"What the hell is going on?" the elder Mongin demanded.

"You've got your money," Riley said. "You and your son get going. You too," he indicating Dillon.

"I think we have the same objective," Dillon said. "I'm staying."

"What's your objective?" Chase asked.

"Finding your son."

"For Mrs. Jenrette, right?" Chase said. "So she can kill him?"

"She hired me," Dillon admitted, "but *my* priority is finding out the truth." He nodded toward the boat racing away. "Given recent events, I have a feeling that the truth of what happened that night isn't what was reported."

"Hold on, hold on," Riley said. "One thing at a time." He pointed at Westland. "Why do you have chopper and sniper support?"

"Cardena and the Cellar," Westland said. "Did Riley tell you about the Cellar?"

Chase nodded.

"Okay," Westland said. "Here's the deal." She noticed the two Mongins edging away with the briefcase. "Hold on," she yelled at them. "Chad needs to hang around because he has something he needs to tell us, first. So I think both of you just sit your butts down for now."

The two Mongins obediently plopped down at the table.

Westland faced Riley and Chase. "Let's deal with Chad and Dillon first, then I'll let you know what's going on with me. All right?"

Both men nodded. Chase went to the table. "Chad. What happened that night at the Institute?"

Chad glanced at his father.

"Tell the truth, son," the old man said. "We're in it too deep now. If Preston killed both Jerrod and Merchant Fabrou, we've got problems. Maybe these people can help."

Chad swallowed. "Preston killed Jerrod. He was hanging there. Like you left him," he said to Dillon. "Preston cut the harness."

"All right," Dillon said. "You know who you're dealing with now, Chad. Preston will as soon as kill you too. There's nothing left to protect. Tell us about the night Greer Jenrette died."

Chad hung his head, and when he spoke, his voice was barely a whisper.

Back to August, over a year ago.

The bathroom was at the very end of the Sinks, underneath the Institute barracks. It had a name among the cadets: Dante's Den. It was off-limits to rats, unless they were ordered to report there; a summons dreaded among the first-year cadets.

There were a select few, though, who anticipated that summons with something more than dread: with the anticipation of the first step of inclusion into the Ring. As legacies of the Ring, they'd been told about it by their father's, as their father's had been told about it by their own. It was tradition. It was a rite of passage.

The summons had come for Wing and Greer twenty minutes before Taps, via a note slid under each of their doors.

Dante's Den

15 minutes before Taps

Uniform: As for PT, under Raincoat, under arms
Bring this note

It was an order, and rats obeyed orders. Both scurried to get into the proper, bizarre, uniform and hustle down the stairs.

Preston, Chad and Jerrod were waiting, dressed in civilian clothes, passing a bottle back and forth. At least Chad and Jerrod were. They'd never seen Preston drink, even though he'd bought the expensive whiskey as they drove back to the Institute after a day on the town.

"Hit the wall!" Chad screamed as Greer Jenrette showed up first. "Present arms!"

"Give me the note," Jerrod demanded, taking it and stuffing the evidence in his pocket.

Greer obediently slammed back against the tile wall of the open-bay shower, chin tucked tight into his chest, his M-14 at present arms, his bayonet in its scabbard, dangling from a starched white belt over his shorts and underneath his raincoat. He wore the gray physical training T-shirt, his name stenciled about the Institute crest.

Chad and Jerrod giggled, passing the bottle once more, but Preston eyed Greer in a way that made the rat very nervous.

"How's your grandmother, Jenrette?" Preston asked.

"Fine, sir!" Greer shouted.

"No. I mean really. How is she? Ready to kick the bucket any time soon?" Preston asked.

"No, sir."

"You sure, old boy?" Preston's assumed accent was kicking in.

"Yes, sir."

"Too bad," Preston said. "You know she didn't invite Cadet Mongin's parents to the Saint Cecilia Ball last year?"

"No, sir."

Chad got in his face. "We not good enough for you?"

When Greer didn't respond right away, Chad was screaming, spittle hitting the plebe's face. "Answer, rat!"

"Yes, sir."

"'Yes, sir' what?" Chad said. "Yes, my family's not good enough?"

"Sir, I do not understand."

Preston laughed. "I'm sure he doesn't." And then Wing was there in Dante's Den, pinging down the hallway and entering the showers.

"Give me the note," Jerrod demanded.

"Against the wall!" Chad screamed. "Present arms."

In a flash Wing was next to Greer, rifle held upright in front of him.

"Are you cold, Wing?" Jerrod demanded.

"No, sir."

"I'm cold," Jerrod said.

"Are you dirty, Wing?" Chad asked.

"No, sir."

"I think you're dirty," Chad said. "I think you're a scummy piece of shit. A fucking mongrel."

A flash of anger passed across Wing's face, exactly what sadistic upperclassmen dug for when hazing. It meant they'd gotten to the rat, touched him emotionally. It was usually the beginning of the end for the rat who displayed it.

Preston leaned close so only Wing could hear. "You're worthless, Wing. You don't belong here. Why don't you go home to China? Or the ghetto? See, that's your problem. Who are you, Wing? Where do you belong? Do you even know?"

A muscle in Wing's jaw quivered in anger, but his lips were sealed.

"I can tell you where you don't belong," Preston said. "Here."

Meanwhile, Chad had gone along the wall, turning on the hot water, leaving a small space for the two rats. As the scalding water poured, steam began to fill the showers.

Jerrod went over to a bench in front of a row of lockers then sat down, bottle in hand. "Whoa, guys." He missed the look of disgust that passed over Preston's face at his expression of weakness.

"Chad, old boy," Preston said. "Welcome the rats to Dante's Den."

And Chad began to run the two rats through the manual of arms. Every time they made the slightest mistake, he harangued them. Even when they were correct, he screamed. It was a lose-lose situation.

Meanwhile, Preston sat down next to Jerrod. "You doing all right, old chap?"

"Bit lightheaded," Jerrod said. He held out the bottle. "I think I've had enough."

Preston took it, but didn't indulge. "You have to think ahead, Jerrod. Plan far, far ahead or you will go nowhere in life. My great-grandfather knew that. He didn't plan for himself. He planned for generations ahead."

Chad's screams echoed off the wall. The sound of water splashing from the showers was loud, magnified by the enclosed space. The steam was so thick one could barely see three feet. Chad and the two rats weren't even visible.

Jerrod didn't quite understand why Preston was regaling him with his family history and the future. He just wanted to get through this evening.

"My grandfather planned for me," Preston said. "My father has done well. Granted. But we can go higher. The Kennedy's were like that. They might have been bloody Yankees but they were bloody smart Yankees. Joe planned for his boys. He was Ambassador to England, but he wanted more for his family."

Jerrod opened his mouth to point out that in the end things had not turned out very well for the Kennedy's, but he knew Preston well enough not to interrupt.

"My family has a plan and I am the culmination." Preston stared at Jerrod through the mist. His eyes were gleaming. He held up the bottle. "That's why I can't drink. It makes a man weak."

"I feel weak," Jerrod joked, but Preston barely heard him.

They were both startled as Wing and Jenrette came hustling by. Their rubber raincoats were stuck to their bodies, their faces drenched in sweat. Their rifles were held out from their body, parallel to the floor. Chad was right behind them, screaming. Wing, blinded by steam and sweat, ran right into the wall and Jenrette bounced into him. The two fell in a tumble.

Chad stopped by Preston and Jerrod. He grabbed the bottle from Jerrod and took a deep swig. "You two going to help? I'm as worn out as they are."

"You're doing a great job, Chad, old boy," Preston said. He tapped Jerrod on the shoulder. "Up to it?"

It was as much a challenge as a question.

Jerrod struggled to his feet, sweat pouring down his face, his golfing shirt soaked through. "Sure."

Chad immediately plopped down on the bench, bottle in hands. He took another deep drink. They could hear Jerrod yelling at the two rats, his voice breaking occasionally. But they were out of sight, somewhere on the other side of the shower room.

"Turn the showers off," Preston said to Chad.

The football player checked his watch. "After Taps now. We probably should shut down."

"We're just beginning," Preston said. "Now for the real test."

Chad peered at him quizzically but when nothing more was forthcoming, he got up off the bench with a grunt and went around the walls, turning off the hot water. As the water stopped pouring, Jerrod's attempts at hazing became clearer. He was continuing the close order drill, but fumbling the commands, which caused the two rats to fumble their responses, which made Jerrod even more frustrated.

Preston ignored everyone. He took a key out of his pocket and slid it in a padlock on one of the lockers. He opened it and pulled out two sets of Army-issue body armor vests, along with Kevlar helmets that had clear visors attached to the front.

"Gentlemen!" he yelled, stopping Jerrod in mid-haze. Both rats slammed back against the tile, chins tucked in tight, weapons back at present arms.

Preston indicated the vests and helmets. "Gear up, rats."

Wing's mouth opened to ask a question. But Jenrette moved quickly forward, grabbing body armor and helmet. He put his rifle down as he slipped the vest over his head.

"Help him," Preston ordered Jerrod.

Wing finally reacted and moved forward to grab the other set.

Jerrod was fastening the Velcro straps, making sure the body armor was tight around Jenrette. Chad moved to help Wing gear up without being told. He jerked on the straps extra hard, causing Wing to exhale in pain.

Everyone was sopping wet from both steam and sweat. When the two rats put the helmets on and fastened the chinstraps, the clear visors misted up.

Preston didn't care.

"Attention!" he yelled.

The two snapped to.

"Order arms!" The butts of the M-14s thudded onto the tile floor as they brought them down to their right side.

"Fix bayonets!" Preston ordered.

Again, Wing hesitated, while Jenrette went right to it. Preston knew that Jenrette's father had probably told him of this tradition, thus he wasn't surprised. It was all new to Wing. And hopefully, after this evening, Wing would be old news to the Corps.

Jenrette's bayonet clicked into place and he resumed order arms.

Wing fumbled with his bayonet, almost dropping it after removing it from the scabbard. He missed putting the hole in the hilt over the barrel the first time, earning a scream of derision and curses from Chad. Wing finally managed to get it right, clicking the blade in place.

The chrome-covered knives weren't very dangerous; the chrome muted the edge into something thicker than a butter knife. Still, they did come to a point. Legend in the Corps was that someone had passed out during a parade while in formation and spitted himself on the bayonet of the man behind him.

But it was just a legend and no one knew if it had really happened.

Both Wing and Jenrette didn't seem that far away from passing out from their ordeal.

"Gentlemen," Preston said. "There is a tradition in the Corps. It is called the Quick and the Dead. Because, as you were taught, there are only two types of bayonet fighters: those who are quick, and those who are dead. Which are you?"

"The Quick, sir!" they screamed, their voices muted by the faceguards.

Preston smiled. At least they remembered the correct response from their abbreviated bayonet training of the past weeks.

"Face each other, gentlemen, weapons at the ready."

Wing and Jenrette squared off, rifles held tensely in front of them, angled up and across their bodies. The mist was slowly dissipating, but visibility was still only about ten feet and the temperature had to be just breaking three digits. Add in the water on the visors, and the two rats were almost blind.

Which was part of the ordeal.

"On guard!" Preston yelled. "A touch of the tip counts as two points. A touch of the down blade as one. No other points are counted, old boys. Attack!"

Chad let out a loud rebel yell as Jenrette thrust. His bayonet tip hit Wing in the stomach, not much power behind it, and the body armor stopped it.

"Two for Jenrette," Preston said.

"Get your head out of your ass, Wing!" Chad screamed.

Jerrod had slumped back down on the bench, alcohol and heat taking the better of him.

The two rats took stock of each other. Wing weakly thrust and Jenrette easily parried it.

"Don't fuck around and play patty-cake with each other you little shits!" Chad screamed. He got up next to Wing, screaming at him. "Attack! Attack, you little shit or I'll beat the crap out of you myself. You fucking mongrel dog. Which one was the nigger? Your mother or your father? Not that is matters. Nigger or chink, both are scum."

Wing surprised everyone by swinging the butt of his rifle in an arc, part of bayonet training, but one they hadn't expected here as everyone tended to get focus on using the blade, even though they'd been taught the entire rifle was a weapon at close quarters. The butt hit Jenrette's helmet on the side with a solid thud, sending the larger rat staggering.

"Fucking A!" Chad screamed.

"Get up," Preston hissed at Jerrod. "This is Jenrette's forging. He'll remember this the rest of his life."

Jerrod forced himself to his feet as Jenrette shook his head, trying to clear it from the blow.

"Follow up, Wing!" Chad screamed. "Didn't they teach you to finish your opponent off?"

Wing's head turned toward Chad, perhaps trying to understand what he'd yelled, and Jenrette took advantage, poking Wing in the belly once more with the tip of his blade.

"Two for Jenrette!" Preston announced. "You're losing bad, Wing. You lose and we will bring you back down here to fight someone new every night until you can win."

"Blood!" Chad screamed. "Blood makes grass grow. Blood, blood!"

"It's tile," Jerrod muttered, unheard by anyone as Chad continued the chant.

Wing thrust widely, aiming for Jenrette's head. It was a mistake as Jenrette parried as he'd been trained, and followed through with a slash, hitting Wing on the shoulder with the edge of his blade. Wing howled in pain, even though no skin was broken.

"I'm sorry!" Jenrette cried out, lowering his rifle. "I'm sorry, Wing!"

The sorries didn't get through, but the pain did. Wing went crazy, thrusting, then slashing in a flurry of moves. Jenrette backed up, forgetting to bring his rifle up, until he hit the tile wall. Chad was on him.

"Defend yourself, maggot," Chad yelled. "There's no goddamn sorries!"

"What are you doing?" a new voice yelled, and there was Harry Brannigan in his shorts and athletic shirt.

Chad grabbed Jenrette, who dropped his rifle, by the raincoat and tossed him toward Brannigan, who backed up, hands raised defensively as Jenrette tumbled into him and they both fell to the floor.

Preston picked up the rifle and removed the bayonet.

"Brannigan!" Preston yelled.

Brannigan got to his knees, Jenrette on his back in front of him.

Preston tossed the knife to him and Brannigan caught it instinctively by the handle. And then Preston jumped on top of the rat, using both hands to grab Brannigan's hand holding the bayonet and aim it as they fell down on top of Jenrette with their combined weight.

The chrome tip hit Jenrette's exposed neck, puncturing flesh, then into the artery. Blood pulsed out onto Brannigan as Preston rolled free.

"Holy shit!" Jerrod screamed.

Brannigan was frozen for a moment, staring down at his classmate. He dropped the bayonet and pressed both hands against the wound, trying to stem the spray of blood.

"What the hell did you do, Brannigan?" Preston asked, standing over the two.

Brannigan looked up, confused. "You did it. You made me."

"He's dying," Preston said. "You killed him."

Brannigan was shaking his head. "No. No. I didn't do it."

"Your hand on the knife," Preston said. "Your fingerprints. You did it." He turned to Jerrod. "Get the duty officer! Now. And an ambulance."

Jerrod raced out of the shower room for a phone.

Chad was frozen, staring down at Jenrette lying in a widening pool of blood. Wing was cowering in a corner. Brannigan still had his hands on the neck, but the flow slowed, then stopped. A dullness appeared in Jenrette's eyes.

"You killed him," Preston said. "They still have the death penalty here, Brannigan."

Harry Brannigan stared up at Preston Gregory for a few seconds and then he acted. He jumped to his feet and ran out of the shower room, covered in his classmate's blood.

Chapter Eleven

Thursday Late Afternoon

When Chad stopped, there was a short silence, then Chase spoke. "You didn't tell the duty officer the truth?"

Chad looked up. "Preston told us what to say. That Brannigan came in acting crazy. Grabbed Wing's weapon. Took the bayonet off and threatened all of us. Killed Jenrette."

"And they believed that bullshit?" Chase asked.

"It's Preston Gregory," Chad explained.

"And it was you and Jerrod Fabrou backing him up," Riley said.

"You're going to tell the truth to the authorities," Chase said.

Chad laughed bitterly. "*What* authorities? Preston's family are the authorities. His dad's a fucking Senator. And Fabrou's dad runs Savannah."

"Why did Preston want to kill Jenrette?" Riley asked.

Chad shook his head. "I don't know. He's always talking about his future. How he's going to be the biggest thing ever. He never really liked Greer. All his money. I think he saw him as a rival."

"Preston took the opportunity that was presented," Westland said. "There's a certain type of person who does that."

"Like Sarah Briggs," Riley said, looking at Chase. "She came up with a non-existent son in a flash, when it was to her advantage."

Dillon spoke up. "What about Jerrod? He was alive when I left him."

Chad grimaced. "He choked to death right in front of us. Preston said he could pin it on you right away. That your fingerprints would be on the nylon and on Jerrod's ring."

"But you know the truth," Dillon said. "You saw the truth."

Chad glumly nodded.

Riley stepped forward. "We know what happened in the past. But right now that's not the key thing. We've got to stop Preston and Sarah from whatever it is they have in the works. We've got to get Doc and Harry back from them."

Chad Senior had put his arm around his son's shoulder as he began to sob, but Riley, Chase, Dillon and Westland ignored that. What was done was done.

Riley looked over at Westland. "And you need to tell us what the hell is going on with you. Why are you here? Why do you have support? What is Cardena's deal in all this?"

Westland nodded toward the Mongin's. "They don't need to hear this."

"Hey!" Chase said, getting their attention. "Go home. And Chad, don't get amnesia. You're going to be telling your story again. The real story."

"What about him?" Riley asked, indicating Dillon.

"You still working for Mrs. Jenrette?" Chase asked. "Looking to kill my son?"

"I'm looking for justice," Dillon said. "Seems to me that's pointed in a different direction now. I think we all have the same problem: Preston Gregory."

"Mrs. Jenrette is coming here tomorrow, isn't she?" Westland asked.

Dillon nodded. "They're closing the Sea Drift deal. Preston will be back, too. And this Sarah woman too, most likely."

"He's going to use us," Riley said, indicating Chase. "He's going to use Doc and Harry as leverage to put us on his and Sarah's side." He looked at Dillon. "But they don't have any leverage on you, do they?"

Dillon considered that. "He's trying to pin Jerrod's death on me. Seems that's Preston's M.O. But we've got Chad's testimony; don't we, Chad?"

Chad reluctantly nodded.

"I don't like Preston," Dillon said. "Didn't like him from the first moment I met him. He tried to bribe me, tell me he could get me into the Ring."

"What's that?" Riley asked.

Dillon held up his hand, Institute ring shining. "It's part of what they were doing that night with Greer Jenrette. Putting him through a rite of passage so he could join this secret inner circle of cadets and graduates of the Institute. The Ring. You have to be born to the right people to be chosen, but Preston offered it to me when I told him I was investigating Jenrette's death. A bribe. I'm seeing this through."

Riley glanced at Chase, who nodded. Then Westland. She agreed also.

"I wouldn't go home," Westland said to Chad Senior and Junior. "Preston might send someone looking. I'd hide out for the next day. Until this is settled once and for all."

The two hurried away to the pier and then got into their boat.

"Now your story," Chase said to Westland.

Westland sighed. "You guys were Army. It's a different deal where I'm coming from. I was CIA when we met, Dave. But a couple of years later I was recruited into another organization. One whose name doesn't matter. But suffice it to say it's not on the books anywhere. We did a lot of dirty work. Wet work. And once you go that deep in the black world, there really isn't any retirement." She lightly tapped the side of her head. "I've got too much in here for them to let go of me. It's a life sentence. So when I wanted to pull the plug, I was given an offer that was essentially an ultimatum. Work for the Cellar when called upon."

"For Cardena," Riley said.

"For him, but really we all work for Hannah. She's hands-on control for every op." She paused, to see if they had any question, and Riley did.

"How does Sarah Briggs come into this?"

"Sarah Briggs," Westland said, as if tasting the name. "That's the alias she's used for this. She's had a lot of names over the years. It doesn't even matter what her real name is any more. She might not even remember it."

"But you know it," Riley didn't make it a question.

Westland nodded. "I said I had a stake in this. It's her. She worked for me a long time ago. Twelve years ago."

"CIA?" Chase asked.

Westland shook her head. "No. The unit that has no name. Sarah, let's stick with that name, was my protégé." She shrugged. "You've got an idea how sharp she is. I saw that potential early on."

"When did she go bad?" Riley asked.

"'When did she go bad'?" Westland repeated. "I remember it quite clearly."

"Okay," Riley said. "This is important, but let's get back to Brams Point first. Kono and Gator should be meeting us there. We need to see if Gator has come up with anything."

Chapter Twelve

"A sniper?" Sarah Briggs didn't seem surprised as Preston relayed what had happened on Daufuskie.

It was dark outside his suite at the Sea Pines Resort, but the lighthouse and the shops and restaurants around it were brightly lit, the glow reflecting in the large sliding doors through a partial screening by trees. One of the doors was partially open and the sound of drunken reverie was in the distance. They were on the second floor, the maximum height allowed to any building in Sea Pines, part of the island's strict building codes.

"Shot my bloody case," Preston groused. He was seated at the desk, papers piled high on top of it.

"But the Mongins made the deal." Sarah stood near the door, away from the window, a position that Preston had noticed.

Preston held up the leather case. "I have the easement."

"Who did the shooting?" Sarah asked. "Riley and Chase were in front of you, right? So it must have been that big Ranger they hang with. Lucky he didn't blow your brains out."

Preston shrugged. "Some woman was giving the orders to the sniper via her phone."

"A woman?" Sarah went very still. "Describe her."

"Older woman. Grey hair with a black streak in it. Tall."

Sarah closed her eyes briefly, then opened them. "I'd like payment now, please. Ten million for Bloody Point."

"What's the rush?" Preston asked.

"I'm done here. Time for me to move on."

Preston stared at her. "You're *not* done here. You're not done until I tell you that you are done. You will not be paid until I have decided I am done with you. I do want you to sign over Bloody Point to me now. So I can focus on Mrs. Jenrette tomorrow."

"If I sign over now," Sarah said, "then you pay me now. Transfer the money and I'll sign."

Preston pulled his phone out and typed a short message into it. Then he leaned back in the chair. "You found Harry Brannigan, didn't you?"

"Yes."

Preston smiled. "I've always enjoyed your directness even though you are quite the deceiver at times. Why didn't you tell me?"

"How did you find out?" Sarah asked.

"I had your phone reprogrammed. We've listened to every conversation. And intercepted the proof of life photo. And you've tried negotiating directly with Mrs. Jenrette, bypassing me."

The double doors to the suite swung open and the three men who'd accompanied him to Daufuskie came in. They didn't have their coats on but each sported a pistol in a holster on their belt. They fanned out behind Preston.

Sarah barely acknowledged their presence. "You can have Harry Brannigan right now too. Along with Bloody Point. Give me my money and you'll never see me again."

Preston laughed. "I've already got Harry and Doc Cleary. My men got them earlier today. Your men, unfortunately, are no longer with us."

"Fine," Sarah said. "You want Bloody Point from me, then pay me."

"Such loyalty to the help."

"Risks of the business."

"Yes," Preston said. "We all face that. But we had an agreement and you violated that by offering to make a deal directly with Mrs. Jenrette."

"Not really," Sarah said. "I believe the way your plan works, if I can guess the script correctly based on what you've done so far that *wasn't* in our agreement, is that you'll end up with all of Sea Drift anyway. In fact, it would have saved you ten million by having *her* pay me, rather than coming out of your share."

"So thoughtful," Preston said. "And Rigney?"

Sarah said nothing.

"I assume you used your feminine wiles on him," Preston said. "But that only goes so far, you know."

Sarah remained silent.

"So what aren't you telling me?" Preston asked. "Who is the woman? Do you know her?"

"Let's just say she's an old acquaintance."

"And she frightens you," Preston said. "So much so that you want to run immediately."

"She doesn't frighten me," Sarah said. "But the organization she works for does."

"'Organization'?" Preston repeated. "What organization?"

Sarah shook her head. "You don't know of it, so it's pointless to discuss it."

"If a new player has entered the game," Preston said, "then I need to be brought up to speed."

Sarah indicated the three guards. "If you didn't feel safe going up against her and her sniper with them today, why do you think it will be any different tomorrow?"

"Because I'll be prepared," Preston said. "Now tell me about this organization? Is it governmental? That can handled quite easily by my father."

Sarah laughed. "I'd like to see that happen. It's called the Cellar. Run by a woman named Hannah."

"Hannah who?"

"Just Hannah. I'd say it's likely your father has heard of her given he chairs the Select Committee on Intelligence."

Preston steepled his fingers, deep in thought. "My dear woman, why would the government be getting involved in our little adventure here? Certainly not because of me. That leaves two possibilities. Misters Chase and Riley still have contacts. But I doubt they would be able to draw in an official agency, no matter how clandestine. They simply don't seem that important."

"They did against Karralkov," Sarah said. "A Hellfire missile from a Predator drone took his boat out. That's pretty official."

"Perhaps," Preston said. "But it's rather amazing that you know this woman. Makes it sound rather personal. I lean toward this being about *you*. Why is the government interested in you?" He didn't wait for an answer. "Ah. That's how you learned things like the poison you gave me to kill Merchant Fabrou. You worked for the government once upon a time, didn't you? Were you a spy?"

"I'm not allowed to speak of it," Sarah said.

Preston was astounded. "You're playing that card? You do understand you are on the wrong side of the law, correct?"

"I was an assassin," Sarah said.

Preston smiled. "Ah! That makes sense. And I assume the gray-haired woman is of the same ilk?"

"Fine," Sarah said. "She's here for me. So give me my money and I'll be gone and she'll be gone."

Preston shook his head. "I don't think so. I don't think you understand who you're talking to. The power of my family. My father will bring this Hannah woman to heel and send your old acquaintance packing. Because even if you leave, we still have to deal with Riley and Chase. And even with Harry Brannigan as *my* ace in the hole, so to speak, I still think they have the potential to cause trouble. And, my dear woman, you also have skills we will possibly need tomorrow. I suggest you catch a good night's rest. Tomorrow promises to be most interesting."

Sarah didn't leave. "You don't understand—"

Preston slapped his palm on the desk, rattling the papers. "No. *You* do not understand even though I have been most patient. My father will deal with this Hannah and her minion. And that will be enough of that." Preston took a deep breath. "You've been in contact with Chase, correct? Leveraging him and Riley and their group?"

Sarah nodded.

"How do you contact them?" he asked.

Sarah pulled out her burner. "They've called twice. I've got the number on the burner they have on speed dial one."

"Give me that."

"If you want to run everything," Sarah said, "then you really have no need for me any more."

Preston nodded. "You're right." His hand came up with a gun in it.

Sarah threw the phone at Preston as she whirled, sensing the presence behind her. With her forearm she blocked the arm with the stiletto that was aimed toward the base of her skull. She followed through the block with her other fist, hitting the assailant in the side of the head, stunning him momentarily. She kept moving, dashing past him, through the open sliding door to the balcony. She vaulted over the railing, rotating her arms and elbows in front of her face as she'd been taught in jump school to prepare for a tree landing.

A tree jump wasn't much different as she hit one of the pines next to the building. She crashed into the branches, breaking the smaller ones, then hitting a thicker one that bounced her off it, into another one, slowing her, then she free fell, bending her legs and hitting the grass with her feet. She went with the impact from balls of her feet, shin, side of her buttocks and then the upper side of her back.

All well and good but the pain of broken ribs from one of the branches took her breath away during the last slam into the ground. She lay there, stunned.

The sound of a suppressed gun firing motivated her to get moving. One of the guards was on the balcony, peering into the darkness below, trying to spot her. Meanwhile he was firing blindly in her general direction.

Sarah rolled to her knees, gasping in pain, but moving, scurrying, getting away as fast as she could move. She sensed a bullet whiz close by and then she was on the path, running, putting the pain at a distance in her mind focusing only on survival.

She was very good at that. An expert.

* * *

The guard came back in, silenced pistol in hand. The man Sarah had hit was on his feet, shaking his head.

"She got away," the guy with the pistol reported.

A spasm of irritation crossed Preston's face. "Is it so hard to get effective help these days? Is it that hard to kill someone? I haven't had a problem with it."

The guards had no response to that.

Preston picked up the phone Sarah had thrown, looked at it, then stuck it in his pocket. Another piece to be played as needed.

Then he pulled out his own phone and made a call to his father in Washington.

* * *

It was late and Hannah's secretary had departed hours ago. That did not mean Hannah had stopped working. She liked the evenings and the long nights alone. It gave her time to peruse the data stream filtering down from the NSA above her head. She was tapped into everything, but could only absorb a fraction of it.

It was like trying to drink from a fire hydrant. But years of experience had taught her how to scan; and which of the analysts were the most perceptive. On top of that, was the Ultra Loop. The most highly classified intelligence loop in the world. Ever since Turing had made the first computer to break the German Enigma way back in World War II, true power had devolved into those who could read, and listen, to the messages of others.

If it was electronic, it could be intercepted and deciphered.

The number of people with access to the Ultra Loop, which still bore the same designation from the early days of World War II, was less than a dozen on both sides of the Atlantic. What was critical, and had been from the very start, wasn't the information. It was making the decision about which information to act on. The danger of knowing everyone's information was that one couldn't let others know you knew; too many actions would tip them off and they'd either go dark and silent or switch their encryption. The latter was a pain because it meant the source 'went dark' during the time it took to break their new system.

Bad things happened in the dark.

Thus it required very judicious use of the pearls that were uncovered.

Nero had liked to tell Hannah, as he trained her, that the decision was based on being a very specific judge of the quality and the long-range importance of each potential decision. They were all pearls, but only the rare, 'black pearls', should be acted on. Often, it was as important what *wasn't* acted on as what was. The events that were allowed to happen in order to keep up the mirage that networks and messages of foreign governments, corporations, organizations, etc. were secure.

Sometimes those events were horrible, but it was all for the greater good. A philosopher might argue the finer points of that, but Hannah and the handful like her in the world, lived in reality. And that 'justice' had a way of eventually catching up to evil and making it pay.

It also required a massive cover-up. Disinformation is as important as information. Documentaries are still being made and aired discussing the 'code-breakers' at Bletchley as if they'd really done an original thing, and not been handed a message that had already been decoded by Turing's machine, the very first computer, and then recoded in an easier manner, one which *could* be broken by the human minds there.

Games within games.

Sometimes the blatant logic that people ignored surprised Hannah, who was very difficult to surprise. But it was simple: If the Turing machine had broken Enigma, then it broke *every* message, not just a magical handful. The magical handful were the ones the powers-that-be, Hannah's predecessors wanted to be known.

The chilling fact that Nero had known, and Hannah now did, was that once Turing and the British broke the German Enigma and then the Americans broke the Japanese Purple, was that those at the very, very highest level, had known every single major operation planned by the other side.

Coventry was the rule, rather than the exception.

The secret had to be kept and wielded only on the very rarest of occasions.

Still, there were exceptions. Which was why Hannah looked beyond the Ultra Loop and checked the analysts' reports. In this new world of the War on Terrorism, many enemies were not states but small groups; much more difficult to keep track of. And, of course, Hannah's primary tasking was to watch over the United States own group of covert organizations, the number of which seemed to constantly be growing.

She had a lot going on besides Cardena's problem in South Carolina. The covert world contained many strange and diverse units; all of which required some sort of policing. She had to put those out of her mind for the moment.

She accessed the keyboard on a shelf underneath her desktop. The computer screens were set in the desk, visible only to her via reflecting off of mirrors through the clear surface. To those on the other side it looked like nothing was on her desk. She constantly had data streaming on those screens. Nero had his folders, but she'd accepted she had to go digital. The key was that it was all one way. Data came into her office, but never out. And she stored no information, instead tapping into the NSA's mainframe with unlimited access.

She also didn't like to do email.

A buzzing noise interrupted her reading. She pulled open a drawer and stared at the phone inside with distaste. She hated talking on the phone as much as she disliked email, but there were some calls she had to take. If a person had this number, then it was such.

Hannah picked up the receiver. "Hannah."

"Ms. Hannah." The voice drooled southern charm so fake it grated on Hannah's nerves like fingernails on a chalkboard.

"Senator. What a surprise to hear from you. Especially at this late hour."

"We who serve our country," Senator Gregory said, "are always on duty."

There was a pause, into which Hannah suspected she was supposed to say something as pithy.

She didn't.

"Now, Ms. Hannah," Gregory began, "I understand you have an operative working down in my neck of the woods."

"Which neck is that?" Hannah asked, having a fleeting vision of strangling the Senator's scrawny neck.

"Down around Hilton Head," Gregory said. "You have a woman yonder who is causing a bit of a ruckus. Seems she took a shot at my son. Makes it kind of personal, don't ya think?"

"I doubt she shot at your son," Hannah said.

"And why is that?"

"Because he'd be dead if she did and he is not, am I correct?"

"You are correct," Gregory admitted. "But still. The propriety of it all. Really. There is nothing in that area that need concern you."

Another pause, which Hannah once more refused to fill. She marveled at the simplicity of unraveling a lie: by calling her so late and telling her there was nothing, he was telling her there was indeed something.

Gregory's voice lost a little bit of its charm. "Do you understand?"

"I understand," Hannah said.

"Very good."

The phone went dead.

* * *

They could see the *Fina* tied up to Chase's floating (sort of) dock. It was dark and the lights along the 240-foot walkway were on, a single bulb every twenty feet or so giving out a feeble glow. Once more the difference between Chase's abode and the houses on either side was apparent as the neighbors were brightly lit.

"Trying to scare off robbers?" Westland asked as they pulled up, noting the illumination.

"Trying to show everyone how much house they have," Chase answered.

"Oh," Westland. "That makes sense. Not."

Riley drove his Zodiac to the inside of the dock, where he tied it off. He led the way up the gangplank to the walkway, with Chase, Westland and Dillon following.

They entered the back sliding doors, into the tree-filled living room, where Gator and Kono were waiting.

"What do you have?" Riley asked Gator without preamble.

Gator held up an iPad. "Got my friend to do the best he could with it. He said the pixies wasn't the greatest."

"Pixels," Westland said.

"And?" Chase pressed.

Gator indicated that it was Kono's turn to contribute.

The Gullah took the iPad. He tapped the screen, expanding the view of the window. "Here."

The others gathered round, but could see nothing special.

"These lines," Kono said and then they could see three thread-like lines crossing the blue sky above the green trees and dark water outside the window. "Power lines far back. If this is the Intracoastal, only a few places where lines like that. One is Hilton Head. Tybee Island another. Some also run north-south along coast. Maybe down by Savannah or the Golden Islands in Georgia. I'd have to run the coast to try and figure it out. Match lines to place."

Chase looked out the window. "Can you do that in the dark?"

Kono nodded. "Night vision. We can run the coast."

"What time is this meeting on Daufuskie?" Gator asked.

"Ten in the morning," Westland said.

"Cutting it tight," Riley said. "We not only have to find where Doc and Harry are being held, then we have to launch an op to rescue them before that meeting."

"Someone still has a story to tell," Chase said, indicating Westland. "Who is Sarah Briggs? What are we facing? We need to get a better understanding before running around in the dark searching for the proverbial needle in the haystack."

"We thought she was dead," Westland said. "She went on an op twelve years ago. HAHO infiltration into Russia."

"What was the mission?" Riley asked.

Westland shook her head. "Still can't talk about that. She was an assassin, all right? So it was wet work as they used to say in the old days. Her jump was clean, there was an open chute. And then nothing. No infil report. No initial entry report. And nothing from the Russians either."

"Did she cut and run?" Riley asked.

A new voice entered the discussion. "She did not."

Everyone turned and reacted with varying speed. Riley was the fastest, weapon at the ready, Chase not far behind. Gator and Kono also drew their pistols.

But Westland didn't.

Sarah Briggs stood in the front doorway of Chase's house, blood running down from a cut in her forehead, cradling one arm, and looking like hell.

"Hello Kate," Sarah Briggs said. "It's been a long time."

She turned to face the others. "I was betrayed. Khan'd," Sarah said. She took a step in. "Do you know what that is? Any of you? I'm not referring to damn *Star Trek*. I'm referring to Inayat Khan, the first woman to jump into Occupied France with a Jedburgh team during World War Two."

Riley lowered his gun. The others shifted their gazes from her to him and Westland.

"What the fuck?" Gator asked, not lowering his weapon. "Thought we were going to kill her?"

Riley sighed and sat down on the trunk of the tree. "Let's hear her story. I know what she's referring to."

"I didn't know," Westland said to Sarah. "I swear. I didn't know."

Sarah came further in. "Doesn't matter whether you knew or not. You wouldn't have had any choice. There was nothing you could do about it. Actually, the whole point is *none* of us know the truth when we work in the black world." She looked around the living room. "We're all played all the time. Don't you get it? By those who *do* know. By those we're supposed to trust. But they aren't trustworthy. I'm not going to be played any more. No more."

"Someone want to clue me in?" Chase asked. He looked at Riley and Westland. "What is she talking about?"

"She was betrayed," Riley said. "I'm willing to bet that when she landed after her HAHO jump the Russians were waiting on her drop zone. Took her prisoner. Tortured her. Extracted what information they could. And believed it, since they got it under torture, except it didn't occur to them that she'd been briefed on false intelligence and gave that up. That's what happened to Inayat Khan. She was pumped full of false intelligence during her mission preparation, then sent into a Resistance network that her handlers knew had been compromised. She was betrayed. Picked up by the Gestapo. Tortured. Naturally, the Germans believed the intel she gave up. It never occurred to them that the 'gentlemen' English would knowingly give her up."

"What happened to this Khan woman?" Gator asked.

Sarah answered. "After they got everything they could from her, they sent her to Dachau where she was shot in the back of the head and thrown into the crematorium."

"How do you all know all this?" Gator asked Riley, the concept of books being rather foreign to him.

"When I arrived at my first Special Forces assignment," Riley said, "the battalion commander gave me a book to read, titled *Bodyguard of Lies*. It's about the covert war during World War Two. Her story was in it. Stuck with me because it always made me think twice every time I got a mission briefing. Wondering whether the mission was actually the mission or a cover for something else."

"You can go crazy thinking like that," Westland said.

"No shit," Sarah said.

"You can end up dead not thinking like that," Riley countered.

"I don't care," Gator said. "We said we'd kill her if we saw her again. Let's do it."

Sarah looked at Chase. "Preston is moving your son. And Doc Cleary. He's got them now."

"So the two of you have turned on each other," Riley summed up the situation.

"So much for searching tonight," Kono said.

"Why are you here?" Chase asked.

"The enemy of my enemy is my friend," Sarah said. "Preston is crazy. I was in this just for the money. He's in it for something else. Power."

Dillon spoke up. "He's killed three people that we know of. Jerrod and Merchant Fabrou. And Greer Jenrette."

Sarah nodded. "And I suspect he's going to use your son, Chase, to get you to kill Mrs. Jenrette. That way he'll own all of Daufuskie."

"Why do I think you were going to do the same when you were in cahoots with him?" Chase asked.

"And what did you do to Farrelli?" Riley demanded of Sarah.

"I killed him," she admitted. "Just like you had Karralkov killed. He was a crook and a murderer. And what I was going to do doesn't matter any more. The field has changed. I'm here to help." She looked at Westland. "Unless of course you're to Sanction me upon sight."

"The final decision on a Sanction is always in the hands of the field agent," Westland said.

"And what have you decided?" Sarah asked.

"I can wait until we see what happens tomorrow," Westland said. She looked over at the men. "It can't hurt to have another gun on our side."

"Are you really on our side?" Riley asked Sarah. "I see no reason to trust you."

"There are ten million reasons for you to trust me," Sarah said. She reached inside her coat, Gator snapping up his pistol in reaction, and pulled out a thin leather satchel. "I still own Bloody Point. There's no way Preston Gregory is going to pay me for it, but Mrs. Jenrette will."

"And why do I think," Chase said, "that you offered up my son to Mrs. Jenrette to fatten the deal?"

Sarah smiled. "You're getting better at this, Horace."

"We're never going to trust you," Chase said.

"There's a lot you don't know," Sarah said.

"Tell us what happened in Russia," Westland said. "And tell us the truth."

"What happened in Russia?" Sarah repeated. "I'd prefer not to go back there, even in words."

"I'd prefer to shoot you," Riley said. "I'm not sure we should believe your story. Either what happened twelve years ago or what happened today. You don't have a very good track record with the truth."

Sarah's gazed blankly out the back windows at the dark night outside, the glow from the lights on the houses on either side impinging on the view of the Intracoastal.

"You have coverage out there, don't you?" she said to Westland, surprising the others.

Westland nodded. "Yes."

"So if you give the signal, I'm dead."

"Yes."

"All right," Sarah said. "Since Preston has already moved your son," she added, looking at Chase, "we have nothing else to do this fine night. I will tell you what happened. You decide whether to believe me or not."

Twelve Years Ago

She exited the Combat Talon at 30,000 feet altitude and offset from the border eighteen miles. Arms and legs akimbo, she became stable in the night air as her mind counted down as she'd been drilled.

She pulled the ripcord and the parachute deployed at an altitude greater than that of Mount Everest. She was on oxygen, had been on it for forty-five minutes prior to exiting the aircraft. The ground, and objective, were over five miles below vertically and over three times that horizontally, leaving no time at the moment for her to enjoy the view.

She had a long way to fly.

She checked her board, noting the glow of the GPS and then double-checking against the compass. She began tracking to the north and east. Then she looked about. She was high enough to see the curvature of the Earth. To the west, there was a dim glow from the sun, racing away from her, leaving her a long night of fell deeds ahead. Far below there were clusters of lights: towns, not many, spread about the countryside. She remembered the nighttime satellite imagery and aligned the light clusters into a pattern to confirm both the GPS and the compass. While she was reasonably certain the aircraft had dropped her in the correct place, mistakes had been known to happen and it was on her, not the crew racing back to the safety of the airfield. She also had to factor in the wind, which would shift directions as she descended through various altitudes.

Her hands were on the toggles attached to the risers of the wing parachute, specially designed for this type of operation. Despite the thick gloves, the minus-forty temperature at altitude was biting into her fingers.

It would get warmer as she got lower.

Hopefully, not too warm.

She'd trained for two weeks in order to be able to do just this jump. The normal time to fully train a Military Free Fall candidate was four weeks: one in the vertical wind tunnel at Fort Bragg, then three out at Yuma Training Ground, in the clear Arizona weather. Like all her training, hers was quicker, harder and compressed. She'd been assigned individual instructors, hard-core Special Ops veterans who knew better than to ask what the female 'civilian' was doing in their school. She didn't even have a name, just a number.

They followed orders, just as she was following orders.

She shook her head. Too much time to think as she descended. The time was necessary as she was crossing from a neutral airspace into not-so-friendly airspace. She'd already passed the border, the 'point of no return'.

It did not occur to her it was only the point of no return as long as she didn't turn the chute around and fly in the opposite direction. If it had occurred to her, she wouldn't be here in the first place, as such people were not recruited into her unit.

Which also had no name. It didn't even have a number. It just was what it was. Those in it, knew they were in it. Those outside of it, didn't know it existed. A simple concept but profound in its implementation and implications.

Her chute did have a slight radar signature, but not a significant enough one to bring an alert, definitely less than that of a plane or a helicopter; more along the lines of a large bird. And she was silent as she flew through the air, a factor that would come into play as she got close to the ground.

She checked her altimeter, checked the GPS, checked the compass for heading, confirmed location by lining up the towns against the imagery she'd memorized.

Halfway there; both vertically and horizontally.

She was making good distance, almost too good. But better to overshoot and track back than fall short. She dumped a little air, to descend faster.

Of course she had to be on time. She had the small window every covert meeting had: two minutes before, two minutes after. Outside of that window her contact had strict orders not to meet. To evade. And the mission would be a scrub. A failure.

It would be a long walk back.

As she passed below five thousand feet, she flipped down her night vision goggles from their position on her helmet. The world below lit up in various shades of green. She could see the outline of the lake she was using as a final reference point, the flat surface reflecting the quarter moon, confirming her location. She focused on the drop zone, a small, square field, barely big enough to allow her to land her chute in it.

A light was flickering in the middle of the field, an infrared strobe light. Invisible to the naked eye, it was a clear beacon in the goggles. It went out for a few seconds, then back on, repeating a pattern.

A pattern that meant it was safe for her to land. At this altitude, if the no-go signal, non-stop flickering, had been present (or no signal at all), she still had time to peel off and land at least a couple of miles away and go into her escape and evasion (E&E) plan.

She dumped more air, quickening her descent, aiming for the light, estimating that she would land about a minute early. At two hundred feet she dropped the rucksack full of gear on its lowering line so that it dangled below her.

As she reached the treetop level, she flared, slowing her descent. The ruck hit terra firma, and then she touched down lightly, right next to the light, the chute billowing down to the ground behind her. She quickly unbuckled her harness, looking about through the goggles. A person appeared, moving out of the tree line toward her.

She was pulling her submachine gun free of the waist strap when the person raised a hand, not in greeting, but with something in it. Her gloved fingers fumbled to bring the sub up.

The taser hit her on the arm, sending a massive jolt through her system and immobilizing her. She collapsed, unable to control her body. As she curled up on the ground, she could see others coming out of the tree line, armed men, weapons at the ready.

Her muscles wouldn't respond. Not even her tongue.

Someone knelt next to her and reached toward her face. Fingers dug into her mouth and probed. The 'suicide' was ripped out of its hide spot in the upper right side of her gum.

How had they known about that?

Compromised. She'd been comprised right from the start.

The person who'd removed her suicide option spoke. "We've been expecting you. We have quite the welcome waiting for you."

Her muscles wouldn't work as her gear was ripped off her body. And then her clothes, until she was lying naked in the small field. Her hands were chained behind her back, the cuffs cinched down, but not too hard, a small fact she processed but found odd.

Her legs were also shackled, but the restraints were padded on the inside, another strange thing.

Like a sack of meat she was lifted by four men and carried. It was cold, the air biting into her naked flesh, but she barely noticed it, her muscles still trying to recover from the massive electrical shock; along with her brain from the betrayal. There was a van underneath the trees and she was tossed in, onto a carpeted floor. Someone grabbed a chain off one wall and locked it to the shackle chain between her legs.

The chains were thick.

She lay on the floor, staring up the ceiling as the engine started and they began driving. There were two men in the back with her. Despite her nakedness, they seemed barely interested in her; they had their weapons at the ready across their knees as they sat on seats on either side and their demeanor told her they were professionals, men who knew how to use their weapons. They had small, bulletproof windows next to their seats and gun ports, and they alternated between glancing at her and watching the world outside.

They drove for a long time, hours. Movement returned to her muscles and she covertly tested the restraints, she had to, one never knew, but these were professionals. She was cold but knew better than to ask for a blanket or her clothing. If they wanted her covered, she'd be covered. Everything they were doing was according to a script, one she knew most likely ended badly.

For her.

The van came to a halt and she heard muted voices. The back doors were thrown open and a light shone in. It swept over her, the two guards, and then the doors slammed shut once more. The van moved again,, stopping after only a minute.

Once more the doors opened and two men stepped in, while the guards overwatched. They unlocked her from the chain around her leg shackles. They dragged her out and put her on a gurney. They strapped her down securely with broad nylon straps, then removed the wrist and ankle restraints. Looking about, she could see that she was in an open space, a concrete ceiling about twenty feet above.

There was a vibe in the air. An odor that was visceral and ancient.

Fear.

She was wheeled down a corridor. Shifting her head left and right she saw they were passing doors. Cell doors. Solid steel. No openings in them, but with a small screen next to each with buttons and knobs below.

Observation. But all the screens were blank at the moment.

She could hear music thumping away behind those thick doors. Heavy metal music. Her mind flashed back to SERE training: Survival, Evasion, Resistance and Escape. They'd also stripped her naked right at the start. It's amazing what the lack of clothes could do to a person. Many broke right then. It was especially troubling to the military, who valued their uniforms, in fact placed great pride and a sense of self in their uniforms and their badges and tabs. Some of them, tough soldiers, had broken right then, stripped of their accouterments.

It didn't bother Sarah that much.

And the music. In the mock prisoner-of-war camp where she'd ended up, they'd played music most of the time, keeping everyone on edge, making it difficult to sleep. She had an idea what was awaited her in whichever cell they tossed her in.

A door swung ponderously open and she was wheeled in. Bright lights lined the ceiling, glaring down at her as she was placed near the center of the room. Another person came in, some nondescript woman with shears and an electric razor. She shaved Sarah completely. Her head and her entire body. The woman was not tender and Sarah's skin was left raw and bleeding in several spots. Then the woman and the two men who'd pushed her gurney left.

And the door swung shut.

She was still bound to the gurney. She looked about, her head nestled in the sheared debris of her hair. The walls were covered with this bright red padding covered them, even the back of the heavy door.

No smashing one's head against a wall to end it.

There were tiny black spots up in each corner: cameras.

She waited.

Someone else might have called out. She didn't. In fact, the longer it went without anything happening, the better. The rule was to hold out for forty-eight hours. She knew that her handler, Westland, back in the States had been informed she'd left the plane and had already noticed she had not sent her infiltration confirmation report. And Westland would soon note that there was no initial entry report as required by SOP.

Those two events would initiate a protocol: whatever information Sarah had that could compromise other operations and personnel would be reviewed and action taken to minimize possible damage.

So every minute that ticked by, while it might serve to un-nerve someone else, was almost soothing to Sarah.

Eventually she had to urinate. So she did.

She noticed it was getting chillier in the room. Temperature modification. Something she expected. Nothing she could do about it. Goose bumps rose on her skin. She began to shiver, vibrating against the restraints.

She had no idea how much time had passed.

She eventually lost consciousness.

She woke to her body covered in sweat, the temperature in the room at least in the high nineties. She was badly dehydrated. She could smell her urine and the gurney below her was soaked.

She heard the door open but didn't turn her head, the only act of defiance left. A woman came into view, hovering over her. A rather striking woman, with short blond hair, well colored, and high cheekbones. She had grey eyes; correction one grey eye. The other was bright red, artificial. No pupil. Just red. She might have been a model (other than the eye), but the lines on her face indicated she was in her thirties at least, past prime for most models and she'd never known the prick of the Botox needle. The heat didn't seem to affect her in the slightest; she looked like she could walk through a sauna and not produce a drop of sweat. Cold, very cold.

Sarah doubted she was a model.

"What do you know of the color red?" the woman asked in perfect English with an American accent.

There was someone else in the room, on the other side. Sarah shifted her eyes. A man dressed in white. He had an IV stand and a cart. He found a vein in her arm, expertly inserted a needle, checked the drip and then left.

"You must be thirsty," the woman said. "We want to keep you hydrated. In fact, you're not really going to be harmed. Physically. Much. No marks at least. Nothing permanent. That's crass and vulgar." She pointed at her red eye. "This was crass and vulgar and totally unnecessary so I know of what I speak. But I adapted. Some think it an ostentatious display, my red eye. But it's a machine. A very expensive one. I can't see through it; a pity. So I have no depth perception. Ended my ability to do my previous line of work, although it is amazing how we can adapt to almost anything. But the eye is quite useful in my new occupation. It registers your temperature and some other things." She shifted gears. "Back to the room. Do you like the red?"

Sarah stared straight up.

The woman waved her hand, indicating the surroundings. "Red is a warm color. It, and its neighbors orange and yellow, have the longest wavelengths. Thus it actually takes more energy to look at those colors than the soothing ones, like blue or green. Red stimulates the brain, raises your pulse and your respiration rate." She gestured toward her red eye. "I can tell both of yours are up. People think a toreador wears a red cape to enrage the bull, but the bull is colorblind. It only responds to the movement of the cape. He wears it for the crowd. The color indicates danger, excitement, hostility and also success. Like the toreador, everything here is designed for you and those like you. Keep that in mind.

"Have you ever noticed how many fast-food restaurants are painted red? It also stimulates the salivary glands and makes us hungry. You're hungry, aren't you? And it hurts the eyes. Casinos use red in high-stakes areas because it tends to make people place larger bets and take greater risks. And it induces us to make faster decisions, which is why 'buy now' buttons tend to be red."

Sarah knew the monologue was the first attempt at making a connection. The woman was letting her know that she was an expert. Also, she wasn't threatening. Not directly. It was all implied. Sarah also knew she had to play her own side of this.

Sarah tried to speak, found it hard with such a dry mouth, but finally managed to get the words out. "So you're my toreador?"

The woman laughed, no warmth in it. "That would make you a bull. Do you feel like a bull right now? Pinned down? Helpless? No. If I were your toreador, this would be a contest. I can assure you, this won't be a contest. The sooner you accept that, the better.

"FSB? SVR?" Sarah asked, using the acronyms of different successors to the KGB.

"That would make you CIA. Which you might have been once upon a time, but no longer. As your unit has no name, mine doesn't either. And this place," she indicated the red walls. "Doesn't exist. A black site, similar to the ones your country has. Not listed on any maps. Not acknowledged. Think of what happens in your black sites. And then accept we are no different."

The woman looked at Sarah, raking her gaze along Sarah's naked body. "I will soon know you better than anyone ever has. Think of that? I will be more intimate with you than any lover you've known."

* * *

During training, Sarah had been taught by a Buddhist monk to meditate, an arcane skill for an assassin and one she hadn't seen the need for at the time.

It was very useful now. The lights never went out and the moment her 'toreador' had left, music began blaring. A form of heavy metal with no discernible beat, a rock band on a very bad trip with no musical talent. Sarah kept her eyes closed and focused on the techniques she'd been taught. She'd just reached an almost peaceful place despite the alternating temperature, light and sound, when the door opened and the sound suddenly stopped.

The silence was surprisingly disconcerting.

"I did not properly introduce myself last time," the red-eyed woman said. "My name is Verusha. We know your name. We know quite a lot about you, actually. And since you never sent your infiltration or initial entry reports, your handler knows you have been compromised. And all that valuable information in your head is no longer timely. So, bravo. According to the tenets of your SERE school, you have lasted the critical first forty-eight hours without giving up anything.

"But that's not what we're interested in. After all, we are not at war with your country. We're not that keen on what you know. What we want to know is who you know. Who they are. It gives us a picture of our counter-parts in your country. Such knowledge is very useful, as you can well imagine.

"Shall we begin?"

Of course it had already begun from the moment she'd been tased.

The weeks that followed merged together. Light. Sometimes pitch-black. Sound. Sometimes, but rarely, absolute silence. Heat. Cold. Interrogations.

Then, once, the door flew open and a quartet of men rushed in. They handcuffed her and hustled her out of the cell, and down the corridor, essentially carrying her. They made a left turn, then a right and an open door beckoned. They carried her out the open door into a courtyard, roughly twenty feet on a side. The walls, other than the steel door, were concrete. The men carried her to one side and shoved her against the wall, where she stood, naked and shivering.

She looked up. A grey, cloudy day.

Never had such a sky looked so beautiful to her.

Then she looked down. The four men had pistols leveled, pointing at her. Looking left and right she saw that the concrete to each side was pitted and cracked. Dull red smears marked it. The brick floor was stained dark.

It was a place of execution.

The steel door creaked open and a man wearing a suit stepped out. He had a piece of paper in his hand. He barely glanced at Sarah, then read in imperfect English: "Enemy of the state. You are condemned to die by firing squad. Today. Sentence to be carried out immediately." He folded the piece of paper then slid it into a pocket on the inside of his suit. Then he nodded at the four men.

"Prepared!" he cried out. They'd been ready from the moment they raised their pistols.

"Aim."

For the first time, for some odd reason, Sarah felt the full extent of her nakedness as the looked at the four pistols aimed at her. The black holes at the end of the muzzles appeared enormous.

"Fire!"

The hammers clicked down.

On empty chambers.

Sarah felt pride that she didn't fall to her knees. The men holstered their guns, hustled forward, grabbed her, and dragged her back to her cell.

She was grateful to have been outside, if only for a moment, and seen the sky.

Eight times the door was opened and she was dragged out to that courtyard. Far above the sky always beckoned. Sometimes it was day, sometimes night. Once they did it in the midst of thunderstorm. Sometimes it was pistols. Sometimes automatic weapons. Sometimes it was four men, then a few more, a few less. Once, a single man, pressing a pistol up to the back of the her head after making her kneel and face the wall, staring into fresh blood smearing the concrete.

Never did the bullet come.

Always she was returned to the cell and strapped down again.

Finally, after what must have been months, she was unbuckled from the gurney and it was removed along with the IV. But she was kept naked in the cell. Food was thrown in onto the floor, slop about whose composition she had no clue. No water. She learned she had to drink when the hose man came in, follow him around, mouth open, desperately gulping water, even as it blasted against her skin and face.

There was no toilet. There was a three-inch wide drain in the center of the rubber mat floor and it all sloped gently down to that. Every so often, at a varying schedule, two men came in, with two guards overwatching with tasers, and hosed the room, and her, down.

Sometimes the lights and sound went out, descending her into pitch black and absolute silence. The mock executions decreased in frequency, but always loomed, with the greater threat of real execution as she knew she was less and less useful to them as they wrung her dry of everything she knew.

She tried doing exercises. But she was so famished and exhausted, her energy was spent quickly and she realized they were not supplying her with enough calories for her to work out. Just enough to survive. So she kept working out, trying to kill herself.

But they knew that one too. She was tased, gurnied, and IVed, just enough to survive. She went through this pattern several times before surrendering to the norm of just enough food to live.

It got to where Sarah looked forward to Verusha's visits. She anticipated them, her only interaction with another human being. The only thing that kept her from becoming a base animal.

Sarah talked. Not much at first, but more and more, trying to draw out the visits as long as possible. She gave up all she knew. And when she had nothing left, she began to make things up because she knew that one day that sky above the courtyard would be the last thing she would ever see.

That was a mistake.

One day the door flew open and five men came in. Covered by the two men with tasers.

Four held her down. The fifth raped her. And then they all switched places.

This happened time and time again, with no visit from Verusha.

It occurred to Sarah, in some portion of her mind where she retained her sanity, that there was some ulterior motive to the rapes, not just punishment.

Everything here had a purpose.

One day the music suddenly stopped and instead of men, Verusha was framed in the doorway. Sarah rushed her, nothing to lose, and was tased by a man standing right behind her. She fell to the matting. Verusha walked in, followed by men with a gurney. Sarah was returned to the condition she'd arrived in.

She was at least thirty pounds lighter than the trim fighting shape she'd been in when she'd jumped out of the back of that Combat Talon; a skeleton with skin on it. It was her mind though, that was the most starved. Empty of almost all but the most base survival instincts.

In essence, she was nothing more than an animal in human form.

Sarah noticed a change. The temperature was normal. Not too hot, nor too cold for her nakedness. The only other times it was like this was the brief transition from freezing to sweltering and vice versa. But this was remaining the same as Verusha walked around her as if inspecting a slab of meat.

"If I wish to absorb fiction I will read my Kindle." She smiled. "Yes, I own one. Love your technology. When you started making things up, I knew you'd told all."

She came to a pause next to Sarah's shaved head. "Now you understand why we don't use rude techniques such as water-boarding or cutting or breaking things. Other than the subject's mind. When the torture is too rapid and intense, the subject tends to go to story-telling too quickly to stop it. At the beginning. Here, we get the stories, the lies, at the end, once everything had been wrung from the subject. So when you began to tell stories, we knew we had it all."

Verusha ran a hand along Sarah's cheek, almost like a lover. "The rapes were to remove your mind from the act of sex. Sex is a tool for people like us. That is all. There is no love. There is no affection. There is only power and leverage. Your body is yours only in how it is useful. It can be more effective than a sniper rifle or a dagger."

"Kill me," Sarah begged. "You've got everything."

"Not everything," Verusha said. "You are a valuable asset. You do know you were betrayed, correct?"

Sarah closed her eyes, but she nodded.

"Good. It's an old technique to send in an agent with false information. As old as Sun Tzu probably. That's why we didn't care about what you knew. Some key elements of it were most *definitely mis-information planted by your handlers to be given up to us under torture in order to mislead. For whatever reason. That's why we focused on who you knew. Our dossiers on those people are now that much thicker."*

Verusha moved down to the strap across Sarah's chest. She loosened it, then tossed it over. She continued, taking all of them off. As she did so, she spoke. "You can't go back. When they sent you on this mission they decided you were expendable, for whatever reason. Even we have heard of your Cellar here. If you go back, they will Sanction you. Rather cynical, or perhaps ironic. You did what they wanted, but nonetheless you are a traitor."

Verusha stepped back as Sarah sat up. "There's clothing under the gurney."

Sarah slid off the gurney and reached underneath. A blue jumpsuit. She carefully put one leg in, then the other, needing the gurney for support because she was so weak. She pulled it up, the cloth feeling foreign against her skin.

"You will be human again," Verusha said. "But you will never be the same. I speak from experience."

Sarah fingers fumbled with the last button, securing it just below her neck. "What use could I possibly be to you?"

"You are a woman of considerable talents," Verusha said. "You still retain those. Except your motivation and attitude are much changed. You won't go back to your old job and—"

"I won't work for you," Sarah finished.

"Of course not. You would fear the same thing happening. It is the nature of our professions. So we are done with you. Killing you is wasteful since everything and everyone has some value." She smiled, without any warmth or humor, which was quite a feat. "So we sold you."

She turned and the door opened. A tall, thin man walked in. His head was almost a skull, the skin pinched so tightly to the bones. But his eyes bulged out slightly, giving him a strange appearance.

"My name is Karralkov," he said in English with a Russian accent. "I run many businesses. Some in the United States. Some in other countries nearby. You will help me. In return, you will be well paid. And some time in the future, if you do your job well, you will be given your freedom with enough money to live the rest of your life in comfort. They use the stick here. I prefer the carrot." He turned to Verusha. "Fatten her up. She looks terrible. My man will be here to take delivery in three weeks."

Chapter Thirteen

"So it all comes full circle," Chase said, when Sarah stopped talking. There had been a long silence, each person in the room processing what she'd related.

"Do you believe me?" Sarah asked, and it wasn't clear if the question was directed to any specific person.

Chase, along with Riley, Gator, Kono and Dillon, all turned to look at Westland. "If I didn't believe her," she said, "I'd kill her right now."

"You worked for Karralkov," Riley said. "So that was over when he died, correct?"

Sarah nodded. "He was working several angles, including the Daufuskie land deal. He had me buy Bloody Point years ago through intermediaries. Among other deals. When SAS got hacked, it was because I let his programmers into the system."

"And then you turned on him." Riley didn't say it as a question.

"No," Sarah said. "He turned on me."

"How did you find my son?" Chase asked.

"I have contacts in many places," Sarah said. "Their boat has a transponder on it that can be activated with the correct signal. I activated it and we went and got them. Before that, to get them close, I pretended to be Erin, asking my long lost son to come visit his mother."

"Did you hurt my son?" Chase said.

"No. They were fine when I last saw them."

"Are they on their boat?" Chase asked, grasping at the possibility.

Sarah shook her head. "No. They were on my boat, but I'm assuming that's at the bottom of the ocean now. I have no idea where Preston would hold them. He's got a lot of resources, both through his father and on his own. He has several million dollars of his own money via a trust fund from his grandfather that's not monitored by anyone."

Dillon spoke up. "I don't get it." He got up and walked back and forth, agitated. "Is Preston simply crazy? How does he think he can get away with all of this?"

"Because he *has* so far," Sarah said. "He's crazy, but not in the way most people think of it. He's a psychopath. Brilliant and with a plan. I think it all started when he jumped on your son," she nodded at Chase, "and killed Greer Jenrette. He'd always hated the Jenrette's. Even though his father is the most powerful political person in South Carolina, the Jenrette's run Charleston and are the richest family in South Carolina. Politics and money. Preston wanted both. He saw Greer as a rival. He took the opportunity and it worked. Think about it. Harry Brannigan is on the run for murder, yet it was Preston who did it.

"He's got it set that he will own all of Sea Breeze tomorrow. And he'll use that money as his base of future power. He wants to be indebted to no one."

"What about Mrs. Jenrette?" Westland asked.

"I have a feeling he'll take care of her in a manner similar to the way he took care of Merchant Fabrou."

Riley checked his watch. "It's late. We're going to need to be sharp in the morning. I want to put in surveillance on Daufuskie before daybreak. Let's all get some sack time."

The group broke apart, heading to their sleepings. Riley took Sarah with him to a small room on the far side of the garage. "You bunk here."

"Keeping me away from the troops?" Sarah asked.

"I believe your story," Riley said. "But that still doesn't make all you've done since then all right."

"I've never hurt a civilian," Sarah said. "Everyone's been a player."

"You played us well to get to Karralkov," Riley said, "but you got lucky in the end."

"We all did," Sarah said. "Karralkov planted me where I was, then he was getting ready to pull the plug. I had to act and I did the best I could."

Riley folded his arms and considered her. "I don't believe you're telling the entire truth. You turn on us, you put us in danger for your own reasons, then I will kill without a moment's hesitation. And that goes for Westland, Kono and Gator."

"And Horace?" Sarah asked.

"He'll shoot you faster than any of us," Riley said. "You're responsible for putting his son in harm's way. Family. It's even stronger than what you went through."

* * *

Across the Intracoastal the sniper had watched it all. The group meeting with Sarah surprisingly showing up. That had caused the sniper a moment of angst, her finger caressing the trigger, but holding because: no order.

She had no idea what the target had said, speaking for so long.

But something was off. Something was different because they all parted to bed down for the night.

As the lights darkened across the way at Brams Point, the sniper rolled on her back and made a satellite call.

* * *

Hannah listened to the sniper's report. She hung up, then punched in a code. It was answered on the second ring.

Westland didn't answer with a greeting. She knew exactly why Hannah was calling.

"Sarah Briggs told us what happened to her," Westland began. She then summarized Sarah's story in a paragraph.

In her office, alone underneath the NSA, Hannah listened. When Westland finished, the silence played out for a few seconds.

"That was under Nero," Hannah said. "And the op was run by the organization you both worked for at the time, which no longer exists. Part of the reason it no longer exists is that it did things like this."

"But you still ordered a Sanction on Sarah Briggs," Westland said. "It's why I'm here."

"Kate," Hannah said, a surprising use of the familiar. "It's a circle. I'm not going to apologize for whoever sent Sarah Briggs to that fate. It's the way it is. You didn't Sanction her upon sight, which means I sent the right person on this mission, correct? Perhaps my motive was larger than simply Sanctioning Sarah Briggs?"

"I've been considering that possibility," Westland said.

"Good. Cardena told me about this Horace Chase. He's a good operative. And you told me Dave Riley is one too. They've been useful. In a way, so has Sarah Briggs. She helped us terminate Karralkov."

"And what is the play now?" Westland asked.

"It's in your hands," Hannah said. "Along with Chase and Riley. I have been contacted by Senator Gregory who told me to back off."

"So you'll deal with him?"

"Of course."

* * *

Chase sat on the dock in the darkness; relative darkness given the lights from his neighbors who still bathed their houses in them even though it was three in the morning. He'd have to wake everyone soon and get moving. Put surveillance into place on Daufuskie before dawn. Try to figure out a way to find where Preston had secreted away Doc and Harry.

He found it odd that Sarah Briggs had met his son, but he hadn't. Not the only odd thing about all of this. He heard footsteps coming down the dock and turned his head, expecting to see Dave Riley, but instead, it was Dillon.

The Institute grad sat down at the table without a word. They stayed like that for a while, a ritual for soldiers on guard duty at night. In tune with the world around them, respecting each other's thoughts.

"You served," Chase said.

"Yes."

"Whose side will you be on tomorrow? Ours or Mrs. Jenrette's?"

"I think Mrs. Jenrette will be on our side once she knows the truth."

"Then you need to tell her before the meeting."

Dillon nodded. "I got a text message from her man. They're coming down via her yacht, just the two of them. They want me to meet them on Daufuskie, but I think I should meet her on the boat before she disembarks. Fill her in."

"Good idea."

"You know," Dillon said, "something Sarah said just triggered a thought. Preston has a boat. If Sarah was keeping your son and Doc Cleary on her boat, it stands to reason Preston's men needed a boat to get to them. And—"

Chase had his cell phone out. He pulled out his wallet and retrieved the card that Zelda had given him. He was a bit surprised when it was answered on the third ring.

"Yeah?" The voice was groggy.

"Zelda, this is Horace Chase."

"You drowning? Your boat sinking?"

"No."

"Then fucking call me when the sun is up."

"I need help," Chase said. "Now. Please. I think my son and Doc Cleary are being held prisoner on a boat and I need to find it. I understand some boats have transponders that can be—"

The grogginess was gone from Zelda's voice. "Whose boat?"

"Preston Gregory."

"That dickhead from Charleston? Hold on."

Chase waited.

Zelda came back on the phone. "It's active. I'm pinging it now." There was a pause. "Okay. I got it. Pinckney Island, in an inlet. Not exactly where normal people anchor. You got that crazy man Kono with you?"

"How do you know that?"

"I talk to Tear. And he talks to me."

"Kono's here."

"Tell him to give me a call and I'll tell him exactly where the ship is."

The phone went dead.

Chase looked at Dillon. "Great idea. Let's go."

The two began running down the dock back toward the house.

* * *

Riley watched them coming, dark figures barely visible in the few bulbs lighting Chase's 240-foot long pier. The cell phone he'd appropriated from Farrelli's two goons began vibrating in his pocket.

"Get Sarah," he said to Westland, who was sitting next to him.

Riley answered. "Yeah?"

"Is this Mister Riley or Mister Chase?"

"Who the fuck are you?"

"I'm the person who has Harry Brannigan."

"So you're Preston Gregory."

"How astute," Preston said. "I assume then, that my former compatriot Ms. Briggs has run to you in the vain hope you might protect her."

Sarah Briggs appeared with Westland.

"So is this Riley or Chase?" Preston asked.

"Riley."

"Why are you getting involved in something that doesn't pertain to you?" Preston asked.

"I have a dog in this hunt," Riley said.

The back door slid open and Chase and Dillon were there. Riley held up a finger to keep them quiet. He hit speakerphone so they could all hear.

"You do know Sarah Briggs is a lying, psychopathic, double-crossing bitch, correct?" Preston asked.

"I've heard it said," Riley replied, looking at Briggs.

Chase was using hand and arm signals and it didn't take a genius to figure out he'd learned where Doc and Harry were. Riley gave him the thumbs-up to indicate he understood.

Gator and Kono appeared, attracted by the activity.

"So why are you involved?" Preston repeated.

"My friend's son is in danger," Riley said.

Preston laughed. "He is in danger if you don't do exactly what I say. I can tell I'm on speaker, so I assume Chase is there? Is Briggs there too?"

"Correct on both counts."

"Who else? The woman with the black streak in her hair?"

Westland shook her head. She gestured north and mouthed: D.C.

"No," Riley answered. "She was recalled to Washington."

Preston laughed again. "That's real power for you. My father probably only had to make one phone call to jerk her ass back there. And since I have Harry and the old man, I have the power over you." His voice shifted, and a bit of an English accent crept into it. "Hello there darling Sarah. Do you believe you are among friends?"

"You're clueless," Sarah said.

"Perhaps," Preston said. "Mister Chase?"

"Yes?" Chase said.

"If you want to see your son alive, you will shoot Sarah Briggs right now in the forehead, immediately take a picture of her dead body, and text it to me on this phone in the next thirty seconds, or your son is dead."

The phone clicked off.

Riley, Chase, Westland, Gator, Kono and Dillon all remained frozen for a moment. But Sarah Briggs reached out, pulled the pistol from Chase's holster, pointed it toward her forehead, and smiled at all of them.

Then she pulled the trigger.

Chapter Fourteen

Preston Gregory peered at the screen of the cell phone. Sarah Briggs lay on a floor, glistening blood covering most of her face, her eyes staring up vacantly.

He hit speed dial one.

"Riley."

"Did you do that or Chase?" Preston asked.

"Does it matter?"

"I suppose not. Impressive response, but I expected no less of men of your caliber. Now. Here's what else you are going to do and then you get Harry and the old man back. Mrs. Jenrette is leaving Charleston at the crack of dawn on her yacht. We'll all meet on Daufuskie at Bloody Point on the old dock just west of the Point. It's secluded and both ships can dock there along with your little dinghy. That's when you're going to give me Sarah's documents. And Mrs. Jenrette will call my father and have him file the appropriation so the money will start flowing and the contracts will be put out.

"And then it gets interesting," Preston continued. "She'll wonder why you're there. By the way, I want just Riley and Chase. If catch a glimpse of anyone else, especially those two whack jobs, Gator and Kono, your boy dies. Along with the old man. Then, and only then, I'll bring out Harry and the old man from my boat. And then it's between you and her who gets him. Should be fun to watch."

Preston hit the off button. Then he stood up from behind his desk in Sea Pines. It was an hour and a half before first light on the first day of his new life.

He felt pretty damn good.

* * *

"A crazy lady," Kono said, as he held the compress against Sarah's forehead, trying to stem the flow of blood.

"You sure she's alive?" Dillon asked. They'd all seen her shift the muzzle at the last moment before firing.

Kono touched her neck with his other hand. "Pulse."

Chase ran over to his footlocker, threw open the lid and pulled out a Quikclot bandage and tossed it to Kono.

The Gullah ripped it open then pressed it against the self-inflicted wound.

"Hold it for five minutes," Chase said. "It will stop the bleeding."

Sarah had turned the gun so it was *almost* parallel to her head then pulled the trigger. The bullet had grazed her skull, stunning her, ripping open the skin to the bone, and dropping her to the floor.

It wasn't exactly something she could have asked someone to do on a moment's notice. And a millimeter deeper and she'd be dead.

"Concussion at least," Kono said, keeping pressure on the wound.

"Do we believe her now?" Dillon asked.

"She didn't kill herself," Chase said.

"Close," Westland said. "Close enough that Preston believed it."

"Shit," Gator said, impressed. "I thought she did it, until I didn't see any brains. Guess that little dipshit never saw the result of a head shot."

Sarah Briggs groaned and Kono helped her sit up.

"What were you thinking?" Chase asked.

"I was thinking I'd better shoot myself before one of you did," Sarah said.

Chase and Riley exchanged a glance, but didn't say anything.

"I'm assuming he bought it," Sarah continued, "because none of you finished the job."

"Yeah, he fell for it," Riley said. "And he wants us to go up against Mrs. Jenrette over Harry and Doc. They're meeting at the old dock on the south end of Daufuskie and he wants just Chase and me there with your documets. He picked that spot because you could blow a pound of C-4 there and no one would notice. Hell, the Air Force dropped a nuke off the coast south of there in 1958 and no one has found it yet."

"Based on Gregory's actions so far," Chase said, "he has to wipe the slate clean so he can move forward."

"And," Riley added, "I have no doubt that whoever comes out standing won't stay standing much longer."

"Except I know where Harry and Doc are," Chase said. "Kono, call Zelda and get the exact location of Preston's boat. She says she has the transponder active."

"Find out where Mrs. Jenrette's yacht is too," Dillon suggested.

"Roger that." Kono stepped out into the back with his cell phone.

"Whoa," Riley said. "Hold on. Let's think this through. We move too fast, bad things could happen."

"We get my kid," Chase said.

"It aint that simple," Riley said.

"Why not?" Chase demanded.

"Because Preston Gregory isn't going to let it be that simple," Riley said.

"He's right," Sarah said. "He's been planning this for a long time and he's ruthless. Even if we get your son away from him, then what? There's still the matter of Greer Jenrette's death. The stakes have gotten too high all around."

"We've got Chad—" Chase began, but even he realized the foolishness of that.

Kono came back in. "I've got Gregory's boat. West side of Pinckney. And Mrs. Jenrette yacht has just departed Charleston and is heading south."

Riley shook his head. "We're not going to be able to approach Preston's boat and get them. We know a hostage rescue is the hardest op and from what we saw on Daufuskie, Preston has some people who know how to use guns. We don't have time to do anything fancy. We need to think for a moment and make the best plan we can with the time we have left."

"All right," Chase said. "Suggestions?"

"We make a clean sweep of it," Sarah said. "We have to follow what Preston said: the two of you make the meet."

"And the rest of us?" Dillon asked.

"First," Chase said. "Are you all in? If anyone wants to walk, now is the time."

"I've been in," Riley said.

"I'm with you," Gator said, since he'd be in with anything that promised mayhem and gunfire and explosions.

"Yah," Kono said. "No more playing around."

"I'm in," Dillon said. "As long as I can tell Mrs. Jenrette the truth."

Riley turned to Westland. "What say the Cellar?"

"I guess we'll find out," Westland said.

"And you?" Riley asked Sarah. "As far as Preston is concerned, you're dead. You can walk away clear and free."

"I could," Sarah said. But she didn't move.

"All right." Riley said. "I know the spot where the meeting is going to take place. Here's the plan."

Chapter Fifteen

Gator cradled his gear in a waterproof case, made sure the 12 foot tow line was attached to it, and then pushed himself off the dive platform on the rear of the *Fina* as the boat kept moving up the waterway between the mainland and Pinckney Island. He was tossed about in the boat's wake, before the water settled.

Gator peered through the dark and island and spotted a small glow through the trees in a lagoon. Bad light discipline.

He rolled onto his back and began finning toward the light, his gear being pulled along behind him on the line.

He was in a good mood because action was pending.

* * *

Sarah Briggs and Kate Westland slid over the side of Riley's zodiac into the dark water off the south end of Daufuskie Island with their gear in waterproof bags. They bobbed in the water, both gave him a thumbs up, then began swimming toward the beach.

* * *

Preston Gregory sat in the back of the Town Car. There was a black Range Rover leading the convoy and one behind his car. Each held four men, part of Pappano's crew of former agents, soldiers and criminals.

Technically, given the things they'd already done, they were all criminals now, but Preston didn't see it that way. He'd studied history and power and had come to the conclusion that laws were for the masses; not the elite. Rules were made to be broken.

Pappano sat across from him, a little white ear-piece in place, the crackle of updates from the other two cars and the boat occasionally breaking the silence.

He almost felt like he was back in the Service, part of the Presidential motorcade. And there was a part of him, deep inside, that had a feeling that one day Preston Gregory might be riding in such.

They were heading off Hilton Head on Route 278. But not to the mainland. They passed over the Intracoastal and while the bridge headed over another arm of water to the mainland, they too an exit onto the island that was between the northern part of Hilton Head and the mainland: Pinckney Island.

As they circled underneath the bridge, they passed a small, empty parking area and came to a metal gate. One of the men hopped out of the lead Range Rover and unlocked the gate. The three vehicles passed through, and then halted, while the trail man locked the gate behind them. They were now in the National Wildlife Refuge.

It was still dark out, dawn still a half hour away.

"How far is the boat?" Preston asked, eager for the day to get underway.

"Not far," Pappano said. "It's secure in a lagoon. And once we get underway, it won't take long to get to Daufuskie."

"The prisoners?"

"Secure." Pappano hesitated, but then asked: "Sir. What is your ultimate plan for them? They're going to recognize you, unless you'd like me to have them blindfolded before we arrive? But after that?"

"You're worried they can identify you and your men," Preston said as they drove on the dirt track deeper into the Wildlife Refuge.

"Partly. The reality is—" once more he stopped.

"The reality is," Preston said, "that we're better off with them dead. And so they shall be. Today we close out this chapter and open a new one with the board clear."

* * *

Kono was talking into the radio, speaking in Gullah, which Dillon could only partially translate. Someone replied in the same, and then Kono turned the wheel, heading the *Fina* west.

"What are you doing?" Dillon asked. "Mrs. Jenrette's yacht will be coming down the coast."

"We have to pick someone up first," Kono said.

The dark mass of the shoreline was directly ahead. It was completely dark, indicating no houses or docks; no sign of civilization at all. Until a small light flashed.

"There is our friend," Kono said.

Dillon didn't ask any more questions, knowing he was along for the ride and at the discretion of Kono. He was still trying to sort through this mess, but it always looped back to Preston Gregory and his insane desire for power.

Or perhaps not so insane, given he'd gotten, and kept, the upper hand so far.

Kono slowed the patrol boat down as they came up on the source of the light: an old man with a long white beard, sitting in a row boat, holding a flashlight.

"Help," Kono simply said as he throttled down and then went to the side where the row boat was. Together, he and Dillon helped the old man on board, then Kono used a small winch to lift up and secure the rowboat on the fantail.

"Dillon, this is Tear."

The old man stuck out his hand and Dillon shook it, feeling the calluses of decades of hard work.

Without another word, Kono climbed back to the cockpit, with Dillon and Tear following. Kono pointed down at the small, glowing screen. "This here," he said, tapping a triangular red dot, "will be Mrs. Jenrette."

And then he opened up the engines, heading in that direction.

* * *

The sniper was waiting on the Little Bird helicopter at Hunter Army Airfield, having been alerted by Westland twenty minutes ago. She was a bit irritated the crew wasn't here yet, but then again, they were Army and even in Special Ops, an alert before dawn on a weekend took a little tie to respond to.

A truck pulled up and the pilot and co-pilot exited. They nodded at her, having learned not to ask any questions or even say hello.

This was business and while they had little clue why they were flying a woman with a sniper rifle around the Low Country, the two grizzled warrant officers had flown enough mission with Task Force 160, the Nightstalkers, in enough strange places around the world, to accept it was what it was.

The sniper made sure her monkey harness was secure, checked that the sling to her rifle was firmly attached to harness (what was commonly known in Ranger School as a 'dummy cord') and then settled down.

"Where to?"

"How long will it take us to get to Bloody Point on Daufuskie?" she asked.

Interestingly, since Savannah was several miles up river from the coast, Daufuskie lay almost due east as the bird, and the helicopter, flies.

"Six minutes."

"Good enough," the sniper said. "How long from a cold start?"

"Not much longer if we don't make it a cold start," the pilot said. "We can crank the engine every so often and keep it ready. Save fuel by shutting down in between."

"That's the plan for now."

* * *

Hannah looked at the text message from Westland and sat up in bed. She swung her feet over, touching the tile floor, collecting her thoughts. She had a lot more going on than events in the Low Country but she had the capability to compartmentalize and right now, this is what needed to be dealt with. She quickly threw on some clothes and left her small living area and went into her office.

For a moment, but only a moment, it struck her how silent and austere the place was. How the only light came from the overheads. No windows. Not even a plant to throw a little color into things.

Then she dismissed the thought.

She sat at her desk and looked at the two files Doctor Golden had left with her. Sitting side by side. Sarah Briggs and Preston Gregory. One person whose trajectory had already burned out. The other thinking they could reach the highest possible positions of power.

Hannah picked up a file in each hand. As if weighing them against each other.

Chapter Sixteen

As far as she knew, Mrs. Jenrette was heading to a business meeting, not showdown, but she didn't trust Preston Gregory as far as she could run, and since she could barely walk these days, that wasn't very far.

"We have company," she said, peering out of the glass of the wheelhouse.

"Kono's boat," Thomas said. He'd earned a captain's license many, many years ago, working on the shrimping boats. And he took Mrs. Jenrette's yacht out every so often; he liked to say for maintenance, but he was truly at peace on the water and sailing through the waterways of the Low Country. He knew this area almost as well as Kono did. His family had lived here for generations, indeed as long as Mrs. Jenrette's.

"What do you make of this, Thomas?" Mrs. Jenrette asked.

"I think things are going to become very difficult. We should have brought more men."

Mrs. Jenrette hadn't wanted anyone but Thomas with her. "This is between you and me," she said.

"Not any more," Thomas said.

Dawn was breaking over the ocean as Kono gently pulled the *Fina* alongside her yacht. The shoreline was about two miles away, the white sand brightly lit from the sun's rays, the lush greenery a sharp contrast just behind the beach.

"It's a glorious morning," Mrs. Jenrette said. "I am going to miss this most of all."

Thomas was looking down at the patrol boat.

"Mister Dillon is with him. And our old friend, Tear."

"I hope Mister Dillon has some answers."

Thomas leaned over from the wheelhouse and waved them aboard, greeting the old man in Gullah. Dillon followed up the stairs. Kono pulled his boat away a safe distance.

"Welcome," Thomas said. Then he nodded at the patrol boat a hundred yards off their port side. "Hard man," he said to Tear.

The old Gullah nodded. "Hard, but has a good heart." He turned toward Mrs. Jenrette. "We must talk to you about your grandson and what waits at Bloody Point."

* * *

Preston Gregory sipped a cup of coffee as he considered Harry Brannigan and Doc Cleary. Both were seated on a couch across from him. Their hands were zip-tied behind their backs and two guards flanked Preston, weapons at the ready. The boat's engines were rumbling and they were heading south, crossing underneath the Route 278 bridge which connects Hilton Head Island to the mainland.

"Your father has been looking for you," Gregory said to Harry. He shifted his gaze to Doc Cleary. "Have you told him about his father?"

"I have."

"Does it bother you, Harry," Preston said, "that your father was never in your life?"

"He was never in my life," Harry said, "because he didn't know I existed until recently."

Preston frowned. "But, Doc, you knew about Horace Chase all these years."

"I didn't know he was Harry's father until two years ago," Doc said. "When Harry came to the island. And I only found about because his grandmother, Lilly, told me. She'd known all along."

Preston chuckled. "Family intrigue. So Horace's own mother didn't connect father to son."

"She had her reasons," Doc said. "And I trusted her."

"And now," Preston said, "here we are. Heading for a family reunion of sorts." He acted like a thought had just struck him. "Oh. Perhaps Lilly was right, since your mother is dead, Harry. Shot by an associate of your father. Quite the mess."

Harry said nothing, absorbing that news without expression.

Preston laughed. "I see your short time as a rat did teach you a few things. Very nice and stoic."

Doc Cleary peered at him over his rimless glasses. "*'The pleasure of those who injure you lies in your pain. Therefore they will suffer if you take away their pleasure by not feeling pain'*."

"Did you make that up, old man?" Preston asked.

Harry spoke. "Tertullian. A Carthaginian author."

"So the two of you weren't just staring at the sea gulls while you were sailing around," Preston said. "Impressive. I imagine you could rattle off a bunch of brilliant sayings. But my take on it? Make up your own shit. Don't use the words of others. Be original."

"Why are you wasting our time?" Doc Cleary asked. "Where are we going?"

"Daufuskie Island," Preston said. "Your father should be there, Harry. You'll get to say hello and thank him for killing your mother. Should be quite interesting."

"Screw you," Harry said. "Doc did tell me about my father while we were at sea. I think you've gotten in too deep this time, Preston. I think you have no idea what you're up against. You act the big shot when you have the system working for you. When you can haze rats, or your father's political power behind you. What's coming for you now is—"

Preston cut in. "A man who can't even be a father." He stood up. "We're almost there. And by the way, Harry. Maybe I'm not the person you should be worried about. We're meeting Mrs. Jenrette there."

Doc and Harry exchanged a glance.

"Feeling a smidge of pain?" Preston asked. "Fear?"

"We'll tell her the truth," Doc said. "That you killed her grandson."

"She's had a while believing the story everyone else told," Preston said. "I don't think you're going be able to change her mind."

* * *

"It's the truth," Dillon said.

Mrs. Jenrette was very still. She was seated in the seat next to the captain's chair She hadn't said a word since Dillon began relating events since he was last with her in Charleston.

Finally, she spoke. "Thomas?"

"Yes, ma'am?"

"Do you believe him?"

Thomas looked to Tear. "What say you?"

Tear was also seated on a bench to one side, hand folded on his beard covering his belly. "I know Merchant Fabrou is dead. His son is dead. Word is heart attack and suicide. Word under the word is dark deeds. This Farrelli. He is dead too. Heart attack. There, the word under the word is murder. All points to Gregory boy. But no one will face him down."

"They're afraid of his father," Mrs. Jenrette said.

"They're afraid of *him*," Dillon corrected. "I think he's more dangerous than his father."

"If he killed Greer . . ." Mrs. Jenrette didn't finish the sentence.

"And Mister Rigney has disappeared," Thomas added.

"That man has no spine," Mrs. Jenrette said. "You were right about him, Thomas. You were right about many things. And I've been very wrong. My grief has clouded my mind."

"Pain does that," Tear said. "You and I. We know that."

"We met many years ago," Mrs. Jenrette said to him.

"I remember," Tear said. "You showed me kindness when I was in pain for a long time. Sunk deep in my own grief. As did you, Thomas."

Mrs. Jenrette turned to Thomas. "Have you spoken to Tear, to anyone, about my plan?"

"No, ma'am. You know I would never speak outside of us, especially about Sea Breeze."

Mrs. Jenrette was lost in thought for a few moments. "So Harry Brannigan and Doc Cleary will be on Daufuskie."

"Most likely," Dillon said. He then proceeded to tell her the best summation they'd come up with concerning Preston Gregory's plan for the day.

When he was done, Mrs. Jenrette nodded. "And I assume your friends, Misters Riley and Chase have a plan of their own?"

* * *

Preston's yacht eased up to an old pier, just west of Bloody Point, that was in a secluded inlet. They were an hour and a half early. By design. A half dozen of Poppano's men deployed, running a perimeter sweep, weapons at the ready, around the dock and the abandoned golf course that lay just inland.

Once they were certain the area was clear, four of them spread out, establishing a perimeter. That left Preston with four guards, including Poppano, to handle the meeting.

Preston Gregory went up to the bridge of his yacht and sat down in the captain's chair. Poppano stood behind him, listening to the reports from his security.

"We're secure, sir," he reported.

* * *

"Let's go," the sniper ordered and the Little Bird lifted off from Hunter Army airfield.

* * *

Mrs. Jenrette had experienced much in her ninety plus years. She'd witnessed lynchings as a young girl, both in the city and out in the countryside, where crowds cheered and jeered and only a handful of people turned away in disgust. Many fought to take part in it, both before and after, literally cutting 'souvenirs' off the corpses. After seeing something like that, she'd learned never to underestimate the cruelty and evil humans were capable of.

She'd also come of age during the lawlessness of prohibition, where many currently wealthy families had earned their first fortune breaking the law. She knew that capitalism dictated a reality much different than the mirage of democracy; and she also knew that the United States had never been a democracy. A republic at best in its early days, it had begun the slide into something very different in just decades; a similar slide which had taken Rome centuries. But the end results would be the same. Now she wasn't sure where things stood and she feared for the future, because despite her disdain for the Stars and Stripes over Fort Sumter, she believed in her country.

She'd known Senator Gregory for decades and while he wasn't the most ethical (she wasn't sure any politician could be), he was nowhere near the depth of depravity and danger of his son now that she finally understood.

"Thomas."

"Yes, ma'am." He was looking forward, drawing a long arc around the shallow sandbars off of Hilton Head's beaches.

"I fear this boy is evil. Rigney said Preston would sell his half to me for the right amount. I fear that was a lie."

"Most likely," Thomas agreed.

"He has done very bad things," Tear said.

Dillon had left the boat before they came in sight of Hilton Head and was with Kono, waiting, just over the horizon. Thomas turned the wheel and they headed landward.

"He's here already," Thomas said.

"I can still see," Mrs. Jenrette said, which she knew wasn't fair. But today had been a day of revelations and she was feeling her years.

Thomas ignored her. "And he has soldiers."

"Of course. He never intended to negotiate or share."

Mrs. Jenrette's yacht pulled into position on the other side of the old pier from Preston Gregory's. He held the higher ground from the open bridge of his boat. They were only fifteen feet apart, the width of the pier separating them.

"Welcome, Mrs. Jenrette," Preston called out. "It is nice to finally meet face to face. I mean, we have met, but only briefly, and you were always too busy to speak with me."

"Does that hurt your feelings?" Mrs. Jenrette called out in a surprisingly clear voice.

"My feelings don't get hurt," Preston said. "I'm a professional."

"Professional what?" Mrs. Jenrette asked.

But Preston was looking past her. "Who is the old man with you?"

"A friend," Mrs. Jenrette said.

"Which do you want first?" Preston called out. "The deal for Sea Breeze or your son's killer?"

"That's not what we agreed on," Mrs. Jenrette said.

"Things change," Preston said. He gestured and Pappano and one of his men pushed Doc Cleary and Harry Brannigan out of a hatch and onto the bridge next to him.

"I believe all we need now is to get the paperwork for Bloody Point—" he gestured out toward the gold course, which had seen better days. The greens were over-grown with weeds, the sand traps littered with leaves and other debris. Preston checked his watch. "I suspect our visitors who are bringing it will be punctual."

"Where is Charles Rigney?" Mrs. Jenrette asked.

Preston shrugged. "No idea." He looked to the right. "Here comes the last piece."

* * *

"I think we're seeing wealth inequality in action," Riley said as he steered his zodiac toward the old pier where the two yachts were docked.

But Chase was looking through binoculars. "Harry."

"Keep it together, Chase," Riley said as he pulled back on the throttle, slowing them down as they came to the end of the pier. "The clock is ticking."

* * *

Gator peered at his watch. Getting to be that time. He reached up and undid the snap link that connected the rope around his legs to a stanchion on the bottom of the six-foot wide swim platform, allowing his feet to swing free into the water. He shook the short piece of rope off, letting it sink down.

Then he released the snap link attached to the rope around his chest, while keeping a tight grip with his other hand on a stanchion. He lowered himself into the water.

His body was a bit battered because Preston's boat's wake had churned the two-foot gap between the bottom of the teak platform and the water's surface considerably during the journey from Pinckney Island to the south end of Daufuskie.

But that simply fit in with Gator's philosophy that 'pain is weakness leaving the body'.

And now Gator was getting ready to do some pain dealing. He opened up the waterproof sack and retrieved his submachinegun.

* * *

"We're docking," Riley reported over the radio to the team.

He pulled up to the end of the pier and Chase jumped off, tying off the zodiac. Riley grabbed Sarah Briggs' leather satchel and took it with him as he joined Chase on the pier.

"Focus," Riley said to Chase as they walked down the pier until they were between Preston and his captives and Mrs. Jenrette, who had only Thomas and Tear at her side. Two men with automatic rifles were tracking Riley and Chase from Preston's boat. One had his gun pointed at Mrs. Jenrette. And another was behind Harry and Doc, holding a gun on them.

Riley held up the satchel, showing it to both Preston and Mrs. Jenrette. "Bloody Point golf course. The deed is signed by the owner. We just have to fill in the name of the buyer."

Chase was staring up at his son. "I'm Horace," he called out.

"Your father," Doc Cleary said to Harry.

"The family reunion can wait," Preston said. "Give me the deed and you get your son." He looked up at Mrs. Jenrette. "Or you can pay for Bloody Point, and then sign over your part of Sea Breeze and Bloody Point to me and I give you your son's killer."

"I believe you over-estimate yourself," Mrs. Jenrette said. She gestured at Tear. "My old friend here knows everything that goes on in the Low Country."

"I doubt that," Preston said. But he spotted something in the distance: the *Fina* racing in toward them. "I told you no interference!"

"You're surrounded," Chase said. "Give up my son and Doc and you'll live to see the end of this day."

"Then your son dies," Preston said.

"Action!" Riley ordered over the radio.

From the sand trap closest to the pier, Sarah Briggs and Kate Westland burst up from beneath the sand. They got to their feet, weapons at the ready, Sarah pointing hers toward Preston's yacht while Westland went back to back with her, aiming outward.

Gator swung himself up on the swim deck, then climbed up into the ship, rushing toward the bridge, submachinegun tight to his shoulder.

Sarah Briggs fired. The round hit Pappano on the side of his head, blowing brains, blood and bone out the other side. He dropped like a stone.

Preston reacted surprisingly fast. He grabbed Harry, pressing his own pistol into the base of his skull, and backing up into the safety of the small alcove leading to the hatchway behind him.

"I'll kill him!"

* * *

Hearing the shot fired behind them, the four perimeter guards turned and began running back toward the pier.

Kate Westland had a 'heavy' SCAR (Special Operations Combat Assault Rifle), chambered for 7.62, to her shoulder. She killed the perimeter guard to the west, as she spoke over her phone. "Take the closest."

* * *

The sniper hit the guard to the east, shifting to the next one even before the first had hit the ground. She fired, a head shot, killing the second as Kate Westland took out the last one. Westland whirled about, shoulder to shoulder with Sarah Briggs.

The sniper leaned into her harness and shifted her target to Briggs. "Ready to Sanction."

"Hold," Westland said.

* * *

Riley didn't believe in the proverbial "Mexican" stand off, but at the moment, with Presto Gregory shielded by the entrance to the hatch, and his gun pressed against the back of Harry Brannigan's head, everything was in a pause.

The three guards on the deck of Preston's ship were trying to regroup, one pointing his weapon toward the sand trap where Westland and Briggs were, another still aiming at Riley and Chase, and the last aiming toward Mrs. Jenrette, Thomas and Tear.

That didn't last long.

Gator came up the stairs onto the main deck, firing, double-tapping. One guard down, two, but then the third wheeled, firing on full automatic, hitting Gator in the chest with two rounds, sending him tumbling back down the stairs.

* * *

"Preston!" Chase called out. "You've got nowhere to go. You've got no one covering your ass any more. Give up. We'll let you walk away."

Preston shoved the gun harder into the back of Harry's head, causing Chase's son to cry out in pain.

"I'll kill him."

Doc Cleary turned toward the two, hands still ziptied behind his back. "I'll take his place. I can pilot this boat out of here. You'll be free to go."

"Bullshit," Preston said. "You're not worth it. Brannigan's the only collateral I have." He looked across to the other yacht. "Mrs. Jenrette! Call these people off and you get the man who killed your grandson and I'll give you Sea Breeze!"

"I'm not in charge of these people," Mrs. Jenrette said.

Kate Westland and Sarah Briggs, sand sliding off their clothes, were walking forward to the pier, weapons at the ready. Riley and Chase had their hands up. Gator was motionless at the base of the stairs.

Preston's head was on a swivel, taking in the suddenly changed tableau. He had one man left.

"Get us out of here," he ordered the surviving guard.

"How?" the guy responded. "I—" and then his head exploded as a round from the sniper's rifle hit in the right temple and blew most of it to shreds.

"Fuck you people!" Preston screamed. "My father is a Senator! You can't touch me. I'll kill him before I let you win! I have a plan! I *will not* allow you people to interrupt it."

"Stop, please," Mrs. Jenrette said. "There's been too much pain. Too many deaths. This isn't worth it."

Preston looked down at the pier. "You. Daddy. What's your son worth to you? Will you call off your dogs for his life?"

Chase took two steps forward, toward the boat, hands raised. "I'll give you my life for my son's."

Sarah Briggs and Kate Westland halted about ten feet away from Chase and Riley. They had their weapons aimed up toward Preston, but they couldn't get a clear shot as he was in the alcove of the hatch with Harry in front.

"Move east, swing around," Westland said into her phone. "Target the man holding the hostage."

"Negative," the sniper responded. "I have to target the Sanction."

"The Sanction has changed," Westland said.

Sarah Briggs shifted her gaze to Westland. "Your Cellar support? Aiming at me? Let 'em shoot. Fuck it. I don't care any more. Maybe it will confuse the little shithead up there and someone else can get a clear shot."

* * *

On board the chopper, the sniper gave the order and the Little Bird lifted out of the trees on Daufuskie and banked hard, heading out over the water so it could swing around and she could have a shot west, toward the boat and the new target.

* * *

Chase took another step forward. "Preston. Let Harry go. I give you my word. My heart for his heart." He thumped his chest. "Shoot me and it's over. The slate is clean." He nodded toward Riley, then Sarah and Westland. "I'm ordering them to stand down if you let Harry go."

"You're full of shit," Preston said. "You fucked everything up! All my plans!"

Chase held his hand over his heart. "My heart for his and yours."

Preston pulled the gun from the back of Harry's head and fired, pulling the trigger as fast as he could.

His first round hit Chase's shoulder, staggering him back. The second and third into his chest, but then Harry slammed backward into Preston, getting space between the two.

And Sarah Briggs fired her SCAR, the round hitting Preston in the left eye, blowing his brains out.

Chapter Seventeen

Horace Chase had been shot before.

But this was different. In Afghanistan there had been pain, blood, gunfire still going off all around, his medic working over him.

But this time he felt strangely calm and still. He was lying on his back on the pier.

No pain. Dave Riley was kneeling over him. "What the hell were you thinking?" Horace could feel Riley ripping open his shirt. Probing. Doing something.

He didn't care. Looking past Riley he saw Sarah Briggs staring down at him. And then his son.

"Harry," Chase said. But he couldn't hear his own words, which worried him that his son couldn't hear them.

He remembered something though, even as he looked at his son. "Gator? Is Gator all right?"

"Vest took the rounds," Riley said, pressing a bandage against Chase's chest. "Biggest problem the dumb lug has is falling down those stairs and hitting his head. You're going to be okay, Chase. You're going to be all right."

Chase smiled. "I *am* all right. A heart for a heart." He suddenly saw his mother, Lilly. Reading to him each night. Often the same letter now in the bottom of his foot locker. So many times, so much love. Chase lifted his blood-covered right hand. And his son leaned over and took it. "*'And, which is more,* you'll *be a man, my son'.*"

And then Horace Chase died.

Epilogue

A single death does not stop the other lives affected by it. It sends them tumbling, staggering, meandering, marching, searching, in different directions.

* * *

Kono leaned over Gator and placed a poultice on his chest. "It will make you better."

"Chase is dead?" Gator asked. He was on the deck of the *Fina*, his chest bruised from where the bullets had hit his armor vest. He also had welts and bruises from his battering from hanging suspended underneath the swim platform of Preston's boat.

Pain might be weakness leaving the body, but at the moment, Gator was feeling a smidge beat up.

"Yes."

"Fuck."

"He died well," Kono said.

Gator looked up at his friend. "There is no dying well. There is just death."

"He gave a life for a life," Kono said. "There is nothing more honorable."

* * *

Cardena watched Senator Gregory leave his mistress's apartment building.

So predictable. And in the covert world, predictable was a kissing cousin of fatal. For the Senator, he probably thought it was no big deal.

He was wrong.

Cardena's men grabbed the Senator quickly and efficiently, snatching off the street in Alexandria as if the man had stepped into a crack in the pavement to Never-Never land. Cardena followed the van to a black site, ironically one Senator Gregory had voted in secret to fund.

What goes around, comes around.

The Senator, once the gag was removed, was screaming threats. It's what those who thought they were powerful did when suddenly transplanted into an environment where they weren't.

"Are you in charge, you fucking asshole?" Gregory demanded of Cardena when he entered the padded cell.

Cardena wiped the Senator's spittle off his face. "No. But I'm as in charge as you're going to meet."

"Who do you work for? Get them here right now!"

"I work for Hannah."

That gave the Senator pause. Cardena could almost see the blocks of thoughts tumbling in the Senator's brain, like dominos heading toward a bad ending. The man, after all, wasn't stupid.

"What is going on?" Gregory asked, in a much more civil tone. "Is this about my asking her to back off in South Carolina? One of her people took a shot at my son, damn it."

"Yes," Cardena said. "But that was just a warning shot. Just think. If you were so upset about that, how upset would you be if your son had actually *been* shot?" He didn't wait for an answer. "It would not be hard to imagine that you might possibly be so upset at losing your only son, you'd take your own life. On top of evidence being uncovered about the impropriety regarding a causeway and Daufuskie? What a scandal."

Gregory's face went pale. "Are you threatening me?"

"What's curious," Cardena said, "is that your first response is to ask if I'm threatening you, without any consideration whether your son has indeed been shot."

"I'm a United States Senator and as such—"

"As such, you serve the people. The problem, Senator, is that your son murdered another cadet at the Military Institute. And since then he's murdered others. Really. Don't see how you can stay in office after all that."

"You can't—"

"You'll be found hanging in your mistress's apartment," Cardena said. "She leaves for work in about twenty minutes. I usually don't say this, since it's such a cliché: if you are a God-fearing man, time to pray. But I doubt very much you fear God. But you do fear death."

* * *

"These are yours," Dillon said, handing the photo and bracelet he'd taken from Brannigan's room at the Institute to Harry.

"Thank you."

Dillon, Harry, Doc, Riley, Sarah Briggs and Kate Westland were gathered on the end of the dock in Brams Point. Riley had a black box containing Horace Chase's ashes. Chase's footlocker was on the planks. Doc's sailboat was tied up on the outside of the dock, while Riley's Zodiac was on the inside.

It was two days after the events on Daufuskie and the Cellar had efficiently policed up the site in just a few hours, leaving behind Kate Westland for the moment.

Doc was looking shoreward, at the house. "I want to go back to sea. At least for a while." He glanced at Harry. "Do you want to stay here or come with me?"

Harry didn't hesitate. "I want to head back out with you. We didn't go everywhere we planned. And we need to talk"

"I can keep an eye on the place," Riley said. "Stop by every so often."

"Thanks," Doc said. "But I think it needs to be occupied." He turned to Sarah Briggs. "Do you need a place?"

Sarah was startled. "What?"

"A place to stay for a while," Doc said. "While you sort things out. Dave told me some of your past. Sounds like you need a place of peace for a while."

Sarah looked at Westland. "Will I be left in peace?"

"My mission is over," Westland said. "Turns out there's a reason the field agent has the final call on a Sanction. We had the wrong target."

"I'd like that very much," Sarah Briggs said to Doc.

Riley held out the black box and Harry took it.

"We'll spread his ashes along the Intracoastal," Harry said. "That way, he'll always be around us."

"And this is yours, too," Riley said, indicating the footlocker.

"Thank you," Harry said, but he was eyeing the footlocker with wariness. "Do you know what's in it?"

"Your legacy," Riley said. "And remember, you can always change it. Your father gave his life for that."

"Hold on," Sarah said. "There's something we need to do first."

They followed her down the dock. She assembled the group in that crazy room with the tree poking down through the roof (which she kind of liked).

"Wait a second." She left and went into the small room, across the garage where they'd given her a bed. She came back with a large Gucci bag.

She opened it, showing them ten million dollars, wrapped tightly in bundles of hundreds. Old Mrs. Jenrette kept her word, Sarah had to give her that. Another surprise, wrapped in many.

"This is ours," Sarah told them. "I'm only going to say this once. Each of you has access to this bag. We all earned it. You all have needs. Wants. Whatever. I know it might overwhelm you right now. But take some. For something you want right now."

No one moved for several moments, but then Gator came forward, stuck his hand in and pulled out a single bundle.

"How much is that?" he asked, holding it up.

"Ten thousand," Sarah told him.

"Cool," Gator said. "There's this really neat long rifle I'd like to get."

And that was it. He walked away, apparently more than satisfied with such a small percentage of the amount, Sarah couldn't even understand it right now.

Kono followed his friend. "I need two. I'm sorry. But I need to have the engines on *Fina* replaced." So he pulled out two bundles. All of twenty thousand dollars out of ten million.

Sarah looked at Dillon. "Thanks for wanting the truth. I think you're good at it. Perhaps a future in that?"

"Law school is expensive," Dillon said.

"Oh, geez," Sarah said. "It's ten million dollars. How much is law school going to cost?"

"The first year will be around thirty thousand," Dillon said, almost apologetically.

Sarah pointed at the bag and Dillon took his first year's tuition.

"Make it through that year and come back for more," Sarah said, not quite believing she was doing this. She'd envisioned Paris.

But what good was Paris alone?

Westland shook her head. "I'm good." But she nudged Riley. "Dinghy?"

Riley flushed. "I only told you that because . . ." he faltered to silence.

"A boat would be nice," Sarah said. "So you could come over and check on things."

"I don't think I have to do that," Riley said. "But there's this used Boston Whaler . . ."

And he took three bundles.

"Doc?" Sarah asked.

"Take care of our house," was all Doc had to say.

Sarah looked at the last man. "Harry?"

He shook his head. "Take care of *our* house. That's all I ask."

Sarah looked around the room, keeping tight control, the control that she'd been trained, tortured into. "All right. Well. I'll be here. Any time."

And with that, farewells were said. Harry and Doc Cleary carried Horace Chase's remains to their sailboat and cast off.

Dillon walked to his car to head back to Charleston.

And Kate Westland climbed into Riley's Zodiac to journey with him back to Daufuskie Island.

They left behind Sarah Briggs, standing alone on the dock. But not for long as Chelsea came walking slowly down the long wooden pier and sat down next to her.

Without thinking, Sarah reached down and ran her hand through the dog's mane.

Her last view of Doc Cleary's boat was Harry Brannigan standing on the aft, slowly spreading his father's ashes into the water.

* * *

Mrs. Jenrette was impressed that an arm of the government could work so efficiently. There was no sign of a gun battle at Bloody Point. She'd been assured by the woman with the black streak in her hair that this would be as if it had never happened. When Mrs. Jenrette had asked about how Senator Gregory would react to the death of his son, the woman had told her that she need not be concerned.

Something in the confident way the woman said it wiped away any doubts Mrs. Jenrette had. It would be handled as efficiently as this had been.

For now, there was just the quiet lap of the waves on the sandy beach. A heron flew by, unconcerned with the three humans standing on the beach. Fifty meters off shore a dolphin breached the surface, dorsal fin cutting through the water, then it was gone.

"Tide is changing," Tear said, eyeing the water line and the currents.

Mrs. Jenrette had her hand on Thomas' arm, needing his strength to stand.

"It is," Mrs. Jenrette said. "Bloody Point has lived up to its name, once more."

"It will be different from here on out," Thomas said.

Mrs. Jenrette held a leather satchel in her other hand. She held it out to Tear.

The old Gullah took it.

"The land goes back to your people, the Gullah," Mrs. Jenrette said. "There will be no causeway built. No development."

"Not just my people," Tear said. "We will welcome those who were here before us. Any Native American will be welcome."

"I fear not many survived in this part of the country," Mrs. Jenrette said. "But that is all up to you now. The island is yours. I trust you will care for it."

"We will," Tear said. "And our children and our children's children. You have done a good thing."

Mrs. Jenrette shook her head. "I never expected it to happen like this. But evil exists. It is good that there are men and women still willing to stand up and fight it."

Thomas spoke up. "This will be a place of peace from now on."

"I am tired, Thomas," Mrs. Jenrette said. "Very tired. Could you help me sit down for a second?"

Thomas gently helped the old woman to a sitting position on the sand. She stretched her withered legs out in front of her. "I remember the beach," she whispered. "Greer and I used to . . ." but her voice drifted off to silence. Her head slumped down.

Before she could fall backward, both Tear and Thomas had their arms around her. Together they lifted her up.

* * *

Hannah had listened to Cardena's after action report on the entire Gregory mess. The old man, the Senator, had been undone by his own son. Almost sad.

But not quite.

Now she was alone, as she normally was. The thick file that had accumulated on Preston Gregory was on a corner of the desk where her assistant would collect it at the end of the day. To be put in a drawer with all the other closed files.

But there was still the thin file of Sarah Briggs, front and center, on her desk.

Most curious.

Hannah opened the bottom right drawer on her desk. There were three other files in there. Hannah picked up Sarah Briggs file and added it to the three.

* * *

On the northern end of Daufuskie Island, Dave Riley sat in a beach chair, a cooler to one side and to the other, Kate Westland in her own chair. He pulled out two cold ones, unscrewed the tops, and handed one to her.

"Nice place," Kate said.

"It is."

"Might be a good place to retire to," Westland said.

"I thought you didn't get to retire."

"Well," Kate said. "How about semi-retire?"

Riley glanced over at her. "Is that an offer, a question or a statement?"

"A question."

"Hell, yeah," Riley said. He held out his bottle and Kate Westland clinked her's against his.

* * *

And outside what used to be Horace Chase's house, Sarah Briggs, who no longer even remembered the name she'd been born with, was hitting the heavy bag hanging down from the walkway out to the dock. Turn kicks. Side kicks. Fist strikes. Sweat poured down her body.

But after a few minutes, she began to slow down and the force of her blows lessened.

Until she dropped to her knees in the sand.

And then she realized she was crying. Tears flowing down her cheeks.

She hadn't cried in twelve years.

The End

To learn how Chase and Riley ended up involved with Sarah Briggs, and Chase learns he is a father for the first time: ***The Green Berets: Chasing the Lost***.

To read about the mission Dave Riley and Kate Westland were on together: ***The Green Berets: Eyes of the Hammer***, which is the very first Dave Riley book. He's younger and faster, but not necessarily smarter. The book is also also free.

To read about the Cellar, it begins with ***Bodyguard of Lies***, which tells Hannah's story when she's picked by Nero; when her file was in that lower right drawer.

For more about Doctor Golden and her theories on profiling and how she works with Hannah, there is ***Lost Girls***.

To read about Horace Chase and his time as Federal Liaison to the Boulder Police where he ends up investigating the apparent rape/murder of a housewife and a secret CIA operation: ***The Green Berets: Chasing the Ghost***.

And Dave Riley, Kate Westland and Sarah Briggs will be back in Green Berets #10, ***Old Soldiers***, in spring, 2018.

An excerpt from Bodyguard of Lies follows author and book info.

About the Author

Thanks for the read!
If you enjoyed the book, please leave a review. Cool Gus likes them as much as he likes squirrels!

Look! Squirrel!
Bob is a NY Times Bestselling author, graduate of West Point, former Green Beret and the feeder of two Yellow Labs, most famously Cool Gus. He's had over 70 books published including the #1 series Area 51, Atlantis, Time Patrol and The Green Berets. Born in the Bronx, having traveled the world (usually not tourist spots), he now lives peacefully with his wife, and labs. He's training his two grandsons to be leaders of the Resistance Against The Machines.

Subscribe to my newsletter for the latest news, free eBooks, audio, etc.

For information on all my books, please get a free copy of my *Reader's Guide*. You can download it in mobi (Amazon) ePub (iBooks, Nook, Kobo) or PDF, from my home page at
www.bobmayer.com

For free eBooks, short stories and audio short stories, please go to
http://bobmayer.com/freebies/
Free books include my next free book constantly updated.
And permanently free:
Eyes of the Hammer (Green Beret series book #1)
Duty (Duty, Honor, Country series book #1)
Ides of March (Time Patrol)
There are also free shorts stories and free audiobook stories.

Never miss a new release by following my Amazon Author Page.

I have over 220 free, downloadable Powerpoint presentations via Slideshare on a wide range of topics from history, to survival, to writing, to book trailers.
https://www.slideshare.net/coolgus

If you're interested in audiobooks, you can download one for free and test it out here: Audible

Connect with me and Cool Gus on social media.
Questions, comments, suggestions: Bob@BobMayer.com
Blog: http://bobmayer.com/blog/
Twitter: https://twitter.com/Bob_Mayer
Facebook: https://www.facebook.com/authorbobmayer
Google +: https://plus.google.com/u/0/101425129105653262515
Instagram: https://www.instagram.com/sifiauthor/
Youtube: https://www.youtube.com/user/IWhoDaresWins

ALL SERIES

THE CELLAR SERIES:
1. BODYGUARD OF LIES
2. LOST GIRLS

NIGHSTALKERS SERIES:
1. NIGHTSTALKERS
2. BOOK OF TRUTHS
3. THE RIFT
The fourth book in the Nightstalker book is the team becoming the Time Patrol, thus it's labeled book 4 in that series but it's actually book 1 in the Time Patrol series.

TIME PATROL SERIES:

THE GREEN BERETS SERIES:

THE DUTY, HONOR, COUNTRY SERIES:

AREA 51 SERIES:

ATLANTIS SERIES:

THE SHADOW WARRIORS:
(these books are all stand-alone and don't need to be read in order)

THE PRESIDENTIAL SERIES:

THE BURNERS SERIES:

All my novels and series are listed in order, with links here:
www.bobmayer.com/fiction/

My nonfiction, including my two companion books for preparation and survival is listed at
www.bobmayer.com/nonfiction/

Thank you!

Excerpt from **Bodyguard of Lies**

BODYGUARD OF LIES
THE CELLAR SERIES
book one

Bob Mayer

Chapter 1

THE OLD MAN SAT alone in the darkness contemplating failure on a scale that historians would write about it for centuries, and the subsequent inevitable need for change. He was one of the most powerful people in the world, but only a few knew of his existence. His position had been born out of failure over sixty years previously, as smoke still smoldered above the mangled ships and dead bodies in Pearl Harbor. For over six decades, he had given his life to his country. His most valuable asset was dispassion, so he could view his own recent failures objectively, although recent was a subjective term. He realized now it had all begun over ten years ago.

His office lacked any charm or comfort. There was a scarcity about the room that was unnerving. The cheap desk and two chairs made it look more like an interview room in an improvised police station than the office of a man so powerful his name brought fear throughout the government he served in Washington. The top of the desk was almost clear. Just a secure phone and a stack of folders.

There were, naturally, no windows. Not three hundred feet underground, buried beneath the 'crystal palace' of the top secret National Security Agency at Fort Meade, Maryland. And not that he could have used windows. The few who knew of the organization sometimes wondered if this location was what had led to its name. While the CIA made headlines every week, the Cellar was only whispered about in the hallowed halls of the nation's capitol. It might have been located underneath the NSA building but it was an entity unto itself answerable only to its founding mandate.

The room was lit only by the dim red lights on the secure phone. They showed the scars on the old man's face and the raw red, puckered skin where his eyes had once rested. There was track lighting, currently off, all three bulbs of which were over the old man's head and angled toward the door. When on, they placed his face in a shadow and caused any guest to squint against the light. The few who had the misfortune to sit across from him didn't know whether the lighting was placed in such a way to blind them as if he was, or to hide the severity of his old wounds.

He was not a man given much too sentimental reflection, but he knew his time was coming to an end, which made him think back to his beginning, as he knew all things were cyclical. He opened a right side desk drawer and pulled out a three dimensional representation of an old black and white photograph. He ran his fingers lightly over the raised images of three smiling young men dressed in World War II era uniforms—British, French and American. He was on the right. The other two were killed the day after the photo was taken.

He left the image on the desktop and reached for the files. The ones he wanted were the first two. He placed them on his lap. Paper files, the writing in Braille. He'd never trusted computers, even though there were ones now that could work completely on voice commands and read to him. Perhaps that was part of the problem. He was out of date. An anachronism.

They were labeled respectively Gant, Anthony and Masterson. He ran his fingers over the names punched on the tabs. He was patient. He had waited decades for plans born out of seeds he had sown to come to fruition. Quite a few similar plans had failed, so there was no reason to believe this one would succeed. But this plan was now in motion, initiated by an event he had had nothing to do with, the way the best plans in the covert world always started to allow deniability.

Despite his gifts of dispassion and patience, he felt a stirring in his chest. It puzzled him for a few moments before he realized he was experiencing hope. He squashed the feeling and picked up the phone to set another piece of the puzzle in motion.

Chapter 2

NEELEY HAD NOT ANTICIPATED waiting to kill people to be so boring. Staying well back in the darker shadows, out of the dim reflection of the few working streetlights, she scanned the ghostly quiet alley. She used the night vision portion of her retina just off the center of vision as Gant had taught her. There was nothing moving. A dumpster, an abandoned car and intermittent piles of refuse dotted the pitted concrete between the two abandoned tenements. There was a way out on either end. She could hear the rumble of traffic from the Bruckner Expressway a few hundred yards away.

Neeley had been here for a day and a half and she could superimpose from memory the details that the night refused to divulge to her naked eye. Looking right, a couple of miles to the east, she could see the aircraft warning lights on top of one of the towers of the Bronx-Whitestone Bridge crossing Long Island Sound.

She picked up a bulky rifle and pressed the scope on top to her right eye, twisting the switch to the on position. After a moment's hesitation, the black night gave way to bright green and she no longer needed her memory for the details the technology provided. Completing a second overall scan from her location in a corner apartment in the abandoned tenement, Neeley then zoomed in on the three locations she had noted during thirty-six hours of observing.

Two of the three men had arrived together four hours ago, just as darkness had slid like a curtain across the alley. Neeley had watched the two set up in separate rooms, on the second floor of the derelict building across the street.

The third man had shown up twenty minutes after the first two. If he'd tried the building, he might have bumped into the first two, but this last man wasn't very smart. He'd positioned himself inside the dumpster on the alley floor, leaving the top wedged open so he could observe the street, south to north. She gave the man an 'A' for effort, getting among the moldy garbage inside the large container, but an 'F' for tactical sense. True, the dumpster had a good ground level field of fire, but the man was trapped in a steel coffin if it became necessary to relocate. The two men in the building had the high ground, always a tactical advantage and the ability to move. Of course, they lacked the element of surprise but Neeley mentally gave them a few points anyway.

Through the scope, she could easily see the glow of one of the men across the street covertly smoking a cigarette, obviously thinking he was secure since he was well back from the window in the darkness of the room. The burning glow, barely visible to the naked eye, showed up like a searchlight in the night-vision scope. She shifted left two windows. The second man was watching the dumpster through a pair of older model, army-issue night-vision goggles. PVS-5s as near as Neeley could tell at this distance.

Nothing else was moving in the street and Neeley didn't expect to see anything until the deal went down. Alleys in the South Bronx were places even most bad people stayed away from at night. A few blocks to the south, prostitutes haunted the streets and docks of the Hunts Point section but this area was a no man's land. Which was why the two sides had chosen it.

The man across the street put out his cigarette. Neeley lay the rifle down and slid back from the window. Pulling a poncho-liner over her head, she completely covered herself. Only then, did she peel back the Velcro cover on her watch, and check the glowing hands. Twenty minutes to twelve. She considered the situation. At least six hours of darkness left. Neeley hadn't allowed herself to sleep since arriving here a day and a half ago. She'd drunk the last of the coffee from her thermos a while back and now her eyes burned with fatigue. Given the presence of the advance guards, odds were the deal would go down soon. She decided to take a calculated chance and pulled a pill out of her pocket. Popping it into her mouth, she washed it down with a swig from a water bottle. Four hours of intenseness. She would need at least an hour, preferably two, on the flip side of the deal to get out of the immediate area and be reasonably secure. Neeley reaffirmed the decision she had made during mission planning: 0300 and she was out of here, deal or no deal. Survival first and stick with the plan.

Her pulse quickened as the speed hit the blood stream. Neeley pushed aside the poncho liner and crammed it into a stuff sack, placing the sack inside a small backpack. She felt around the floor with her hands. Nothing left out. Just the pack and rifle. Methodically, she did a mental inventory of her actions of the past day and a half and all the equipment she had brought with her. The room was sterile, everything accounted for. Rule number four: Always pack out what you pack in. There were some rules you just couldn't break and the remembrance of one of Gant's rules brought a wry smile to Neeley's lips.

Neeley laid the pack down three feet inside the window and sat on it, laying the rifle across her knees. She was used to waiting. She'd spent most of her thirty-two years learning that patience was a virtue; a life-saving one.

She picked the rifle back up, the feel of plastic and steel a familiar one. It was an Accuracy International L96A1, a venerable sniper rifle of British design, firing NATO standard size 5.56mm by 51mm rounds, each of which Gant had reloaded to reduce velocity to sub-sonic speeds. A bullet that broke the sound barrier made a cracking noise as it left the muzzle and the special load eliminated that noise. On the end of the barrel was a bulky tactical suppressor, which absorbed the other large noise source for the rifle, the gasses that came out of the end of the barrel upon firing. In essence, the suppressor was a series of washer-like baffles around the end of the barrel that took the force of the expelling gasses. It was good for about ten shots before it had to be retooled. The combination of the two made the rifle almost noiseless to operate although they did drastically reduce the range and change the trajectory of the rounds, both of which Neeley was prepared for after many hours on the range firing it.

A pair of headlights carved into the northern end of the alley. Neeley tried to control the adrenaline that now began to overlap the speed. She watched the car roll slowly down the alley and come to a halt, the dumpster and its hidden contents thirty meters ahead.

Looking through the scope, Neeley saw one of the men in the building across the street, the one on the left speak into his hand.

The car was an armored limo. Another pair of headlights came in from the south. This one was a Mercedes. Not obviously armored, as it rode too high for that. It came to a halt thirty-five meters from the limo, headlights dueling. The dumpster flanked the Mercedes, to its right front.

The doors on the limo opened and four men got out, two to a side. Three had submachineguns. The fourth a large suitcase. The Mercedes disgorged three men, all also heavily armed. One went back and opened the trunk.

"I want your man out of the window up there," one of the men from the Mercedes yelled. The guy in the dumpster had seen the glow from the same cigarette that Neeley had. This also confirmed that the man in the dumpster had communication with the Mercedes.

After a moment's hesitation, the man with the suitcase pulled a small Motorola radio off his belt and spoke into it. A minute later, the man who had been smoking walked out of the building and joined the other four.

"Satisfied?" the suitcase man yelled back.

"Yes," the chief Mercedes man answered.

Neeley adjusted the scope's focus knob, zooming in. The remaining man across the way was now resting the bipods of an M60 machine gun on the windowsill. She shifted back to the standoff in the alley.

The men from the Mercedes unloaded two heavy cardboard boxes from the car's trunk and stacked them ten feet in front of the headlights. The five men from the limo side moved forward, fanning out, the man with the suitcase in the middle.

Neeley placed the crosshairs of the night-scope on the head of the suitcase man. She began to note the rhythm of her heart. The tip of her finger lay lightly on the trigger, almost a lover's caress. She slowly exhaled two-thirds of the air in her lungs, to what Gant had called the natural respiratory pause, and then held her diaphragm still. In between heartbeats, she smoothly squeezed the trigger and, with the rifle producing only the sound of the bolt working in concert with a low puff from the barrel suppresser, the 7.62-millimeter subsonic round left the muzzle. In midstride, the target's head blew apart.

Reacting instinctively, not knowing where death had winged its way from, the other four men swung up their submachineguns and fired on the Mercedes crew. The dumpster man replied, only to be lost in the roar of the machine gun in the window. In the ensuing confusion, and on the same paused breath, in between new heartbeats, Neeley put a round into one of the limo men.

After ten seconds of thunderous fire, an echoing silence enveloped the street. All the Mercedes men were down. The M60 had swiss-cheesed the dumpster. Two of the limo men were still standing.

Neeley took another breath and slowly exhaled, then paused. In between the next three heartbeats, she fired three times. First round, a headshot blowing the M60 gunner backwards into the darkened room across the way. Second and third rounds finishing the two-left standing before they even realized that death was silently lashing out of a window above their heads.

Satisfied that all were down, Neeley pulled out a red lens flashlight and searched the dirty floor of the room. She collected the five pieces of expended brass and placed them in a pocket on the outside of the backpack, insuring the Velcro cover was tightly sealed. She listened to the earpiece from the portable police scanner in her pocket as she swung on the backpack and started down. She was on the street before the first call for a car to investigate shots fired came over the airway. The police would not respond with any particular alacrity. Shots fired were common calls in the South Bronx at night. Cops tended to band together here and only became excited if the radio call was 'officer down'.

As she headed toward the Mercedes, movement from one of the bodies caused her to swing the muzzle up; one of the men was still alive. Neeley watched the figure writhing on the ground for a few seconds. She stepped forward, and with one boot, shoved the body over, keeping the muzzle pointed at the man's head. The man's stomach was a sea of very dark, arterial blood: gut shot. Neeley's training automatically started scrolling through her consciousness, outlining the proper procedures to treat the wound.

The bulky barrel of the rifle mesmerized the man's gaze. Looking above it, into Neeley's dark pupils, his own widened with surprise. They searched for mercy in the depths of Neeley's thickly lashed eyes. Neeley's entire body started sweating and the adrenaline kicked up to an even higher level. The muzzle didn't waver.

The round entered a small black dot between the man's eyes. The bullet mushroomed through the brain and took off the entire rear of the head, spraying the dirty street. Neeley watched the body twitch and become still. She automatically scooped up the expended brass casing and stuffed it into her pocket.

Moving to the cardboard boxes, she pulled a thermal grenade out of one of the pockets of her loose fitting black leather, knee-length overcoat and pulled the pin. She placed the grenade on top of the boxes and released the arming lever, pocketing both it and the pin. Acting quickly, trying to make up for the seconds lost dealing with the wounded man, she tore the briefcase out of the limp hand still holding it and jogged to the end of the alley. A subdued pop and a flicker of flames appeared behind her as two million dollars worth of cocaine began to go up in flames.

Satisfied she was out of immediate danger, and before reaching the corner, Neeley twisted the locking screw and broke the rifle down into two parts. She hung the barrel on the inside right of her coat and the stock on the left, securing them with specially sown in bands of Velcro.

Turning the corner, Neeley settled into a steady, swift walk. From the confused babble on the scanner, she had six to eight minutes before the first police arrived.

She made three blocks and then turned left. Here were the first signs of life. This area was more populated, but still well within the urban battle zone known as the South Bronx. Covert eyes watched her as she moved and Neeley slid a hand up, loosening the 10mm Glock Model 20 pistol she wore in a shoulder holster.

Her purposeful stride and appearance deflected any thoughts of evil intent from those lurking in the shadows. Neeley was tall, an inch shy of six foot. She had broad shoulders and a slender build. Her short, dark hair had seen better days and could use styling. Her face was all angles, no soft roundness, with two very dark eyes that took in everything in her surroundings. She moved with a sense of determination, her long overcoat half open, allowing her easy access to the weapons inside.

Two more blocks, no interference encountered, and she reached her parked pick-up truck, nestled among other battered vehicles. She unlocked the door and threw the suitcase in. The first sirens were wailing in the distance as Neeley got behind the wheel and cranked the engine.

For the first time she paused. She held her hands in front of her face. They were shaking slightly. Neeley took a deep breath and held it. The vision of the man looking up at her flickered across her eyes, then was gone. She shivered; shaking her head in short violent jerks, then was still again. She put the truck into gear and drove off.

Sticking with the route she had memorized, Neeley drove, keeping scrupulously to the speed limit. After ten minutes of negotiating side streets, she reached an on-ramp for the Cross Bronx Expressway and rolled up it, heading northeast for New England.

The suitcase on the passenger seat nagged at her. Neeley held her patience for two hours, until the city was over eighty miles behind her, and she was well into Connecticut, just south of Hartford. Finally, she pulled into a rest area. Parking away from other vehicles, Neeley turned on the dome light and put the suitcase on her lap.

She checked the exterior for any indication it was rigged. Nothing. Flipping both latches, she slowly lifted the lid an inch. She slid a finger in and carefully felt the edges. Then she opened it all the way. A wadded piece of cloth lay on top, covering the contents. Neeley peeled the cloth away. Stacks of worn hundred dollar bills greeted her. She didn't count it. She knew exactly how much was there.

Finally accepting she was safe, Neeley allowed herself to think of Gant. She wondered how it would have been to open the suitcase with him. She knew he would have been proud of her. Gant had talked about this mission endlessly. He had a source, someone he called his Uncle Joe, although he said the man was not family by blood, who had called him just two weeks ago with word of this meet. Somebody who must have owed Gant a lot, but Neeley understood owing Gant.

She remembered all the nights she had lain with her body curled into his. Talking about it and perfecting the plan. Every ex-Green Beret's dream, he'd called it.

Neeley closed the suitcase and with it the memories of Gant. There was still much to do.

* * *

The day her life as she knew it came to an end, Hannah Masterson forced herself to stroll casually down the carpeted hallway. They were all trying hard not to stare but Hannah was certain they were. She doubted that they knew about John, but she'd always known that people could sense bad news. Hannah had an urge to walk the length of the long hallway, stopping at every desk, and explain in great detail to every person that she had been a good wife, never shirked her duties, always smiled and appeared happy, and that John wasn't really gone. He was just away for a little while. On business.

Of course they wouldn't believe her. She didn't believe it either. Not that she hadn't been a good wife, but that John was really gone. Men like John, with six-figure salaries and power jobs, didn't just dump the wife, career, house and two cars for no reason at all. Something had happened to him, she was convinced of it; well, had been. The day-old postcard in her purse had forced her to acknowledge other possibilities.

With relief, she found the door to Howard Brumley's office open and aimed herself toward a vacant char. One look at Howard's face told Hannah that there was to be no reprieve during this appointment. His normal ruddy complexion was pale; the dancing, flirting eyes were gone, replaced by shaded 'I hate to tell you this' pupils.

Howard picked up a file and tapped the corner nervously. "You look good."

Hannah's wasn't a natural beauty, but more the result of money meeting good bone structure. Her blond hair was thick and shiny, flowing to her shoulders in natural waves. Her eyes, hidden now by the dark glasses, were the color of expensive chocolate left in a hot car. The few worry lines around her eyes and mouth were deepened by the stress of the past week and were the only thing that made her look older than her 31 years. She was a shade under five and a half feet and weighed what any self-conscious woman of means would weigh.

Howard, the family lawyer, was dodging. Hannah knew it was difficult to talk to a woman whose husband had apparently taken the perpetual golf trip. That was how John had done it. Left early on a beautiful Saturday morning the previous week with his golf bag and whistling a happy tune. Glanced back once. Whether to look at her, or the house, maybe both, she would never know. The Country Club had returned the car on Monday. John had taken his clubs. Even with the car back in the garage though, Hannah couldn't believe he was gone.

Howard put down the file folder and leaned back in his chair. "Have you heard anything else from John?"

"Just the card from the islands. If it was John who sent it," she amended.

"Is it his handwriting?" Howard asked.

Hannah reluctantly opened her bag and handed the card over. "It looks like his writing, but it could be a forgery."

Howard shook his head, staring at it. "I can't believe he would do something like this."

"Maybe the card is just--" Hannah began, but Howard was shaking his head again and his attention was no longer on the card.

"No." Howard gestured to the file folder. "I mean I can't believe he would do anything like this."

"You think he's really gone?" Hannah asked. "Off to some south sea island like this card says?"

Howard sighed. Hannah was watching him carefully. John was hurt. That was it. "He's been in an accident, hasn't he?" She picked the postcard up from the desk. "This was John's way of trying to keep me from knowing, isn't it?"

"He's not hurt, not that I know if." Howard blinked. "Hannah, I've known John a long time and two weeks ago I would have trusted him with the lives of my children." Howard took a deep breath. "I don't know what to say."

Hannah sat still and waited to hear something so bad it would render a lawyer speechless.

Having taken the plunge, Howard continued. "Evidently John was planning this for some time. He cleaned out everything: IRA's, mutual funds, stocks, real estate, you name it. You should have had your name on all of it. It was too easy for him. He did leave you fifteen thousand in your household account. But here comes the bad news."

Hannah's head snapped from an imaginary upper cut. She was a little behind Howard, taking it one-step at a time. "He's gone? He's really gone?"

Howard was in a rush to get it over with. "The house, Hannah. It's the house."

"No. That's mine." Her voice was level and hard. "When we paid the note off last year John filed a quitclaim deed and put the house in my name."

She remembered the night well. John had said it was a symbol of his love and devotion. Hannah who had spent most of her childhood in a succession of foster homes felt safe for the first time that night. Her house, it would always be her house.

"John forged your name and took out a new note on the house. It's mortgaged to the max. If you sell it now you can pay the bank. As it is you have a payment of a little over six thousand dollars due in seven days. You don't have enough money to stay there more than two months."

Hannah shook her head. "John wouldn't do that. He wouldn't do that with the house. Not the house."

Howard must have seen too many war movies with shellshock victims as he slapped Hannah with his words. "Hannah, John's gone. He left you and stole everything that wasn't nailed down. And what was nailed down he sold out from under you."

Hannah held up a thin, manicured hand. "But that's illegal." It was beginning to sink in. "What about the cars?"

"Both leased," John said. He glanced in the deadly folder. "The Volvo is five hundred and forty. The BMW is eight-twenty, both payable the first of the month."

Howard cleared his throat. Could there be more? Hannah wondered.

There was. "I also received mail from John yesterday." Howard was holding several legal sized pieces of paper. "It's a marital dissolution agreement."

"You're joking," Hannah sputtered. "John wants to divorce me after stealing everything?"

Howard looked distinctly uncomfortable. "Apparently so."

"But . . ." Hannah shook her head. "I don't . . ."

"It's an unusual situation," Howard said.

The understatement of the year, Hannah thought. She found it strange that the only thing that resounded in her mind was that she hadn't seen it coming. She didn't really care about the cars or the money—the house, of course, was a different matter, for a different reason—but she hadn't seen this coming.

Howard's voice took on his professional lilt. "You have to realize that some of what John did *is* illegal and not just toward you. The bank he took the new mortgage out from will not be very happy either. You're probably going to have to divorce him to keep the bank and others he defrauded from coming after you, Hannah."

"Coming after me?" she repeated. "I didn't do anything."

"Divorcing him, and a thorough check of your lack of assets, will help convince them of that," Howard said. "But as it looks now, you're a party to everything he did. Divorcing him will be the best thing you could do."

"Divorcing John is a good thing?" Hannah pressed her hands against her temples. "I don't understand. Until a week ago I thought I had a good marriage. John seemed as happy as ever. Something's wrong with this picture, Howard. Either something awful happened to John or my entire adult life has been a sham. After all these years for him to do this now means I'm an idiot."

Howard's voice softened. "No. You're a lovely, lovely woman who married a snake. But now's not the time for pity. Now's the time for action. You have to rise above this, Hannah. We have to take care of the dirt John left you. Then you can start a new life."

Hannah stared. A new life? She didn't even know how she'd lost the old one yet.

Howard kept the words coming. "Hannah, you're a beautiful woman with lots of talents. You can get a job or another husband in no time."

Even through the numbness, that struck a painful chord. "I can't believe you said that, Howard."

He held up both hands, defensively. "I didn't mean it like that."

"How else could you possibly have meant it?"

"Hannah, please!" Howard was standing. He had an envelope in his hands that he was running one thumb along the edge of. "Do you need help?"

Hannah was puzzled by the inane question.

"Haven't you been seeing someone? A professional?" Realizing he wasn't getting through, Howard cut to the chase. "A psychiatrist?"

How did he know about Dr. Jenkins, Hannah wondered. John must have told him, she immediately realized. Hannah gave a bitter laugh. "How can I pay for a psychiatrist now?"

"You're still covered by John's health plan; for a while at least. I think you really should go see him. Get some help."

Hannah stood. "I have to go."

Howard started coming around his massive desk. "I'm sorry, Hannah. Please don't leave like this. With everything you have to worry about I'd hate it if I were the cause of any more trouble. I was just trying to help."

Hannah didn't say anything. She walked quickly out the door. As the elevator doors shut Howard was still calling after her, telling her they had to take care of this now. Clear it up before it was too late.

Hannah leaned against the brass wall letting the cool surface soothe her forehead. She was still willing herself not to faint when the doors slid open. The man in front of her shot an appreciative glance as he entered the elevator.

"Nice day."

She stared at him as she pushed by him into the lobby, awed by the fact that the world was going to go on.

Hannah fumbled her way out of the office building and stood in a daze on the sidewalk. All around her office workers were hitting the streets of St. Louis for lunch. After she was bumped a few times she realized it was time to move on. She couldn't quite remember where the car was parked and it didn't seem to matter. The car John had brought home one day. She hadn't even asked if he'd bought it or leased it. Those were questions that simply had never occurred to her after so many years of allowing John to take care of everything.

Hannah wondered if anything was ever going to matter again. This morning her main concern had been John and his safety. Clutching her purse to her chest, she now knew that John was never coming back. Beyond that was dangerous territory for her mind to go.

The Adam's Mark was just ahead. Two weeks ago she might have wandered into the hotel bar and waited for her successful husband to join her for lunch. Today she didn't know if she had enough money for a sandwich and a coke. She fumbled with her purse and checked. She had a couple of dollars in cash. She had no idea what the status of the credit cards was.

The bar was cool and dark and occupied by a lone female bartender. Hannah took a seat at the bar and waited. She noted that the bartender was about her age but looked it. Hannah's carefully tended thirty-one years had been shielded from the direct hit of aging, until this week of course.

"Are you OK?"

Hannah was startled by the bartender's sudden question. She nodded.

"How about a cup of coffee?"

Hannah indicated in the affirmative, thankful that she would have a moment to compose herself before the woman returned. Hannah noticed that the woman's nametag pronounced her Marty. She was eyeing Hannah suspiciously from the end of the bar as she poured the coffee. She carried the cup the length of the bar and set it carefully in front of Hannah.

"Let me see if I can guess: man trouble."

Hannah tried to smile and failed. "Yes. He left me."

Hannah surprised herself. Even though John had been gone a week, this was the first time she had uttered those words aloud. It was as if by refusing to say them she had been able to negate the fact that he was no longer there. She had simply refused to consider the possibility. Even the post card's intent had been ignored.

"He left you?" Marty emphasized the latter pronoun as the look on her face passed from sympathy to incredulity. "I don't mean to be funny but if you got left, I don't figure any of us are safe."

Hannah took a sip of her coffee. The scalding liquid bit at her lips and she put the cup back on the polished surface of the bar. "Maybe nobody is safe."

Marty was leaning on the bar. "Was this guy your husband?"

"Yes. Next month would have been our tenth anniversary."

"He just up and left? Took his stuff and split?"

"Not really. He didn't even take a change of clothes. He just never came back home. For the past week I was afraid something terrible had happened to him and then yesterday I received a post card with palm trees all over it saying he wasn't coming back. I went to our lawyer and he had the divorce papers all ready."

Marty wiped the bar top. "Sounds like he went a little bit nuts. Maybe he's gonna come back after he gets regrooved and everything will be fine."

"He can't come back now. He forged my name on some real estate papers. He left me with nothing."

Marty wore a mask of outrage. "Oh man, that's the worst thing I ever heard. Don't sign the divorce papers. Nail the asshole. Get your own lawyer."

Hannah wondered why she was sharing this with some woman she would never speak to again, and realized that was the reason. She could hardly talk about this with the women in her limited social circle. She had kept John's disappearance as quiet as possible, telling only Howard and calling the people at John's office trying to find out, without saying *she* didn't know, if they knew where John was. But no one had had a clue as to his hereabouts. Hannah had even considered calling the police, but Howard had told her to wait a little bit. Howard's position had been that John's sensitive job at the company should be protected.

Hannah watched as Marty returned her thoughts to the bar. Hannah drained the last of the coffee and decided that it was time to go home.

She left the three-dollar bills that were all she had and mumbled some polite words to Marty. She passed through the hotel foyer focused on the green marble floor, ignoring the businessmen of assorted ages checking her out, noting the rings that marked her as taken and bagged by one of their own. They all gave her the soft smile and nod that they expected from other men for their own wives. They didn't expect Hannah to notice them just as they didn't expect their own wives to alert to the nods of other men.

She found the car around the block from Howard's office. The big black BMW that John had loved to drive. It was odd to discover that she didn't own it; that she didn't own anything. She thought about that for a minute, feeling the anxiety that threatened to overwhelm her. She pulled up to the garage attendant and panicked, realizing she had no money to pay the parking fee. She flipped open the console and slid quarters out of their holder. She had to go halfway down the dime column before she had enough. She was relieved when the gate released her and she burned rubber pulling away.

That little incident was more telling than anything Howard had said. Hannah moved some numbers around in her head and knew she needed a plan. The money that John had left would be swallowed by house expenses in no time. Howard was right: she was going to have to sell the house and then turn in the cars. But that left her without a job, home, car, anything. Hannah's mind was churning. She could sell the contents of the house. Maybe she could generate enough to lease an apartment.

She had to get a job. The very thought brought a tightness to her throat. Not because she didn't want to work, but because she felt she had nothing to present a future employer. She had dropped out of college to put John through graduate school, working two jobs, one as a substitute teacher and the other waiting tables. Instead of going back and finishing her degree, she had become a full-time wife. John's career had been so demanding and financially rewarding that she had simply never given a thought that she would need to support herself one day. That was the deal-- the word stuck in her consciousness-- the deal they had made without even bothering to verbalize it. It had just happened.

Excerpted from **Bodyguard of Lies**

Copyright

Cool Gus Publishing

http://coolgus.com

CHASING THE SON by Bob Mayer
COPYRIGHT © 2015 by Bob Mayer

ISBN-13: 9781621251859